BY SOPHIE KINSELLA

Confessions of a Shopaholic
Shopaholic Takes Manhattan
Shopaholic Ties the Knot
Can You Keep a Secret?
Shopaholic & Sister
The Undomestic Goddess
Shopaholic & Baby
Remember Me?
Twenties Girl
Mini Shopaholic
I've Got Your Number
Wedding Night
Shopaholic to the Stars
Finding Audrey
Shopaholic to the Rescue
My Not So Perfect Life
Surprise Me
I Owe You One
Christmas Shopaholic
Love Your Life

Love Your Life

Love Your Life

A Novel

SOPHIE KINSELLA

THE DIAL PRESS

NEW YORK

Copyright © 2020 by Madhen Media Ltd

All rights reserved.

Published in the United States by The Dial Press, an imprint of Random House, a division of Penguin Random House LLC, New York.

THE DIAL PRESS and the HOUSE colophon are registered trademarks of Penguin Random House LLC.

Published in the United Kingdom by Bantam Press, an imprint of Transworld Publishers, a Penguin Random House UK company.

LIBRARY OF CONGRESS CATALOGING-IN-PUBLICATION DATA
Names: Kinsella, Sophie, author.
Title: Love your life : a novel / Sophie Kinsella.
Description: New York : The Dial Press, [2020]
Identifiers: LCCN 2020026668 (print) | LCCN 2020026669 (ebook) |
ISBN 9780593132852 (hardcover) | ISBN 9780593132876 (ebook)
Subjects: GSAFD: Love stories.
Classification: LCC PR6073.I246 L68 2020 (print) |
LCC PR6073.I246 (ebook) | DDC 823/.914—dc23
LC record available at https://lccn.loc.gov/2020026668
LC ebook record available at https://lccn.loc.gov/2020026669

International edition ISBN 978-0-593-24147-9

Printed in the United States of America on acid-free paper

randomhousebooks.com

2 4 6 8 9 7 5 3 1

FIRST U.S. EDITION

Title-page image: © iStockphoto.com

Book design by Dana Leigh Blanchette

In memory of Susan Kamil

Love Your Life

One

As I reach for the doorbell, my phone bleeps with a text and my head instantly fills with a roll call of possibilities.

- Someone I know is dead.
- Someone I know won the lottery.
- I'm late for an appointment I'd forgotten about. Shit.
- I was witness to a crime and now I need to give very specific, detailed evidence about something I can't remember. *Shit.*
- My doctor was looking back through her notes. (Why? Unclear.) And she found something. "I don't want to worry you, *but* . . ."
- Someone sent me flowers and my neighbor took them in.
- A celebrity just tweeted something I need to see. Ooh. What?

But as I take out my phone, I see that it's from Seth, the guy I had a date with last week. The one who said nothing, the whole evening. *Nothing.*

Most guys have the opposite problem. They drone on about themselves and their brilliant achievements and as you're paying your half they ask as an afterthought, "What do you do again?" But Seth stared at me silently through his close-set eyes while I babbled nervously about the butternut squash soup.

What does he have to say? Does he want another date? Yikes. My stomach cringes at the very thought, which is a sign. One of my major rules of life is: You should listen to your body. Your body is wise. Your body *knows.*

It's fine. I'll let him down gently. I'm pretty good at letting people down.

Hello, Ava. After consideration I have decided our relationship is not something I can continue with.

Oh. Hmph. I see.
Whatever.

I eye-roll very deliberately toward the phone. Although I know he can't see me, I have this very slight theory that you can somehow convey emotions through your phone.

(I haven't shared this theory with anyone, because most people are quite narrow-minded, I find, even my best friends.)

You may have thought I was contacting you to ask for another date, in which case I'm sorry to have raised your hopes.

My hopes? My *hopes?* He should be so lucky.

You'll want to know why.

What? No. I don't, thanks very much.

I mean, I can guess.

No, scratch that. I can't.

Why should I have to guess, anyway? Who wants to *guess* why someone doesn't want to date them? It sounds like some awful TV game show called *Is It My Bad Breath?*

(It's not my bad breath. Whatever it is, it's not that.)

I'm afraid I cannot date anyone who thinks butternut squash soup has a soul.

What?

I stare at the phone, incensed. He has *totally* misrepresented me. I did *not* say butternut squash soup has a soul. I simply said I thought we should be open-minded about the way the physical and spiritual interlink. Which I do. We should.

As if he can read my mind, Harold gives a sympathetic whine and rubs his nose against my leg. You see? If that doesn't prove the world is interconnected, then what does?

I want to text back, **Sorry not to be closed-minded enough for your limited outlook on life.** But that would indicate that I've read his texts, which I haven't.

Well, OK, I *have,* but the point is, I'm deleting them from my mind. All gone. Seth who? Date? What?

Exactly.

I ring the doorbell, then let myself in with the key Nell's given me. It's what we all do, in case Nell's having an episode. It's been awhile, but they can flare up viciously out of nowhere.

"Nell?" I call.

"Hi!" She appears in the hall, grinning widely, her hair pink and spiky.

"You've gone back to pink!" I exclaim. "Nice."

Nell's hair color has changed about 106 times over the years that I've known her, whereas mine hasn't changed once. It's still the same dark auburn, straight down to my shoulders, easy to swish into a ponytail.

Not that hair is really on my mind right now. I was distracted momentarily by Seth's texts—but now that I'm inside the house, my throat is starting to tighten. My stomach feels heavy. I glance down at Harold and he turns his head inquiringly toward me in that adorable way he has, whereupon my eyes start to prickle. Oh God. Can I really do this?

Nell squats down and holds out her hands to Harold. "Ready for your holiday?"

Harold surveys her for a moment, then turns back to me, his liquid brown gaze fixing mine piteously.

If anyone thinks dogs can't understand everything we say and do, then they're *wrong*, because Harold *knows*. He's trying to be brave, but he's finding this as hard as I am.

"I can't take you to Italy, Harold," I say, swallowing hard. "I've told you that. But it won't be long. I promise. A week. That's all."

His face is crunched into a heartbreaking "why are you *doing* this to me?" expression. His tail is gently thumping on the ground in an encouraging, hopeful way, as though I might suddenly change my mind, cancel my flight, and take him out to play.

I've sworn I won't cry, but tears are brimming in my eyes as I gaze at his bright, intelligent face. My Harold. Best beagle in the world. Best dog in the world. Best *person* in the world.

"Harold can't *wait* to stay with me," says Nell firmly, ushering us both into the living room. "Can you, Harold?"

In answer, Harold screws up his face still more and gives a soul-shattering whine.

"That dog should go on the stage," says Sarika, glancing up at him from her laptop with an amused look. Sarika isn't really a dog person—she admits as much—but she's a Harold person. You can't meet Harold and not be a Harold person.

I found Harold at a rescue center four years ago when he was just a puppy, and it was instant, utter devotion. He looked up at me, his eyes bright, his breath all snuffly and excited, and he seemed to be saying, "There you are! I knew you'd come!"

I'm not saying it was plain sailing. I'd never had a dog before. I'd longed for one as a child, but my parents were the type who keep vaguely promising, then it never happens. So I was a beginner at looking after a dog. And Harold was a beginner at being looked after. Because, believe me, he was *not* looked after by the people who abandoned him on the side of the A414. That was *not* looking after him. Just thinking about it makes me feel hot and bothered.

Anyway, so it's been a learning curve. When Harold first arrived at my flat, he had a freak-out. He was quite clearly saying, "What have I *done,* agreeing to live with you?" And I had similar wobbles. There was quite a lot of howling, on both sides. But now I can't imagine life without him. Yet here I am, planning to leave him for a week.

Maybe I should cancel. Yes. I should cancel.

"Ava, stop stressing. You realize he's *trying* to make you feel bad?" says Nell. She turns to Harold and surveys him sternly. "Listen, mate, I don't fall for your hammy act. Ava can go on holiday without you. *It's allowed.* So stop giving her a hard time."

For a long moment Harold and Nell lock eyes—two huge personalities confronting each other—then at last Harold subsides. He gives me another reproachful look but pads over to the hearth rug by Nell's chair and settles down.

OK, maybe I won't cancel.

"Do *not* apologize to him," says Nell to me. "And do *not* waste all week mooning over videos of Harold instead of writing your book."

"I won't!" I say defensively.

"We'll be fine," she reiterates. *"Fine."*

I don't have many life tips. But one of them is: If you're ever feeling sorry for yourself, visit Nell. She's tough in all the right places. She bounces back stupid thoughts at you. Her matter-of-fact attitude whips through you like a gust of sharp, cold air.

"Here's all his stuff." I dump my massive bag on the floor. "Bed, water bowl, blanket, food . . . Oh, his essential oils!" I suddenly remember, taking the bottle from my bag. "I've made him a new blend, lavender and cedarwood. You just have to spritz his—"

"Bedding." Nell cuts me off. "Ava, relax. You've already

sent me five emails about this, remember?" She takes the bottle from me and scrutinizes it briefly before putting it down. "That reminds me, I've been meaning to ask. Whatever happened to your aromatherapy qualification?"

"Oh," I say, halted. "I'm still . . . doing it. Kind of."

My mind flicks back to my aromatherapy books and bottles, shoved to the side in my kitchen. I'm doing an online course, and I *must* get back to it, because I'm definitely still interested in becoming a part-time aromatherapist.

"Kind of?" queries Nell.

"It's on pause. It's just, with work, and writing this book . . . You know." I heave a sigh. "Life gets in the way."

My job is writing pharmaceutical leaflets and online copy, which I can pretty much do in my sleep by now. I work for a drug company called Brakesons Inc., based in Surrey. It's fine, I like the firm, and they let me work mostly at home. But I'm always trying to expand my horizons. If you ask me, life's too short *not* to expand your horizons. You should always be thinking: *This is OK . . . but what* else *could I be doing?*

"All the more reason to go to Italy and focus on writing your book," says Nell firmly. "Harold *wants* you to do that. Don't you, Harold?"

In answer, Harold emits a soulful "wahoo!"—sometimes he sounds just like a wolf—and Nell laughs. She ruffles Harold's head with her strong stubby hand and says, "Idiot dog."

We've been friends since Manchester uni. Nell, Sarika, Maud, and I all met in the university choir and bonded on a tour to Bremen. Sarika had barely spoken a word till then; all we knew about her was that she was studying law and could sing a top C. But after a few drinks she revealed she was secretly sleeping with the conductor and their sex life was getting a bit "dark." So now she wanted to dump him but also stay in the choir, and what did we think? We spent a whole night drinking German beer and discussing it, while also trying to elicit what "dark" meant, exactly.

(In the end, Nell crashed her glass down and said, "Just bloody *tell* us, OK?")

(It was a bit gross. Not worth repeating, or even thinking about.)

Anyway, Sarika did dump the conductor, and she did stay in the choir. That was fourteen years ago now (how did *that* happen?) and we're still friends. Of the four of us, only Sarika still sings in a choir—but, then, she was always the most musical one. Plus she's constantly on the lookout for a man whose interests chime with hers, and she reckons London choirs are a good place to start. Along with cycling clubs. She joins a new choir every year and switches cycling clubs every six months, and there's been a pretty good yield of guys.

I mean, three serious possibilities in two years. Not bad, for London.

We all live near one another in north London, and even though our lives are different in a lot of ways, we're closer than ever. We've been through a few roller coasters these last few years. We've shrieked and clutched one another's hands, both literally and . . . whatsit.

Not-literally.

Metaphorically? Figuratively?

Great. I'm going on a weeklong writing course tomorrow and I don't know what the opposite of "literally" is.

"What's the opposite of 'literally'?" I ask Sarika, but she's tapping intently at her laptop, her dark shiny hair swishing the keys. She's often to be found tapping intently at her laptop, Sarika, even when she's round at Nell's. (We tend to gather at Nell's place.)

"No smokers," Sarika mutters, presses a key, and peers closely at her screen.

"What?" I stare at her. "Is that work?"

"New dating site," she says.

"Ooh, which one?" I ask with interest. Sarika has more cash than any of us, being a lawyer, so she's the one who can afford to join the expensive dating sites and then report back.

"No psychics," replies Sarika absently and presses another key, then looks up. "It's called Meet You. Costs an arm and a leg. But, then, you get what you pay for."

" 'No psychics'?" echoes Nell skeptically. "How many psychics have you dated, exactly?"

"One," says Sarika, swiveling toward her. "And that was more than enough. I told you about him. The one who reckoned he knew what I *really* liked in bed and we argued about it and I said, 'Whose body is it anyway?' and he said, 'It's for both of us to enjoy.' "

"Oh, *him*," says Nell, light dawning in her eyes. "I didn't realize he was a psychic; I thought he was an arsehole. Is there a 'no arseholes' filter?"

"Wouldn't work," says Sarika regretfully. "No one thinks they're an arsehole." She turns back and taps at her key-

board again. "No magicians." She types briskly. "No dancers. What about choreographers?"

"What's wrong with dancers?" objects Nell. "They're fit."

"Just don't fancy it," says Sarika, shrugging vaguely.
"He'd be out every night, dancing. We should keep the same
hours. No oil-rig workers," she adds as an afterthought, typing again.

"*How* does this site work?" I say, baffled.

"It starts with all your deal-breakers," replies Nell. "It
shouldn't be called Meet You, it should be called Sod Off
You. And You. And You."

"You're making it sound really negative," protests Sarika.
"It's not about telling people to sod off, it's about being
super-specific, so you won't waste time looking at unsuitable
people. You keep honing your target match until you've got
the perfect shortlist."

"Let me see." I head round the sofa to look over her shoulder. The screen of her laptop is filled with male faces, and I
blink at them. They all look nice to me. The guy with the
stubble in the righthand corner looks particularly cute. His
expression says, "Pick me! I'll be kind to you!"

"He looks sweet." I point at him.

"Maybe. OK, what next?" Sarika consults a typed list on
her phone. "No vegetarians."

"What?" I stare at her in shock. "*No vegetarians?* What
are you saying? Sarika, how can you be so narrow-minded?
Your sister's vegetarian! *I'm* vegetarian!"

"I know," she says equably. "But I don't want to date my
sister. Or you. Sorry, babe. You know I love your halloumi

crumble." She reaches out an arm to squeeze my waist affectionately. "But I want someone I can roast a chicken with."

She clicks on *Filters* and a box appears with four headings: *Yes Please!, Don't Mind, Not Ideal,* and *Deal-breaker.*

"Deal-breaker," says Sarika firmly, starting to type *Vegetarian* in the box. After two letters, the word *Vegetarian* autofills and she clicks on it.

"You can't rule out all vegetarians," I say in utter horror. "It's prejudiced. It's . . . is it even *legal?*"

"Ava, lighten up!" retorts Sarika. "Now, watch. This bit is fun. *Apply filter.*"

As she clicks, the photos on the screen start to shimmer. Then, one by one, big red crosses appear in front of faces, scattered over the screen. I glance at the cute guy—and feel a nasty lurch. There's a cross in front of his face. He looks as though he's been sentenced to execution.

"What's going on?" I demand anxiously. "What is this?"

"It's called 'Last Chance,'" explains Sarika. "I can reprieve any of them by clicking on them."

"Reprieve him!" I say, pointing to my favorite. "Reprieve him!"

"Ava, you don't know anything about him," says Sarika, rolling her eyes.

"He looks nice!"

"But he's vegetarian," says Sarika, and presses *Done.*

The screen shimmers again and all the guys with crossed-out faces disappear. The remaining guys swirl around the screen and then assemble again in neat rows of photos, with new ones taking the place of the vanished.

"Great," says Sarika with satisfaction. "I'm getting somewhere."

I stare at the screen, slightly traumatized by this culling process.

"It's brutal," I say. "It's heartless."

"Better than swiping," puts in Nell.

"Exactly!" Sarika nods. "It's scientific. There are more than eight hundred possible filters on the site. Height, job, habits, location, political views, education . . . The algorithms were developed at NASA, apparently. You can process five hundred guys in, like, no time." She consults her list again. "Right, on to the next. No one over six foot three." She starts typing again. "I've tried super-tall. Doesn't work with me."

She presses *Apply Filter*, three red crosses appear, and within seconds a new selection of guys is gazing out from the screen.

"Apparently one woman kept on applying filters until there was only one guy left on the screen, and she contacted him and they're still together," Sarika adds, scrolling down the typed list on her phone. "That's your ideal."

"It still feels wrong," I say, watching the screen in dismay. "This can't be the way."

"It's the only way," Sarika contradicts me. "Basically everybody dates online now, right? *Eve-ry-bo-dy*. Millions of people. Billions of people."

"I guess so," I say warily.

"Everybody dates online," Sarika reiterates clearly, as though she's giving a TED Talk. "It's like going to a cocktail party and everybody in the world's standing there, trying to catch your eye. That's never going to work! You need to narrow it down. Ergo." She gestures at the screen.

"ASOS is bad enough," puts in Nell. "I searched for *white shirt* yesterday. You know how many I got? Twelve hundred and sixty-four. I was like, I don't have time for this shit. I'll take the first one. Whatever."

"Exactly," says Sarika. "And that's a shirt, not a life partner. No more than ten minutes from tube station," she adds, typing briskly. "I've had enough of schlepping to flats in the middle of nowhere."

"You're ruling out guys who *live more than ten minutes from the tube*?" My jaw sags. "Is that even a *thing*?"

"You can create your own filters, and if they like them they add them to the website," Sarika explains. "They're considering my one about hair-washing frequency."

"But what if the perfect guy lives eleven minutes from the tube station?" I know I'm sounding agitated, but I can't help it. I can already see him, drinking his coffee in the sunshine, wearing his cycle shorts, listening to his Bach playlist, longing for someone just like Sarika.

"He'll lie about it," says Sarika comfortably. "He'll put *ten minutes*. It's fine."

She's really not getting the point.

"Sarika, listen," I say in frustration. "What if there's an amazing guy who's six foot five and vegetarian and he lives twenty minutes away from Crouch End . . . and you've ruled him out? This is nuts!"

"Ava, stop freaking out," says Sarika calmly. "You have to have *some* deal-breakers."

"No you don't," I say adamantly. "I don't have any deal-breakers. I want a good man, that's all. A decent, civilized human being. I don't care what he looks like, what his job is, where he lives . . ."

"What about if he hates dogs?" says Sarika, raising her eyebrows.

I'm silenced.

He couldn't hate dogs, because only really strange, sad people don't like dogs.

"OK," I concede at last. "That's my only deal-breaker. He has to like dogs. But that's the only one. Literally."

"What about golf?" chips in Nell craftily.

Damn her. Golf is my Achilles' heel. I'll admit I have an irrational loathing for the game. And the outfits. And the people who play it.

But in my defense, it's because I used to live near the snootiest golf club in the world. There was a public footpath across the land, but if you even *tried* to go for a walk on it, all you got was furious people in matching sweaters flapping their arms at you, telling you to be quiet, or go back, were you an *idiot*?

It wasn't just me who found it stressful; the council had to have a word with the golf club. Apparently they brought in a new system of signs and it's all fine now. But by then we'd moved away, and I'd already decided I was allergic to golf.

However, I'm not admitting that now, because I don't like to think of myself as a prejudiced person.

"I don't have a problem with golf," I say, lifting my chin. "And anyway, that's not the point. The point is, two matching lists of attributes aren't *love*. Algorithms aren't *love*."

"Algorithms are the only way," says Sarika, squinting at the screen. "Mmm, he's nice."

"OK, where's the algorithm that tells me what a guy smells like?" I retort, more passionately than I intended. "Where's the algorithm that tells me how he laughs or the way he ruffles a dog's head? *That's* what matters to me, not all these irrelevant details. I could fall in love with a scientist or a farmer. He could be five feet tall or seven feet. As long as there was chemistry. *Chemistry.*"

"Oh, *chemistry*," says Sarika, exchanging grins with Nell.

"Yes, chemistry!" I retort defiantly. "That's what matters! Love is . . . is . . ." I grope for words. "It's the ineffable, mysterious connection that happens between two humans when they connect, and they feel it . . . and they just know."

"Ava." Sarika regards me fondly. "You are a love."

"She's getting in practice for her romantic-writing course," suggests Nell. "You realize Lizzy Bennet had a zillion deal-breakers, Ava? *No arrogant snooty types. No idiot clergymen.*" Nell nods at Sarika. "Put that one in."

"*No idiot clergymen.*" Sarika pretends to type, grinning at me over the top of her laptop. "Shall I put, *Only those with stately homes need apply?*"

"Very funny." I sink down next to her on the sofa and Sarika puts a conciliatory hand on mine.

"Ava. Babe. We're different, that's all. We want different things. I want to bypass all the time-wasting. Whereas you want . . . chemistry."

"Ava wants magic," says Nell.

"Not *magic*." I flinch slightly, because my friends always

make out I'm too romantic and rosy-tinted, and I'm *not*.
"What I want is—" I break off, my thoughts a little jumbled.

"What *do* you want?" asks Nell, and she sounds genuinely curious. At last I draw breath.

"I want a guy who looks at me . . . and I look at him . . . and it's all there. We don't have to say anything. It's all there."

I break off into a misty silence. It has to be possible. Love *has* to be possible—otherwise, what are we all doing?

"I want that too." Sarika nods, breaking the spell. "Only within ten minutes from a tube station."

Nell guffaws with laughter and I raise a reluctant smile.

"I've got a date tonight, actually," I reveal. "That's why I can't stay."

"A date?" Sarika's head jerks up. "You're telling us this now?"

"I thought you were packing for Italy," says Nell, almost accusingly.

"I am packing. After my date."

"Exciting!" Sarika's eyes sparkle at me. "Where did you meet him, at the ice cream social?"

"No, at the assembly rooms," says Nell. "He helped her when her carriage wheel got stuck."

"He wrote a note with his quill pen and stuck it into her bonnet." Sarika giggles.

"Ha ha." I lift my eyes to heaven. "Online, obviously. But I didn't set up a million artificial deal-breakers, I went by *instinct*."

"Instinct?" echoes Nell. "Meaning . . ."

"His eyes," I say proudly. "There's a look in his eyes."

After the disastrous date with Seth, I came up with a new

theory: It's all in the eyes. I *never* liked Seth's eyes. That should have told me. So I went online and searched for a guy with gorgeous eyes . . . and I found one! I'm actually quite excited. I keep looking at his picture and feeling a real connection with him.

"You can tell a lot about someone from his eyes," concedes Sarika. "Let's see."

I summon up a photo and look at it lovingly for a moment before showing it to Sarika, then Nell. "He's called Stuart," I tell them. "He's in IT."

"Nice eyes," concedes Nell. "I'll give you that."

Nice? Is that all she can say? They're wonderful eyes! They crinkle with warmth and intelligence and wit, even in a tiny photo on a phone. I've never *seen* such amazing eyes, and I've looked at a lot of dating profiles. . . .

"Harold!" Sarika suddenly shrieks, and I leap up in alarm. "That's my chicken wrap! *Bad* dog!"

While we've been talking, Harold has silently crept over to Sarika's side of the sofa and swiped her Pret A Manger wrap out of her bag, still in its plastic. Now he's looking from her to me to Nell as though to say, "What are you going to do about it?"

"Harold!" I chide. "Drop!" I take a step toward him and he backs away a step. "Drop!" I repeat, without much conviction.

Harold's bright eyes travel around the room again, as though he's assessing the situation.

"Drop." I try to sound commanding. "*Drop.*"

"Drop!" echoes Nell, her alto voice booming round the room.

I lean slowly toward Harold and his eyes follow me, inch by inch, until I make a sudden grab. But I'm too slow. I'm always too slow for Harold. He scrabbles and slides to the corner behind the TV where no one can get him, then starts chewing furiously at the wrap, pausing every so often to regard the three of us with an expression of triumph.

"Bloody dog," says Nell.

"Shouldn't have left it in my bag," says Sarika, shaking her head. "Harold, don't eat the *plastic,* you total moron."

"Harold?" A familiar voice comes wafting in from the hall. "Where's that gorgeous dog?"

A moment later, Maud appears round the door, holding the hands of two of her children, Romy and Arthur. "*Sorry I'm late,*" she declaims in her theatrical way. "*Nightmare* at school pickup. I haven't seen Harold for *ages,*" she adds, turning to beam at him. "Is he looking forward to his little holiday?"

"He's not a gorgeous dog," says Sarika ominously. "He's a bad, naughty dog."

"What did he do?" says Arthur, his eyes lighting up in delight.

Harold is a bit of a legend in Arthur's year-two class. He once starred at show-and-tell, where he swiped the school teddy, escaped into the playground, and had to be rounded up by three teachers.

"He stole my chicken wrap," says Sarika, and both children roar with laughter.

"Harold steals everything," proclaims Romy, who is four. "Harold steals *all* the food. Harold, here!" She holds out her hand encouragingly, and Harold lifts his head as though to say "Later," then resumes chomping.

"Wait, where's Bertie?" says Maud, as though only just noticing. "Arthur, where's Bertie?"

Arthur looks blank, as though he'd never even realized he had a brother called Bertie, and Maud clicks her tongue. "He'll be somewhere," she says vaguely.

Maud's basic conundrum in life is that she has three children but only two hands. Her ex, Damon, is a barrister. He works insanely hard and is pretty generous on the money front but not on the showing-up front. (She says, on the plus side, at least her kids' lives won't be ruined by helicopter parenting.)

"Sarika," she begins now. "You *don't* happen to be driving through Muswell Hill at five o'clock on Thursday, do you? Only I need someone to pick up Arthur from a playdate, and I *just* wondered . . ."

She flutters her eyelashes at Sarika, and I grin inwardly. Maud asks favors all the time. Will we mind her children/take in her shopping/research train times/tell her what tire pressure her car should be at? This isn't since becoming a single parent—this is ever since I've known her. I still remember meeting Maud at choir. This amazing-looking girl with tawny, mesmerizing eyes came over, and her very first words to me were, "You couldn't *possibly* buy me a pint of milk, could you?"

Of course I said yes. It's almost impossible to refuse Maud. It's like her superhero power. But you *can* resist if you try, and we've all learned, the hard way. If any of us said yes to all Maud's requests, we'd basically become her full-time bondslaves. So we've informally agreed on a rough ratio of one to ten.

"No, Maud," says Sarika, without missing a beat. "I couldn't. I work, remember?"

"Of *course*," Maud says with no rancor. "I just wondered if perhaps you had the afternoon off. Ava—"

"Italy," I remind her.

"Of course." Maud nods fervently. "Impossible. I see that."

She's always so charming, you *want* to say yes. She should basically run the country, because she could persuade anyone to do anything. But instead she runs her children's ridiculously complicated social lives, plus an online furniture-upcycling business, which she says is going to start making a profit any month now.

"Well, never mind," she says. "Shall I make some tea?"

"You didn't ask me," comes Nell's voice, upbeat but just a little tense. "Don't leave me out, Maud!"

As I turn to look at Nell, she's smiling broadly enough— but in her Nell-ish way. It's a determined smile, Nell has. A strong smile. It says, "Just for now, I'm not going to punch you, although I can't speak for the next five minutes."

"Don't leave me out," she repeats. And she's kind of joking—but she's not. I force myself not to glance at her cane in the corner, because she's having a good patch at the moment and we don't bring up the subject except when she does. We've learned that over these last few years.

"Nell!" Maud looks stricken. "I'm *so* sorry. What an oversight. Will you pick up Arthur for me?"

"No," shoots back Nell. "Sod off. Do your own chores."

Sarika snuffles with laughter, and I can't help grinning.

"Of course," replies Maud, in the same earnest way. "I *totally* understand. By the way, Nell, my sweet, I meant to say, there's a revolting-looking man standing by your car, writing a note. Shall I have a word?"

At once, Sarika lifts her head and glances at me. Sensing the atmosphere, Harold gives an ominous whine.

Nell frowns. "Does he look like a miserable git?"

"Yes. Gray trousers. Mustache. That kind of thing."

"It's that bastard John Sweetman," says Nell. "Moved in a month ago. He's always on at me. He wants to have that space for unloading his shopping. He knows I've got a blue badge, but . . ." She shrugs.

"No bloody *way*," says Sarika, clapping her laptop shut and getting on her feet. "These people!"

"You stay here, Nell," I say. "We're on it."

"You don't need to fight my battles for me," says Nell gruffly.

"Not for you. With you." I squeeze her shoulder and follow the others out into the forecourt of Nell's block, our faces equally set and determined.

"Hello, good evening, is there a problem?" Maud is already greeting the man in her posh boarding-school voice, and I see him taking in her appearance, a little stunned.

I mean, she's quite a sight. Six feet tall in platforms, trailing red hair, drifty skirt, two equally stunning red-haired children at her sides, and a third clambering onto her shoulders from the top of a nearby 4X4. (*That's* where Bertie was.)

"Spider-Man!" he yells, before climbing back onto the car roof.

"Is there a problem?" Maud repeats. "I believe my friend is parked here *entirely* legally, and writing this unfounded note would count as—"

"Harassment," chimes in Sarika deftly. She's whipped out her phone and is taking photos of the guy. "Harassment on several counts. How many letters is it you've written to my client?"

The man's eyes bulge at the word "client," but he doesn't retreat.

"This is a blue-badge area," he says tetchily. "Blue badge. Disabled."

"Yes." Nell steps forward. "I've got a blue badge. As you can well see. You, on the other hand, do *not* have a blue badge."

"The point is, my flat is right there," he says testily, pointing to the window behind Nell's car. "In the absence of any genuinely disabled persons, I should be able to park in this space. It's common sense."

"She's got a blue badge!" exclaims Sarika.

"You're disabled?" He scoffs at Nell. "Young healthy woman like you? Do you mind sharing the nature of your ailment?"

I can see him taking in her appearance, and I look at Nell through his eyes for a moment. Her squat, determined body, her jutting chin, her six earrings, her pink hair, her three tattoos.

I know Nell would rather keel over in the street than have this guy feeling sorry for her. For a few moments she's silent. Then, with the deepest reluctance, her face like thunder, she says, "I have . . . a chronic condition. And even that's none of your bloody business."

"My friend has a blue badge from the authorities," says Maud, her eyes flashing dangerously. "That's all you need to know."

"The authorities can be mistaken," persists John Sweetman, undeterred. "Or hoodwinked."

"Hoodwinked?" Maud's voice rises in rage. "*Hoodwinked?* Are you seriously suggesting—"

But Nell raises a hand to stop her.

"Don't waste your energy, Maudie," she says a little wearily, then turns to John Sweetman. "Fuck. Off."

"Seconded," says Maud briskly.

"Thirded," I add.

"Fourthded," puts in Sarika, not to be outdone.

"Spider-Man!" yells Bertie from the top of the 4X4, and lands with an almighty thump on John Sweetman's shoulders. John Sweetman gives an agonized yell and I clasp my hand over my mouth.

"Bertie!" exclaims Maud reprovingly. "Do *not* thump the man and call him ignorant."

"Ignorant!" yells Bertie at once, and punches John Sweetman. "Ignorant!"

"Children these days," says Maud, rolling her eyes. "What *can* one do?"

"Get him *off*!" John Sweetman's voice is muffled and furious. "Argh! My leg!"

"Harold!" squeals Romy gleefully, and I realize that Harold has dashed out to join in. He's grabbed John Sweetman's trousers between his teeth and is snuffling with excitement, and any minute now we'll be paying for a new pair of gray flannel slacks.

"Come *here*." I grab Harold's collar and with a supreme effort manhandle him away, while Maud reclaims Bertie. Somehow we all make it back inside, close the door of Nell's flat, and look at one another, breathing heavily.

"Fuckers," says Nell, which is what she always says.

"Onward," says Sarika firmly, because she's all about eyes forward, stay tough.

"Drink?" says Maud, which is what she always suggests. And now it's my turn to pull everyone in for a group hug.

"It'll be OK," I say into the dark, cozy warmth of us, our foreheads touching; our breaths mingling. The rest of the world is shut out; it's just us four. Our squad.

At last we draw apart, and Nell pats me reassuringly on the back.

"It'll be OK," she says. "It always is. Ava, go and have your hot date. Go to Italy. Write your book. And do not give that bad dog a *single thought*."

Two

⌇

Hot date. What a joke. What a *joke*.

The most humiliating thing is: I'm still thinking about it. Here I am at my expensive writing retreat in Italy. Our instructor, Farida, is giving her introduction to the week, and my pen is poised dutifully over my notebook. But instead of listening properly, I'm having flashbacks.

It felt wrong from the first moment we met in the pub. He was different from how I expected—which, to be fair, they always are. All online dates. They walk differently from how you imagined, or their hair's longer, or their accent isn't what you conjured up in your head. Or they just smell wrong.

This guy smelled wrong *and* drank his beer wrong *and* sounded wrong. He also had a lot to say about cryptocurrency, which . . . you know. Is only interesting for *so* long. (Ten seconds.) And the more I realized that he was wrong, the more I felt like a fool—because what about my instincts? What about the look in his eyes?

I kept peering at his eyes, trying—but failing—to find the life and intelligence and charm that I'd seen in his profile photo. He must have noticed, because he gave an awkward laugh and said, "Have I got foam on my eyebrow or something?"

I laughed, too, and shook my head. And I was going to change the subject—but I thought, *Sod it, why not be honest?* So I said, "It's weird, but your eyes don't look *exactly* like they did on the website. Probably the light or something."

Which is when the truth came out. He looked a bit shifty and said, "Yeah, I've had some problems with my eyes recently? They went a bit septic. Gunky, you know? This one was kind of greeny-yellow." He pointed to his left eye. "It was *bad*. I went through two lots of antibiotic cream."

"Right," I said, trying not to heave. "Poor you."

"So hands up," he continued. "I didn't use my own eyes in my profile picture."

"You . . . what?" I said, not quite following.

"I photoshopped in someone else's eyes," he said matter-of-factly. "Same color, so what's the difference?"

In disbelief, I got out my phone and summoned up his profile picture—and at once it was obvious. The eyes opposite me were flat and dull and insipid. The eyes on the screen were crinkly and charming and inviting.

"So whose eyes are these?" I demanded, jabbing at them. He looked even more shifty, then said with a shrug, "Brad Pitt's."

Brad Pitt's?

He lured me into a date with *Brad Pitt's eyes?*

I felt so angry and stupid, I could barely get out another word. But he didn't seem to notice that anything was wrong. In fact, he suggested that we go on to a restaurant. What a nerve! As I left, I nearly said sarcastically, "FYI, my boobs are Lady Gaga's." But that might have sent the wrong message.

I should complain to the website, only I can't be bothered. I can't be bothered with any of it. I'm having a pause from men. Yes. That's what I'm doing. My instincts can just have a holiday—

"The most important thing, of course, will be for you to stay focused." Farida's voice penetrates my thoughts. "Distraction is the enemy of productivity, as I'm sure you know."

I look up, to realize Farida's gaze is resting appraisingly on me. Shit! She knows I'm not listening. I feel a tremor, as though I'm in fourth-form geography and have been caught passing notes. Everyone else is listening. Everyone else is concentrating. *Come on, Ava. Be a grown-up.*

I glance around the ancient, high-ceilinged stone room we're sitting in. The retreat is taking place in an old monastery in Puglia. There are eight of us, sitting on well-worn wooden chairs, all dressed in the plain linen kurta pajamas we were given this morning. That's one of the rules of this retreat: You can't wear your own clothes. Nor can you use your own name. Nor can you have your phone. You have to hand it in at the start of the week and you only get it back for half an hour a night, or for an emergency. Plus there's no Wi-Fi. At least, not for guests.

On arrival, we were given lunch in our own bedrooms so that we wouldn't meet before this afternoon. The rooms are

old monks' cells with whitewashed walls and paintings of
the Madonna all over the place. (They've also been knocked
through, if you ask me. Don't tell me monks had enough room
for king-size beds, writing tables, and hand-embroidered ot-
tomans, available for purchase in the gift shop.)

After lunch I sat on my linen bedspread, trying to focus
on my plot and only occasionally scrolling through photos
of Harold on my laptop. Then we were individually ushered
into this space and asked to remain silent. So I'm sitting with
a group of utter strangers with whom I haven't exchanged a
single word, just a couple of shy smiles. Five other women
and two men. They're all older than me, apart from a thin
bony guy who looks to be in his twenties and a girl who
looks like she's a college student.

It's all quite intense. Quite strange. Although in fairness,
I knew it would be. I read a stack of online reviews before I
booked this course, and 90 percent of them described it as
"intense." Other words that cropped up were "eccentric,"
"immersive," "challenging," and "lot of bloody nutters."
But also "sublime" and "life-changing."

I'm choosing to believe "sublime" and "life-changing."

"Let me now explain to you the philosophy of this writing retreat," says Farida, and she pauses.

She pauses a lot as she speaks, as though to air her words
and consider them. She's in her fifties, half-Lebanese and
half-Italian. I know this because I've read her book about
dual heritage, called *I and I*. At least I half-read it. (It's a bit
long.) She has sleek dark hair and a calm demeanor and is
wearing the same kurta linen pajamas as the rest of us, except they look far better on her. I bet she's had hers tailored.

"This week is not about how you look," she continues. "Or what your background is. Or even what your name is. It is purely about your writing. Remove your self, and your writing will shine."

I glance at the skinny, dark-haired woman sitting next to me. She's writing *Remove your self and your writing will shine,* in her notebook.

Should I write it down too? No. I can remember it.

"I have run writing retreats for many years," Farida continues. "In the early days, I had none of these rules. My students began by introducing themselves, sharing their names, backgrounds, and experiences. But what happened? The conversations grew and mushroomed. They chatted about publishing, children, day jobs, holidays, current affairs . . . and none of them wrote!" She smacks one hand against the other. "None of them wrote! You're here to write. If you have a thought you want to share, *put it into your writing.* If you have a joke you want to make, *put it into your writing.*"

She's quite inspiring. If a little intimidating. The thin bony guy has raised his hand, and I admire his guts. I would not be raising my hand at this point.

"Are you saying this is a silent retreat? Can't we talk?"

Farida's face creases into a broad smile. "You can talk. We will all talk. But we will not talk about ourselves. We will release our minds from the strain of small talk." She eyes us all severely. "Small talk depletes creativity. Social media stifles thought. Even choosing an outfit every morning is needless effort. So, for one week, we will let all that nonsense go. We will engage instead with *big* talk. Character. Plot. Good and evil. The right way to live."

She picks up a basket from a heavy carved side table and walks around, handing out blank name badges and pens.

"Your first task is to choose a new name for the week. Liberate yourselves from your old selves. Become new selves. Creative selves."

As I take my name badge, I feel quite excited by becoming a new creative self. Also, she's right about the outfits. I knew in advance about the kurta pajamas, so packing was easy. Pretty much all I needed was sunblock, hat, swimsuit, and my laptop to write my book.

Or, at least, finish my book. It's a romantic story set in Victorian England, and I'm a bit stuck. I've got up to my hero, Chester, riding off on a hay wagon in the golden sunshine, exclaiming, "When next you see me, Ada, you will *know* I'm a man of my word!" but I don't know what he does next, and he can't stay on the hay wagon for two hundred pages.

Nell thinks he should die in an industrial accident and help to change the archaic labor laws of the day. But that seems a bit gloomy to me. So then she said, "Could he be maimed?" and I said, "What do you mean?" which was a mistake, because now she keeps googling horrendous accidents and sending me links with titles like, *Could he lose a foot?*

The trouble is, I don't *want* to write about Chester being mangled in a thresher. Nor do I want to base the evil landowner on Maud's old chemistry teacher. The thing about friends is, they're very helpful, but they're almost *too* helpful. They all suggest their own ideas and confuse you. That's why I think this week away will be really helpful.

I wonder what Harold's doing.

No. *Stop.*

I blink back to reality as I notice the woman next to me putting on her name badge. She's called herself "Metaphor." Oh God. Quick, I need to come up with a name. I'll call myself . . . what? Something literary? Like "Sonnet"? Or "Parenthesis"? Or something dynamic like "Velocity"? No, that was a team on *The Apprentice.*

Come on. It doesn't matter what I call myself. Quickly I write *Aria,* and pin my badge onto my pajama top.

Then I realize Aria's almost exactly my real name.

Oh well. No one will ever know.

"Well done." Farida's eyes gleam at us. "Let us introduce our writing selves."

We go round the room and everyone says their "name" out loud. We're called Beginner, Austen, Booklover, Metaphor, Aria, Scribe, Author-to-Be, and Captain James T. Kirk of the Starship *Enterprise*—the bony guy. He goes on to inform us he's writing a graphic novel, not a romantic one, but his screenwriter friend told him this course was good, and you can learn from anything, right? Then he starts on some rant about the Marvel Universe, but Farida gently cuts him off and tells him we'll call him "Kirk" for short.

I already like the look of Scribe. She's got cropped salt-and-pepper hair, a tanned face, and a mischievous smile. Beginner has cotton-candy white hair and must be eighty at least. Author-to-Be is the guy with gray hair and a paunch, and the student is Austen. Booklover looks about forty and has exchanged a friendly smile with me—meanwhile Metaphor has already shot her hand up.

"You say we shouldn't talk about ourselves," she says a bit snippily. "But surely we'll reveal elements of ourselves *in our writing*?" She sounds as if she wants to catch out Farida, thus demonstrating how clever she is. But Farida just smiles, unruffled.

"Of course you will reveal your souls as you write," she says. "But this is a romantic-fiction writing retreat. The art of fiction is to present reality as though it's unreality." She addresses the whole room. "Be artful. Use disguises."

That's a good tip. Maybe I'll change my heroine's name from Ada to something a bit less like Ava. Victorienne. Is that a name?

I write down *Victorienne* in my notebook, just as Farida resumes speaking.

"Today we look at the principles of story," she says. "I would like each of you to say what story means for you. Just one sentence. Beginning with Austen."

"Right." Austen colors bright red. "It's . . . um . . . wanting to know the end."

"Thank you." Farida smiles. "Author-to-Be?"

"Crikey!" says Author-to-Be with a throaty chortle. "Put me on the spot, why don't you! Er . . . beginning, middle, end."

"Thank you," says Farida again, and she's about to draw breath when there's a rattle at the huge wooden door. It swings open and a woman I recognize as Nadia, the course administrator, beckons Farida over. They have a hurried whispered conversation, during which we all glance at one another uncertainly, then Farida turns back to address us.

"As you know, there are three different retreats taking

place in the monastery this week," she begins. "Writing, meditation, and martial arts. Unfortunately, the leader of the martial-arts retreat has been taken ill and a replacement has not been found. Those guests have been given the opportunity to join one of the other retreats instead—and three have chosen to join our writing group. I would ask you to welcome them."

We all watch, agog, as the door widens. Two men and a woman walk in—and my heart jumps. That taller, dark-haired guy. Wow.

He smiles round the room and I feel my throat tighten. OK. So it turns out my instincts don't want a holiday, after all. My instincts are leaping up and down and pulling in the extra emergency-instincts team and yelling, "Look, look!"

Because he's *gorgeous*. I've been on thirty-six online first dates—and not one has sent a streak of electricity through me like this.

He's got to be in his late thirties. He's well built—you can see that through the fabric of his kurta pajamas. Wavy black hair, faint stubble, a strong jaw, deep-brown eyes, and a fluid, easy motion as he takes his seat. He smiles at his neighbors a little uncertainly as he takes a name badge and pen from Farida and regards them thoughtfully. He's the most good-looking person in the room by a million miles, but he doesn't even seem to have noticed.

I'm blatantly gobbling him up with my eyes, I realize. But that's OK, because you're allowed to be observant if you're a writer. If anyone asks, I'll say I'm making mental notes for a character in my book, and *that's* why I'm gazing so intently at his thighs.

Kirk seems quite taken by one of the other new arrivals, I notice, and I swing round to survey her quickly. She's pretty attractive, too, with tawny hair and white teeth and amazingly toned arms. The second guy is incredibly pumped up, with mammoth biceps—in fact, our whole group is suddenly about 50 percent more good-looking on average. Which maybe says something about martial arts versus writing.

The entire mood of the room has lifted, and we watch, rapt, as the newbies choose their names. The girl goes for Lyric, the super-muscled guy is Black Belt, and the dark-haired guy chooses Dutch.

"It was the name of my childhood dog," he says as he introduces himself—and I melt. His voice is *good*. It's deep and resonant and honest and ambitious but noble and humorous, too, with a hint of past sadness but rays of future sunshine and a thread of rare intelligence. And OK, I know I've only heard him utter eight words. But that's enough. I can tell. I can feel it. I just know he has a big heart and integrity and honor. *He* would never photoshop in Brad Pitt's eyes.

Plus he had a childhood dog. A dog, a dog! I feel almost giddy with hope. If he's single . . . if only he's single . . . and straight . . . and single . . .

"We try not to reveal details of our lives on this retreat," says Farida with a gentle smile, and Dutch clicks his tongue.

"Right. You said. Sorry. Messed up already."

A new appalling thought hits me. If we're not talking about ourselves, how am I supposed to find out if he's single?

He's got to be. He's giving off single vibes. Also: If he's attached, where's his partner?

"Now that everyone has been introduced," Farida is saying, "we can carry on with our discussion. Maybe, Dutch, you could tell us what story means to you?" Dutch's face jolts and he looks alarmed.

"Story," he echoes, clearly playing for time.

"Story." Farida nods. "We're here to create story. That's our task in this retreat."

"Huh. Right. Story." Dutch rubs the back of his neck. "OK," he says at last. "Here's the thing. I came here to learn how to kick the shit out of my opponent. Not this."

"Of course," says Farida softly. "But do your best."

"I'm not a writer," Dutch says at last. "I can't tell stories. Not like you can. I don't have your skills or talent. I'd like to learn, though." As he looks around, his eye catches mine and my stomach twangs.

"I'm sure you will learn," I say throatily, before I can stop myself.

At once I curse myself for being too uncool and eager, but Dutch seems disarmed.

"Thanks." He squints to read my name badge. "Aria. Nice name. Thanks."

Three

〰️

At break we mill around in the courtyard with glasses of homemade lemonade. I sip mine for a while, then let my eye catch Dutch's, casually.

Super-casually.

Like, barely interested at all.

"Hi!" I say. "How did you find the writing exercise?"

We've all just written the first sentence of a book and handed them in to Farida. We're going to discuss them later in the week. Mine's quite dramatic; it goes: *Emily's bosom dripped with blood as she gazed at the love of her life.*

I'm quite pleased with it, actually. I think it's pretty riveting. Why is Emily's bosom dripping with blood? Any reader would be *dying* to know. (The only thing is, I'm not sure myself; I must think about that before we get to the discussion.)

"I froze," says Dutch regretfully. "Didn't write a word.

My brain . . ." He bangs his forehead with his fist. "Just won't do it. I was never any good at this kind of thing. Give me a practical task. Or numbers. I'm good with numbers. But creative writing . . ." A tortured expression passes over his face.

"That's OK," I say encouragingly. "It'll come."

"It's interesting, though," he continues, as if determined to be positive. "I liked hearing what everyone else thought. Interesting crowd." He spreads his arms to take in everyone wandering around the courtyard. "You know. It's different. Sometimes it's good to step outside your comfort zone. Try something new."

"This courtyard is beautiful, isn't it?" I can hear Scribe saying behind me.

"Oh, it's *stunning*," Metaphor replies in a loud, definitive voice, as though she's the only person who can pronounce on what's stunning or not and no one else had better even try. "The ancient, craggy stones, worn down by a thousand foot-steps," she continues in declamatory tones. "The echoing cloister, full of history. The scents of herbs, mingling with the cascading blooms of flowers all around us, while swal-lows speed through the cobalt sky, tumbling and shooting like endless darts of . . ." She hesitates for only a moment. "Quicksilver."

"Absolutely," says Scribe after a polite pause. "That's just what I was going to say."

I want to turn around and catch Scribe's eye, but before I can, Black Belt approaches.

"Hi," he greets Dutch. "Hot out here."

He's taken off his pajama top and I'm trying not to stare, but *those muscles*. I've never seen anyone that ripped in real life. Basically he looks like a less-green Hulk.

"It's weird, huh?" He addresses Dutch. "This no-name shit. Did you write anything?"

"No."

"Me either.

"You write anything?" He's turned to Lyric, who is walking up to us, holding a glass of lemonade.

"A bit." She shrugs. "Not really my thing. I thought it would be more interesting."

She's gazing at Dutch over her drink, I suddenly notice. In fact, she can't take her eyes off him. Oh *God*. The horrible truth suddenly hits me: I have a rival. A rival with tawny hair and toned arms and slimmer legs than mine.

As I gaze anxiously at her, Lyric seems to become prettier before my eyes. Her hair is feathery and frames her face perfectly. She's chewing her lips in an adorable way. She probably looks incredibly hot when she kickboxes. Of course she does.

"Are you into this?" she suddenly demands of Dutch, almost aggressively, and he flinches at her tone.

"Don't know. Maybe."

"I'm not," says Black Belt flatly. "I think it was a mistake. Shall we take off?" He addresses Dutch directly. "We can still get a refund."

What?

Panic shoots through me, but somehow I summon a relaxed smile. Relaxed-ish, maybe.

"Don't leave!" I say lightheartedly, making sure I address all of them, not just Dutch. "Give it another chance. Come to the next session, see how it goes."

Farida is banging the little gong that signals us to return to the group, and I can see Dutch is conflicted.

"I'll try another session," he says at last to the others. "I'm not bailing yet. We've got until tomorrow to decide."

Black Belt rolls his eyes but drains his lemonade and dumps the glass on a nearby trestle table.

"If you say so," says Lyric without enthusiasm. "But I think it's pretty shit. I think we should go for the refund. We could go and have a drink now, in the town. Have some fun. Get on a flight tomorrow morning."

"You don't have to stay," says Dutch, sounding defensive. "But I want to have another go. I like listening, even if I can't write. Maybe I'll pick up some tips."

He turns and heads back toward the doorway leading to our meeting room. Lyric watches him for a moment, then clicks her tongue as though in frustration and follows him in, along with Black Belt.

She's *so* after him.

As we take our seats, I sneak a few glances at her and she's gazing at Dutch, an unmistakable look in her eye. It's so blatant. So obvious. I mean, it's inappropriate, if you ask me. This is a *writing retreat*.

"And now it's time for the improvisation exercise that I mentioned earlier." Farida's voice interrupts my thoughts. "Don't be scared! I know some of you are shy. . . ." She pauses, and there's a nervous laugh around the room. "But do your best. I want you to improvise a character in turmoil, thinking about his antagonist; his enemy. Any character. Any turmoil. Dig deep. Kirk!" She smiles as he leaps to his feet. "Go ahead."

Kirk makes his way to the center of the room, looking supremely confident, and draws breath.

"Where do I even begin?" he demands emphatically. "Here I am, cast out from Zorgon, holding the secret of the Third Rock of Farra but unjustly banished from the Sixteen Planetary Nations. And, Emril, I blame *you,* you vile monster; you've always hated me, since we were kids . . ."

As Kirk carries on his tirade, I find my gaze drifting back to Lyric. She's still staring at Dutch, her mouth half open. She's fixated. It's unhealthy! Plus, her kurta pajama top is hanging sexily off one shoulder. Don't tell me that happened by accident.

". . . so, Emril, Empress of the North, believe me. It's *on,*" Kirk concludes menacingly, and we all applaud.

"Very good!" says Farida. "I really felt your anger there, Kirk, well done. Now, who's next?" Her face jolts in surprise as Dutch raises his hand. "Dutch!" She sounds astonished and pleased. "You have a character you want to work on?"

"Yes," says Dutch shortly. "I think I do."

We all watch curiously as he comes to the center of the space, his brows knitted as though he's deep in thought.

"Tell us about your fictional character," says Farida encouragingly.

"He's pissed off," says Dutch, his voice resounding around the space. "Someone won't leave him alone. And it's becoming . . . intolerable."

"Good!" says Farida. "Well, Dutch, the floor is yours."

I'm intrigued as Dutch draws breath. And I can tell everyone else is too. It's pretty impressive, to go from zero to improvisation in front of a class, in less than a day.

"I've *had* it," Dutch says, glowering at an imaginary person in the wall. "I've just *had* it with you." There's a breathless silence—then he blinks. "That's it," he adds to Farida.

That's his entire improvisation?

I hear a snort of laughter from someone, and I bite my lip
to stop a giggle—but Farida doesn't flicker. "Maybe you
could elaborate?" she suggests. "Turn that very powerful
and succinct opening into more of a monologue?"

"I'll try," says Dutch. He looks dubious but turns to address the wall again. "Just *stop*. I can't take any more. You're
so . . ."

He seems to search fruitlessly for words, his expression
more and more exasperated . . . until suddenly he executes a
side kick. "You're just—" He chops the air angrily with his
hand, breathing hard. "You know? You should just . . ."
Again he gropes vainly for words, then in frustration leaps in
the air with a furious cry, one leg kicking out strongly in attack.

We all gasp in shock, and Beginner gives a little terrified
cry.

"Awesome!" shouts Black Belt encouragingly as Dutch
lands. "Nice technique, man."

"Thanks," says Dutch, panting slightly.

"Dutch!" Farida leaps up from her seat and puts a hand
on his shoulder before he can perform any more maneuvers.
"Dutch. That was very convincing. However, this is a writing
group. Not a martial-arts group."

"Right." Dutch seems to come to. "Sorry. I lost it for a moment."

"Please don't worry," Farida reassures him. "You found a form of expression, and that's a start. Clearly you were expressing powerful emotions?"

"Yes," says Dutch after a pause. "It was frustrating. I *felt* it." He bangs his chest. "Just . . . couldn't find the words."

"Indeed." Farida nods. "The plight of the writer in a nutshell. But, please, no more kickboxing. Although I do applaud your vivid portrayal of antagonism. We're here to write romantic fiction." She addresses the group. "And love is closer to hate than any other—"

"Romantic fiction?" Black Belt interrupts her, his face convulsed with horror. "*Romantic?* They said 'Writing.' They didn't say anything about 'romantic.'"

"Of course, you don't *have* to write romantic fiction—" begins Farida, but Black Belt ignores her.

"I'm outta here. Sorry." He gets to his feet. "This isn't my bag. Jeez."

"It's not my bag either," says Lyric, standing up and glaring around generally, as though it's all our faults. "It's superweird and I want a refund."

She's going? Yesss!

Angels are singing *hallelujah* in my head. She's leaving!

"Shame," I say in the most regretful tone I can muster.

"You coming?" says Black Belt to Dutch, and Lyric turns to him expectantly too. The singing angels dwindle away inside my head, and my throat clenches in fear. He can't leave. He mustn't.

Don't go, I silently beg him. *Please don't go.*

I feel as if the whole retreat will be ruined if he goes. Or even my whole life. Which is ridiculous—I only just met him. But that's how I feel.

"I think I'll stay," says Dutch at last, and I breathe out, trying not to give away how relieved I am.

Supper is around a long wooden table in a paved garden filled with massive terra-cotta pots of agapanthus and herbs and spiky cactuses. There are huge candles everywhere and painted pottery plates, and the waiters pour wine into short stubby glasses. Apparently the meditation group are having supper in a different courtyard. So that we don't pollute their meditation, I guess.

I'm at the end of the table, sitting next to Metaphor and Scribe. I tried to sit next to Dutch, but somehow he got swept to the other end, which was incredibly frustrating.

"This place is so inspiring, don't you think?" says Scribe, clinking her wineglass with mine. We've all changed into indigo linen kurta pajamas for the evening, and I must say, hers are very flattering. "My mind is absolutely *humming* with ideas for my book. Is yours?"

"Er . . ." I take a sip of wine, playing for time. The truth is, I haven't given my book a thought. I'm obsessed with Dutch.

He's so handsome. Self-deprecating, but confident too. And he's good with his hands. A few moments ago, it transpired that the massive wooden pepper grinder didn't work. Booklover wanted to tell a waiter, but Dutch said, "Let me try." Now he's taken the whole thing to bits and is staring at the mechanism intently, ignoring the conversation around him.

"During the break, I entirely replotted my story," Scribe tells me. "And it's only day one!"

"Great!" I applaud her, suddenly feeling guilty. I've neglected Chester and Clara (I've renamed her). I should focus on my task. Am I here to write a book or find a man?

Man! yells my brain before I can stop it, and I splutter my wine.

"I'm finding inspiration in everything," Metaphor announces grandly. "Look at these dishes. Look at the sky. Look at the shadows in the garden."

A waiter puts a bowl of bean broth flecked with green herbs in front of each of us, and Scribe says happily, "Mmm, yum."

"I love the way the broad beans rest in their broth," says Metaphor, "looking so contented. As though they've finally found home. *La casa.* A spiritual rest."

They what? Broad beans have found spiritual rest? I catch Scribe's eye and quell a giggle.

"I must write that down," adds Metaphor. "I may use it." She shoots each of us suspicious looks, as though we're planning to pinch her idea.

"Good idea," says Scribe blandly.

At the other end of the table, there's a conversation going on about love and relationships, which I would *far* rather be part of, but I can only just hear it.

"Look at the story we studied today," Booklover is saying, dipping her bread into artichoke dip. "If that's not about trying again—"

"But they don't try again," Author-to-Be interrupts. "That's it. *Finito*."

"I think we have to believe they might reconcile," chimes in Austen shyly. "Isn't that what love is—forgiveness?"

"But there's a limit." Author-to-Be turns to Dutch. "What about you, Dutch? Are you a forgiving type? Do you believe in second chances?"

My heart leaps at the sound of his name, and I try my hardest to hear what he says above the sound of Metaphor, who's now droning on about the Italian landscape.

Dutch raises his head from the pepper grinder and shrugs easily. "I don't know about a forgiving type, but I try to be rational," he says. "I look at the evidence. There's a quote I like. 'When the facts change, I change my mind.' "

" 'Look at the evidence!' " Author-to-Be gives a short laugh. "That's romantic!"

"That's just how I am—" Dutch breaks off, and his face suddenly lights up as though he's spotted someone he knows. "Hey, beautiful."

My throat seizes up. Beautiful? Who's beautiful? Who just arrived? His wife? His Italian girlfriend? The waitress he's somehow already started a relationship with, this afternoon, without my noticing?

Then I see a huge white dog padding through the garden, weaving its way between the giant terra-cotta pots. Dutch holds out his hand invitingly and the dog makes straight for him, as though it knows, out of all of us, Dutch is the guy to choose.

Scribe is saying something to me, but I can't hear. I'm gripped by the sight of Dutch. He's talking to the dog, coaxing it, stroking it, smiling down at it, ignoring everyone else. I know it when I see it: He doesn't just like dogs, he loves dogs. As the dog puts a paw playfully up to him, Dutch throws back his head and laughs, in such a natural, engaging way that I feel another tug at my heart.

Now Metaphor's trying to get my attention, but I'm deaf to anything but Dutch. And as I watch him . . . his strong, muscled arms . . . candlelight flickering on his face . . . his easy smile . . . I feel as if I'm floating. My heart is bursting with hope and exhilaration.

As though he's reading my mind, Dutch lifts his head and looks at me for a few seconds. He smiles as though he's trying to say something, and I find myself nodding and smiling back as though I understand, my heart going hippity-hop in my chest.

I feel about sixteen right now.

No. Younger. When did I have my first ever mammoth crush? That age.

Then a waiter comes up to take Dutch's plate, he looks away, and the moment's over. Reluctantly, I turn my attention to my neighbors and force myself to listen to what Metaphor's saying about some Booker Prize winner. But all the while, my thoughts are turning over and over.

What if . . . ? I mean, what *if* . . . ? He's handsome. Positive. Thoughtful. Good with his hands. And, oh my God, *he loves dogs.*

Four

By the next evening, my heart has hipped and hopped all over the place. I'm getting ready for supper, staring at myself in the tiny cracked mirror in my room (everything here is old and picturesque), unable to think about anything except: What are my chances?

I'm slightly wishing I looked more Italian right now. All the Italian staff at the retreat have such glossy dark hair and smooth olive skin, whereas my skin freckles in the sun. I'm what they call "fine-featured," which can seem like an asset until you see a luscious nineteen-year-old girl with blunt bobbed hair and a snub nose and rounded, dimpled shoulders—

No. Stop it. I shake my head impatiently to clear my thoughts. Nell would say I'm being a moron. She would have no time for this. At the thought of Nell, I automatically think of Harold—and before I can stop myself, I'm summoning up the *Harold* folder on my computer.

Scrolling through photos of him calms my heart a little. Harold. Beloved Harold. Just seeing his bright, intelligent face makes me smile, although even the video of him trying to get into the laundry basket can't fix all my problems. As I shut the folder down, I'm still twitchy and uncertain. It's been that kind of day.

The morning session was a blur. While all the other participants discussed their writing goals and made studious notes on daily routines, I was focused on Dutch. He was sitting between Scribe and Booklover when I arrived (damn), but I took the chance to sit opposite him.

Our eyes met a few times. He smiled. I smiled back. When Farida mentioned confrontation in fiction, I made a jokey martial-arts gesture at him and he laughed. It was kind of a thing.

As we disbanded for lunch, I felt 100 percent hopeful. I also had a plan: Bag a seat next to him, pull out every flirtatious trick I had, and, if all else failed, ask blatantly, "How do you feel about holiday romances?" (If he looked appalled, I could pretend it was the plot of my next novel.)

But he didn't turn up. He *didn't turn up*!

How can you not turn up to lunch? Lunch is part of the package. It's free. And delicious. Nothing made any sense.

Then it got worse: He didn't turn up to the afternoon yoga session either. Farida even came up to me and asked, "Do you know where Dutch is?"

(Note: She asked *me*. This says people have noticed we have a connection. Although what good is a connection if he's not here?)

At that stage I gave up. I thought, He's left. He's not inter-ested. In writing *or* me. Then I cursed myself bitterly for having been distracted this morning, because, after all, this course wasn't cheap. I decided to refocus, forget love, and do what I came here to do: *Write*. Not think about holiday ro-mances. *Write*.

I sat on my bed, staring at my manuscript printout for a bit, wondering if Chester should get off the hay wagon or if maybe the hay wagon should catch on fire. Then I thought: What if Clara hides on the hay wagon and she gets burned to death? But that would be quite a short, sad book—

And then the miracle happened. I heard a voice through my bedroom window, which looks out onto one of the clois-tered courtyards. It was Booklover, exclaiming, "Oh, Dutch! We thought you'd gone."

Then I heard him replying, "No, I just took off for the afternoon. How was yoga?"

Then they had some conversation I couldn't hear prop-erly, and Booklover said, "See you at supper," and he said, "Sure thing," and my heart started pounding while my man-uscript slithered to the floor.

And now hope is dancing unstoppably round my body. I close my laptop, spray on a final spritz of perfume, tug at my indigo pajamas, then head through the candlelit corridors and courtyards to the paved garden where supper is served. I can see Dutch already—and an empty chair beside him. I'm having that chair.

Picking up my pace, I reach it just before Austen and grab it with a viselike grip.

"Why don't I go here?" I say in the most nonchalant tone I can muster, and quickly sit down before anyone can comment. I breathe in to compose myself, then turn to Dutch.

"Hi." I smile.

"Hi." He smiles back, and my insides crumple with desire.

His voice *does* things to me. It stirs up reactions in all kinds of places. And it's not just his voice—his whole presence is setting me alight. His eyes look as though they already know what I want. His body language is strong. His smile is irresistible. As he reaches for his napkin, his bare forearm brushes against mine and I feel a tingle throughout my body. No, more than a tingle. A craving.

"Excuse me," I murmur, leaning over on the pretext of pouring him water—and for the first time I inhale his scent. Oh *God*. Yes. I want more of that too. Whatever combination of hormones and sweat and soap and cologne that is . . . it works.

A waiter has poured us both wine, and Dutch lifts his glass to toast mine, then turns to face me properly. His gaze is intent and focused, as though the rest of the table has disappeared and it's just us two.

"So," he says. "We can't make small talk."

"No."

"I can't ask you anything personal about yourself."

"No."

"The more I'm told I can't do something, the more I want to do it." His dark eyes are fixed fully on mine and I catch my breath, because I'm suddenly imagining what else he might want to do. And what else I might want to do.

Unhurriedly, his gaze unmoving, Dutch sips his wine.

"I'd like to know more about you." He leans forward and lowers his voice to a whisper. "We could break the rules."

"Break the *rules*?" I echo, shocked. I feel as though I'm in a nineteenth-century novel and a gentleman has asked if he might write me illicit letters. Dutch laughs, seeming tickled by my reaction.

"OK, you don't want to break the rules. How about we ask each other just one personal question?"

I nod. "Good idea. You start."

"OK. Here's my question." He pauses, running a finger round the rim of his wineglass—then looks up. "Are you single?"

Something seems to flash through my body. Something joyous and strong and urgent all at once. He *is* interested.

"Yes," I say, my voice barely working. "I'm . . . Yes."

"Great." His eyes crinkle at me. "That's . . . Glad to hear it. Now you ask me a question."

"OK." My mouth flickers into a smile, because we're playing a game now. "Let me think. Are you single?"

"*Oh* yes." There's an emphasis to his answer which in another conversation I would pick up on—but I'm out of questions.

"So now we know everything," I say, and Dutch laughs.

"Everything for now. Maybe we ask each other one question every night. That could be our ration."

"Sounds good."

We're interrupted as a waiter comes to give us plates of pasta, and I take the opportunity to gaze at Dutch surreptitiously again, at his strong jaw and dark lashes, and at his tiny endearing crow's feet, which I didn't notice before. I don't know how old he is, I realize. I could ask him tomorrow night. That could be my question.

But, then, do I care how old he is? No. No! I don't!

I feel suddenly exhilarated. I feel liberated! I don't care about the facts or the details or what his profile might be on Match.com. He's here and I'm here and that's all that matters.

"Wait, I have another question," I say, as Dutch turns back from passing the olive oil along. "I *think* it's allowed. . . . Where were you this afternoon?" I shoot him a mock-reproving look. "You ditched yoga!"

"Oh. Right." He takes a forkful of pasta, looking amused. "I'm not a yoga fan, to be honest. I'm more of a—"

"Stop!" I raise a hand. "Don't tell me! Too much personal information!"

"Jeez!" exclaims Dutch, looking for the first time genuinely frustrated. "How are we supposed to talk, even?"

"We're not," I point out. "We're supposed to write."

"Ah." He nods. "Touché."

"Or, in your case, kick the shit out of things," I add, and Dutch laughs.

"Touché again."

I take a mouthful of orecchiette, which is the local pasta. It's served with greens and rosemary and tastes sublime. But while last night I couldn't stop rejoicing over the food, tonight I can't stop rejoicing over this delicious, tantalizing conversation. Or non-conversation.

Dutch is silent for a few moments, munching pasta, then says, "Actual fact, I hired a car and went exploring down the coast a little. There are some coves . . . nice villages. . . . It was fun." He swallows his mouthful, turns to me, and adds carelessly, "I was thinking of doing the same tomorrow. You want to come?"

As we bowl along the coastline the next afternoon, I feel giddy. How has life fallen so stunningly into place? How do I find myself being driven through gorgeous Italian scenery, the sun blazing down, the radio playing, next to the most perfect guy in the world?

I'm trying to take an intelligent interest in the beautiful, stark landscape around us, but my attention keeps being drawn back to Dutch. Because he just gets better and better.

He drives confidently. He doesn't get stressed out by being lost. Five minutes ago, he asked an old guy for directions in a terrible mishmash of English and bad Italian. But his smile was so charming, the guy ended up summoning an English-speaking woman from inside his house, who drew us a map. And now here we are, at a tiny cliff-top car park, with nothing in view except olive groves, rocks, and the endless blue Mediterranean.

"What's this place called?" I ask, so that I sound intelligent. (I don't care what it's called.)

"No idea," says Dutch cheerfully. "But the woman knew where I meant. I came here yesterday. It's fun."

"I intended to learn Italian before I came out here," I say regretfully. "But there isn't time for everything. . . . Do you speak any other languages?"

"I try," says Dutch. "But they don't stick."

He sounds so unapologetic, I can't help smiling. A lot of people would resort to bullshit at that point, but not him.

I follow him down a stony path to a little rocky cove with a pebbly beach and the clearest aquamarine water I've ever seen. There aren't any sun beds or beach bars; it's not that kind of place. The beachgoers are mostly older Italian women, sitting on towels with scarves protecting their hair, and clutches of shouting teenagers.

On either side of the cove are rocky cliffs, and there are teenagers at every level, climbing, sunbathing, smoking, and drinking beer. As I scan the scene, a girl in a red bikini hurls herself off a rocky outcrop, screeching and fist-pumping the air before plummeting into the sea. A moment later, she's followed by a teenage boy, who jumps with flailing legs and lands with a massive splash.

They skirmish in the water for a moment, then he holds her bikini top up out of the water with a triumphant yell, while the girl laughs hysterically. His audience of teenagers on the rocks bursts into cheers, and Dutch gives me a wary glance.

"It wasn't quite this wild yesterday," he says. "We could find somewhere quieter."

"No, I like it." I smile at him. "It feels . . . you know. Real. Wow," I add, watching another girl leaping off the rocky ledge. "That's high."

"It's fun."

"You *did* that?"

"Of course." He laughs at my expression. "I mean, it's safe. Water's deep. You want to have a go?"

"Er . . . sure!" I say, before I can think whether this is a good idea or not. "Why not?"

We find an empty patch on the pebbly beach and I take off my caftan, sucking in my stomach as I do so. Although I'm careful not to look in his direction, I can sense Dutch checking me out in my swimsuit. It's black and low cut and I know it's a sexy number because Russell used to call it Instant—

No. I stop my own thoughts abruptly. I'm *not* thinking about Russell. Why would I recall an obnoxious ex-boyfriend at this moment?

I fold up my caftan, demurely looking away from Dutch as he strips off but also managing to sneak some glances at him. He's in navy swim shorts and clearly visits the gym. His thighs are muscled, and he has a hairy chest. I like a hairy chest.

I feel a trickle of sweat on my forehead and wipe it away. It's even more baking down here than it was on the cliff, and the splashing of the waves is unbelievably inviting.

"It's hot," I say, and Dutch nods.

"We should get in the water. You want to . . . ?" He gestures at the rock-jumpers, and my stomach flickers with nerves. I'd be quite happy paddling. But I'm not admitting that, so I say, "Of course!" and Dutch grins.

"Cool. This way."

He leads me to a tortuous path, looping back and forth up the side of the cliff. We clamber up craggy rocks, past caves, pausing once or twice to let rowdy groups of teenagers rush past us. As we finally emerge at the rocky ledge and look down at the white-flecked water below, I feel elation and terror, all at once.

"Ready?" Dutch gestures at the edge, and I laugh nervously.

There's a guy of about twenty standing behind us, not hiding his impatience, and I step aside. We both watch as he takes a good run-up, leaps off the cliff, and plummets into the blueness below.

"Long way down," I say, trying to sound conversational rather than petrified.

"That's what makes it fun," says Dutch with enthusiasm.

"Definitely!" I nod several times, then add casually, "I mean, there's a line between 'fun' and 'terrifying.' "

Dutch laughs. "Yup." Then his expression suddenly changes to one of concern. "Wait. Are we over that line for you? Sorry. I dragged you up here. I don't know where your limits are."

I can sense him suddenly thinking, *I don't know this person at all; why am I encouraging her to jump off a cliff?*

"You want to go down a level?" he adds, standing aside to let a group of three teenagers jump off. "We can do that."

For an instant I'm tempted. But then I recall what he said the other day: "Sometimes it's good to step outside your comfort zone."

"I don't know," I say, staring at the glittering sea, feeling a stab of frustration at myself. "I don't *not* want to do it. I think I'm finding out where my limits are."

"OK," says Dutch cautiously. "Well, where are you right now?"

"I want to do it," I say, trying to convince myself as much as him. "It's just . . . how many feet is that?"

"Don't get hung up on those kinds of thoughts," says Dutch reassuringly. "Just think about the excitement. The rush."

"Uh-huh." I nod. His words are helping. Although I'm still not moving toward the edge.

"I saw two little kids in a playground once," Dutch continues. "One was psyching himself up to go on the monkey bars and his friend was trying to help him. He said, 'You learn by scaredness.' I've never forgotten it."

"You learn by scaredness," I repeat slowly. "I like that. So what do you learn, jumping into the sea?"

"You learn you can do it." He smiles at me, a broad, infectious smile. "Shall we do it together?"

"OK." I nod. "Come on. Let's do this."

I may die, I think calmly as we step forward. This is possible. On the plus side, it's a good way to go. *Girl perishes jumping into sea with handsome guy.* That would do.

Dutch takes my hand, and I want to say, "No, I've changed my mind!" but somehow my mouth doesn't move. I'm not really going to do this, I think crazily, as his grip on mine tightens. Surely. I'm not going to . . .

"One, two, three . . ."

And we're over.

As I fall, the air is sucked from my body. I don't know what to feel. I *can't* feel. My brain has been emptied. Gravity is the only force in my life right now. I look over at Dutch's smiling, encouraging face, feel him squeeze my hand briefly, then let go, as we land in the sea.

The water crashes against my body with more force than I predicted. My legs have been flung akimbo and I'm descending through the cold sea, unable to stop. Down . . . still down. I need to float up. Why aren't I floating up? My lung capacity is too small for this. . . . I *am* going to die, I knew it. . . . Wait, I'm rising again. . . .

And then suddenly I've surfaced, spluttering and gasping and spitting out salty water. There's hair all over my face and my swimsuit is wedged halfway up my bum and my heart is nearly exploding with triumph. My chest is pumping, my blood feels on fire, my mouth won't stop grinning. . . . That was *awesome*!

Dutch is about ten feet away, already swimming toward me with an exultant expression.

"You did it!" He high-fives me and I whoop. "It's amazing, isn't it?"

"Yes! Incredible!"

Nearby, another teenage boy crashes into the sea, and the wash of waves surges toward us. It's quite hard work, treading water like this. Not that I'll admit it, because I like to think I'm pretty fit.

"I have an admission," I say, above the sound of splashing and cheering. "I was shit scared."

"You're kidding," says Dutch teasingly.

"I thought I hid it," I say mock-indignantly, and he laughs.

"No chance. Are you OK?" he adds, as a wave catches me in the face.

"Fine," I say spluttering a little. "Thanks."

Another swell pushes us together, and suddenly our chests

are meeting. Underwater, my legs are bumping against his with the ebb and flow of the waves. Instinctively, Dutch grabs my waist—then at once lets go, looking alarmed, and says, "Sorry. I didn't mean to . . ."

"No."

"That wasn't—" He cuts himself off.

"No," I say, a little breathless. "I know."

"Not that I don't—" He stops himself again, and something unreadable flickers across his face.

For a moment we stare at each other, breathing hard, hair plastered to our heads, arms moving automatically and rhythmically through the water.

"So," says Dutch at last, as though changing the subject. "Want to have another go?"

"Sure!" I say, although I can't concentrate properly, because, was that . . . ? Did we nearly . . . ?

He swims away, toward a metal ladder set into the rock, and I follow, my mind churning. I clamber up the ladder, and then we both start climbing back up the path to the ledge. It's a narrow track, and as we round the cramped corners, his wet skin brushes against mine. One minute we're in the shade; the next, the sunshine is beating ferociously down on us. Neither of us speaks, although we're both breathing heavily. Is that because of the heat or the climb or because . . . ?

Oh God. I can't stand this. I need to nudge things along. As we emerge onto a broad, sunlit stretch of rock, I come to a halt. Dutch turns and pauses questioningly, his eyes crinkled up against the sun. My heart is hammering, but what the hell? I jumped into the sea; I can do this.

"I'm allowed one personal question, right?" I say bluntly.

"Oh." He seems taken aback. "Now?"

"Yes, now."

"Fine. Shoot. What do you want to know?"

"OK. Just now, in the sea, it felt like—" I break off. "It felt like we might— But—" Again, I stop myself. "Anyway. That's my question."

Dutch looks baffled.

"What's your question, exactly?" he says after a moment. "Nothing you've said is a question."

Oh, right. He has a point.

"My question is, just now, in the water, I felt we might be going in a certain . . . *direction*." I force myself to meet his gaze full-on. "And I'm interested in . . . in where?"

There's an answering glint in his dark eyes and my stomach clenches. That's his answer. Right there. That expression. And the slow smile spreading over his face.

"Maybe I don't know how to answer," Dutch says after a pause. "I don't have all the words like you writers do."

As he steps toward me, he's blatantly running his gaze over my swimsuit. (OK, not the swimsuit.) I take a matching step toward him so we're only inches apart, my face tilted upward.

"You know what they say," I say softly. "Show, not tell."

I don't know what I'm inviting. A chaste, romantic kiss, maybe. Like Chester and Clara shared before he boarded the hay wagon. But as Dutch's lips meet mine, all ideas of being chaste fly out of the window. I don't want chaste, I want him. This mouth. This faint roughness of stubble against my skin. All of him. Right now.

He's deepening the kiss, expertly, intently, his hands at the straps of my swimsuit as though any minute he'll yank it down. He tastes salty and manlike. Somehow our bodies have become melded together, damp skin against damp skin, with the sun blazing down on our heads and backs. He's already hardening, I'm already melting, if we weren't in public . . .

I hear someone laughing nearby—at us? But I'm too lost in sensation to move my head. It's fine. We're allowed to kiss in public. This is Italy, home of passion. They *invented* sex. And I can't stop. My craving is limitless.

"*Ciao, bella!*" A screechy whistle makes me jump, and I glance round. It's the teenagers, all clustered to watch us, about five feet away. Drat. They *are* laughing at us. And now they're all wolf-whistling. We should stop. We're probably in fact breaking a bylaw or something.

With an almighty effort, I wrench myself away from Dutch and stare up at him, breathing hard. I'm not sure I can speak, and he looks pretty dazed himself.

The teenagers are still catcalling us, and I try to block them out. Probably we shouldn't have had our first sexual encounter in a public space with a jeering audience. But, then, everything's easy in hindsight.

"So," I manage at last.

"Uh-huh." Dutch smiles again.

I know I'm supposed to have all the words, but I can't even frame a sentence right now. I'm still too transfixed.

"I'm allowed a personal question too." Dutch's low voice takes me by surprise. "Right?"

One hand is roaming beneath the seam of my swimsuit

while the other caresses my ear. His touch is somehow soft and firm at the same time. *He knows what he's doing,* crosses my mind, and for a moment I savor this delicious thought. Then I realize he's waiting for me to reply.

"Uh, yes." I come to. "Yes. I guess."

What does he want to ask?

I wait for Dutch to speak—but he's silent for a few moments, his eyes gleaming as though with secret thoughts. "Good," he says, and touches my nose gently. "Might save mine up for later on."

That afternoon, I feel as though I've unleashed a fearless genie inside me. We rock-jump again and again, yelling and waving at each other, midair. We splash and swim and kiss in the sunshine, mouths salty with the sea. Then, when we're exhausted, we head off the main beach into the shade of a nearby olive tree and spread our towels on the ground. The sun is dancing through the branches and I close my eyes, loving the feel of it on my face.

"I think Italian sun is different," I say dreamily. "They fob us off in England. They keep the good sun in a cupboard because they think we'll get spoiled if we have it too much. Then they let it out but only for twenty-four hours. And never when we expect it."

Dutch laughs. "No wonder the British are obsessed by the weather."

While we're talking, he's idly constructing a tower from the big, smooth pebbles that lie scattered around. As I watch, he places a large, fairly ambitious pebble on top and the whole thing falls down—whereupon he laughs and begins again. When he pauses, I add my own pebble to the stack, and he glances up with a grin.

"How many do you think we can stack? I say eight."

"I say ten," I counter at once, reaching for another pebble. For a while we're silent, concentrating on the task. But at last we have a teetering pile of ten stones. Dutch reaches his hand out to high-five me, but impulsively I shake my head.

"One more! Let's make it eleven."

"Eleven!" Dutch raises his eyebrows teasingly. "I like your style. Go on, then."

As I reach for another pebble, I suddenly feel ridiculously nervous. I know it's only a game, but we made this pebble stack together, and I really don't want to knock the whole thing down when I could have settled at ten. In fact, I'm not sure why I even wanted to add another pebble. I guess it's that voice inside me, constantly asking, *What* else *could I be doing?*

Tentatively, I place the new pebble on top and withdraw my hand—and it stays put!

"Result!" Dutch lifts his hand again, and this time we do high-five and I feel absurdly elated at our joint achievement.

"This takes me back to my childhood," says Dutch lazily, lying back down on his towel. "I love architecture, design, that kind of thing. Guess it began with building sandcastles on the beach."

"I used to love building sandcastles on the beach!" I say eagerly. "And I love design too. I collect interesting furniture. It's, like, a hobby of mine."

"Furniture?" Dutch lifts his head with interest. "What kind? Because I'm—"

"Wait!" I cut him off with a horrified gasp. "Sorry! I shouldn't have said that. We're not supposed to reveal our hobbies."

"Too late." He chuckles.

I've also just hinted that I live in England, it occurs to me. Honestly, I'm *rubbish* at this.

"I'm not necessarily from England, by the way," I say quickly. "I might have been double bluffing. Maybe I don't even have a permanent abode."

"Aria." Dutch shakes his head incredulously. "Do we need to stick to the rules?"

"Yes! We need to try, at least. Only one personal question each, and you still haven't asked yours. But here's an idea," I add in sudden inspiration. "Let's talk about the future. When you're ninety, what will you be doing? Give me a snapshot."

"OK." Dutch nods and thinks for a moment. "I'll be looking back over a full life. I hope I'll be content. In the sunshine somewhere. The *good* sunshine," he clarifies with a quick grin. "And I'll be with friends, old and new."

He sounds so sincere, I feel a little pull at my heartstrings. He could have said so many other things. He could have said, "I'll be on my yacht with my fifth wife." That's what Russell would have said. In fact, now I recall, that's what Russell *did* say.

"That sounds perfect," I say in heartfelt tones. "And . . . same. Good sunshine, friends around me. Plus I'll be eating ice cream."

"Oh, so will I," says Dutch at once. "For sure. The only reason I came on an Italian holiday is because of the ice cream."

"What flavor?" I demand.

"Is that tomorrow's personal question?" counters Dutch, and I laugh.

"No! I'm not wasting a personal question on that. Forget it. I don't need to know."

"Shame." His eyes crinkle at me. "Then you'll never know how much I love nocciola."

"That *is* a shame." I nod. "And you'll never know how much I love stracciatella."

I lie back down on my towel, too, and Dutch's hand idly strays over to take mine. Our fingers enmesh and I can feel his thumb circling my palm, and then he's pulling me all the way over to his towel and finding my mouth with his.

"You taste better than nocciola ice cream," he murmurs in my ear.

"You don't really mean that," I murmur back, and Dutch seems to think.

"OK, tied," he allows. "Tied with nocciola ice cream. And you beat mango sorbet."

"I beat mango sorbet?" I open my eyes wide in mock-amazement. "Wow. I don't even know what to say. That's a compliment I'll never forget."

And of course I'm joking . . . but at the same time I'm speaking the truth. I'll never forget this charmed, intoxicating, sunlit day.

As afternoon turns to early evening, we finally stir. We've been lying, kissing, dozing, and idly chatting all afternoon. As I get up, my limbs are stiff and my legs are patterned with the imprint of twigs, but I can't stop smiling dreamily.

We gather our things and head back toward the car and,

as we do so, pass some teenagers playing a game of football on a stretch of scrubby land. The ball suddenly veers toward us, hitting Dutch on the head. He catches it, smiles, then heads it back into the game.

"*Signor!*" In a stream of Italian, one of the teenagers invites him to join in. Dutch pauses for a moment, then says to me, "Two minutes."

As he joins the game, he instantly becomes utterly absorbed in it, and I watch, fascinated by seeing him in a different setting.

He seems to understand what the teenagers are yelling, even though they're speaking Italian. (I guess they're all communicating in the international language of "football.") When one of the players slams into him with an aggressive tackle, Dutch brushes off his apology with an easygoing nod. He has a natural authority, too, I notice. The kids are deferring to him, even while they're challenging him. Everything is another clue to who he is. Everything is another insight.

At that moment Dutch glances over at me and says, "I have to go now, guys, thanks for the game."

The teenagers start exhorting him to stay (even I can translate that), but Dutch lifts a hand in smiling farewell and comes to rejoin me. "Well played!" I say, whereupon he laughs, takes my hand, and we turn our steps toward the car.

As we drive away with the evening sun still baking through the windscreen, I look back, trying to imprint this precious place on my memory, until we've turned the corner and are speeding along a main road.

"I wish we could have brought the pebble tower with us," I say wistfully, and Dutch laughs again.

"I'm serious!" I say. "It would have been an amazing souvenir of the holiday."

"You would have carried those eleven heavy stones back to the car?"

"Yes."

"And all the way back home on the plane?"

"Of course!"

"And how would you have remembered what order they were piled up in?"

I pause, because I hadn't quite thought that through. "I would have had a system," I say at last with dignity. "And then every time I'd seen the pebbles back at home, I would have remembered—"

I break off abruptly, because if I'm not careful, I'll say too much. I'll open my heart too wide; I'll scare him off.

I would have remembered the most amazing man I've ever met.

I would have remembered the most perfect day of my life.

I would have remembered heaven.

"It would have been nice," I say at last, in lighter tones. "That's all."

As we arrive back in town, I still feel heady, as though I'm in a dream. A blue-skied, filmlike dream, spiked with adrenaline and lust and sunshine. I'm lolling against the hot plastic seat of the car, sipping an ice-cold Orangina we picked up en route. My hair is mussed up, my skin is salty, and I can still feel the imprint of Dutch's mouth on mine.

I know there's a delicious free supper waiting for us at the monastery, but when Dutch says, "Shall we grab some pizza?" I nod. I don't want to share him with anyone. I don't want to have to explain anything or make small talk. Farida is right, it distracts from the main event, which right now is Dutch.

Dutch parks the car in a deserted quarter of the town, with shadowed squares and stark streets lined with studded wooden doors.

"Found a pizza vendor yesterday," he tells me as he leads me along. "It's not a restaurant, it's just a guy in a booth. . . . Is that OK?"

"Great. Perfect!" I squeeze his hand and we round the corner into a smaller backstreet, even less well lit.

We take a few steps along the street. Ten, maybe. And then, in an instant, everything changes. From nowhere, two teenagers appear in our path. Skinny and tanned, like the guys Dutch was playing football with, but not like them, because they're sullen and pushing at Dutch and saying aggressive things in Italian. Are they drunk? High? What do they *want*?

I'm trying to rationalize what I'm seeing, so my brain takes forever to realize the truth—this is a situation. An actual situation. In the space of three seconds, my heart goes from calm to pumping in fright. Dutch is trying to lead me past the boys; he's trying to be amicable, but they won't— They're angry— Why? I can't even— What—

And now—no, no, *please,* God, no—one of them has reached into his jacket and I see the heart-stopping metal flash of a knife.

Time stands still. A knife. A *knife.* We're going to be stabbed, right here, right now, in this backstreet, and I can't even move. I can't make a sound. I'm frozen in utter terror, like a mummified, petrified creature from the Ice Age—

Wait, what? What is that? *What's happening right now?*

Before my eyes, Dutch is wrenching the arm of the guy with the knife and twisting it in some efficient practiced maneuver, and somehow he's got hold of the knife. How did he do that? How?

All the time he's shouting, *"Run, run!"* and suddenly I realize he means me. He wants me to go.

But before I can run, the teenagers do. They sprint away, up the street, around the corner, and I sag against Dutch in shock. It's only about thirty seconds since we rounded the corner, but I feel as though the world has stopped and started again. Dutch is breathing very hard but simply says, "Are you OK?" then adds, "We should get to the car. They might get some stupid ideas about coming back."

"How . . . how did you *do* that?" I stutter as we move along the street, and Dutch shoots me a look of surprise.

"What?"

"Get that knife off them!"

"Learned," says Dutch with a shrug. "Everyone should learn. You should learn. It's basic safety. I live in a big city—" He breaks off. "Right. Sorry. No personal details."

"I don't think that matters right now," I say with a laugh that is perilously near to a sob.

"Aria!" Dutch looks stricken and stops to pull me close. "It's OK," he says in a low voice. "It's over."

"I know," I say against his firm chest. "Sorry. I'm fine. I'm overreacting."

"You're not," says Dutch firmly. "Anyone would be shaken

up. But I think we should keep walking," he adds, holding my hand tighter as we move on. "Don't worry. I'm right here with you."

His voice soothes my jangled nerves and strengthens my trembling legs. As we walk, he starts reading out all the road signs in deliberately bad pronunciation, making me laugh. And by the time we're in the car, driving back along the coast road, munching pizza from a different vendor, it's almost as though the whole thing never happened. Except that every time I look at him, my heart melts even more.

He saved my life. He's hot and he loves dogs and we jumped off rocks together and he saved my life.

We drop the car at the hire garage, then walk the hundred feet or so back to the monastery, letting ourselves in through the massive wooden door. The entrance courtyard is empty and I pause, looking around its tranquil candlelit cloister. It's like another world from the one we've been in. Swallows are wheeling against the indigo sky, and I can smell verbena in the air.

"Quite an afternoon," says Dutch with a wry laugh. "You came here for a peaceful writing retreat and instead you've had an adrenaline roller coaster. Is your heart still thumping?"

"Uh-huh." I smile and nod.

My heart *is* thumping. But not for that reason anymore. It's thumping because of where we are in the evening.

All afternoon I've been thinking with anticipation, *Tonight . . . tonight . . . maybe tonight . . .* And now here we are. The two of us. With an empty night in Italy ahead of us.

As I meet his eyes again, my chest feels constricted with

lust. It's almost painful, this desire of mine. Because we're not done. We are so not done. I can still feel his mouth, his hands, his hair entwined in my fingers. My skin is longing for his. My *everything* is longing for his.

"No point joining the others," says Dutch, as though reading my mind, and his fingers brush against mine.

"No."

"My room's at the end of the corridor," he adds conversationally. "Kind of secluded."

"Sounds great," I say, trying to contain the tremor in my voice. "Can I . . . see it?"

"Sure. Why not?"

Without any further words, we turn and walk along the corridor, our footsteps matching, our fingertips touching. My breaths are short. I'm nearly dying of need here. But somehow I manage to put one foot in front of the other like a normal person.

We get to a wooden studded door and Dutch produces an iron key. He gives me a long look which makes my stomach swoop, then reaches to unlock the door.

"Your personal question," I say, remembering suddenly. "You *still* haven't asked it."

A trace of amusement appears on Dutch's face. He surveys me for a moment before leaning forward to kiss me, long and hard, his hands gripping my hips. Then he bends in still farther, gently bites my neck, and whispers, "We'll get to that."

Five

~~~

Oh my *God*.

I can't move. I can't think. I've had barely any sleep. My skin prickles every time I think back over the night we've just had.

There's a rustle of sheets and Dutch turns over, blinking as a ray of light catches his eyes. For a moment we look at each other. Then slowly his face creases into a smile and he murmurs, "Good morning." He draws me in for a long, lingering kiss, then gets out of bed and pads to the bathroom.

As I flop back on my pillow, my head feels like a marshmallow. All sweetness. All bliss. Dreamy and soft. When Dutch reappears, freshly showered, I say impulsively, "I missed you!" and it's true. I don't want to be apart from him for a second. It's not chemistry we have, it's magnetism. It's a pull. It's a scientific force. It's inescapable.

But does he feel like that too? Where *are* we with this?

Where do we go from here? I sit up and wait till Dutch looks round from putting on his shirt.

"What now?" I say momentously—then remember that this is what Clara asks Chester as he gets on the hay wagon. For a ridiculous moment I imagine Dutch saying, "When next you see me, Aria, you will *know* that I am a man of my word!"

But instead he blinks and says, "Breakfast, I guess."

"Right." I nod.

I mean, that's the obvious answer.

As we walk along, brushing shoulders, the morning sunshine dances on our heads and I feel lighter than I have for months. Years. We approach the courtyard and I suddenly realize we've been absent since yesterday lunch. It might seem conspicuous; people might ask questions. . . .

But as we join the group around the big wooden table, no one bats an eyelid. It turns out quite a lot of people ducked out of yoga yesterday afternoon—and a few went out to supper at a local restaurant. (Verdict: not as good as the food here, don't bother.)

So no one asks or guesses or hints at anything. And I'm glad. I don't want any scrutiny. I want to be able to gaze at Dutch over my orange juice, undisturbed, thinking delicious, private thoughts.

Except I need to share this with the squad. (That still counts as private.) After breakfast I get my phone from reception, citing a family emergency, and head out to the corner of the street, where I've heard there's a patch of good 4G. And after standing there for five seconds, my phone starts to come alive. It's kind of magical, as though the world is talking to me again.

All my WhatsApp groups flood with notifications, and I feel a pang of longing. I can't believe I've gone this long without chatting to anyone. But somehow I force myself to ignore the 657 messages beckoning me. I've promised I won't look, because once I look, I'll get sucked in. Instead, I turn to a new group, entitled Ava's Emergency Hotline, which Nell set up for exactly this eventuality.

Hi, I type, and after only ten seconds, Nell starts typing a response. It's almost as though she's been waiting for me to make contact. A moment later it arrives:

He's fine.

Then a photo of Harold pops onto my screen with a caption: See? He's happy. Stop stressing. Go and write!!

A moment later Maud chimes in:

Ava! How's the book?

Now Sarika is typing too:

How come you have your phone? Isn't this against the rules?

They're all online, I realize. This is perfect timing. Joyfully, I type:

Never mind the rules. Because, guess what, I've found a guy. I've found the perfect guy!!!

I send it off and watch the responses arrive, my mouth curving into a smile.

What??!?!?!

Wow.

That was quick!

Have you been to bed?

Spill!!!!

I can't help laughing out loud, their excitement is so infectious.

Yes, we have been to bed, thank you for asking. And he's amazing. He's wonderful. He's . . .

I'm running out of words, so I type sixteen heart emojis and send them. Immediately the answers bombard me.

Got it. :))

Good to know ? ☺

More details!!! What's his name????

I type my answer—Dutch—and wait for the barrage.

Dutch!

Dutch??

Is that a name?

Does that mean he is Dutch?

I'm about to type No when I realize I don't know. Maybe he *is* Dutch but was brought up in the UK so he has a British accent. You can't assume anything.

I'm not sure what nationality he is.

???

Well, where does he live???

Don't know

What does he do??

Don't know

You don't know????

I heave a sigh of slight frustration and start typing again.

Everyone's anonymous on this retreat. That's the joy of it. It's different. We're communicating as humans. Not as lists of statistics. Details don't matter. Nationalities don't matter. Jobs don't matter. CONNECTION matters.

As I finish typing, I feel quite inspired, and I wonder if what I've said will give my friends pause for thought. But at once the replies start popping into my phone again.

???

What's his income bracket?

Not relevant, Sarika!!!

Yes it is, sorry to be so pragmatic

I'm guessing she doesn't know

You can guess, surely?

Ava, sweetheart, not wanting to rain on your parade . . .
but what DO you know about him??

As I'm reading the conversation, I realize I'm in the way
of a bent old woman with a shopping trolley, and I skip aside
apologetically, saying, "*Scusi!*"
The woman smiles and I smile back, taking in her ancient
lined face and thinking both *She looks so wise* and *Oops, I
forgot to put on sunscreen.* Then I turn my attention back to
the conversation. I feel a bit surreal, standing in a remote
Italian street, trying to explain this amazing development in
my life to my friends, so far away. But after some thought I
start typing again:

This is what I know. His hair is dark and thick. His eyes
are gleaming. He just has to look at me to make me
ripple inside. When he laughs he throws his head back.
He's confident, but he doesn't brag. He values friendship. And he loves dogs.

I add another stream of heart emojis, eighteen this time,
then press SEND.
There's silence from the other end. Then the responses
start piling in.

????

That's it?

What's his other name? Dutch what? I'm googling him.

That is so typical of Sarika. I quickly type:

Don't know.

Then, after some hesitation, I come fully clean.

Actually, Dutch isn't his real name. I don't know his real name.

This time the replies come more swiftly than ever.

You don't know his name???

Let me get this clear, you don't know his name or his nationality or what he does or where he lives.

So it's just sex.

I stare at the phone, feeling nettled at Maud's comment. First of all, what's that supposed to mean, "Just sex"? Sex with the right person is transcendental. It informs you about a person's soul. Someone who is generous in bed is going to be generous in real life.

And, anyway, it's not just sex. I *know* Dutch. I've built a pebble tower with him. I've seen him play football with kids. I've leaped off rocks with him. That's what's important. Not "What does he do?" but "Would you leap off a rock with him?"

Feeling a little tetchy, I type again:

It's more than sex. I sense the core of him. He is a good person. He's kind. He's intrepid. He's brave.

I pause a few seconds, then add my clincher:

He saved me from a knife attack. He saved my life.

You can't argue with that. He saved my life. *He saved my life!* But if I thought my friends might respond to the romance of this, I was wrong.

A knife attack????

What the FUCK is going on out there?

Ava, stay safe.

I think you should come home.

This guy might be an ax murderer!!

I know they're half teasing, but I also know they're half serious, and it's unsettling me. I type again, my fingers a little jabby.

Stop it. It's fine. It's all good. I'm happy.

Then I add:

I have to go. I'm on a writing retreat, in case you'd forgotten.

There's a momentary pause, then the farewells come into my phone:

OK, we'll talk soon xxxxx

Stay SAFE xoxox

Enjoy!! ;) ;)

And finally another photo of Harold appears, with a photoshopped speech bubble coming out of his mouth: "FIND OUT HIS NAME!!"

Huh. Hilarious.

As I wander back to the monastery, I feel conflicted. Of *course* I'm curious. Of *course* I've speculated. Part of me is desperate to know his real name. And his age. And which big city he lives in. (Please, *please*, not Sydney.)

But part of me doesn't want to go there. Not yet. We're in the most magical bubble, and I want to stay in it for as long as possible.

Should I at least find out *one* detail? His real name?

I pause at the entrance to the monastery, thinking this through.

The trouble is, if I know his name, I'll google him. I won't *intend* to . . . I won't *want* to . . . but I will. Just like I quite often don't *want* or *intend* to order a muffin with my coffee, but, oh, look, there it is on my plate, how did that happen?

I can already see myself making an excuse, getting my phone, feverishly waiting for the results to load. . . .

And that would puncture the bliss.

Slowly, I open the heavy wooden door with my latchkey and step inside the thick stone walls. I hand my phone back at reception, then walk into the main cloister. I can see Farida talking to Giuseppe, who is the porter, driver, and general helper, but as she sees me, she nods to him and turns in my direction.

"Aria!" she greets me, her hair flowing immaculately down her back, her amber beads clicking together. "I'm just on my way to our first session. Are you ready?"

"Yes!" I say, and fall into step with her, trying to drag my thoughts back to the main task.

"Are you finding the retreat helpful so far?" she asks as we walk.

Well, it's helped me get laid.

"Yes," I say earnestly. "Yes, very much so."

That morning's session is called "free writing." We all have to work on anything we like, then share it with the class. Some people are writing in their rooms; others have found shady corners in the garden or courtyard.

Dutch announces he'll write in his room, and I don't really feel I can join him there. So I wander around until I find a secluded bench next to a huge rosemary bush. I sit on it with my feet up, my laptop balanced on my thighs, absently rubbing sprigs of rosemary between my fingers. I still feel exhilarated. And dreamy. All I can think about is sex. And last night. And Dutch.

But that's OK. In fact, it's *good*. It's going to power my writing. Yes! I'm bubbling over with words and feelings to give to my lovers, Chester and Clara. I'm going to speed up their affair. I can see them now, tumbling on the ground, Chester tugging urgently at Clara's bodice—

Wait, do they need to get married first? I'm a bit hazy about Victorian standards. Maybe the hay-wagon driver could also happen to be a vicar and they get quickly married as they're moving along?

Whatever. Don't care. The crucial thing is, they have sex.

Soon. I've never written about sex before, but somehow it's bursting out of me today.

He drove into her with a gasp, I type briskly, then cringe and delete it quickly. Maybe . . . *He plunged into her.*

No, this is too soon. I need to build up to the plunging.

As he ripped off Clara's bodice, he moaned like a . . .

Like a . . . ?

My mind's blank. What moans? Apart from a guy having sex?

OK, I'll come back to it. I'll pop back to that patch of 4G outside and google "things that moan."

He transported her. He intoxicated her. The touch of his fingers set her on fire. The sound of his voice made her head spin. Everything else in life seemed irrelevant. Who cared what job he had or what his name was—

Wait. This isn't Clara I'm writing about. This is me.

Lifting my hands off the laptop, I breathe out and look up into the endless blue sky. He does transport me. And he does intoxicate me. The truth is, all I can think about is Dutch.

Even so, by the time we reconvene, I've managed to write a passage. In fact, I'm so engrossed that I'm late arriving and Dutch is already seated between Scribe and Author-to-Be This is absolutely typical, but never mind.

As Farida invites us to share our morning's work, I feel suddenly intrepid. If I can leap off rocks, I can read my scene out loud.

"I'll go," I say, raising my hand. "This morning I wrote a . . ." I clear my throat. "Well, actually, it's my first ever sex scene."

Scribe immediately whoops and a few people applaud, laughing.

"Good for you!" says Author-to-Be. "Read away!"

I hold up my printout and clear my throat. I'm quite pleased with the scene actually, because as well as the love aspect, I've got a bit of social commentary in there.

"So, this is from the novel I'm working on that I've told you about," I begin. "Just to remind you, it's set in Victorian England." I hesitate, then start reading aloud:

" 'You are my wife,' growled Chester. 'And I claim my conjugal rights.'

" 'This is an outdated practice,' snapped Clara, the fire of feminism in her eyes. 'I foresee that in future generations, women will be equal.'

"The sweat of shame passed over Chester's brow.

" 'You are right,' he said. 'I will join the fight, Clara. In future years I will be a male suffragette.'

"But then Chester could hold back his throbbing desire no longer.

"As he ripped off Clara's bodice, he moaned like a . . ." I hesitate ". . . a Heleioporus eyrie frog."

"A what?" says Metaphor at once, raising her hand.

"It's a frog," I say defensively. "It moans."

"Carry on, Aria," says Farida softly. "Let's keep all queries and comments till the end."

"As his breeches descended, she knew his manhood."

I wince inwardly, because I wasn't wild about "manhood," but what else could I say? I turn the page and feel myself getting into my stride.

"He was inventive. He was thoughtful. They carried on all night. As the moon shone down, they sat on the big stone windowsill, drinking wine and nibbling grissini, knowing that their hunger for each other was building again; knowing that it would be sated. They were practically strangers. They knew so little about each other. But their connection was so real. Later, as he slept, she gazed at his true, honest face. His thick dark hair. His powerful, muscular stature. She was mesmerized. Tantalized both by what she knew of him and what she didn't know. He seemed to her like a wonderful new land, waiting to be discovered."

I come to a halt, and there's a round of applause.

"Well done," says Farida, smiling at me encouragingly. "Writing about such intimate moments isn't easy. . . . Yes, Metaphor? Did you have another question?"

"Just a few." Metaphor shoots me a snide look. "Grissini? In Victorian England?"

Oh. Oops. I was picturing Dutch and me last night. I should have said "sweetmeats."

"Just a little slip," I say easily. "If that's all—"

"No, it's not all," says Metaphor. "I thought Clara and Chester grew up together in the village. Why are they suddenly strangers?"

"I wondered about that," agrees Scribe.

"I have a question too," puts in Austen in her mild way. "I thought Chester had blond hair and was slim built? But now he's suddenly dark and muscular."

Metaphor glances meaningfully at Dutch, then raises her eyebrows at Austen. Has she *guessed*? I push back my hair, feeling rattled. How did I forget Chester was blond?

"It's . . . a work in progress," I say, avoiding everyone's eye. "Anyway, let's hear from someone else." I fold up my printout before anyone else can catch me out.

"It was very good, Aria," adds Austen quickly. "Very . . . you know. Realistic."

"Thanks." I smile at her, as Farida says, "Who would like to read their work to us next?"

At once Dutch puts up his hand, and everyone goggles at him.

"Dutch!" Farida sounds fairly astonished herself.

"I know, right?" He gives a self-deprecating laugh. "Last person you expected. But I was inspired today." He holds up a page covered in handwritten words, and Scribe, who is sitting next to him, exclaims, "Wow!"

"I've never been inspired to write before. But . . ." He shrugs, his face creasing into his infectious smile. "Somehow today the words flowed."

"This is a special moment, then," says Farida, her eyes gleaming softly.

"Well done, old bean!" exclaims Author-to-Be, clapping Dutch on the back.

"You see? Everyone can become a writer with the right inspiration." Farida smiles around at us all. "This is very exciting, Dutch. We can't wait to hear what you've written."

Dutch glances down at his page, then adds, "I don't have a plot or anything like that yet. I guess I was finding my voice. Like you told us yesterday?" He looks up at Farida.

"You told us to be bold and honest. That's what I went for. Bold and honest."

"Bravo!" says Farida. "Indeed I did. Let's hear this bold, honest voice, Dutch."

There's a moment of silence, then Dutch draws breath and begins: *"They fucked."*

As his voice rings through the space, there's a jolt of slight surprise.

"That *is* bold," murmurs Booklover, next to me, as Dutch continues.

"It was incredible. She was hot. And she was loud. Louder than he'd expected. It was intense. Afterward, they drank wine and ate grissini. Then . . ."

He pauses, frowning at his own handwriting. There are prickles of interest around the room, and I feel a few glances coming my way.

"Grissini," murmurs Metaphor. "Who'd've thought?"

I'm feeling a bit unreal here. I somehow want to signal to Dutch, but he's drawing breath to read again.

"Her skin was beautiful, like—"

Dutch breaks off and says, "Sorry, I can't read my own . . . Is that *silk*? Or . . ." He turns his head and scrutinizes my leg as though for a prompt, and his brow suddenly clears. "Oh, right, I remember—*milk.*"

"Sorry to interrupt, Dutch," says Metaphor, raising her hand politely, "but since we're on a pause: Is this fiction?"

Dutch looks caught out. "Of course," he says after a moment. "Fiction. For sure."

"What are your characters' names?" inquires Metaphor with a sweet smile.

"Names?" Dutch looks flummoxed. He glances at me and away again. "I haven't got to that."

Oh God. Doesn't he realize how *obvious* this is? I'm squirming on my chair, but Dutch turns the page and resumes confidently. "*She had the longest orgasm, like a cry of abandon in the evening air.*"

No. He did *not* just say that. My cheeks flame red. Does anyone think it's me? As I glance around the room, I can tell: They *all* think it's me. Frantically, I try to meet Dutch's eye and convey the word "stop," but he's already reading again.

"*And she was adventurous. More than he could have predicted. For example—*"

"This is powerful stuff, Dutch," Farida interrupts him hurriedly. "Is it all in . . . this vein?"

"Pretty much." Dutch looks up, his face glowing. "Like I said, I was inspired. I see why you guys love writing now. It gives you such a *buzz*, doesn't it? Writing this gave me—"

He breaks off again, as though he can't even describe what it gave him.

Although I have an idea.

"Well, I suggest we leave it there for now," says Farida pleasantly. "Thank you so much for sharing your . . . work."

"Wait, I'm coming to a good bit," says Dutch, and turns back to his text: "*They did it on a chair with a high back. It was mind-blowing. She wrapped her legs around his—*"

"Enough!" Farida cuts him off almost desperately and places a hand on his page for good measure. "Enough. Let's move on now. Many congratulations to Dutch for . . . finding his bold new voice. Who would like to read next?"

She spreads her hands invitingly, but no one answers. Everyone's looking at either me or Dutch or the high-backed chair I'm sitting on.

"I don't know about anyone else," says Kirk at last in a throaty voice. "But I'm happy to hear more from Dutch."

Six

As the group finally disbands for lunch, I can't look any-one in the eye. Not *anyone*. I wait until everyone else has wandered off, then grab Dutch and pull him into an alcove.

"What was that?" I demand. "Everyone knew it was us!"

"What?" Dutch looks blank.

"Your writing! The sex! It was obvious you were writing about . . . you know. Us. Last night. *Grissini?*" I add mean-ingfully.

"It was fiction," says Dutch, looking a bit offended. "Ev-eryone knew it was fiction."

"No they didn't! You can't just change the names and it's fiction. Anyway, you didn't even bother to change the names," I add, suddenly remembering. "You didn't disguise it at all! Everyone was looking at us and basically picturing us doing it on the chair."

"What? No they weren't!" Dutch pauses, and I can see

him belatedly processing the idea. "Oh. OK. Maybe a couple of people thought it was us."

"Everyone thought it was us," I contradict him firmly. *"Everyone."*

"Well, then . . . they were jealous." His eyes glint wickedly, and in spite of myself I smile. Then he pulls me closer and adds, "I wish we *were* doing it on the chair. I missed you this morning."

"I missed you too," I murmur. My indignation seems to have melted away. It's the spell he puts on me. " 'Mind-blowing,' huh?" I add teasingly. "Is that your five-star review?"

Dutch gives a low chuckle.

"Let's grab lunch quickly," he suggests. "And have a siesta."

"Good idea."

He's so close I can feel his breath on my skin. As we gaze at each other I can see the thoughts playing in his eyes, and I shiver with anticipation.

"Shall we go?" he says, as Scribe crosses the courtyard, along with Beginner and Booklover.

"Yes. No. One more thing." I wait until everyone's out of earshot, then say a little tentatively, "I was going to ask you your name. As my personal question of the day."

"Right." I can see a slight wariness in his eyes. "OK."

"I was *going* to." I hold up a hand to stop him blurting it out. "I know it's against the rules of the retreat, but I thought, if we were . . . you know, together, then . . ." I draw breath. "But then I changed my mind."

"Oh, really?" He peers at me as though he can't follow

my thoughts, which to be fair, he probably can't. No one can follow my thoughts. Nell calls me Alice in Wonderland because I end up wandering down so many mental paths at once.

Which isn't strictly speaking what Alice in Wonderland does, but—

Oh, OK. I'm wandering again. Focus, Ava.

"We're in a bubble here." I gaze at him, trying to convey the strength of what I'm saying. "And it's kind of magical. At least, I think it is."

This is Dutch's cue to say, "So do I," but he just carries on gazing at me, as though waiting for me to continue.

I suppose at least he didn't say, "No it's not."

"This getting to know each other without names and postcodes and family background and all that crap . . ." I exhale. "It's a *luxury*. We should enjoy it. Savor it."

"Yes." He finally comes alive. "I agree. Fully."

"It's real. What we have feels . . ." I hesitate, because is this too much, too soon? But I can't stop myself. "You might just think this is a holiday fling." My voice trembles a little. "But I think . . . I already feel like it's . . . more."

There's an unbearable silence between us. I can hear a distant gale of laughter coming from the lunch table, but I'm rapt.

"I think it's more too," Dutch says at last in a low voice, and he squeezes my hands tight.

"Well . . . good." A stupid smile spreads over my face. "I'm . . . I feel really . . ."

"Me too."

He smiles back, and for a moment neither of us speaks.

And I don't exactly believe in auras, but we are in some kind of aura right now. I can *feel* it. All around us.

"Anyway," I say, coming to. "What I was going to say is, shall we *not* ask any more personal questions of each other? Shall we *not* try to find out . . . I don't know, what our middle names are and where we live? Not till we leave here, anyway. Let's stay in the bubble."

"Sounds good." Dutch nods. "I like the bubble. In fact, I love the bubble."

"I love the bubble too." I feel my face softening as he leans down to kiss me. "Oh, wait, though. There's one thing I think we should know. Do you . . . have kids?"

The thought crossed my mind during the session, and now it won't leave me alone. Not that it would be a *problem,* of course not, it's just . . .

"Kids?" Dutch's face starts in surprise. "No. Do you?"

"No." I shake my head emphatically. "I . . . I have a dog, though."

As I say the words, I feel myself tensing up with almighty nerves. Because Harold *is* my kids. If Dutch has some kind of, I don't know, objection . . . or problem . . .

As I wait for his reply, I'm so fearful I can hardly breathe. Because it could all be over, right now. And then I would die. I would actually die.

He can't have a problem, says an optimistic voice in my mind (Alice). *He loves dogs!*

You don't know that, answers the Red Queen, who is always making trouble and scoring points. *Maybe he only likes white shepherds.*

"I love dogs," says Dutch easily, and I nearly collapse.

"Great!" I say, my relief tumbling out. "That's . . . He's called Harold. He's . . ."

Shall I show him a photo? No. Too soon. Anyway, I've already divulged enough.

"I bet he's a wonderful dog," says Dutch.

"Oh, he is," I say eagerly. "He is."

Just the idea of Dutch meeting Harold floods me with emotion. My two centers of love, together.

Wait. Do I mean "love"? I've only just met Dutch. Am I using the word "love," even in my thoughts?

"Shall we go?" Dutch tugs at my hand. "I have an appetite for grissini." He winks at me. "And shall we not hide anymore? Because if you're right, it's no secret that we've hooked up. And it gives me a kick to be with the prettiest girl in the place." He links his arm firmly through mine. "You know, you mentioned grissini in your piece too," he adds as we cross the cloister. "So you needn't be so high and mighty." He winks at me again and I feel a flood of . . . what?

Come on. Be honest. There *is* only one word for what I'm feeling right now.

I love him. I don't know anything about this guy. Not his age, not his job, not even his name. But I love him.

By Friday, we're a couple. We're *the* couple. We walk around hand in hand, and we sit next to each other in sessions. People leave two adjoining chairs for us at supper, as a matter of course. They say "Aria and Dutch" when they're talking about evening plans.

I've never felt so heady and happy and intoxicated in my

life. Dutch's face when I wake up. His laugh. His strong hand in mine.

On Friday afternoon, Giuseppe drives the whole group out of the monastery to a hillside olive grove, for a picnic. All the writing sessions are done, and Farida has explained that this is when we can relax, unmask, introduce ourselves, and say our good-byes.

As I get down from the minibus, I'm feeling huge pangs, because I've loved it here. The sunshine, the food, the writing, the people . . . I'll even miss Metaphor. Nearby, Austen, Scribe, and Author-to-Be are already talking about booking next year, and I don't blame them.

Giuseppe is unloading a massive hamper from the minibus, and some others are carrying blankets. I'm about to go and help when Author-to-Be comes up, brandishing a piece of paper at me. "Aria! Have you entered the competition?"

"Competition?" I blink at him.

"Guess the name. Two people have got you down as Clover."

"Clover?" I take the paper from him and look down, starting to laugh. There are seven guesses against my name and all of them are wrong.

After a bit of thought, I fill in my own guesses. It's so random and silly, but I do feel like Author-to-Be might be Derek, and Kirk might be Sean.

"Well done." Author-to-Be takes back the paper. "Now let's get some drinks poured and we can have the big reveal!"

"Actually . . ." I put a hand on his arm. "Dutch and I aren't revealing our names yet. We want to leave it until we absolutely have to."

This was my idea. We're not leaving till tomorrow morning. We're in paradise right now. Once we reveal our names, the whole cascade of information will come out . . . and what's the benefit? Why burst our precious bubble any earlier than we have to?

"Fair enough." Author-to-Be twinkles at me. "I'm not above a bit of role play myself."

I stare at him in indignation. *Role play?* This isn't *role play*—it's real, connected love! I'm about to tell him so, but he's already heading over to where the group is sitting on amazing embroidered blankets (available for sale at the gift shop).

I gaze at the scene for a moment, wanting it to last forever. There's prosecco going round and plates of cured meats and Farida is laughing at something and the sunlight is dappled through the olive trees and it's just idyllic.

Dutch is chatting to Giuseppe as they carry the last hamper together. He winks at me, then comes to join me, and we find a place on one of the rugs together. I sip my prosecco while Beginner proposes a toast to Farida, whereupon Farida makes a nice speech about what a particularly charming and talented group we are. (I'm sure she says that every week.)

Then Author-to-Be tinkles a fork in his glass. "Attention! Time for the big identity reveal! I will now read out all the names that you *think* I might be. Derek. Keith. James. Simon. Desmond. Raymond. John. Robert. And the truth is . . ." He pauses for effect. "I'm Richard! And I'm a geography teacher from Norwich."

Everyone bursts into applause and whooping, while Richard beams around, then says, "Next up . . . Scribe!" He passes the paper along to her while Kirk calls out, "Wait! Scribe, can I change my mind? I think you're called Margot."

Scribe *isn't* called Margot but Felicity, and she's a stay-at-home housewife. Metaphor is called Anna and works in London in HR. Kirk is called Aaron and is doing a postdoctorate in computer science. Beginner is called Eithne and has eleven grandchildren! It's actually really fun, hearing everyone reveal their true identities, and for a fleeting moment I wonder if we should join in. . . . But, then, don't the best things come to those who wait?

And anyway, the truth is, I have a fair idea about Dutch already. I'm pretty intuitive. Not psychic, exactly, but . . . I pick things up. I have sensitive radar. He's good with his hands and lit up when I mentioned furniture at the beach. He loves design and he once let a comment slip about being in "the workshop," so, putting that all together, I think he's a carpenter. He probably makes beautiful marquetry or something like that, and I *think* he might work with his dad.

He also has a name with foreign origins. He blurted that out by mistake two nights ago. And it could be anything, obviously . . . but the name "Jean-Luc" instantly popped into my brain.

I just have a *feeling* about it. Jean-Luc. He *looks* like a Jean-Luc.

Hi, this is Jean-Luc. He's a carpenter.

Yes. That feels real. It feels like Dutch.

I don't know where he lives, and that's a bit scary. But it's a city and it's not Australia or New Zealand. (I couldn't survive without asking him that.) So we'll make it work. Whether it's Manchester or Paris or Seattle. We will.

"So. Dutch and Aria." Finally Richard turns in our direction. "You're not giving away your identities yet."

"Their names are *way* too embarrassing," says Kirk, and there's a roar of laughter.

"I know it seems weird," I say with an abashed smile. "But we just want to prolong the magic. This has been *so* special. . . ."

"Holiday flings always are," says Anna, in that sweet, bitchy way she has, and I flinch, because why did she have to say that? This *isn't* just a holiday fling.

I can see Dutch looking from her to me and realizing that I'm hurt. And before I can even draw breath, he's stood up. He beckons to me to join him, and, feeling confused, I stand too. Everyone swivels to look up at us, and Richard tinkles his glass again.

"Pray silence for the bride and groom!" he announces in jocular tones—and I know he's only playing around, but still a *frisson* passes through me. I glance hesitantly at Dutch—because this was his idea—and he draws breath.

"OK, you guys win," he says in his easy way, looking around at the expectant faces. "You've got to me. I never thought about romance till I came on this course. I never thought about 'love.' But now it's all I *can* think about . . . because I love this woman." He turns to me. "Not just for the week. Not just as a holiday fling. But for keeps."

I stare back at him, speechless, my eyes instantly full of tears. I never expected this. I never expected him to make a public declamation, or to be so forceful about it, or to gaze at me like he's gazing at me now, his eyes warm and loving.

For keeps.

"Dutch . . ." I begin, then swallow hard, trying to get my thoughts together. I barely notice Scribe—or, rather, Felicity—creeping up toward me with a plaited garland of greenery. She pops it on top of my head with a mischievous smile, then retreats. And now I really *do* feel like a bride, standing in an olive grove in my white drifty dress with a wreath on my head. Oh God. I'm not sure I can cope.

"Dutch," I start again, trying to ignore the tear which has edged onto my cheek. "I came on this course to learn about writing fictional love. Fantasy love. But I've found the real thing." I squeeze his hands tight. "Right here. The real thing." My voice has started to tremble, but I force myself to continue. "And I want to pledge to you, Dutch, that no matter what your real name is . . . no matter what you do . . . no matter where you live in the world . . . we'll make this work."

Dutch gazes at me wordlessly for a moment, then pulls me in for a kiss, and everyone erupts in whoops, cheers, and clapping. Richard is singing the bridal march, because he's the type to milk a joke, and I'm sure Anna is sneering, but I'm not even going to *glance* in her direction. I'm in bliss. I'm in delicious, hazy, romantic bliss, and—

"*Scusi.*" Giuseppe has appeared out of nowhere, holding a pile of paper slips, and reluctantly I swivel my gaze toward him. "Taxi vouchers," he announces to Dutch and me. He consults the slips, then holds out one to each of us. "BA flight to Heathrow. Yes? The taxi leave at eight A.M."

He nods briskly, then moves to distribute vouchers among the other guests, while Dutch and I stare at each other, taking in this thunderbolt. Heathrow. Heathrow! I'm stunned.

(In fact, I'm *almost* let down, because I'd imagined romantically battling the odds of a long-distance relationship.)

"Heathrow," says Dutch. "Well, that makes things simpler. You live in London?"

"Shhh!" I bat my hands at him. "That's . . . Not yet."

The stars are in alignment, I'm thinking in giddy joy. That's what this is. Of all the places in all the world Dutch could have come from . . . it's London!

"I always assumed you did," he adds, and I jolt in astonishment.

"How on earth did you assume that? I could have lived anywhere! I could have lived in . . . Seattle! Montreal! Jaipur!" I cast around for another random place. "Honolulu!"

Dutch stares at me blankly for a moment.

"You sound like a Londoner," he says with a shrug. "Plus I was chatting to Nadia and she said over sixty percent of the class came from London."

"Oh."

"They have London-centric marketing," he adds. "We were talking about how they could expand their targets regionally. It was interesting."

OK, I feel we're getting slightly off topic here. To recapture the mood, I reach up to kiss him again, then press my cheek against his strong, stubbly jaw.

"We're meant to be," I murmur in his ear. "That's what this is. We're meant to be."

Seven

～～～

By the time we board our plane the next morning, I'm bursting with anticipation. I'm finally going to find out about Dutch! And Dutch will find out about me . . . and our happy life together will begin.

We've decided we won't spill our details to each other on the plane. (At least, I decided.) Even though I'm dying with curiosity, the moment needs to be *right*. We've waited this long; we can wait a little longer.

So my plan is this: We arrive at Heathrow, find a bar, sit and face each other, take a deep breath—and reveal everything. Meanwhile, just for fun, we're going to write down a few guesses on the flight. Name, job, hobbies. That was my idea too. I was going to add "age," and then I suddenly realized what a terrible idea that was and amended, "Everything *except* age."

A few of us from the course are on the plane, all scattered around. Dutch has been seated four rows ahead of me, but that's fine. We don't need to sit together. We've got the rest of our lives to be together.

We're both wearing normal clothes by now. I'm in a floaty dress and Dutch is in jeans, with a linen shirt he bought from the monastery gift shop. His outfit doesn't give much away, although I've noticed a nice watch. He's tanned and brawny and he's wearing flip-flops. He looks *just* like a carpenter.

I write down *carpenter* and *Jean-Luc* and then lean back in my seat, trying to picture where he might live and work. I can *definitely* picture his workshop. And him in it, wearing a frayed gray undershirt. Maybe he saws a few planks and builds up a sweat, then heads outside with a cup of coffee and strips off his undershirt to do martial-arts training in the sunshine. Mmm.

This is such a delicious vision that I close my eyes to imagine it even more vividly, and then I guess I must have fallen into a doze, because it seems about five minutes later that we're preparing for landing. The London sky is white and cloudy as we descend, and I feel a pang of longing for Italy— but it's soon swamped by excitement. Not long now!

We've agreed to catch up with each other at the baggage carousel, and as I arrive there I see Eithne and Anna. (It still feels weird not to call them Beginner and Metaphor.)

"It was *wonderful* to meet you," says Eithne, hugging each of us tightly before leaving.

Anna doesn't hug us but says, "Good luck," with one of those snarky smiles of hers, and I force myself to beam back pleasantly and say, "You too!"

Then finally our cases appear and we're wheeling them toward the exit.

"Where shall we go?" I ask as we pass through the arrivals gate into the melee of drivers holding up signs. "One of the airport hotels, maybe? Sit at the bar? Order some wine?"

"Good idea." He nods.

"So, did you make any guesses about me on the plane?" I can't resist asking, and Dutch laughs.

"Actually, I did guess a few things. I mean, I'm sure I'm wrong," he instantly backtracks. "It's just speculation."

"I like speculation," I say. "Tell me."

"OK." Dutch pauses for a moment, grinning and shaking his head, as though embarrassed by his own thoughts, then blurts out, "I think you might be a perfumer."

Wow. A perfumer! That's actually pretty close to aromatherapist! Which I will be once I've done the course.

"Did I get that right?" he adds.

"That would be telling." I smile at him. "All in good time. Why a perfumer?"

"I suppose when I think of you, it's sitting with flowers all around you," he says after a moment's thought. "Wafting their scent round you. You're so tranquil and serene. So . . . I don't know. Unruffled."

I gaze at him, enchanted. Unruffled! Serene! No one's ever called me serene before.

"And you know what they say about dogs," continues Dutch, warming to his theme. "They always suit their owners. So I'm thinking you have a whippet. Or maybe an Afghan hound. A beautiful, elegant dog with beautiful, elegant manners. Am I right?"

"Er . . ." I root in my bag for a lip balm, slightly dodging the question. I mean, Harold's beautiful for a beagle. And his manners *are* beautiful, too, in their own way, only you have to get to know him. Which I'm sure Dutch will.

"How about me?" says Dutch, as we step outside into the English air, which feels chilly after Italy. "Have you worked me out yet?"

"Oh, I think I've gleaned quite a lot, here and there," I say teasingly, and he shoots me a rueful smile.

"I guess I'm an open book, right?"

"I'm pretty certain I know what you do for a living"—I nod—"and I have an *idea* about your name . . ." I break off as I hear my own name being called from a distance.

"Ava! *Ava!* Over here!"

Huh? What—

Oh my *God*! No *way*!

My heart lifts in disbelieving joy as I take in the familiar faces of Nell, Sarika, Maud, and the children. It's the squad! And Harold! They came to meet me! We had a brief Whats-App chat this morning—but they never told me they were planning this!

The only thing is, they seem to be involved in some sort of scuffle. Harold is snarling at a uniformed chauffeur and biting at his legs, while Bertie tries to haul him off. Oh God. Harold hates uniforms, and this one is particularly ridiculous. Who needs all that braid?

"Get that dog off me!" the chauffeur is exclaiming furiously.

"Take off your hat, then," Bertie retorts insolently. "Harold doesn't like your hat. It's not his fault."

"Children should be seen and not heard," snaps the chauffeur, in livid tones. "Will you *stop that dog*?"

"Seen and not heard?" Nell instantly squares up to him. "You want to silence children? Maybe you want to silence women too. What's your fucking *problem*? Ava! Is that your carpenter?" she adds more cheerily. "Bring him over!"

"Jean-Luc!" exclaims Maud, clapping her hands together in excitement. "He's dreamy! Is he really called Jean-Luc?"

I glance at Dutch to see if he responds to the name Jean-Luc, but he's gazing at the scene with a weird expression.

"Are they . . . with you?" he says disbelievingly.

"Yes," I say joyfully. "They're my friends. Come and meet them."

As I utter the words, Harold starts to run round and round the chauffeur's legs, binding them with his lead, barking uproariously. Bertie's given him too much slack, I realize. But, then, he's only a child.

"I'm calling the police," yells the chauffeur. "You're a disgrace!"

"Is that . . . your dog?" says Dutch, sounding a bit shell-shocked.

OK. So this isn't the most ideal way for Harold to introduce himself. But Dutch is a dog person. He'll understand.

"He hates uniforms," I explain. "Harold!" I call out. "Darling! I'm back!"

At the sound of my voice, Harold turns, and an expression of utter joy comes over his face. He tries to gallop toward me, nearly pulling over the chauffeur before Nell grabs the lead.

"Mr. Warwick!" The chauffeur gazes desperately in Dutch's direction, and I feel an almighty jolt of shock.

"Wait. Is he . . . with you?"

"That's Geoff," says Dutch shortly. "And yes."

Dutch has a *driver*?

My brain seems to be short-circuiting. This is all wrong. Carpenters don't have drivers. What's going on?

I hurry forward, take Harold's lead from Nell, and extricate it from the chauffeur's legs.

"I'm *so* sorry," I say breathlessly. "Are your legs all right? My dog's just quite highly strung. He needs soothing."

"Soothing!" expostulates the chauffeur. "I'll soothe him all right!"

I bend down to hug my precious Harold and whisper in his ear how I've missed him *so* much but I have a new friend for him to meet. Then I rise again, turn to Dutch, and say in tremulous tones, "So, meet Harold!"

It takes me a moment to realize that Dutch isn't even looking at Harold. He's addressing the chauffeur in irritable tones. I've never even heard him sound irritable before.

"Geoff, what are you *doing* here?"

"They want you at the conference," says the chauffeur. "And the dinner. Mr. Warwick, Sr., says you know about it. He told me to come and drive you straight to Ascot."

Dutch closes his eyes as though trying to control himself. "I said I wasn't doing the conference. I made it quite clear."

"That's what he said," replies Geoff implacably. "They're expecting you."

"I need to make a call," says Dutch to me, jabbing tensely at his phone. "Sorry. This is . . . This *really* wasn't the plan. . . . Dad." He strides away out of earshot, and I stare after him, nonplussed.

"I thought he was a carpenter," says Maud, who has been watching, agog, with all the others.

"I thought he was too," I say confusedly. "I . . . don't know. I must have picked up the wrong vibes."

"So, what *does* he do?" says Nell.

"What's his name?" chimes in Sarika.

"Don't know," I admit.

"You still don't know his bloody name?" Nell sounds incredulous. "Ava, what are you *like*? What's his name?" she demands of Geoff. "Your boss there. What's he called?"

"He's called Mr. Warwick," says Geoff stiffly. "*Not* that it's any of your business."

"My friend's planning to spend the rest of her days with him and have his babies," retorts Nell. "So it *is* my business."

Geoff eyes me with a supremely dubious look but doesn't reply. I'm not sure what to say, either, so we all stand there waiting for Dutch to return—and when he does, it's with a thunderous frown on his face.

"I'm sorry," he says directly to me. "I'm so sorry. I have to go and do a work thing."

"On a Saturday?" I can't hide my dismay.

"It's a weekend conference. It's . . ." He exhales. "Sorry. But I'll be back. As soon as I can. Tomorrow. And we'll . . . take it from there."

He looks so miserable and apologetic, my heart melts. I don't know what went on during that phone call, but his brow has darkened and I know he doesn't want to leave.

"Don't worry!" I say, trying to sound cheerful. "Go and do . . . whatever you have to do. And I'm sorry about Harold," I add to Geoff, who just sniffs in reply.

"Nice to meet you." Dutch lifts a hand in greeting to my friends. "And you, Harold. I hope to make better acquaintance with you another time. But I have to go." Then he turns to me and for a moment we're both silent, gazing into each other's faces. "I guess the bubble had to burst sometime," Dutch says at last.

"I guess so."

"But this doesn't change anything. I love you."

"I love you too." I swallow hard. "*So* much."

"And we're going to make this work."

"Yes."

"*Yes.*"

"Oh, look at them!" I can hear Maud exclaiming to Nell. "They're adorable!"

Dutch has taken hold of my hands and I'm not sure I can bear to let go—but Geoff is making impatient noises, so at last, feeling noble, I release him and say, "Go. Do your thing."

I watch as Dutch follows Geoff to a nearby big black corporate-looking car and slides into the back. That is *so* not the car I was expecting him to have. Nor a driver who opens the door for him. Nor the *Financial Times* waiting for him on the backseat.

"Wait!" I say, as Geoff is preparing to shut the car door. "What *is* your thing? What do you do?"

"It's a family company," says Dutch, looking even more tense than before. "So . . . Anyway. That's it."

"But you talked about a workshop," I say in confusion.

"Yes. There's a workshop in the design studio."

"But what do you *do*?" I say in slight frustration. "What does the company *do*?"

"We make dollhouses."

"What?" I stare at him, thinking I must have misheard.

"Dollhouses," he repeats. "And dolls. We've been making them forever. People collect them all over the world. . . . It's a thing."

He's in *dollhouses*? I didn't see that coming either.

"Right," I say, trying to think of something to say about dollhouses. "Well . . . that's super-cool! I'll see you soon."

"Can't wait. It's been amazing." He meets my eyes again. "Truly."

"I'll miss you!" I say impulsively.

"Me too." He nods, then turns away. "OK, Geoff."

Geoff closes the door and gets into the driver's seat. The engine fires up and the car is moving away when I realize the most dreadful, horrendous thing. I pelt after the car, Harold barking madly, and bang on the glass till the car comes to a halt and the window winds down again.

"You haven't got my number!" I blurt out.

"*Shit.*"

"I know!" We stare at each other, both wide-eyed at the enormity of what nearly just happened—then I whip my phone out. "Type it in here," I say breathlessly. "Oh, and one last thing. What's your name? I'm Ava. Who are you?"

"Oh, right." Light dawns on his face. "I never told you." He finishes typing in his number, then looks up. "I'm Matt. Short for Matthias."

"Matt!" I smile, because Matt is a good name, even if it

isn't Jean-Luc. I save his contact under *Dutch/Matt,* ping him a text, and breath out in relief. "Hi, Matt. Nice to meet you."

"Hi, Ava." His eyes crinkle. "Nice to meet you. Good save."

He closes the window again and I watch the car move off, my mind turning over this new information. Matt. Matthias. Dollhouses. (*Dollhouses?*) Matt Warwick. Matt. *Meet my boyfriend, Matt. Hi, this is Matt. Have you met Matt?*

It feels right. It feels familiar. I think I knew he was called Matt all along.

Eight

By the time I'm standing on a street corner the next afternoon, I feel almost limp with the exertion of waiting to see Matt again. My head has ached. I've paced around. I've checked my phone every five seconds for a text from him. It's only been twenty-four hours, but I've barely survived.

My body has *actually* been pining for him. I don't want to sound overdramatic, but he's crystal meth. In a good way. My physiology has changed. I can never not be with him again.

As I see him emerging from the tube station, I feel such relief and exhilaration I could almost burst into tears . . . mixed up with a sudden shyness. Because here's the weird thing: This guy in his black jeans and gray T-shirt isn't Dutch. He's Matt. Matt with his driver and his job and his life. And I don't really know Matt, not yet.

He looks a little trepidatious, too, and we both laugh awkwardly as he nears me.

"Hi! You made it."

"Good to see you."

He wraps his arms round me, and as we kiss I close my eyes, remembering the taste and feel of Dutch. For a moment I'm back in Italy, back in the glorious bubble . . . but as we draw apart, my eyes open and we're in London again, and I don't even know if he has a middle name.

"So! Come and meet my . . . my life, I guess!" I say, trying to sound relaxed as I lead him along the street. "I'm not too far from the tube."

As I say the words, I have a sudden mad flashback to Sarika's deal-breaker and imagine Matt replying severely, "Well, as long as it's not more than ten minutes."

The very thought makes me want to laugh. It just shows how messed up modern love has become! Deal-breakers are wrong. Deal-breakers are anti-love. If you ask me, deal-breakers are the work of the devil.

Matt has taken my hand and we're walking in step together, and right now I can only pity all those tragic people who place such weight on artificial factors that have nothing to do with genuine love. I mean, I love Sarika to bits, but *no dancers*? What kind of rule is that? What if, like, the main guy at the Royal Ballet asked her out? What then?

"Do you believe in deal-breakers?" I can't help saying aloud as we walk along. "I mean, do you have any?"

"Deal-breakers?" Matt looks startled. "What, you mean—"

"Do I need to worry?" I clarify teasingly. "You know, like, some guys won't date a girl who's a smoker, or . . ." I think a moment. "Drinks instant coffee."

This is a real one. A few months ago Sarika saw an article

saying 53 percent of people would never drink instant coffee or date anyone who did. Whereupon she sent round a Whats-App to the squad: Urgent!!! Throw out your instant coffee!!! I didn't have any, but I had some instant carob substitute drink, which I moved to the back of my cupboard, just in case.

But Matt seems perplexed by the idea.

"Jeez," he says after a moment. "No. That's not how I think. You can't define . . . I'm not *wild* about smoking, but . . . You know." He shrugs. "Everything depends."

"That's how I think too," I say eagerly. "It's not about deal-breakers. I don't have any either. I can't even *imagine* having any." We walk on for a few minutes, then I add, "I read up about your family company. It sounds amazing!"

It didn't take much sleuthing. Googling *Matt Warwick* brought him up straightaway. *Chief operating officer, Warwick Toys Inc. Brands: Harriet's House, Harriet's World, Harriet's Friends.*

And of course, once I read the words "Harriet's House," I realized. It's those dollhouses with the thatched roofs. Harriet is the doll with the red hair and the tartan skirt. Loads of my friends had one when I was a kid. I never had the house or the doll, but I had a secondhand pony and a couple of Harriet's rabbits.

According to the website, there are seventy-six different houses, plus more than two thousand figures and accessories to collect. Which I can believe because one girl at my school had a whole roomful of the stuff. What I didn't realize was that Harriet's House is a *global phenomenon,* according to the website. There are even Harriet's House theme parks in Dubai and Singapore. Who knew? (Not me, obviously.)

The company is still "proud to be family run," so I got a good look at Matt's dad, who is CEO and has his own page on the website. He's very good-looking—a lot like Matt, just with gray hair and a warm, craggy face. I have an instinct that we'll really get on.

"Yup," says Matt. "Well . . . it's a thing."

He doesn't sound like he wants to talk about his family company much, and it *is* Sunday, so I decide to drop it for now. It's not like we'll be short of topics.

As we approach my house, I feel prickles of excitement. I'm so proud of where I live. I've decorated and furnished it with love. I've been creative with my ideas and really pushed myself. Nothing's *bland*.

"Well, this is me!" I say as I usher Matt through the main front door. "At least, I'm on the top floor. It's up the stairs."

I fell in love with my attic flat the minute I saw it. It's so original. It's so quirky. It has cornices and original fireplaces and even an old wrought-iron fire escape leading down from the kitchen, which I *love*. I've filled every step with scented herbs in pots, and sometimes I take a glass of wine out and perch on the top step. It gives Harold a route out into our little garden too.

As we climb the last flight of stairs, I can hear Harold yelping excitedly—he knows I'm coming—and I beam at Matt.

"Harold's waiting. I can't wait for you to meet properly."

I open my front door, and Harold leaps on me with joy,

barking and snuffling and lifting up his front paws in expectation.

"Sorry," I say, smiling apologetically over his head at Matt. "We have this routine when I come home. . . . I *missed* you." I address Harold lovingly and kiss his head. "I *missed* you. I *missed* you." I'm holding Harold's paws and waltzing round with him, and I suddenly wish Matt was in this with us.

"Join in!" I say invitingly, and extend a hand to him, but Matt gives us a slightly frozen smile.

"It's OK," he says. "I'm good. Were you out all day or something?"

"No," I say over my shoulder. "I just popped to the tube to meet you."

"Right." Matt seems baffled. "So . . . you do this dance every time you come home?"

"It's our thing. Isn't it, Harold, my love?" I kiss his head one last time, then release his paws, and he trots off to the kitchen. "He's a rescue dog," I tell Matt. "He was found abandoned by the A414 when he was a puppy." Just the thought gives me a stabbing pain in my heart. Who could abandon a dog as adorable as Harold? *Who?*

"That's rough." Matt winces.

"But I gave him a home, and—" I break off before I get too emotional. "Anyway. He's happy now."

"Good for you." Matt takes a step down the hall, looking around with an expression I can't quite read. It's not the widest hall, but I've brightened it up with turquoise paint and lots of Portuguese beaded hangings, which I got on holiday. Plus gold paint on the cornices, which is an idea I saw in a design magazine.

There's also a huge, ugly shelving unit blocking the way, which I hasten to explain.

"Remember I said I was into furniture? Well, that's going to be upcycled."

"Right." Matt stares at it for a silent moment. "When you said you were into collecting furniture, I thought . . ." He seems to stop himself. "Anyway. No. Great!"

"My friend Maud upcycles furniture with chalk paint. She's *amazing,* only she's got a backlog at the moment. . . . Careful, don't get a splinter," I add as he takes another step. "It needs to be sanded."

"Got you." He nods, edging carefully past it. "Nice plant," he adds, looking at my yucca in the corner.

He's saying *all* the right things. I love him even more.

"That's my rescue yucca." I beam at him.

"Rescue yucca?"

"I found it in a skip. These people had just thrown it out!" I can't help sounding indignant. "A living plant! They shouldn't be *allowed* to have plants. So I thought, I'll give you a home, lovely." I touch its leaves affectionately. "And now it's thriving. So. Anyway. Come and have a drink."

I lead him into the main room, which is a living-room-cum-kitchen. It's a drop-dead gorgeous room, even if it needs a bit of a tidy, and I survey it with bursting pride. It's decorated in the same turquoise as the hall, with purple-painted bookshelves everywhere I could fit them. It has multicolored floral House of Hackney feature wallpaper in the chimney breast. And—pièce de résistance—two *amazing* sixties chandeliers in orange glass, which complement the dark-green sofa perfectly.

For a moment Matt stands in the doorway, seemingly speechless at the sight.

"Colorful," he says at last.

"I love color," I say modestly. "It's my thing."

"I see that." Matt nods a few times. "Yes. I see that."

"Glass of wine? Or a beer?"

"Beer, thanks."

As I head to the fridge, Matt surveys the nearest bookshelf—and when I join him, he glances up with a furrowed brow.

"*Drystone Walling in the Vales. Theory of Modular Electronics.* You have eclectic tastes."

"Oh, those." I hand him his beer. "Cheers."

"Cheers." He swigs his beer, then adds, "*The Chevrolet: A Guide,* published 1942. Seriously? And this one's in . . ." He pulls out a hardback. "What language is this? Czech? Do you read Czech?"

"A lot of these books I didn't exactly buy to *read,*" I clarify. "I suppose they're like . . . rescue books."

"*Rescue books?*" Matt looks dumbfounded.

"Sometimes I go into a junk shop and I see an old book . . . and it *speaks* to me. I think, if I don't buy this book, no one will. And then it'll be destroyed. It'll be pulped! I feel as though it's, like, my responsibility to buy them." I run a sweeping hand along my bookshelf. "These would all be pulp if I hadn't rescued them!"

"Oh." Matt swigs his beer. "Would that matter?"

I stare at him in shock. *Would that matter?* For the first time ever, I feel a tiny tension between us—because what kind of person doesn't care about the plight of *books*?

But, then, we can have our little differences, I remind my-self. It's not a big deal.

"Sit down. Let's have some music." Smiling at Matt, I find my favorite playlist on my phone and hook it up to my Buddha speakers. I sit next to Matt on the sofa and sip my drink contentedly as the music fills the room. Then I blink. Did Matt just *wince*?

No. He couldn't have winced. No one winces at music. Especially music as relaxing as this.

"What is this?" he says after a pause.

"It's called Mexican spirit power music," I explain eagerly. "They use special pipes and flutes. It's guaranteed to calm you."

"Huh," says Matt after another pause.

"What kind of music do you like?" I ask conversationally.

"Oh, all sorts."

"Me too!" I say quickly. He might prefer chimes, I'm thinking. Or the harp. I'm already summoning up my Spotify playlists when he adds, "I guess mostly Japanese punk."

I stare at him, a bit dumbfounded. Japanese punk?

"Right," I say, after a long silence. "Awesome. Er . . ." I glance down at my phone. "I'm not sure I've got *that* much Japanese punk . . ."

The closest I have probably is "Cardio Energizing Music," and I'm not sure that's very close at all.

"This is fine." He smiles and swigs his beer, then surveys a nearby poster, which I bought from a gallery. Its frame is covered in silk petals and it's gorgeous.

" 'You can cut all the flowers, but you can't stop spring from coming,' " he reads aloud.

"I love that, don't you?" I say. "Isn't it inspiring?"

Matt looks at the poster again with a puzzled frown. "Well, actually, you would," he says.

"What?"

"You would stop spring from coming. Surely. If you cut every single flower before it had a chance to set seed. And what about pollination? If you cut every flower literally at the moment it bloomed, bees would die out. Cut all the flowers, what do you have? Dead bees."

Dead bees? He looks at a lovely inspirational quote about flowers and sees *dead bees*?

"Although I suppose it depends what you're defining as 'spring,'" he continues thoughtfully. "Cutting all the flowers wouldn't affect the earth's rotation; it's more of a biodiversity issue."

I'm feeling a weird emotion rising inside me. Is it . . . annoyance? No. It can't be annoyance. Of course it's not. This is Dutch. This is Matt. This is my love.

"I don't think it's supposed to be *literally* about flowers," I say, making sure to smile.

"OK." He gives an easy shrug, and my heart melts again, because he's not trying to score points, is he? He's just a logical person. Super-logical. (Possibly *over*-logical.)

"Come here," I say, and pull him in for a kiss, and as soon as I do, I forget I ever felt even a smidgen of annoyance with him. Because, oh *God,* I love this man. I want to kiss him forever. I want to be with him forever.

At last, reluctantly, I pull away and say, "I'd better check on the food."

"Cool." He touches my cheek softly, then says, "Where's the bathroom?"

As Matt disappears into the loo, I take the opportunity to whip out my phone, because I've promised to let the squad know how it's going, and frankly, I'm looking forward to telling them it's all going brilliantly.

They've all been so cynical. So negative. Especially Nell, who keeps saying, "But you don't *know* him." Even Maud, who is generally a very positive person, said, "Ava, you need to stop using the word 'love.' You don't love this man. You don't know enough about him to love him." And Sarika predicted he would ghost me.

Ghost me? I was so insulted. Ghost me? This is *Dutch*. I mean, this is *Matt*. He would never ghost anyone!

Sure enough, as I open up our WhatsApp chat, it's full of messages:

So? Ava?

Come on, spill!

Are you married yet???

Firmly I type:

All wonderful!! A-plus date!!! We're 100% compatible!!

Which is true. We are. Apart from a couple of minute details like the Japanese punk. But that makes us 99.9 percent compatible, and I'm rounding up.

In the kitchen, my tagine is bubbling away nicely, and as I lift the lid, it fills the air with delicious, spicy fumes.

"Wow," says Matt appreciatively as he enters. "Looks fantastic."

"Thanks!" I beam at him.

"Your back doorframe has gone soft," he adds, prodding it. "Dry rot, maybe. And the glass doesn't look too secure. Did you know?"

"Oh, it's been like that forever." I smile at him. "It's fine."

"Isn't that a security risk?" he says, undeterred. "You should get someone to look at that. Or replace it with double glazing."

Double glazing? Replace my quirky original door with *double glazing*?

"Don't worry." I laugh. "We're really safe here." I stir my tagine a few times, then add, "Could you pass the harissa?"

"Harissa?" Matt's brow crinkles as though he doesn't understand the question.

"Harissa paste," I elaborate.

Maybe he uses some different word for it. An authentic Lebanese word. Although, wait, isn't "harissa" Lebanese?

"Harissa paste?" repeats Matt blankly, and I swivel round, feeling equally baffled.

"*Harissa,*" I say, reaching for the little jar. "Spice paste. Ottolenghi."

"What's Ottolenghi?" replies Matt with interest, and I nearly drop my spoon on the floor. *What's Ottolenghi?* I peer at him to see if he's joking, but I don't think he is.

"He's a cook," I say faintly. "He's quite famous. Really famous. Like, incredibly, incredibly famous."

I'm waiting for the light to dawn in Matt's eyes. For him to exclaim, "Oh, *Ottolenghi.*" But he doesn't.

"Huh." He nods, watching as I stir in the harissa. "So . . . what's in the stew?"

"Um . . . um . . ." I try to get past the fact he's never heard of Ottolenghi and focus on my dish. "Adzuki beans, onions, sweet potatoes . . ."

"Cool." Matt nods again, then adds, "What meat?"

"*Meat?*" I swivel on my heel and stare at him, baffled. He's not joking. Oh my God. My stomach has plunged to my heels, because how can he . . . *Meat?*

"Is it chicken?" says Matt, peering at the tagine.

"I'm vegetarian!" I say, more shrilly than I intended. "I thought you realized! I thought . . ." I swallow. "I thought *you* were vegetarian."

"Me?" He seems astounded. "*Vegetarian?*"

"The monastery was vegetarian," I point out, trying to contain my agitation. "I've only ever seen you eat vegetarian food."

"I know, right?" He grimaces. "I was, like, it's only a week. I'll survive. But I tell you, last night I *fell* on a burger."

For a moment I can't quite answer.

"Right," I say at last. "Right. Well. I'm a vegetarian. So. That's . . . So."

I'm stirring my tagine in agitation, my face hot. How can he not be vegetarian? I almost feel like he fooled me. He deceived me.

It's not the end of the world, I tell myself desperately. It's just . . . Oh God. It was all so perfect.

"But you have a bone simmering on your hob," says Matt, gesturing at the stove with a baffled look. "How is that vegetarian?"

I focus on the stove anew. Oh, right. *That's* why he got confused. Actually, that's quite funny. I'm so used to Harold's food by now, I almost blank it out.

"It's for Harold," I explain. "He follows a special canine organic diet. I know some dogs are vegetarian, but I went to a consultant and Harold has quite specific dietary needs."

I wait for Matt to ask about Harold's specific dietary needs, but instead he's peering with interest at the pan.

"What's that, beef?"

"It's a lamb bone," I explain. "I'm going to use the broth to make up his week's food."

"Wow." Matt seems fixated by the bubbling meaty liquid. "It looks good. *Really* good. Could I taste it?"

Out of nowhere, I feel a sudden flare of indignation, and before I can stop myself, I snap, "Are you saying the dog's food looks better than what I've cooked for you?"

Belatedly, I add a little laugh—but Matt's head has already risen.

"God! What? Of course not. No!" His eyes scan my face warily as he seems to realize his error. "This looks amazing," he emphasizes, gesturing at the tagine. "I was just . . . No. Anyway. Can I help lay the table?" he adds, hastily moving the subject on.

I show Matt where the cutlery lives, and as he's gathering knives and forks, I take a few deep breaths. Then I ask, in the most super-casual tones I can muster, "So, Matt . . . do you think you could ever be vegetarian?"

My stomach is clenched as I wait for him to answer. I mean, this isn't a *deal-breaker* or anything like that. God, no. I don't even believe in deal-breakers, so how could it be?

But on the other hand . . . I'm interested in his answer. Put it like that. I'm simply interested.

"Me?" His eyes have widened. "No. I don't think—I know we should all eat less meat, but give it up *completely*?" He catches my expression. "But . . . whatever," he backtracks. "Maybe. Never say never."

Already my stomach has relaxed. There we are. It's all fine! *Never say never.* That's all I needed to know. I can see that I've overreacted; in fact, it's all very clear to me. I'll convert him! The vegetarian gods have sent him to me for this very purpose!

"What should I do with this?" Matt adds, nodding at a pile of papers, and I click my tongue. I intended to tidy that away earlier.

"Er . . . put it on the bench under the windowsill. It's my stuff for my course."

"Right." He nods. "The aromatherapy."

"Different course, actually," I say, chopping fresh coriander. "Career coaching. I want to take that up part-time."

"You have a lot of interests." He raises his eyebrows. "When will you finish your aromatherapy qualification?"

"Not sure," I say, slightly defensive, because don't people realize how hard it is to fit everything in? "Anyway! The food's nearly ready. Have a crisp."

I pass him a bowl of posh crisps which I bought especially for tonight, and Matt takes a couple. But before they can get to his mouth, Harold appears from nowhere, adeptly leaps onto the bench, removes the crisps from Matt's hand, and crunches them. He jumps down and scoots quickly away while I try not to laugh, and Matt gazes at him in astonishment.

"Did he just take that out of my hand? I didn't even *notice* him."

"He's pretty deft." I grin. "You have to hold food at chest level or else. Vamoose."

I'm expecting Matt to laugh, but he still looks astonished. Even . . . disapproving?

"You allow him?"

"Well, no, obviously, I don't *allow* him," I say, feeling caught out. I turn to Harold and say, a bit self-consciously, "Harold, darling, Matt is our friend and we don't steal food from friends. OK?" As Harold buries his nose in my hands, I rub his head. "No stealing food!"

I kiss him on the head, then look up to see Matt watching me with a flummoxed expression.

"What?" I say.

"No. Nothing. I . . ." He stops himself. "No."

"You were going to say something." I stare at him, my eyes narrowed. "What?"

"Nothing!" He shakes his head. "Really. Let's . . . have another drink."

I don't believe him, but nor do I want to force the issue. So in bright tones I say, "Glass of wine?" and fetch a bottle I bought in Italy.

Just the *glug-glug-glug* sound soothes away whatever tension was in the air. We clink our glasses and smile at each other, and as I taste my first sip, it's Pavlovian. Or do I mean Proustian? Whatever it is, I could be back there, in Puglia, in the courtyard with the herbs and the agapanthus and the birds silhouetted in the sky.

"The last time we had this wine we were at the monastery," I say, and Matt's brow relaxes.

"Seems an age away already."

"I know."

He's leaning against the counter and I come to join him. I lean into his broad chest, inhaling him, remembering him as he was then. Dutch. My Dutch.

"It's good to see you," I say softly. "Missed you."

"You too."

There's a moment of silence, then Matt puts down his wineglass and I put down mine. And the moment we're kissing, I can't think why we've waited this long. I'm devouring him, remembering him, wanting him more desperately than ever.

"I haven't thought about anything except you," I whisper into his ear.

"Yesterday, all I could think about was you," returns Matt, his stubble pressed against my neck.

"I never even asked you how your meeting was," I say, with sudden self-reproach.

"I don't want to think about my meeting," he growls back. "Fuck that."

He's already undone my bra; I've unbuttoned his shirt. . . . Whatever tiny tensions were between us have vanished. We're in synch with each other. Moving with each other. In the zone together. This man is all I want or need. . . .

Then a timer suddenly pings, and we both jerk in shock.

"Oh. I set that earlier. Sorry." I wince. "It's . . . doesn't matter."

"We could eat," suggests Matt. "And then . . ." He raises his eyebrows, and as I remember what we got up to in Italy, I feel a cascade of responses all over my body.

"OK. Let's do that."

I ladle out my tagine into two shallow pottery bowls and usher Matt to the table.

"Interesting chairs," he says, eyeing my vintage school chairs. I found them at a car-boot sale and they're quite rickety, but Maud is going to upcycle them as soon as she's done the shelving unit. "Don't tell me. Rescue chairs?"

"Of course," I say, laughing at his expression. "All my furniture is rescue furniture, pretty much. 'Adopt, don't shop.' "

"Not your bed, surely," he says, looking slightly repulsed.

"Especially my bed! I found it in a skip," I say proudly. "Maud painted it and it's as good as new. I just hate new furniture. It's so blah. It's so . . . *functional*. It has no character."

"If you say so." Matt sits down and picks up his fork. "*Bon appétit.*"

As we both take our first mouthfuls, I hear a sound a bit like a twig cracking. I can't quite tell where it came from, though.

"What was that?" I say in puzzlement. "Was that—"

But I don't get to finish my sentence, because the next moment there's the sound of splintering wood and Matt yells with shock—and before my eyes, his chair collapses with him on it, as if he's in "The Three Bears."

"Oh my *God*!" I shriek in horror.

"Shit!" Matt sounds like he's in actual pain. "What the *fuck*?"

"I'm so sorry!" I say desperately.

I'm already on my feet and I try to help Matt up from the mess of wood, although Harold is barking frenziedly and capering around and generally getting in the way.

"Right now . . ." says Matt heavily, as he finally gets to his feet, "right now, I would probably take function over character."

"I'm sorry," I say again, feeling waves of mortification. "I'm so sorry . . . Wait, your *arm*." I feel a stab of dread as I see his sleeve. It's drenched with red. *What has my rescue furniture done to the man I love?*

Wordlessly, Matt pulls up his sleeve to reveal a horrible gash which has gone right through his shirt.

"Shit." My stomach is hollow. "Shit! But how—what—"

"Nail." He nods at a huge rusty nail sticking out of my salvaged kitchen dresser, which is also on Maud's upcycling list. "Must have caught me when I went down."

"Matt, I don't know what to say," I begin, my voice trembling. "I'm so *incredibly* sorry. . . ."

"Ava, it's fine. Not your fault." He puts his uninjured hand on my arm. "But maybe I should go to A&E, get a tetanus jab."

"Yes. Right. I'll get a cab." Flustered, I whip out my phone to call an Uber. I can't quite believe it. This is *not* how things were supposed to go.

"Don't stress. Shit happens." He squeezes my arm. "And apart from that, it's been a great evening," he adds. "Really, it has. Thank you. I loved the . . . um . . ." He stops as though he doesn't know how to finish the sentence. "I loved the . . . the . . ." He pauses again, and I can see him scrabbling for the next word. "I loved . . . *you,*" he finishes at last. "I loved seeing *you* again."

"Well, me too. Cab's on its way."

I soak a tea towel and wash his arm, wincing at the blood, then grab a packet of biscuits from the cupboard.

"We might have a wait at the hospital," I say, nodding at them.

"Ava, you're not coming with me," says Matt, looking taken aback. "It's not necessary."

"Of course I am!" I stare at him. "I'm not going to *leave* you. And . . . d'you want to come back here afterward?" I ask tentatively. "The rescue bed won't collapse," I add in earnest tones. "I promise. It's sturdy."

At the phrase "rescue bed," a weird, fixed look comes over Matt's face, which I can't quite read.

"Let's see how we go, shall we?" he says after a long silence. "We could come back here, yes, we could do that." He pauses again, his eyes running over the heap of broken rescue chair. "Or we could always go to my place."

Nine

~~~~

I'm feeling upbeat and undeterred as I stand in an unfamiliar corner of west London the next evening, waiting for Matt. OK, so we didn't have the best outcome last night—but it doesn't matter. Tonight will be different.

We were at A&E until 1 A.M. By the time Matt had got patched up and signed all the forms, it felt too late to embark on anything more romantic than going home and collapsing in our separate beds. We agreed to start again tonight after work, and Matt said he'd come and meet me at the tube station.

So I've drawn a mental line under everything. We're starting afresh tonight. Harold and I are going to stay at Matt's place, and finally I'm going to see his life!

"Are you excited?" I say fondly to Harold, at my side. "We're seeing Matt! Our new friend! Oh, look, there he is!"

God, he's an impressive sight. I mean, *anyone* would say he's gorgeous. He's walking down the street with that easy gait, his dark hair glowing in the sun, his eyes crinkling into a smile, his muscles rippling as he moves. (OK, so he's wearing a suit, but I can fill in the muscles for myself.)

He greets me with a kiss and takes my enormous case.

"Hi!" I say, then add anxiously, "How's your arm?"

"Fine," says Matt cheerfully. "Wow," he adds, hefting the case. "This is massive. What have you got in here?"

"Harold's stuff," I explain. "I brought his bed and his blanket . . . a few toys. . . . We're both so excited to see your place!" I add excitedly. "And meet your flatmates!"

We start walking and I look around with bright eyes, because this is Matt's neighborhood. This is part of him. And it's a glorious area of London: one pretty street after another. And, look, a garden square! My fingers are crossed that he lives in a square just like this and has a key to the garden. I can see us, lying on the grass in the sunshine, lazily scratching Harold's head and drinking wine and just enjoying life. Forever.

"So, tell me about the people in your life," I say eagerly. "Start with your parents."

I'm always interested to hear about the parents of guys I date. It's not that I'm looking for new parents, it's just . . . Well. I like hearing about happy families.

I told Matt about my parents last night while we were sitting on plastic chairs in A&E. I told him about my dad, who's still alive but divorced my mum and moved to Hong Kong when I was small. And how we *do* see each other sometimes . . . but it's not like other people's dads. It's not easy and familiar. It's more like seeing an uncle or a family friend or something.

Then I told him about my mum dying when I was sixteen. I tried to paint a picture of her for him. Her blue eyes and her artist's smock (she was an art teacher) and her cigarette habit. Her endearing way of getting the joke just slightly too late and exclaiming, "I see, oh, I *see*, oh, that's *funny!*"

Then I described Martin, who was my stepdad for twelve years. His friendly face; his love of jive clubs; his famous six-bean curry. I explained how he was devastated when Mum died but he's since found a lovely woman called Fran and two more stepchildren and how I'm thrilled for him, of course I am, but it's weird for me. They ask me for Christmas every year and I tried going once, but it didn't really work. So the next year I went to Maud's, which was noisy and chaotic and distracting in the best possible way.

Then I really opened up. I told Matt how I sometimes realize how very much on my own I am in the world, with just a distant dad and no siblings. And how it feels scary. But then I remember I have my friends and I have Harold and I have my rescue projects and all my work. . . .

I suppose I talked quite a lot. But there wasn't a lot else to do in the A&E waiting room. And I was going to ask Matt about his family, but before I could, we were called by the nurse.

So now it's time for me to hear about his background. I want to learn all about his parents. Their lovable quirks . . . their heartwarming traditions . . . the important lessons they've given him as he's grown up . . . Basically I want to learn why I'm going to love them.

Nell once said to me, "Ava, you don't have to be ready to love anything and everything you come across," but she was exaggerating. I don't. And anyway, this isn't "anything," this is Matt! I love him! And I'm ready to love his family too.

"Tell me everything about your parents," I reiterate, squeezing his hand. "*Everything*. Don't leave anything out."

"OK." Matt nods. "Well, there's my dad."

We walk along a bit in silence while I wait for Matt to continue. Till I realize that's it.

"What's your dad like?" I prompt, and Matt furrows his brow as though I've hurled some impossible problem at him.

"He's . . . tall," he says at last.

"Tall," I say encouragingly. "Wow!"

"Not *extreme*," Matt clarifies. "He's about six foot two. Maybe six foot three. I can find out if you like." He gets out his phone. "I'll text him."

He summons up his contacts page and I hurriedly say, "No! No, it doesn't matter what his exact height is. So, he's pretty tall. Amazing!"

I'm hoping Matt might carry on with more details, but he just nods as he puts his phone away again and we walk on, while I feel tiny prickles of frustration.

"Anything else?" I say at last.

"He's . . ." Matt thinks for a bit. "You know."

I quell an urge to retort "No, I *don't* know, that's the point." But that would ruin the mood, so instead I say brightly, "What about your mother? What's she like?"

"Oh." Matt thinks for a while again. "She's . . . You know. It's hard to say."

"Just anything!" I say, trying not to sound desperate. "Anything about her. Any detail. Big or small. Paint a picture."

Matt is silent for a while, then says, "I guess she's pretty tall as well."

She's tall too? That's all he has to say? I'm starting to picture a family of giants here. I'm about to ask if he has any siblings when Matt says, "Here we are!" and my head jerks up in surprise. Followed by stupefied horror.

I've been so preoccupied, I haven't noticed our surroundings changing as we've been walking. We're not in a pretty garden square anymore. Or a pretty street. We're standing in front of the ugliest building I've ever seen in my life and Matt is gesturing proudly at it. "Home!" he adds, just in case there was any doubt. "What do you think?"

What I *honestly* think is, I can't believe anyone ever designed this. Or built it. It's made of concrete with sinister-looking circular windows and odd rectangular structures extending in all directions. There are three blocks in total, linked by concrete walkways and stairways and weird angular bits. As I look up, I can see a distant, high-up face peering out of a glass stairwell as though in prison.

But then I feel guilty for having critical thoughts. London's a nightmare to find a home in. It's not Matt's fault that this is all he could find.

"Wow," I say. "This is . . . I mean, London property's expensive, I know it's hard, so . . ." I smile sympathetically at him and he beams back.

"Tell me. I was lucky to see this place on the market. I had to fight off three other bidders."

I nearly fall over in the street. *Three other bidders?*

"It's a great example of 1960s brutalism," he adds with

enthusiasm, opening the main front door and ushering me into a concrete-clad hallway.

"Right," I respond faintly. "Absolutely! Brutalism."

I'm sorry, but if you ask me, no word that contains "brutal" is a good word.

We travel up to the fourth floor in the kind of lift that belongs in a violent thriller, and Matt opens a black-painted front door into an atrium. It's painted matte gray and contains a metal console table, a leather footstool, and a piece of wall-mounted sculpture straight ahead that makes me jump in fright.

It's an eyeless face made from clay, straining out of a panel on a long neck as though it wants to scream or eat me. It's the most grotesque, creepy thing I've ever seen. In revulsion, I swivel away—to see a similar piece of art on the adjacent wall, only this is ten hands all reaching out at me like something from a nightmare. Who *makes* this? I reach down to Harold for some reassurance and say, "Isn't this . . . great, Harold?"

But Harold is whining unhappily at the face sculpture, and I don't blame him.

"Don't be scared!" I say. "It's art."

Harold gives me a desperate look as though to say, "*Where* have you brought me?" and I pat him, soothing myself as much as him.

"Take your coat?" says Matt, and I hand it over, trying desperately to think of something positive to say. In my peripheral vision I can see yet another sculpture, which seems to depict a raven. OK, I can cope with a raven. I walk up to it, intending to say something complimentary, then notice that in the raven's mouth are human teeth.

I emit a scream before I can stop myself, then clap a hand over my mouth.

"What?" Matt looks up from putting our coats in a cupboard which is so discreet I hadn't noticed it. "Are you OK?"

"Yes!" I try to gather myself. "I was just . . . reacting to the art. Wow! It's really . . . Does it belong to you?" I'm seized by a sudden hope that it's his flatmate's, but Matt's face brightens.

"Yeah. It's all by Arlo Halsan?" he says as though I might recognize the name. "I was never really into art, but I saw his stuff at a gallery, and I was like, I *get* this artist. Blew me away. I have another piece in my bedroom," he adds with enthusiasm. "It's a hairless wolf."

A hairless wolf? A hairless wolf is going to watch us have sex?

"Great!" I say in a strangled voice. "A hairless wolf! Awesome!"

Matt closes the cupboard and opens another door, which I hadn't noticed either because everything is so uniform and sleek and monochrome. "Come and meet the guys," he says, and ushers me through the door.

The first thing I notice is how huge the space is. The second is that everything is black or gray. Concrete floor, black walls, metal blinds. There's a seating area with black leather sofas, three desks with an array of computers on them, and a punching bag hanging from the ceiling, which is being thumped by a thickset guy in shorts with his back to us.

On one of the leather sofas is a guy in jeans and massive sneakers. He has headphones on and is intently gaming. I swivel to see the screen—and bloody hell, it's *massive*.

"Ava, Nihal. Nihal, Ava," says Matt by way of introduction, and Nihal raises a brief hand.

"Hi," he says, and flashes me a sweet smile, then turns his attention back to the gunfire on the screen.

"And that's Topher," says Matt, gesturing at the guy whacking the punching bag. "*Topher!*"

Topher stops punching and turns to face us, and I feel an inner jolt. Whereas Nihal is skinny and quite conventional-looking, Topher is arresting. He's powerfully built, with a face which is . . .

Well. I don't like to use the word "ugly." But he's ugly. So ugly he almost comes full circle. His eyes are sunk into his face. His dark eyebrows are massive. His skin is bad. Yet somehow he's compelling. He radiates personality, even standing there, all sweaty in his sports shorts.

"Hi," he says in a gravelly voice, and gestures at his ears with his gloved hands. "AirPods."

"Nice to meet you!" I say feebly as he resumes bashing the punching bag. Then something at floor level catches my eye, and I stare in disbelief. There's some sort of *robot* approaching us over the concrete floor. Like the kind people have to vacuum their houses. But this one is holding cans of beer.

Harold spots it at the same time as I do and starts barking frenziedly. I grab for his lead before he can attack it, and we both watch agog as the robot glides toward Nihal.

"I'm sure Harold will get used to that," says Matt.

"But what *is* it?" I say, bewildered.

"Robot." Matt shrugs. "We have a few. One for beer, one for pizza, one for crisps . . ."

"But *why?*" I say, even more bewildered, and Matt peers at me as though he doesn't understand the question.

"Makes life easier?" He shrugs. "Come and see my room, then I'll get you a drink."

Matt's room has black walls, a gray concrete floor, and the hairless wolf sculpture over the bed, which I try very hard not to look at as I unpack Harold's things. (Why *hairless?*)

I set out Harold's bed and blanket and spritz everything with his essential oils. As Matt enters, holding a glass of wine and a beer, I exclaim, "All ready for the sleepover!"

"In my family, dogs aren't allowed in the bedroom," responds Matt, and I laugh, because he has a really dry sense of humor. Then, as I stand up and see his frown, my heart plunges. That wasn't humor. He means it. He *means* it?

"Harold always sleeps in the same room as me," I explain, trying to hide my rising anxiety. "He'll get lonely if he doesn't."

"I'm sure he'll be fine in the kitchen," says Matt, as though I haven't spoken. "We can put his bed there; he'll be very comfortable. Won't you, Harold?"

The *kitchen?* Who makes their beloved family member sleep in the *kitchen?*

"I don't think he will, actually," I say. I'm trying to smile in a relaxed way, but I feel super-unrelaxed. My dog is not an appliance, and he's *not* sleeping in the kitchen. "He'll miss me. He'll whine. It won't work. That's just . . . you know. How it is. Sorry."

Not sorry, my eyes add silently.

Matt's eyes run over Harold, over the dog bed, and up to me again. I'm still smiling, but my chin has tensed and my hands have curled into fists. I mean, basically this is nonnegotiable. And I think Matt's realizing it.

"Right," he says at last. "So . . ."

"It'll be fine," I say quickly. "It'll be fine. You won't even *notice* him."

I won't mention that Harold always starts off sleeping on his own bed but joins me under the duvet at some point during the night. We can cross that bridge when we come to it.

"I put some stuff in one of the drawers in the bathroom," I say brightly, changing the subject. "The left-hand one."

"Cool." Matt nods. "That's where Genevieve always used to—" He stops himself and there's a prickly silence, during which my mind whirs.

There was a Genevieve?

Of course there was a Genevieve. Of course he has a past. We're grown-ups; we both have pasts. The *real* question is: What do we want to know about those pasts?

Matt has been darting wary looks at me, and now he draws breath. "Genevieve was my—"

"Yes!" I cut him off. "I get it. Girlfriend. You have history. We both do."

Matt and Genevieve. No, it sounds crap. *Matt and Ava* is far better.

"But this is what I think," I continue before Matt can blurt out something unhelpful like how great she was in bed.

"We were lucky. We met in a magical, wonderful bubble. We didn't know anything about each other. We had no baggage. *No baggage,*" I repeat for emphasis. "And in this day and age, that's a precious gift. Don't you think?"

"I guess," says Matt.

"I don't need to know anything about Genevieve," I say, trying to emphasize the point. "I'm not interested in Genevieve! Couldn't care less! And you don't need to know about Russell."

"Russell?" Matt stiffens. "Who the hell is Russell?"

Oh, OK. Maybe I shouldn't have mentioned Russell by name.

"Doesn't matter!" I make a brushing-aside gesture with my hand. "Ancient history! Baggage! We're not *doing* baggage. OK? This is a hand-luggage-only relationship." I walk over so I'm standing directly in front of Matt and survey his strong, handsome, honest face. "This is us," I murmur. "Right here, right now. And that's all that matters." I brush my lips gently against his. "Agreed?"

"Agreed." Matt's eyes crinkle fondly as he gazes at me. "And, yes, we were lucky." As Harold pads over to us, Matt reaches down and caresses his head. "As for *you,*" he addresses Harold in mock-stern tones, "you'd better not snore."

"He doesn't snore," I assure Matt earnestly. Which is true. Sleep-whining isn't snoring; it's a completely different sound.

I'm just pulling Matt close for another kiss when his phone buzzes and he pulls it out of his pocket. He clicks his tongue with annoyance and says, "Sorry. Work. Do you mind? Make yourself at home. . . ."

"No problem!" I say. "Take your time!"

As he answers the phone, I head out to the main living space and look around expectantly.

I'm already getting used to the black. But maybe I could suggest a few brighter accessories to cheer it up. Yes! Like a throw. He needs some throws and cushions.

Topher is now wearing a hoodie over his shorts and sitting at one of the desks, squinting at the screen.

"Hi, Topher," I say, approaching him with a smile. "We didn't meet properly. I'm Ava, and this is Harold. We look forward to getting to know you better."

"Oh, OK." Topher glances up briefly. "Good to meet you. But you won't like me. Just FYI."

"I won't *like* you?" I can't help laughing. "Why not?"

"People don't."

"Really?" I decide to play him at his game. "Why not?"

"I have unfashionable emotions. Melancholy. Envy. Wrath. *Schadenfreude.*" He types something in a sudden energetic flurry. "Plus, you know. I'm a bastard."

"I'm sure you're not."

"I am. I'm mean-spirited. I don't give money to beggars in the street."

"You started a charity," observes Nihal, walking past on the way to his desk. "Topher talks bullshit," he adds to me. "Don't ever listen to him."

"I started a charity to meet girls," says Topher without missing a beat. "Girls love charity. I bet you love charity, Ava." He glances up at me with his deep-set eyes. "Of course you do. 'Oh, *charity*. I just love *charity*. Let's have sex, because you gave a fuckload of cash to *charity*.'"

"Who did you have sex with?" asks Nihal with interest.

"You know who I had sex with," replies Topher after a slight pause. "And you know she broke my heart. So thank you for dragging it up."

"Oh, her." Nihal makes a face. "Sorry. That was a while ago, though," he adds, practically whispering. "I thought maybe you meant someone else."

Topher raises his head and glowers at him. "The snack robot needs reloading."

"It's your turn," says Nihal timidly.

"*Fuck.*" Topher smacks his hand on his desk with a Shakespearean level of despair. "That is the worst household job. The *worst.*"

I can't tell if he's joking or psychotic. Or maybe both.

"The worst household job?" I challenge him. "Loading up a robot with snacks?"

"Yes, of course," says Topher, picking up his phone and tapping at it with a frown. "The more convenient and helpful a machine is, the more enraged I feel when I actually have to *do* anything about it. Like, unloading a clean dishwasher. I wash dishes by hand just to avoid unloading, don't you?" His expression suddenly clears. "Nihal, you lying shit, it's your turn." He brandishes his phone at Nihal. "I have it logged. Your. Turn."

"I don't have a dishwasher," I inform him.

"OK." Topher nods. "Well, if you ever get one, you'll love it for a week. From then on, you'll take it for granted and complain when you have to give it the barest care and attention. Humans are ungrateful shits. My job is in human nature," he adds. "So I know."

"Human nature?" I stare at him curiously. "What do you do?"

"I run polls." Topher gestures at the three computers on his desk. "Opinion polls. I gather viewpoints, crunch numbers, and tell politicians and companies what people think. And it's not pretty. Humans are terrible. But you probably knew that."

"Humans aren't terrible!" I reply indignantly. I know he's joking. (I think he's joking.) But I still feel the need to put in a more positive viewpoint. "You shouldn't go around saying humans are terrible. It's too depressing! You have to think *positive*!"

Topher looks highly amused. "How many humans have you questioned in your time, Ava?"

"I . . . I mean . . ." I flounder. "Obviously I *talk* to people. . . ."

"I have the data." He pats one of his computers. "Humans are weak, hypocritical, sanctimonious, inconsistent. . . . I'm *ashamed* of humans. I include myself, naturally. Nihal, are you going to load up the fucking robot or what?"

"I have to send an email," says Nihal, with mild-mannered determination. "I'll do it in a minute."

"What do you do?" I ask Nihal.

"Nihal runs Apple, only he's too modest to say so," says Topher.

"Stop *saying* that, Topher," says Nihal, looking flustered. "I'm not that senior. I'm like . . . It's not . . ."

"But you work for Apple."

Nihal nods, then says politely, "What do you do, Ava?"

"I write pharmaceutical copy for a company called Brakesons," I explain. "They make drugs and medical supplies."

"I know Brakesons." Nihal nods again.

"But I also want to go into aromatherapy, and I've got a novel on the go," I add, "so . . . you know. A few things. I like challenging myself."

"Cool," says Nihal shyly, then puts his headphones on and resumes typing. Both guys are so absorbed in their work, I'm not sure what to do next. But then, in a sudden gesture, Topher pushes back his chair.

"*Fine,*" he says. "I'm going to load up the robot. Nihal, you owe me a kidney."

As Topher strides into the kitchen, Matt reappears from the bedroom, his gaze downcast.

"Hi!" I say, feeling more relieved than I want to admit that he's back. "Everything OK?"

"Oh." Matt focuses on me with what seems like an effort. "Yes. Have you got a drink? Are you all right? Have the guys been looking after you?"

"Yes!" I say. "I'm having a lovely time!"

I wait for Matt to respond—then realize he didn't even hear me. He looks stressed out. Oh God, has something bad happened at work?

"I want to hear all about what you do," I say encouragingly. "Shall we go and sit down? Or . . . shall I give you a massage?"

"Sorry." Matt rubs his forehead. "No, it's fine. Just . . . I have a couple of things to think about. Give me ten minutes?"

"Take your time," I say, trying to sound reassuring and soothing. "I'm happy here. I can amuse myself."

As I look around vaguely for something to do, I notice a whiteboard covered in writing. I head over to see what it is— then stare, nonplussed. It has *BASTARD CHART* scrawled in capitals at the top. Underneath is a list: *Topher, Nihal, Matt,* and each of them has a tally. Nihal is on 12, Matt is on 14, and Topher is on 31.

Nihal sees me staring and politely lowers his headphones.

"What's a bastard chart?" I ask, puzzled.

"If someone's, like, a total bastard or really annoying, they get a strike on the chart. The loser buys drinks every month. It's always Topher," he adds. "But if we didn't have the chart, he'd be *way* worse."

"Wait, Nihal," I say quickly, before he replaces his headphones. "I can't imagine you ever being a bastard."

"Oh, I am," he says earnestly.

"Like what?" I demand. "Give me an example."

"I told Topher his new sweater looked like shit." Nihal's eyes gleam through his glasses. "He was really upset. It cost him a lot of money. He gave me six strikes. But it does look like shit."

He replaces his headphones and starts typing again. I've pretty much explored the whole room by now, so I head to a nearby black leather barstool and check my phone. Sarika is out shopping for dresses and has sent over about sixteen photos from shop changing rooms for opinions, so I start scrolling through them and chiming in with my thoughts.

Short black is gorgeous!!! Blue beaded OK but weird
sleeves? Which shoes?

All this time, I keep glancing at Matt. He's been standing
stock still, scrolling through something on his phone and
scowling. When at last he moves, I'm expecting him to go to
his desk. But he heads to another concealed cupboard, opens
it, and takes out . . .

What? My stomach clenches. Surely that's not—

"Hey, Matt!" I say casually. "What's that?"

"Putter." Matt lifts it up, so I can see. "Golf club. Helps
me think."

Golf?

As I watch, aghast, he gets out a couple of golf balls and
places them on a strip of green carpet I hadn't noticed before, because it was masked by the leather sofas. He hits one
of the balls toward an artificial golf hole, then waits as some
sort of machinery rolls it back to him, his forehead creased
in thought. Then he hits it again. And again.

"I thought you were into martial arts, Matt!" I say, trying
to sound lighthearted. "Not golf."

"Both," says Matt, glancing round.

"Both!" I clench my glass tighter. "That's . . . great! *So*
great. I mean, all hobbies are great."

"Matt's whole family is into golf," says Nihal, who has
come noiselessly over to one of the leather sofas and is loading up another computer game. "It's like your family obsession, isn't it, Matt?"

"Not obsession," says Matt, giving a short laugh. "But I

guess we take it pretty seriously. My grandmother was Austrian ladies' champion back in the day, and my brother turned pro. So."

I splutter on my wine, then cough frantically, trying to hide it. *Now* I learn this?

"You never mentioned that," I say with a forced smile. "Isn't that funny? All that time we spent together, and you never mentioned golf! Not once!"

"Oh," says Matt with an unconcerned shrug. "Huh. Guess it didn't come up."

"Do you play?" Nihal asks me politely.

"Um . . ." I swallow. "That would be a no—"

"*Madame.*" Topher's deep voice interrupts from behind me. "Feast your eyes on this."

I swivel around and scream before I can stop myself. He's holding a white platter on which are four raw, red, quivering steaks. I can smell their odious fleshy smell. I can see blood oozing from them.

"Steak night," Topher elaborates. "Choose your cut. You'd like it rare, I assume?"

"Could you . . . could you possibly move that away from me?" I manage, almost wanting to hurl.

"Oh, Ava's vegetarian," says Matt, lining up his shot. "I should have mentioned."

"Vegetarian!" says Topher, halted. "OK." He looks at the steaks again. "So . . . medium-well?"

Is that supposed to be a joke? Because I still have revolting meat fumes in my nose, and those steaks were once an *animal*.

"It's fine, I'll just eat some vegetables," I say faintly.

"Vegetables." Topher looks taken aback. "Right. OK. Vegetables." He thinks. "Do we have those?"

"We have some peas," says Nihal vaguely, staring at the screen. "Although they're ancient."

"If you say so." Topher moves toward Nihal. "OK, Nihal, which is it to be?" He lowers the platter so Nihal can see the steaks—and there's a blur of brown and white, accompanied by the scrabbling sound of paws.

Oh my God. *No.*

"Harold!" I cry out in dismay, but he's already on the other side of the room, a dripping raw steak in his mouth.

"What the *hell*?" Topher gapes at the platter, which now has only three steaks on it. "Did that dog just steal one of my steaks? I didn't even *see* him."

"What?" says Matt, putting down his putter and looking up incredulously.

"He came out of nowhere," says Topher, looking shell-shocked. "He's a stealth missile."

We all look at Harold, who eyes us with mischievous defiance, then falls on the meat like the happiest dog in the world.

"That's a grass-fed, dry-aged filet steak," says Topher, staring at Harold. "I took out a mortgage to pay for it."

"I'm sorry," I say desperately. "Could I . . . reimburse you?"

"Well, it was yours," says Topher. "So, you know. Sort it out with Harold."

As Harold polishes off the remaining steak, Nihal starts laughing, which is the most endearing sight. His face screws right up like a baby's and his glasses mist over.

"Topher, you looked so freaked out," he says gleefully. "Topher never gets freaked out," he adds to me. "That was worth the price of a steak."

"I was *not* freaked out." Topher has regained his composure.

"You *so* were—" Nihal breaks off as a buzzer sounds. "Who's that?"

"I'll get it," says Matt, heading to the answerphone. "Probably a delivery. Hello?" There's a crackly, inaudible response, and he peers at the little video screen. "Hi? Hello? I can't . . ." Then his face changes. "Oh." He swallows. "Mum. Dad. Hi."

Ten

~~

Oh my God, oh my God! I'm beyond excited. And nervous. In fact, I'm a bit hyper. Matt's parents are on their way up, and I don't want to overdramatize it, but meeting them is basically one of the biggest moments of my life.

Because let's *suppose* that Matt and I stay together forever. Just *suppose* we do. Then . . . this is my new family! They'll be part of my life for good! We'll have nicknames and in-jokes and I'll probably do little errands for them and we'll laugh happily at the antics of the children Matt and I will have—

Shit. Wait a moment. I clutch at my glass of wine, halted in my thoughts. Does Matt want children? I haven't even asked him.

I feel a bit stunned by this realization. How has this not come up? I asked if he had any children and he answered "no." But that's a different question. Maybe he doesn't have any because he's taken a vow not to overpopulate the world. Or he's infertile. (If so, would he adopt or foster? Because I would be so up for that.)

I need to find this out right now. He's nearby, reading something on his phone, and I grab him by the arm.

"Matt!" I drag him out of the main living space into the scary atrium and lower my voice to a hiss. "Listen! I have something really urgent to ask you."

"Oh." He looks concerned. "What?"

"Do you want children?"

Matt gapes at me. "Do I *what*?"

"Children! D'you want to have them?"

"*Children?*" Matt seems staggered. He glances toward the living space as though afraid of being overheard and takes a few steps away. "Are we doing this now?" he whispers. "It's hardly the time—"

"It is the time!" I contradict him a little wildly. "It's exactly the time! Because I might be about to meet the grandparents of my future babies!" I gesticulate at the front door. "*Grandparents!* That's a big deal, Matt!"

Matt looks utterly baffled. Doesn't he follow my logic? I've been perfectly clear.

"And if you *don't* want children—" I stop dead midsentence, because I'm drawn up short by the enormity of a dilemma which is presenting itself, right here, right now.

I love Matt. I *love* him. As I gaze at his perplexed face, I feel an overwhelming rush of affection for him. If he doesn't want children, even adoptive or foster ones, then he'll have his reasons. Which I will respect. And we'll carve out a different sort of life. Perhaps we'll travel . . . or we'll open a donkey sanctuary and the donkeys will be our children. . . .

"I do want children." Matt's voice punctures my thoughts. "In the future. You know." He shrugs, looking awkward. "In theory."

"Oh!" I sag in relief. "Oh, you do! Well, so do I. One day," I hastily clarify. "Way in the future. Not *now*." I laugh to show what a ridiculous notion this is, even as my brain is conjuring up an image of Matt holding twin babies, one in the crook of each manly arm.

Maybe I won't share that thought with him just now.

"OK." Matt is scanning my face warily. "So, is this conversation done?"

I smile happily up at him. "Yes! I just think it's good to get things straight, don't you?"

Matt doesn't reply. I'll take that as a yes. Then a distant *ping* sounds and I stiffen. It's the lift arriving! It's them!

"What are your parents like?" I blurt out to Matt. "You've hardly told me anything! Fill me in, quickly."

"My parents?" He looks flummoxed. "They're . . . You'll see."

You'll see? That's no help.

"Should we cook something?"

"No, no." He shakes his head. "They're just dropping something off on the way to the theater." He hesitates. "In fact, if you didn't want to meet them, you could stay in the bedroom."

"You mean *hide*?" I stare at him.

"Just if you want to."

"Of course I don't want to!" I say, bewildered. "I can't wait to meet them!"

"Well, they're only staying for a moment—oh, here they are," he adds as a chiming bell sounds.

He heads to the front door of the apartment while my mind whirs. It's the first five seconds that count. I need to make a good impression. I'll compliment his mother's bag. No, her shoes. No, her bag.

The door swings open to reveal a man and woman, both in smart coats, both very tall. (Matt wasn't wrong.) As I watch them hug Matt, my brain furiously processes details. His dad is handsome. His mum is quite reserved; look at the way she hugs him lightly with gloved hands. Expensive shoes. Nice maroon leather bag. And blond highlighted hair. Should I compliment that instead? No, too personal.

At last Matt turns and beckons me over.

"Mum, Dad, I'd like you to meet Ava. Ava, these are my parents, John and Elsa."

"Hello!" I say in an emotional rush. "I love your bag and your shoes!"

Wait. That came out wrong. You don't say both. You pick one.

Elsa looks disconcerted and glances at her shoes.

"I mean . . . your bag," I hastily amend. "That's a great bag. Look at the clasp!"

Elsa glances blankly at the clasp of her bag, then turns to Matt and says, "Who is this?"

"Ava," says Matt, with tension in his voice. "I just told you. Ava."

"Ava." Elsa holds out a hand and I shake it, and after a moment, John does the same.

I'm waiting for Elsa to say, "How did you two lovebirds meet?" or even, "Well, aren't you adorable?" which is how Russell's mother first greeted me. (Russell's mum was a lot nicer than Russell, it turned out.)

But instead, Elsa eyes me in silence, then turns to Matt and says, "Genevieve sends her love."

I feel a tiny jolt of shock, which I conceal with a wide smile. Genevieve sent her love?

I mean, Genevieve's allowed to send her love. Of course she is. But, you know. How come?

"Right." Matt sounds strangled.

"We met for lunch," adds his mother, and I force my smile even wider. It's *good* that they had lunch. I'm super-relaxed about it. Everyone should be friends.

"Great!" I exclaim, just to prove I'm not threatened, and Elsa shoots me a strange look.

"We had a lot to discuss," she continues to Matt, "but first, let me show you this."

She pulls a shiny new hardback book out of her bag. It has a photo of a dollhouse on the front and the title *Harriet's House and Me: A Personal Journey.* At once I spot a chance to be supportive of the family business.

"Wow!" I exclaim. "I used to love Harriet's House!"

Elsa eyes me with a flicker of interest. "Did you have a Harriet's House?"

"Well . . . no," I admit. "But some of my friends did."

The interest in Elsa's face instantly dies away and she turns back to Matt.

"This is straight from the printer's." She taps the shiny cover. "We wanted you to see it, Matthias."

"We're very pleased with it," puts in John. "We're already in talks with Harrods about an exclusive edition."

"Right." Matt takes the book. "It's come out well."

"I'd love to read that," I say with enthusiasm. "I bet it's really interesting. Who wrote it?"

"Genevieve," says Elsa blankly, as though it's obvious.

Genevieve?

Matt turns the book over, and a stunning woman of about thirty stares out of the back cover. She has long blond hair, a delightful sparkle in her blue eyes, and beautiful, elegant hands, which she's resting her chin on.

I gulp inwardly. That's Genevieve? Then I realize that I've seen her before, in a photo on the Harriet's House website, though I didn't clock her name. I remember thinking at the time, *She's pretty.*

"Wow!" I try to sound light and careless. "That's great. So Genevieve works for you?"

"Genevieve is an ambassador for Harriet's House," says John gravely.

"Ambassador?" I echo.

"She's a superfan," Matt mutters to me. "She still collects. That's how we met, at a Harriet's House convention. It's pretty much, you know, her life."

"The work she does for us is wonderful. Simply *wonderful*." Elsa makes it sound as though Genevieve is a NATO peacekeeper.

"Matthias, I think you should call Genevieve and congratulate her," says Matt's father heavily. "She is such an asset to us."

Matt doesn't react for a moment. Then, without looking up, he says, "I don't think that's necessary."

His father's face tightens, and he glances at me. "Could you give us a moment, Eva?"

"Oh," I say, taken aback. "Right. Of course."

"Ava," Matt corrects his dad, looking pissed off. "It's *Ava*."

I retreat into the main space of the flat and the door closes firmly. A muffled conversation begins, and I turn away, telling myself not to eavesdrop. Although I can't help hearing Elsa saying, "Matthias, I *hardly* think . . ."

What does she hardly think?

Anyway. None of my business.

After a minute or two, the door opens again and the three of them enter. Elsa is holding the book so that Genevieve's face shines out at us, even more luminous and beautiful than before. Matt looks stressed out and doesn't meet my eye.

"Good evening!" comes Topher's voice from the doorway to the kitchen, and he lifts a hand in greeting.

"Evening, Topher," says John, hailing him back.

"Are you staying for dinner?"

"No, they're not," says Matt before his father can reply. "In fact, shouldn't you go? Won't you miss your show?"

"There's plenty of time," says Elsa. She deposits her bag on a nearby low stool and starts flipping through the book. "There was a particular photograph I wanted to show you," she adds to Matt. "It's a lovely one of Genevieve as a child."

She continues flipping backward and forward and is just saying, "Ah, here we are," when I hear a vigorous scrabbling sound. I turn to see Harold rushing across the floor in our direction and have an instant, horrifying realization. He's going to grab her bag.

Harold has a thing about handbags. He hates them. It's *not* his fault—I think he had some sort of traumatic handbag encounter as a puppy and sees them as the enemy. I have about three seconds to react before he grabs Elsa's bag and mangles it.

"Sorry!" I gasp. "Sorry, that's my dog, and you might want to move your— Quick!"

I make a desperate lunge for the bag, but at the same time Elsa moves defensively toward it, and I don't know *what* happens, but there's a ripping sound, and—

Oh God.

Somehow as I lunged, I caught the book, and now I've ripped the jacket. Right down the middle of Genevieve's face.

"Genevieve!" cries Elsa hysterically, as though I've attacked her in person, and whips the book away. "What have you *done*?"

"I'm so sorry." I gulp, cold with horror. "I didn't mean to— Harold, no!"

I snatch up the handbag from the stool before Harold can sink his teeth into it. Elsa gasps in fresh horror, grabs it from me, and clutches both book and bag protectively to her.

For a moment no one speaks. One of Genevieve's eyes is gazing straight at me, while the other flaps around on the torn bit of paper. And I know this is irrational—but I feel like Genevieve can see me through the book. She knows. She *knows*.

I glance at Matt, and his lips are compressed. I can't tell if he's livid or amused or what.

"Well," says Elsa at last, gathering herself. "We need to go. I'll leave this here." She places the book on a high shelf.

"Lovely to meet you," I say feebly. "Sorry about . . . Sorry."

Elsa and John both give me stiff nods, and Matt ushers them out while I sag in utter dismay. That has to be one of the worst three minutes of my life.

"Nice work," says Topher's voice behind me, and I turn to see him regarding me in amusement. He nods at Genevieve's ripped face. "Destroy the ex. Always a good first move."

"It was an accident," I say defensively, and he raises his eyebrows.

"There *are* no accidents," he says in mysterious tones. "I like how you and Harold operate as a team, by the way," he adds more matter-of-factly. "You secure the area; he goes in. Very slick. Good comms."

I can't help smiling at the idea of Harold and me having "comms." But I'm not having Topher start some rumor that I attacked a book deliberately. I love books! I take in rescue books!

"I would *never* hurt a book," I say stonily. I glance again at Genevieve's glossy torn face and wince as though it were a real injury.

"They can do wonders with plastic surgery these days,"

says Topher, following my gaze, and I give a half laugh in spite of myself.

"It's not just the damage to the book. It's . . . you know. My first meeting with Matt's parents and it ends like that. You can have the best intentions, the *very* best intentions, but . . ." I heave a hopeless sigh.

"Listen, Ava," says Topher, his voice more serious, and I look up, hoping for some wise word of advice or kindness. "Here's the thing." He pauses, his face creasing up in thought. "Do you count pasta as a vegetable?"

Eleven

~~~~~~~~

Two hours later, I'm in a more positive frame of mind. We've had supper (I had pasta and peas, which was fine) and we've taken Harold out to a local park for his nighttime walk. Now I'm sitting on the bed, reading the questions which the others have been firing at me on WhatsApp:

How's it going?????

What's his place like????

Details please!!!

I consider for a moment, then type:

It's amazing! He has a great flat. Really cool!

My eyes drift toward the hairless wolf and I shudder. I've been thinking about Matt's weird art and have decided my strategy is this: I just won't look at it. I can easily learn how to get about this flat with my eyes averted from the hairless wolf and the scary raven and all the rest. Of course I can.

There's no point mentioning the freaky art on WhatsApp; it'll only sound negative. So instead I type:

Very industrial. Great flatmates. And I met his parents!!!

At once the replies start buzzing into my phone.

His parents???!!!!

Wow, that's quick!!!

I glance up to see Matt coming into the bedroom, put my phone away, and smile at him.

"OK?" he says.

"Yes! Great!"

I wait for him to continue the conversation, but he doesn't, and we lapse into silence.

Something I've noticed about Matt is that he's quite happy with great tranches of silence. I mean, I love silence, too, obviously. Silence is great. It's peaceful. It's something we all need in this hectic modern life, silence.

But it's also quite *silent*.

To fill the gap, I open up WhatsApp again and read Nell's latest comment:

What are his parents like?

I quickly reply:

Fab!!!

Then, before I get asked for any more details, I close down WhatsApp and survey Matt again. Words are bubbling in my brain. And one of my theories of life is: It's unhealthy not to let words out of your brain. Otherwise they curdle. Plus, you know, *someone* has to speak.

"So, Genevieve, huh?" I say lightly. "What's the story there?"

"Story?" Matt looks instantly on guard. "There's no story."

"Matt, there must be a story," I say, trying to hide my impatience. "Every couple has a story. You were together—then what happened?"

"Oh, right. Well . . . OK. Yes. We were together." Matt pauses as though thinking how best to describe his relationship with Genevieve. Finally he draws breath and concludes, "Then we broke up."

I feel a tiny flicker of frustration. That's *it*?

"There must be more to it than that," I persist. "Who ended it?"

"I don't remember," says Matt, looking hunted. "Really. I suppose it was mutual. It was over two years ago. I've had another girlfriend since her; she's dated some other guy. . . . She just happens to be a Harriet's House superfan, so she's still, you know. Around."

"Right. Got it." I digest this new information. He broke up with her two years ago. Good. But then he had another girlfriend?

"Just out of interest," I say casually, "when did you break up with the other girlfriend? The one after Genevieve? In fact, what was her name?"

"Ava . . ." Matt exhales and comes over to face me. "I

thought we weren't going to do this. What happened to 'hand luggage only'? What happened to 'Let's stay in the bubble'?"

I want to retort, "Genevieve gate-crashed the bloody bubble, that's what happened!" But instead I smile and say, "Of course. You're right. Let's not go there."

"We're here," says Matt, taking my hands and squeezing them. "That's all that matters."

"Exactly." I nod. "We're with each other. End of story."

"Don't worry about Genevieve," Matt adds for good measure, and instantly I feel a prickle of fresh irritation. Why did he have to say that? The minute you tell someone not to worry, they worry. It's a law of nature.

"I'm not *worried*," I say, rolling my eyes.

I turn away and do an elaborate yoga stretch to demonstrate my lack of concern, and Matt wanders out of the room again. Suddenly I hear a loud yell of shock. Then Matt reappears at the bedroom door, holding a torn mess of blue poplin.

"Ava," he begins. "I hate to say it, but I think Harold got hold of one of my shirts, and . . ." He gestures at the shredded shirt and I wince.

"Oh God, sorry. I should have told you: Harold has a real thing about men's shirts. They have to be kept out of his reach or he worries them to death."

"Men's shirts?" Matt looks astounded.

"Yes. He's very intelligent," I add, unable to hide my pride. "He can tell the difference between my clothes and a man's shirt. He thinks he's protecting me. Don't you, Harold?" I add lovingly to him. "Are you my chief protector? Are you such a clever boy?"

"But . . ." Matt frowns, looking confused. "Sorry, I thought it was handbags Harold had a thing against. Now you're saying it's shirts?"

"It's both," I explain. "It's different. He's *scared* of handbags. He attacks them because of some trauma he experienced involving a handbag when he was a puppy. Whereas with shirts, he's just asserting himself. He's roughhousing. He's like, 'Take that, shirt! I'm the boss!' "

I glance down at Harold, who gives a little approving whine as though to say, "You understand me completely!"

Matt gazes silently at his mangled shirt, then at Harold's perky face, then finally at me.

"Ava," he says. "Do you know for a fact Harold experienced a trauma with a handbag when he was a puppy? Or have you invented it to account for his behavior?"

Instantly I feel my hackles rise on Harold's behalf. What is this, the Spanish Inquisition?

"Well, obviously I don't have detailed notes about the terrible abusive life Harold had before he was rescued," I say, a little sarcastically. "Obviously I can't go back in time. But I'm surmising. It's obvious."

Harold is looking from me to Matt with a bright, intelligent gaze, and I know he's following the conversation. After a moment he trots over to Matt and looks up at him with hopeful, apologetic eyes, his tail gently thumping. Matt's face softens, and after a moment he sighs.

"OK. Whatever. He didn't mean any harm."

He reaches down to ruffle Harold's head and my heart melts all over again. *Just* when I think things are getting the tiniest bit prickly between Matt and me . . . something happens to make me remember why we're meant to be.

I walk over, wrap my arms around him, and draw him into a long, loving kiss. After a few moments he kicks the bedroom door shut. And soon our clothes are all over the floor and I'm remembering exactly why we're meant to be.

But by 5 A.M. I've learned that Matt's bed and I are *not* meant to be. It's the worst bed in the world. How can Matt sleep in it? How?

I've been awake since the Harold drama at 4 A.M., which was when Harold jumped on the bed to snuggle up, as he always does. It was *so* not a big deal. But Matt woke up and exclaimed, "What the hell!" and tried to push Harold off, still half asleep. Then Harold jumped up again and Matt said quite sternly, "Go to your bed, Harold!"

Whereupon I blurted out, "But he always ends up sleeping in bed with me!" and Matt said, aghast, "What? You never told me *that*."

I mean, in hindsight, it wasn't ideal, arguing about Harold in the middle of the night, both bleary and bad-tempered.

We tried to get Harold to sleep in his bed, but he whined and howled and kept jumping back on the bed till at last Matt snapped, "Fine. One night in bed. Now can we go to sleep?"

But Harold was all jumpy and playful by then. Which *wasn't* his fault. He was confused, being in a strange place.

Anyway. He's finally asleep now. And Matt's asleep. But I am very much *not* asleep. I'm staring into the darkness, wondering how Matt can put up with this terrible, evil bed.

The mattress is super-hard—in fact, I'm loath to call it a mattress. It's more like a wooden plank. The pillow is tough. And the bed cover is the flimsiest sheet of nothingness I've ever tried to sleep under. Every time I move, it rustles.

I try to wrap it around me, close my eyes, and drift off . . . but it won't work. It's not a lovely squashy duvet which warms you and cocoons you. It's too thin and shiny and unfriendly.

Harold's warming my feet, but the rest of me is freezing. It's not just the bedcover, it's the room. It's too cold. I'm wearing the cotton pajamas I brought with me—but I'm still actually shivering. I try to edge toward Matt for body heat, but he murmurs in his sleep and rolls away, and I don't want to risk waking him up again.

I can hear the distant ticking of a clock. I can hear the occasional siren from the London streets below. I can hear Matt breathing, in . . . out . . . in . . . out. I don't dare look at my phone or switch on the light to read a book. I don't even dare move. Lying awake next to a happily sleeping person is *agony*. It's *torture*. I'd forgotten that about relationships.

It wasn't like this in Italy, I think morosely. That super-king mattress at the monastery was the most comfortable one I've ever slept on. The quilt was gorgeous. When Matt and I slept together, it worked. We were both out like lights.

I close my eyes and try to start a relaxation meditation. *My head feels heavy . . . my shoulders feel heavy. . . .* But just then, Matt mumbles something in his sleep and turns over, taking the rustly cover with him and leaving me cold and exposed—and I nearly scream in frustration. OK, that's it, I've had it. I'm getting up.

Carefully, in tiny gradual movements, I edge off the bed and into a standing position. I glance down at Matt to ensure he's still sleeping, then creep out of the room. Luckily the floor doesn't squeak, which is the only plus point of this place.

I tiptoe into the kitchen, turn on the light, and switch on the kettle to make myself a comforting cup of tea. You can't have a cup of tea in the middle of the night without a biscuit, but as I poke around the cupboards, I can't find any snacks, except roasted nuts and crisps. Where are the biscuits? Everyone has biscuits in their kitchen. No one doesn't have biscuits.

As I exhaust one cupboard, then another, my search becomes more urgent. I'm not giving up. They *have* to have some biscuits. "All I want is a digestive," I mutter to myself furiously, as I search behind bottles of ketchup and cans of baked beans. Or a Hobnob. Or a shortbread, a custard cream, anything . . .

And then, as I'm investigating an unlikely cupboard full of tonic water, I gasp in glee. Yes! A tub of chocolate rolls! I don't care who they belong to, I don't care what the flatmates' rules are, I am sitting down with a cup of tea and two chocolate rolls right here, right now, and no one can stop me.

My mouth is already salivating as I grab the tub. I *need* these. I will love Matt far better if I can just have a couple of chocolate rolls, and maybe he should know that. As I prize off the lid, my fingers are quivering in excitement—but then I freeze in horror. What the . . . *What?*

As I gape down, I can't believe it. The tub is full of phone chargers, all twisted around one another. There's no chocolate. *No chocolate.*

"Noooo!" I wail, before I can stop myself. *"Noooo!"*

I desperately empty out the phone chargers onto the counter, in case they're somehow only the top layer—but there's not a scrap of a chocolate roll. Not a crumb.

And now rage is starting to brew in me. What kind of twisted, warped person puts *phone chargers* in a tub labeled *chocolate rolls?* It's playing mind games, is what it is. It's gaslighting.

"Ava." Matt's voice makes me jolt and I look up to see him at the kitchen door, peering at me with sleepy eyes. His hair is on end, his face is sleep-crumpled, and he looks alarmed. "What happened?"

"Nothing," I say, my voice a little tense. "Sorry if I woke you. It's just . . . I thought there were chocolate rolls in here."

"What?" he says in puzzlement—then his eyes focus on the tub. "Oh. We keep chargers in that."

"Oh, *really?*" I say, but Matt's not quite awake yet and he doesn't seem to notice my tone.

"Why are you up at five A.M.?" He comes into the room, looking anxious.

"Couldn't sleep."

"Well." He rubs his face. "They do say that if you allow a dog in your bed—"

"It's not *Harold*!" I exclaim indignantly. "Harold's not the problem! It's the room! It's freezing!"

"*Freezing?*" He seems astounded. "My room?"

"Yes, your room! It's like an igloo! And your bed is . . ." I catch sight of his worried face and rein myself in. "It's just . . . you know. Different from mine."

"Right," says Matt, digesting this. "I guess it would be." He comes up to me and puts an arm round me. "Ava, let me run you a warm bath. Does that sound good?"

"Yes," I admit. "That sounds wonderful. Thank you."

I take my cup of tea back to bed and sit stroking Harold, letting his presence soothe me, listening to the bathwater run into the tub.

"It's ready," says Matt at last, and I peel off my pajamas, already cheering up at the prospect. Matt's bath is generously sized, and I can smell some kind of nice musky bath essence. "Thank you so much," I say gratefully to Matt as I step into the scented water and sit down. Then I gasp forcefully as the lukewarm water meets my skin. What the hell is *this*?

"Sorry!" I exclaim in dismay. "This is . . . It's not . . ." I'm already standing up, water streaming off me. "It's tepid! I'll freeze in here! Sorry."

"Tepid?" Matt gapes at me. "It's warm!" He dips his arm into the water. "Warm!"

Is he telling me I'm wrong? About my own body temperature?

"It's not warm enough for *me*." I can hear tension in my voice again. "I like it *really* warm."

"But . . ." Matt's arm is still in the water, and he's gazing at me in disbelief.

For a moment we stare at each other, both breathing hard.

Things feel almost . . . confrontational. Then, as though realizing this, Matt removes his arm from the bath and steps back, drying it on a hand towel.

"Let's not sweat it," he says carefully. "You let some water out, Ava, run it the way you want it."

"OK," I say, equally carefully. "Thanks."

I step out, wrap a large towel round me, let out half the bath and start running hot into it. Apart from the sound of the streaming water, there's silence. We seem to be good at silences.

As I swoosh my hand back and forth, I'm letting a few unwelcome thoughts stray into my head. I *know* Matt's the perfect man for me, I *know* he is, but there are just a few aspects of his life which are . . . what? Not negative, definitely not, but . . . *challenging*. The weird art. The golf. The meat. The parents.

I glance at Matt, and he seems to be brooding too. I bet he's thinking along similar lines. He's probably thinking, *She's turned out to be a vegetarian whose dog mangled my shirt. And she doesn't like Japanese punk. Can we make this work?*

The thought gives me an unwelcome jolt. We've only been back in the UK for a few days and already we're having *doubts*?

As I turn off the bathwater, I say impulsively, "Matt?"

"Yes?" He looks round warily, and I can tell, he *is* having the same thoughts as me.

"Listen. We have to be honest with each other. Agreed?"

"Agreed." He nods.

"Things are . . . We've had a couple of hiccups. But we

can do this. We can make it work. After all, we built a pebble tower together, remember? We leaped off rocks together. We both like ice cream. We're a great team!"

I shoot him a hopeful, encouraging smile, and his own face flickers, as though with fond memories.

"I want to make it work," he says firmly. "Believe me, Ava. I do."

He wants to make it work. *I* want to make it work. What's the problem, then? My brain is whirring in frustration.

"Though I guess my life is like a foreign country to you," Matt adds—and something twangs in my brain.

A foreign country. That's it. I remember thinking that Matt was a wonderful new land waiting to be discovered. Well, now I'm doing the discovering. And so is he.

"That's exactly it!" I say with new animation. "That's how we need to look at things!"

"What is?" Matt doesn't seem to be following.

"We're like two different countries," I explain. "Call them Ava-land and Matt-land. And we need to acclimatize to each other's cultures. So, for example, in Matt-land it's perfectly reasonable to keep phone chargers in a tub labeled 'choco-late rolls.' Whereas in Ava-land that's a capital offense. We just have to *learn* about each other," I emphasize. "Learn and become accustomed to each other. You see?"

"Hmm." Matt is silent for a few moments, as though taking this in. "In Matt-land," he volunteers, "dogs sleep on the floor."

"Right." I clear my throat. "Well . . . we'll have to decide how and where we take on each other's customs. We'll have . . . er . . . negotiations." I unwrap my towel, hoping to distract him from the subject of dogs. "But meanwhile, let me introduce you to one of my most important customs. In Ava-land, *this* is what a bath should be like."

I get into the full bath and sigh with pleasure as my skin responds to the water. It's hot. It's restorative. It's a *proper bath*.

Matt comes over, and as he feels the temperature of the water, his eyes widen. "Are you for real? That's not a bath, that's a *cauldron*."

"You can get in if you like." I grin at him, and after a moment he strips off his T-shirt and boxer shorts. As he gingerly steps into the water, he looks genuinely pained.

"I do not get this," he says. "I do not get this at all. Ow!" he exclaims as he sits down. "It's *hot*."

"Love me, love my bathwater," I say teasingly, and tickle his chest with my toes. "You're in Ava-land now. Enjoy."

Twelve

〰️

It's nearly three weeks later, and as I shower in Matt's bathroom, I'm pensive. Not in a *bad* way. God, no. Of course not. Just in a thoughtful way.

I keep picturing Matt—and it's almost as if there are two men in my head. There's Dutch, the man I fell in love with in Italy. Dutch, with his kurta pajamas and smoldering eyes and general air of being some sort of hunky artisan carpenter. Then there's Matt, who gets up every day and puts on a suit and sells Harriet's House dolls and comes home and putts golf balls.

And they're the same exact guy. That's what's quite hard to reconcile.

I do still see glimpses of Dutch; he's still *there*. We've started doing tai chi together most evenings before bed, which was my idea. I told Matt I'd love to learn more about the ancient tradition of martial arts, except I wasn't going to fight anyone. So tai chi was the perfect solution—and we do it in our kurta pajamas from the monastery. (Also my idea.) We follow this great YouTube video and Harold joins in sometimes—at least, he tries—and it's such a happy time. We both spend the whole ten-minute routine smiling at each other and laughing when we get it wrong. It's fun. It relaxes Matt. It gets us in sync with each other. It's exactly like we *should* be.

So that's good. And sex is still great. And the other night, when Matt told me this long story about his friend learning to ski, he was so hilarious I thought I would die laughing. When he loosens up, he's *funny*.

But we can't do tai chi all the time. Nor have sex, nor tell funny stories, nor wander romantically through the streets, hand in hand, as though we don't have a care in the world. (We've done that twice.) The trouble is, there's life to deal with too. Actual life.

On the plus side, I'm getting more accustomed to Matt-land. I can now approach his ugly building without flinching, which I see as major progress.

However. Being a fair-minded and unbiased person—which I definitely am—I would say that whereas my life is quite straightforward and easy to learn, his is a tortuous maze. Every time you think you're getting somewhere, you find yourself faced with a socking great hedge, usually in the form of his family business. *God,* it's intrusive. How can one international toy company with a presence in more than 143 countries be so intrusive?

OK, maybe that's not exactly what I mean. What I mean is, why does Matt need to work so hard?

The more I learn about Harriet's House, the more I lurch

between awe at its stature and frustration at the way Matt's parents run it. They seem to have this pathological need to call Matt every night. They run tiny decisions past him. They make him read all their emails. They make him take people out to lunch. They make him wear stuffy suits, because it's "tradition."

They're very old school, that's no secret. I've explored the Harriet's House website a bit, and the rule appears to be that every sentence will contain the word "tradition," except the ones that contain the word "legacy." There's also quite a lot about how the Warwick family *will never tire in its dedication to Harriet's House fans all over the world.*

I mean, I admire that dedication. I admire Matt's strong work ethic. I admire his family loyalty. I even admire the new Eco-Warrior Harriet doll, which I saw a sample of the other day. I'm full of admiration!

I suppose what I'm missing is any *enthusiasm* from Matt. Whenever I try to engage him on the subject of Harriet's House, he gives me quite short, functional answers. Which I can understand: He's tired and he's talked about it all day at work. But still. It's his body language too. It's the whole picture. Let's say I have mixed vibes.

So that's one challenge. Another is the amount of time Matt spends putting on his golf machine. (Quite a lot.) A third is the way that he's showing no interest in turning vegetarian, despite all my education and encouragement. Quite often, when I ask, "What did you have for lunch?" hoping he might say, "Tofu—and it was delicious!" he answers, "A burger," as though it's obvious.

Also—and this is more recent—he's been a bit moody. But when I've asked him what's wrong, he won't answer. He goes silent. He almost turns into a rock.

By contrast, I am never a rock. My work is not intrusive. Nor do I have weird art, nor a flat kept at an antisocial temperature. (I *know* he keeps turning the thermostat down when he thinks I won't notice.)

I'm not going to pretend I'm perfect or anything. I'm sure he finds Ava-land difficult sometimes. Like . . . Matt's quite tidy. This is really coming home to me. He's quite tidy and I'm quite untidy. So there's been the odd *tiny* tension between us when I've buried his phone under a pile of my batik work, for example.

(I've just taken up batik. It's amazing! I'm going to make batik cushions and sell them on Etsy.)

But honestly, after scrupulously racking my brain, this is all I can think of. There's nothing else negative to say about my life. I have a wonderful life! I live in a gorgeous, welcoming, warm flat. I make food with imaginative ingredients like harissa and okra. And when Matt comes round, I'm never making work calls or hitting golf balls. I'm *chatty*. I'm *engaged*. The other evening, I decided to make him a bespoke aromatherapy oil. I got him to smell lots of different essences and wrote down his responses, and I told him what each oil was for, which he had *no* idea about. We had music playing and scented candles, and Harold sang along with the music, and it was just . . . mellow. It was lovely.

By contrast, last night Matt was on the phone till late. I still haven't got used to his stupid hard rustly bed, so I hardly slept a wink. And then he had an early kickboxing session, so he rushed off at 6:30 A.M. It's uncivilized. Nothing in life should involve rushing off somewhere at 6:30 A.M.

As I finish my shower and get dressed, something else is bugging me, which is Genevieve. I can't stop googling her, which I know is a mistake, but she's so *googlable*. She's always doing something adorable on Instagram or announcing some new piece of Harriet's House merchandise on her You-Tube channel. Plus I've heard Matt mentioning her on the phone to his parents. He was saying, quite forcefully, "Dad, you need to listen to *Genevieve*. She *gets* it." Which kind of made me blink.

I was going to ask him about it afterward. I was going to say, "What's Genevieve so wise about?" with a careless little laugh. But then I decided that I would sound paranoid. (Even with the careless little laugh.) So I left it.

But then yesterday I came across an old video of Genevieve and Matt presenting together at a toy conference, three years ago. And it made me feel just a bit prickly, because they had such amazing chemistry. They were relaxed and confident with each other and they finished each other's sentences and Genevieve kept patting Matt's knee. They looked like some sort of incredible über-couple with a sexy spark between them.

I watched it twice, then I turned it off and gave myself a talking to. I reminded myself that their relationship is over. What does some old spark matter when the flame is extinguished?

But then I remembered those hideous raging forest fires that start because someone *thought* the campfire was extinguished and walked away without paying attention . . . *but it wasn't! The spark was still alive!*

And that niggling worry hasn't really left me. Only I can't say any of this to Matt, obviously. If I'm going to bring up the subject at all, I need to be subtle.

Maybe I'll be subtle right now.

"Matt," I say as he wanders into the bedroom, still in his exercise clothes. "I'd like to talk."

"Right. OK." He starts the calf-stretching exercise he does every morning. "What's up?"

"OK," I begin. "So, we've decided not to discuss romantic baggage, and I think that was the right decision. I mean, God, Matt, I have *no* desire to know about your ex-girlfriends. *None*." I fling out a hand, just to demonstrate how little I want to know about them. "It's the *last* thing I want to think about, believe me!"

"Right," says Matt again, looking confused. "Well, let's not talk about them, then. Sorted."

"But it's not as simple as that, is it?" I continue quickly. "If we're really going to know each other as rounded people, then we need *context*."

"Do we?"

"I think so," I say firmly. "A bit of romantic context. Just for information. For a fuller picture."

"Uh-huh," says Matt, looking less than enthusiastic.

"So I have a new idea," I continue.

"Thought you might," mutters Matt, so quietly that I can barely hear him.

"What?" I narrow my eyes.

"Nothing," he says hastily. "Nothing. What's your idea?"

"We do what we did at the monastery. We can ask one question each about ex-partners. I mean, five questions," I amend quickly. "Five."

"*Five?*" He looks appalled.

I want to retort, "Five is nothing, I have fifty!" But instead I say, "I think that's reasonable. I'll start!" I add before he can protest. "First question: How serious was it with Genevieve?"

Matt looks speechless, as though I've asked him to explain string theory in three words.

"Depends what you mean by serious," he answers at last.

"Well . . . did she stay over here?"

"Sometimes."

I suddenly remember that I already knew that and curse myself for wasting a question.

"How often?"

"Couple of times a week, maybe."

"And did you . . ." I hesitate. "Did you tell her you loved her?"

"Can't remember," says Matt after a pause.

"You can't *remember*?" I say in disbelief. "You can't *remember* if you told her you loved her?"

"No."

"Well, OK. Did she—"

"You're out of questions," Matt interrupts, and I stare at him, bewildered.

"What do you mean?"

"You've asked five questions. Conversation over."

Furiously I count back in my head. One . . . two . . . oh, for God's sake, that's not *fair*. That was *not* five proper questions. But I know Matt. He's literal. I have to play the game accurately; otherwise he'll never do it again.

"OK." I lift my hands. "Your turn. Ask me anything."

"Fine." Matt thinks. "How serious was it with Russell?"

"Oh *God*." I breathe out as I consider the question. "Where do I start? Did I love him? I told him I did, but did I even know what love was? It was a weird relationship. He started off so wonderful, so kind, so . . . I don't know, *attentive*. He loved Harold . . . he loved my flat . . . he sent me all these lovely long emails. . . . For five months it was just amazing. But then at the end—"

I break off, because I don't particularly want to get into how he ghosted me, not to mention how long it took me even to realize what he was doing. I made every excuse for him under the sun. And I *still* don't understand how he went from someone who said, "You're my soulmate, Ava, everything about you is so perfect it makes me want to weep," to someone who blanked me. (Nor do I want to remember calling his mum in desperation and her getting all flustered when she realized it was me and pretended to be the Polish cleaner.)

"Huh." Matt is silent a minute, digesting this. "Did *he* stay over?"

"No," I say after a pause. "He never did. He wanted to, but his job was quite demanding, so . . . I mean, it would have been the next step."

"Huh," says Matt again. Silently, he pulls off the rest of his exercise wear, and as I watch him, I feel a growing intrigue. His face is brooding and intent. What's he thinking about? What's he going to ask me? Then he reaches for a towel.

"OK, I'm having a shower. What time are we leaving for this picnic?"

"*What?*" I peer at him. "What about your other three questions?"

"Oh, right," says Matt, as though he'd forgotten. "I'll get to those another time."

He disappears into the bathroom and I gaze after him, flabbergasted and just a little offended. He had three more questions! How could he not be burning to know more? I still have a zillion questions about Genevieve.

Feeling disconcerted, I head out to the living space. There weren't supposed to be any glitches today. I'm taking Matt to meet my friends at Maud's birthday picnic, and it was all supposed to be wonderful and happy and perfect.

I mean, it *is* wonderful and happy and perfect, I remind myself quickly. I just wish Genevieve hadn't got under my skin.

Then I notice Nihal and Topher getting breakfast in the kitchen, and an idea hits me. I head toward them swiftly, glancing over my shoulder, just in case.

"Morning, Ava," says Nihal politely, as he pours cereal into a bowl.

"Morning." I give him a super-friendly smile. "Morning, Topher. Listen . . ." I lower my voice. "Could I pick your brains really quickly, without you telling Matt?"

"No," says Topher uncompromisingly. "Next question?"

"Oh, please," I wheedle. "It's nothing bad. I just want to know a bit more about . . ." I lower my voice. "Genevieve. But we've agreed not to talk about our exes. Like, at all."

"Well, that's a stupid idea," says Topher, rolling his eyes, and I sigh.

"Maybe it is, but that's what we're doing. So I can't ask Matt. But I *have* to know—" I break off and rub my face.

"What?" says Topher, looking mildly intrigued, and Nihal pauses, his hand on the milk carton.

I feel an inner squirming, because I already feel paranoid and ridiculous, but on the other hand, I *need* to talk about it with someone.

"How much did Matt love Genevieve?" I whisper.

This has been my deep-down fear since I saw that video: that they were hopelessly in love in a way that I can't understand or compete with. And that she'll come back and wield some sort of magic over him.

"Love?" echoes Topher blankly.

"Love?" Nihal crinkles up his face. After a moment he resumes pouring his milk, and I feel a spike of frustration. Both of them have dodged the question, I notice.

"Well?" I say, a little impatiently.

"I mean, *love* . . ." Topher looks confounded—then his face clears. "I'd say it's irrelevant. If you're going to start looking at Matt's exes, the one you want to worry about is Sarah."

"What?" I blink at him. "Who's Sarah?"

"The girlfriend Matt had after Genevieve. Irrational. Used to turn up at his office with no warning. *She's* your problem."

"Problem?" I echo, feeling stung. "I don't have a problem!"

"You do, or you wouldn't be in the kitchen questioning us," says Topher with implacable logic.

"Didn't Sarah move to Antwerp, though?" ventures Nihal. "And start dating another guy?"

"Doesn't mean anything," retorts Topher. "You know she once called me up and asked me to check Matt's phone to see if he was getting her texts? Psycho."

"What about Liz?" suggests Nihal. "Remember her?"

"Only lasted a week or two." Topher shrugs. "A very intense week or two . . ." He gives a sudden reminiscent chuckle.

Liz? How many bloody girlfriends has Matt had?

"I don't need to hear about every single one of Matt's exes!" I say, trying to sound more lighthearted than I feel. "I just wondered if Genevieve was . . ."

"A threat to you?" supplies Nihal.

"Yes."

"Anything's possible." Nihal makes an apologetic face. "I wouldn't feel right saying 'a hundred percent no.' "

"Nihal, you're a moron," says Topher dismissively. "Genevieve isn't a threat to Ava."

"She's more of a threat to Ava than Sarah is," says Nihal, in his mild, obstinate way.

OK, I could really do without hearing the phrase "threat to Ava."

"Genevieve's on the spot," Nihal persists, counting off on his fingers. "And everyone loves her. The Harriet's House fan base is huge," he adds to me. "It's a bit nuts."

"Yeah, that's true," concedes Topher, turning to me. "There's a bunch of crazed Harriet's House fans who would pretty much lynch you for tearing Genevieve's face on that book."

"Really?" I say anxiously.

I suddenly envision a furious mob of Harriet's House fans running toward me with pitchforks.

"Also, Matt's parents worship Genevieve," Topher adds. "But you knew that."

"Oh yes," Nihal agrees earnestly. "You should really try to impress Matt's parents, Ava. Matt values their opinion."

"Ripping that book was . . . you know." Topher gives a sudden snort of laughter. "Unfortunate."

I'm utterly frazzled by this conversation.

"You know, you're really not making me feel better!" I say, a little shrilly, and both men look baffled.

"Oh. Sorry," says Topher, shooting Nihal an "uh-oh" look. "We misunderstood. Did you come in here wanting to feel better?"

"We didn't realize that was the brief," says Nihal politely. "We thought you wanted information."

I give up. Why can't Matt have female flatmates?

"Well, thanks anyway. And please don't tell Matt I was asking about his exes," I add, glancing warily at the door. "We're trying to have a baggage-free relationship."

"No such thing," says Topher at once. "Doesn't exist."

"Hand luggage only, then," I clarify, and Topher gives a bark of scoffing laughter.

"Impossible. You can't have a hand-luggage-only relationship in your thirties. You can only have a six-extra-heavy-cases-and-fines-on-all-of-them relationship."

"Well, that's your opinion," I say, feeling ruffled.

"It's everyone's opinion," he asserts. "Nihal, have you finished the Shreddies, because if so, you are getting ten bastard strikes, you utter bastard."

God, he's exhausting. He's relentless. How does Matt live with him?

As I head back to the bedroom, Topher's words about ripping the book are still in my mind. I glance over at the bookcase and wince as I see the damaged Harriet's House book. You can't see the rip, but I know it's there and I can still remember Elsa's anguished cry.

How am I going to make up for my crap start with Matt's parents? Whenever I've brought up the subject with Matt, he's said vaguely, "Oh, it doesn't matter, they'll have forgotten it." But I'm more inclined to believe Topher. Elsa doesn't look like a woman who forgets anything. She's probably sticking pins into an Ava dolly right now.

I decide to calm my nerves by watching a YouTube eyeshadow tutorial. By the time I've finished that, and three different attempts at contouring (disastrous), and done my hair, it's almost time to leave for the picnic, and my spirits have risen. As I glance out of the window, I see that the sun is shining, and I feel even more cheered.

Never mind about baggage. Never mind about Genevieve or Sarah or whatever that other one was called. I'm going to focus on the *now*. On *us*.

"Where's Matt, Harold?" I say, and Harold appears from under the bed, with what looks like a sausage roll in his mouth. Shit. Where did he get that?

Actually, I don't want to know.

"Eat up!" I instruct him, *sotto voce*. "Get rid of the evidence! Matt, are you ready?" I call in a louder voice.

I grab my bag and head out to the main living space. There I find Matt staring intently at a screen on Topher's workstation.

"Forty-two percent," Matt's saying. "Shit. Unbelievable."

"I called it," says Topher calmly, taking a swig of Coke. "Called it all along."

"Nihal, forty-two percent!" Matt calls across the room.

"Wow," says Nihal, looking up politely from where he's tinkering with the snack robot. "What?"

"New poll on voting intentions," says Matt, still gazing at the screen over Topher's shoulder.

Matt adores talking to Topher about his work. In fact, this scenario is a pretty common one in Matt-land: Matt and Topher huddled together in front of the screens, talking about percentage points as avidly as though they're discussing the Kardashians, while Nihal quietly works on his robot. I've learned that it's Nihal who bought and customized the snack robots, but now he's gone more ambitious and is making one from scratch.

"How's it going?" I say politely as I catch Nihal's eye.

"Oh, really well," says Nihal, brightening at my interest. "It's going to have a moving arm. Full rotation."

"Great!" I say encouragingly. "What will it do?"

"What would you *like* it to do?" answers Nihal, perking up. "If you were buying a robot, Ava, what functionality would you look for?"

I can't tell him the truth—that I wouldn't buy a robot in a

million years—so I say vaguely, "Not sure! But I'll think about it."

I find the robot thing a bit alien, to be honest. It's a bit like having a pet. But if you want a pet, have a dog. A *dog*.

"They can't maintain this lead," Matt is saying, now peering intently at a pie chart. "What are the other polls saying?"

"Other polls?" Topher sounds highly offended. "Fuck off. Other polls? Only our poll counts." He consults his phone. "See? *The Times* have already run it."

Topher's company is always being quoted in the papers. He's actually quite a big shot, I've learned. He has a big team and lots of influence with important people. Although you wouldn't know it from looking at him in his ratty T-shirt.

"Have you ever thought of going into politics, Topher?" I ask, because it's something I wondered the other day. "You seem so interested in it."

Immediately Matt bursts into laughter, and I can hear Nihal snuffle with mirth too.

"Topher stood for parliament in the last election," Matt tells me. "As an independent candidate." He summons up an image on his phone and snorts again. "Here he is."

He passes me the phone and I find myself looking at an election poster. It consists of a photo of Topher (quite unflattering), glowering as though he's exasperated with everyone. Underneath him is the slogan: *For a better, sexier Britain*.

I can't help giggling.

"*For a better, sexier Britain?*" I turn to Topher. "That was your campaign slogan?"

"Who doesn't want things to be better and sexier?" retorts Topher defensively. "Name one person."

"How many votes did you get?" I ask, at which Topher scowls without replying, turns away, and starts typing furiously.

"Shh! Don't mention the votes," says Matt in a fake whisper, drawing his finger across his neck and wincing comically at me.

"Sorry! Well, er . . . what were your policies?"

"They were many and complex," says Topher without breaking off from typing. "I took inspiration from a number of political ideologies across the spectrum."

"Some of them were quite challenging," says Matt, winking at me.

"They required vision," replies Topher stonily. "The electorate wasn't ready for them."

"Well, better luck next time," I say diplomatically. "Stupid voters. Matt, we really need to go. Harold, come on!"

Matt grabs his jacket and says, "See you," to Topher and Nihal—and we're just walking out when Nihal suddenly calls out, "Hey, guys! The counter!"

As though responding to some sort of code-red military command, Matt instantly pivots back to Topher's workstation.

"Loading," says Topher urgently. "Come on, you bastard . . . *there*."

There's silence as he and Matt stare at the screen, while Nihal gazes at his phone, gripped. I'm not watching. I refuse to. This is the stupidest fixation I have ever known. All of them are obsessed by the number of Internet users in the world. There's a live Internet counter that you can watch. Every so often it reaches some key number and they all stand breathlessly watching the numerals turning over.

I was there when the count reached 4.684 billion and had the whole thing explained to me. I stood there, absolutely baffled, while we watched the counter go from 4,683,999,999 to 4,684,000,000. All three guys high-fived. Nihal actually cheered.

And now they're avidly watching again. The number of Internet users in the world. I mean, why? It's so weird. It's so *random*.

"Yes!" erupts Topher as the number rounds up to a row of zeroes. He high-fives Matt, then Nihal, who is already posting on Instagram a photo he took of the screen.

"Yay!" I say politely. "Super-fun. OK, can we go now?"

"Sure," says Matt. Then he seems to notice me for the first time. "Wow, Ava, you look great!"

"Thanks," I say, blossoming as he runs his eyes over me. "You do too."

Unlike any other man I've dated, Matt has this way of looking at me that says he's *actually* noticed me—he's not just going through the motions. He focuses. He sends me little messages with his eyes, and I send my own back. It's like a delicious, silent conversation.

And as I lose myself in his affectionate, steady gaze, I feel ridiculous. All my concerns about Genevieve seem to fall away. Those worries are in my *head*, I remind myself, whereas this man is *here*. With me. And that's what counts.

Thirteen

~~~~~~~

We're meeting for the picnic at Maud's local park, and when we're a few streets away, I take the opportunity to prime Matt on my friends.

"You'll get used to Maud," I say encouragingly. "The important thing to remember is, *don't* say yes to her."

"'Don't say yes'?" Matt frowns, puzzled. "What does that mean?"

"She'll ask you for favors," I explain. "She'll be really charming. And you'll want to say yes to everything, but you have to say *no*. Got it? Say *no*. Otherwise, you'll turn into her slave."

"Right." Matt seems somewhat alarmed by the prospect of Maud, so I hastily move on.

"Nell can be a bit . . . She's a character. She has views. And Sarika's quite perfectionist. But I love them all, and you have to as well. They're part of the deal."

"Don't worry, that's pretty obvious," says Matt with a wry expression, and I peer at him, puzzled.

"What do you mean?"

"Well, you WhatsApp your friends all day and all night, Ava." He raises his eyebrows. "No one could miss the fact that they're part of the deal."

We walk on in silence as I digest his comment. It seems a little exaggerated to me. All day and all night? Really?

"Do you have a *problem* with me WhatsApping my friends?" I say at last.

I don't want to have a disagreement. But on the other hand, this is something we need to be clear on, preferably before we arrive at the picnic. Because my friends are my friends, and if you love me, you love them.

"Of course not," says Matt, and there's a slightly prickly silence. "But . . ." he adds, and I inhale sharply. I *knew* there was a "but," I *knew* it.

"Yes?" I say shortly, ready to launch into a six-page speech about my friends and our bond and our support and how I thought he *valued* friendship. My friends are my tiger cubs and I'm ready to lash out with a gigantic roar if he so much as—

"Maybe not during sex?" says Matt, and I stare at him, brought up short. Sex? What's he talking about? I don't WhatsApp during sex!

"I don't," I retort.

"You do."

"I wouldn't *ever* WhatsApp during sex! I'm not that kind of person!"

"Last time we had sex," Matt says calmly, "you broke off and sent a WhatsApp."

What? I rack my brain, trying to recall—then suddenly a flush comes to my cheeks. *Shit.* I did. But it was only really quick. I had to wish Sarika good luck in her assessment. I thought he would barely notice.

"Right," I say after a long pause. "I forgot about that. Sorry."

"It's fine." Matt shrugs. "Just . . . I believe in boundaries."

Is he joking?

"Oh, right," I can't help shooting back. "That's why you make work calls at eleven P.M. Because you have such great boundaries."

Matt looks jolted, and his brow creases. We carry on walking silently while I try to take deep breaths and clear my head.

"Right," says Matt at last. "Touché. I'll try to rein the work in."

"Well, I'll switch off my phone when we have sex," I say, as though it's a major concession.

Then, as I hear myself, I realize how appalling that sounds. I have an image of myself scrolling through Twitter while in the midst of sex, which is pretty heinous. (Especially as I actually possess a book called *Mindful Sex,* which I must read.)

"I'll turn off my phone," I repeat, "*unless* there's a major celebrity story breaking. Obviously." I shoot Matt a tiny grin to show I'm joking. "Then, sorry, I'll have to multitask. I'll still have one spare hand. . . ." Matt peers at me uncertainly, as though to make sure that I'm teasing—then his expression clears and he laughs.

"Fair enough," he says. "You won't mind me checking the cricket score, then?"

"Of course not."

"Or watching *The Godfather, Part Two*?"

Now it's my turn to laugh. I squeeze Matt's hand and he squeezes back, and I feel a lift of relief, because look! We're sorting out our differences with empathy and humor. It's all OK after all.

"Ava, I don't want to fight," says Matt, as though reading my mind. "And I want to hit it off with your friends. I know they're important to you."

"They are." I nod. "We've been through a lot over the years. Sarika has issues with her mum, and as for Nell—" I break off. "There's been . . . stuff."

I don't dare reveal any more details right now. I love Nell to bits, but she can be scary when she lashes out, even after all these years of friendship. And she's at her scariest when she thinks someone's breached her privacy. Or when she feels vulnerable. Nor is she always consistent. (For which I do *not* blame her, but it's the truth.)

Anyway, it's best to play safe. Nell will tell Matt what she wants to tell him, in her own time.

We're nearly at the park now, and I suddenly want to make sure everything is totally secure between Matt and me before we see the others. I feel I have something to prove here. I want—no, I *need*—us to arrive as a happy couple. A blissful couple. A happy, blissful, fully compatible couple.

"Matt," I say quickly. "There aren't any other things bothering you, are there? About us? Like, little glitches we need to iron out or whatever?"

There's silence—then Matt says, "No, of course not." I can't see his face, because we're crossing the road and he's looking out for cars, but he sounds sincere. I think. "What about you?" he says, his face still averted. "Any issues you want to . . . er . . . discuss?"

He doesn't sound overwhelmingly thrilled at the prospect. And although *Your freezing-cold bedroom* has already flashed through my mind, I'm not going to get into that now.

"No!" I say brightly. "I mean . . . You know. Tiny, silly things. Nothing worth . . . No. Nothing." I put my arm around him. "Really, nothing."

The park is busy with picnickers and families playing with Frisbees. It takes a while to spot the others, but then I glimpse Nell's pink hair and exclaim, "There's Sarika and Nell!"

They're too far away to hear me, but as though they're psychic, they both turn and wave, then stare at Matt with undisguised curiosity.

"Why do I feel like I'm on trial?" says Matt with a nervous laugh.

"You're not on trial!" I say reassuringly. (Truthfully, he kind of is.)

"You'll look after me, won't you, Harold?" says Matt, and I laugh.

"Don't worry! Anyway, you've already met my friends, and everyone *loves* you."

Matt's phone buzzes, and as he sees the caller ID, his face looks momentarily rocklike, which means it's work. I want to say, "Don't answer," but I won't, because we've had that argument before.

"Sorry," he says. "Sorry. It's my dad. I *have* to take this. It's about— Sorry. I'll be quick."

"Don't worry," I say generously, because, actually, I don't mind having a quick moment with Sarika and Nell. As Matt wanders off, talking on the phone, I hurry over the grass toward them, feeling a wash of euphoria. My wonderful new guy and my best girls, all together in the sunshine. What could be better?

"Hi!" I clasp Sarika in a tight hug, then Nell.

"Where's he gone?" demands Nell at once. "Run away?"

"Phone call. How're you doing?" I automatically scan her face for signs of pain or fatigue, but she smiles back easily.

"I'm great! A hundred percent." She hesitates, then adds, "I was just saying to Sarika, it's been three months since— Well, since any symptoms at all. Three *months,* Ava. So . . . who knows? Maybe I'll be able to give up my blue-badge space to bastard Sweetman after all."

There's hope in her face—and it makes her look so vulnerable, my stomach squeezes. Nell doesn't normally do hope. Not since she got ill. She describes her life philosophy as "managed pessimism." If she's looking like this, she must be really hoping she's turned a corner for good.

"Nell, that's awesome!" I lift a hand and high-five her.

"I know. Pretty cool. Anyway, enough about me and my

boring health," she quickly adds. "Ask this one about her love life." She prods Sarika, who shakes her hair back, looking pleased with herself.

"I'm down to a shortlist of three guys," she tells me. "All really eligible. Two in IT, one accountant, all in the right salary bracket."

"Three eligible guys!" I exclaim encouragingly. "That's great! Do they all live within ten minutes of a tube station?" I add, meeting Nell's eye.

"Of course," says Sarika, looking surprised, and I bite my lip.

"That's great! So, are you going to meet them all?"

"I'm going to apply some more filters first," says Sarika thoughtfully. "Take the process to the max. See who lasts the course. Maybe one will really stand out."

"Like *The Hunger Games*," I suggest, and she narrows her eyes, not sure if I'm joking or not. To be honest, I'm not sure if I'm joking or not either. I suddenly visualize these three poor guys standing on pedestals, waiting for whatever firebomb Sarika throws at them next, and have an awful urge to laugh.

But I mustn't. This is just Sarika's way. It suits her.

"Good for you," I say encouragingly. "I'm sure you'll end up with the perfect guy."

"Speaking of which . . ." Sarika raises her eyebrows sardonically. "How's *your* perfect guy?"

"Perfect," I reply with a blissful smile. "I mean . . . more or less."

"Here he is," observes Nell, as Matt strides over the grass toward us. He's put his phone away and his face is open and eager, and I feel a flash of pride because, well, just *look* at him. He could live ten hours from a tube station and he'd still be the right guy for me.

"Hi," he addresses Nell and Sarika. "Good to meet you again."

He shakes Sarika's hand, then Nell pulls him in for a hug, and then, not to be outdone, Sarika kisses him.

"You realize you're an inspiration to us all?" she says, addressing both of us. "You meet on holiday, you know absolutely nothing about each other, you're practically strangers . . . and here you are! The perfect couple!"

"I know!" I say, glancing fondly at Matt. "Isn't it amazing?"

"Some people invest hours and money in dating the logical, scientific way," continues Sarika, "but you two just stumble across each other. It's a dating miracle!"

She eyes Matt closely, waiting for him to respond . . . and then I get it. Sarika is a lovely, generous person—but even so, she's *dying* to find something wrong. Because our love story disproves all her theories of dating, and Sarika's used to being the clever one.

"Yes, it *is* a miracle, really," I say, dragging Matt closer to me and wrapping my arm around his waist. "Sarika's into online dating," I add to Matt. "She believes in the power of the algorithm. But I don't. I mean, be honest, would you have gone for me if you'd seen my profile on a dating site?" Even as I'm saying the words, I realize I don't actually want Matt to answer this question. "Whatever!" I hastily chime in as he draws breath. "Maybe you would, maybe you wouldn't, it's irrelevant! Because here we are. And what brought us together wasn't a *computer*." I allow myself a tiny, disparaging smile. "I'm not guided by a piece of code that some stranger wrote. I'm guided by my own internal, natural code. My *instinct*." I bang my heart. "My instinct was that we would be compatible, and it was right!"

"So—no flies in the ointment?" Sarika sounds teasing, but I can tell she seriously wants to know. "No clouds on the horizon?"

"None," I say, trying not to sound smug. "All blue sky."

"Amazing," says Sarika, looking unconvinced. "Do you agree, Matt?"

"Hundred percent," says Matt at once, and I feel a surge of love for him. "We have so much in common, Ava and I. We both love . . ." He pauses as though searching for words. "We both really enjoy . . ." He stops again, apparently stumped.

I feel a slight tweak of annoyance, because can't he think of one thing we both like? There are so many! There's sex . . . and there's . . .

"Tai chi!" I suddenly recall. "We do tai chi together every day."

"Yes." Matt's brow clears. "Tai chi. That was Ava's idea," he adds. "She has great ideas. Always coming up with plans."

"You have great ideas too," I counter at once, but he shakes his head.

"I'm not as creative as you. I was a lucky guy, meeting Ava," he concludes stoutly. "Best day of my life." At this, Sarika's face melts into a misty smile. (For all her talk, she's secretly a bit of a romantic.)

"That's so lovely. How did you hurt your head, by the way?" she adds, looking at the Band-Aid on Matt's forehead.

"Oh." Matt smiles ruefully and raises a hand to touch it. "Pile of stuff fell on me at Ava's flat. It's pretty crowded in there, and there's shit all over the place. I bumped into a dresser and a load of painting palettes and brushes fell on me."

"It was only a small cut," I say defensively, and Matt nods.

"At least I didn't end up in A&E this time," he says, and both Sarika and Nell goggle at him.

"*A&E?*" echoes Nell.

"Oh, didn't I mention that?" I say evasively. "Matt had a tiny accident the first time he came to mine."

"I sat on Ava's 'rescue chair' and it collapsed," explains Matt, and Nell snorts, then claps a hand over her mouth.

"Sorry," she says. "Matt, have a drink. So, big question," she adds as she pours him a cava. "Do you get on with Harold?"

There's a long pause. I can see both Sarika and Nell waiting for Matt's answer.

"Harold's a character," says Matt. "Definitely a character."

"Do you have a dog?" asks Sarika.

"No, but my family keeps dogs." He pauses again. "Although, you know, we train them pretty thoroughly. So. Bit different."

I can see both Nell's and Sarika's eyes widening.

"Harold's trained!" I say defensively. "He sits, he stays . . . sometimes. . . ."

"Harold's *trained*?" Matt echoes with a laugh. "Are you kidding? I mean properly trained. If you saw my family's dogs, you'd understand."

"What are they trained to do?" demands Nell suspiciously, and I want to hug her for leaping to my side. "Jump through hoops?"

"Be civilized companions for their owners," says Matt easily, and I feel a tiny stab of annoyance, because he *knows* I don't like the word "owner."

"I think it's about communication, not training," I say, trying to stay lighthearted. "And I'm not Harold's owner, I'm his *friend*." I reach down to ruffle Harold's head but, slightly annoyingly, he's gone over to Matt.

"He could do with some training," says Matt, as though I haven't spoken. "But he's a great guy, Harold. Aren't you, boy?" He addresses Harold fondly. "I can't believe I let you in the bed. Dogs should *not* sleep in beds." He looks up at Sarika and Nell. "Anyway, yes, Harold and I have bonded. Mostly because we're the two meat-eaters in the house," he adds cheerfully, at which Sarika's jaw drops open.

"You're a *meat-eater*?" She swivels to me. "Ava, you told us you'd found a vegetarian artisan carpenter!"

"Called Jean-Luc," adds Nell with a wicked grin.

"The Jean-Luc thing was a misunderstanding," I say, ruffled. "Anyone can have a misunderstanding."

"And I'm a meat-eating capitalist," says Matt robustly. "Sorry about that," he adds, sounding not at all apologetic.

"But you're on the *way* to becoming vegetarian," I say, still trying to sound lighthearted. "You're considering it, at least."

"Nope." Matt shakes his head, and I feel a surge of indignation, which I try to quell. How can he be so closed-minded? Didn't he hear *anything* I told him about the planet?

I'm suddenly aware that Nell and Sarika are scrutinizing me, and I hastily plaster on my loved-up euphoric smile.

"Anyway," I say quickly, "it's no big deal."

"No big deal?" Nell peers at me, staggered. "Meat is *no big deal* to you?"

"No," I say defensively. "It's not. We're in *love*." I clutch Matt again. "The details are just details."

"Right," says Nell, looking skeptical. "Well, cheers to that." We clink glasses, then I say, "Maud will be here in a moment. I'll just assemble my vegetable mini-wraps."

"Need a hand?" says Matt at once, and I can't help shooting a triumphant look at the others as though to say, "See how helpful he is?"

"Don't worry," I say affectionately. "You chat with Sarika and Nell. I won't be a minute."

I spread out my picnic blanket next to Nell's, take out my Tupperware containers, and start constructing my little wraps with vegetable strips and spicy sauce. I can hear Matt and my friends talking, but I'm concentrating so hard, I barely catch a word, until Sarika exclaims, *"Golf!"* in such a high-pitched, incredulous tone that half the park must hear her.

Oh shit. How did they get onto that? Now she'll say she can't believe I'm dating someone who's into golf and make *that* a big thing. I should have told Matt not to refer to the golf. I could have said, really casually, "By the way, let's never mention that you play golf."

Then I catch myself. No. Don't be ridiculous. I don't want to lie to my friends. Obviously. But it's quite annoying, them being so forensic and knowing so much about me.

As I finish the wraps and stand up, shaking my legs out, Nell's voice travels through the air: "No, Ava never mentioned any art."

"She described your flat," chimes in Sarika. "It sounds wonderful. But she never mentioned the art."

"For real?" Matt replies, sounding astonished. "Well, I'm quite a serious collector. One artist in particular. He's a genius. I have his pieces everywhere."

"Which artist?" demands Nell, and Matt says, "Arlo Halsan."

Instantly, Nell and Sarika whip out their phones. I just know they're going to google Arlo Halsan, and I feel a sudden dread. Why did they have to bring up art?

"Ava!" says Nell chidingly as she sees me standing up. "You never told us about Matt's art collection! Is it amazing?"

"Oh! Yes!" I force myself to sound enthused as I walk over. "It's incredible."

"Which is your favorite piece, Ava?" Matt turns to me eagerly. "I've never even asked you."

I stare at him, frozen.

"It's . . . hard to decide," I say at last. "They're all so . . ."

"Oh my *God*," says Sarika, blinking in shock as her phone loads with images of the hairless wolf and disturbing sculptures of eyeless faces. "*Wow.*" She looks up at me, her mouth twitching, and I stare desperately back at her. " 'Incredible' is the word."

"Jesus!" Nell recoils from her phone as the same images appear. "Very . . ." She searches for a word. "Distinctive."

"Search 'Raven Three,' " suggests Matt eagerly. "I have

that piece in my hall. I got it at auction. Cost a lot, but . . . wait till you see it."

There's silence as Sarika and Nell both google it, then Sarika makes a muffled, exploding noise, which she hastily turns into a cough. Nell gazes at the screen, apparently speechless, then looks up and says in heartfelt tones, "I don't even know how to respond."

"I know, right?" says Matt, his eyes lit with enthusiasm.

"Are those *human teeth* inside that beak?" Sarika is peering at the image, looking freaked out.

"What do *you* think of it, Ava?" says Nell brightly, and I silently curse her.

"Well." I rub my nose, playing for time. "I love art. So."

Sarika gives another suppressed snort and Nell bites her lip. Then she seems to have an idea.

"Hey, Matt, I was going to bring crisps for the kids, but I forgot. Would you mind getting some? There's a kiosk by the gates."

"Sure," says Matt easily, batting away the fiver she offers him. "Back in a moment."

He saunters off, and the others watch him before swiveling to me.

"Golf?" says Sarika in a hysterical undertone. "*Golf?* Does Matt know your views on golf, Ava?"

"He clearly has no idea about your taste in art," says Nell with a gurgle of laughter. "Or are you saying you like this freaky stuff?"

"Stop it," I say crossly. "It's irrelevant."

"Don't you think you need to be a little bit honest with him?" Sarika looks suddenly earnest. And I know she means well, but I'm not in the mood for a lecture about relation-ships.

"No!" I say. "I mean, I am!" I give a huge yawn before I can stop myself, and Nell peers at me.

"Ava, sweets, you look a bit shit, if you don't mind me say-ing so. Are you coming down with something?"

"No." I hesitate. "It's just . . ."

"What?" demands Nell.

"I can't sleep at Matt's place," I admit. "His bedroom's freezing. And his bed is like a plank of wood."

"Have you told him his bed is like a plank of wood?" que-ries Nell.

"Yes. But he says it's really comfortable and he has no idea what I'm talking about." As I look at my friends, I can feel my veneer slipping a little. "Look, Matt and I *are* com-patible. We really are. But there are just a few tiny areas where we need to find a middle ground."

"Oh, Ava." Sarika wraps her arms around me, laughing. "You're a love. I'm sure you'll make it work, but not if you float around in denial."

"If his art collection is the worst thing, it's not so bad." Nell shrugs.

They're both being so nice and supportive, I feel a sudden urge to confide in them fully.

"It's not the worst thing," I confess. "The worst thing is I met his parents and they hate me."

(I can't admit the worst thing is I keep googling his ex-girlfriend. That does not sound cool.)

"How can they hate you already?" Sarika looks as-tounded, so I tell her and Nell about the book and Genevieve's face being ripped in two, and they both burst into fresh hysterics.

"Glad you think it's funny," I say morosely.

"Sorry," says Sarika, calming down. "But honestly, Ava, you do get into situations."

"What about this ex-girlfriend?" says Nell, her eyes narrowing. "Is she an issue?"

"Dunno. There are two ex-girlfriends, actually. Or maybe three. But it's Genevieve who works for the family company. And his parents love her."

"Well, sod his parents," says Nell robustly. "Ignore them. Refuse to engage, if they can't be more polite."

But already Sarika's shaking her head.

"Bad strategy. Ava, you don't want them complaining about you to Matt, putting a wedge between you. I'd say go the other way. Win his parents over. Go on a charm offensive."

"Why the hell should Ava have to go on a charm offensive?" says Nell combatively, and Sarika sighs.

"She shouldn't. I'm just being pragmatic."

Nell rolls her eyes. "You're such a bloody *lawyer*," she says, and Sarika grins, because she and Nell have some version of this argument about three times a year. (Usually in the context of Nell telling Sarika to leave her job and her shitty bosses and stick it to the man. Whereupon Sarika ignores her advice, stays, and gets a pay rise.)

"Ava, Matt's parents *will* love you," reiterates Sarika, putting a hand on my arm. "They just don't know you yet. You need to spend time with them. Next time Matt visits his parents, go along too. Bond with them. And *don't* take Harold."

"Sarika's right," chimes in Nell. "Don't take Harold. I'll have him."

"But—"

"If you take Harold, it's over," Sarika cuts me off bluntly. "You think ripping the ex's face in half was bad? Wait till he eats the lunch."

"Or all the shoes," says Nell.

"Or the priceless new goose-down pillow."

They both gaze at me adamantly, and I fold my arms, not wanting to admit they have a point.

"Let's wait till I get an invitation, shall we?"

"Anyway, I think Matt's lovely," says Sarika supportively. "What does he think of *us*?"

"Oh, he loves you," I say automatically, then suddenly focus on Matt, who is approaching over the grass. He's holding about ten bags of crisps in his arms, accompanied by Maud, who is talking very intently at him in a way I recognize.

"Oh *God*," I say. "Maud's got him."

"Shit," says Nell.

"Uh-oh," says Sarika, biting her lip.

"I told him to say no," I say. "I told him! But look at him, nodding away!"

"Poor love," says Sarika, laughing. "Didn't stand a chance."

Matt is clearly captivated by Maud. I mean, everyone's captivated by Maud, what with her amazing auburn hair and lustrous eyes and instant way of making you feel you're special. He's still nodding, and she's clutching his arm, and as they get nearer, I hear her saying, "Thank you *so* much," in her confident, penetrating voice. "You're *such* a star, Matt. So, you'll phone the storage company, will you?"

"Er . . . no problem," says Matt, sounding a bit startled.

"You're an angel." Maud bats her eyelashes at him. "Now, tell me, you don't know any MPs, do you? Because—"

"Maud!" I cut her off brightly. "Happy birthday!"

"Oh, thank you!" says Maud, blinking at me as though this greeting is a complete surprise. "What a lovely day."

"Where are the children?" inquires Nell, and Maud looks around vaguely.

"They *were* here. . . . Now, Matt, that reminds me, you don't have an electric mower by any chance, do you?"

"No, he doesn't," I say quickly. "Matt, a word?"

I drag him away a little distance and say in a stern undertone, "You have to say 'no' to Maud, remember? We went over this."

"I'm not just going to say a flat 'no' when someone asks me a favor," says Matt, frowning. "I'm a decent human being."

"That's how she gets to you!" I retort. "She makes you feel like a decent human being, she flutters her eyelashes gratefully . . . and then boom. You've been got. I love Maud, but it's true."

Matt laughs and bends to kiss me.

"Thanks for your concern," he says. "But I can look after myself."

Fourteen

Famous last words. Sure enough, two hours later, Matt looks utterly beleaguered. *God* knows what he's agreed to do for Maud, but she's been monopolizing him and saying things like "I'll text you the details" and even handing him Royal Mail notices about parcels. In the last conversation between them, I overheard the phrases "passport office," and "school run," and "*so* kind."

Well, he'll learn.

By now we're all sprawled on the picnic rugs, searching for the last of the cava. Maud's children were eventually located trying to cadge food from another family picnic and corralled back to ours. Now, having heard that Matt does martial arts, they're attacking him with "kung fu" punches.

"I'm going to beat you up!" Bertie yells at Matt for about the hundredth time.

"Stop it, Bertie, my love," says Maud, glancing up briefly. "Matt, I'm so sorry, only he does adore martial arts."

"It's fine," says Matt good-humoredly, although I see him flinch as Bertie prepares to kickbox him again.

"I've found it," Nell addresses Matt, looking up from her phone. " 'The fundamental problems with Harriet's House: a feminist viewpoint.' It's a blog. I knew I'd seen it. Have you read it?"

"Can't remember, I'm afraid," says Matt, looking even more beleaguered. He and Nell have been debating Harriet's House all afternoon—at least, Nell has been telling him how patriarchal and misogynistic it is, and he's been occasionally offering replies like, "We have a new feminist line of character dolls," which barely causes her to break stride.

" 'Who buys into this capitalist, exploitative version of girlhood?' " Nell reads out with a thunderous frown. " 'What architects of bullshit think to create such a misleading fantasy world?' You should read the piece, Matt," she adds, offering him her phone. "It's good."

"Right," says Matt, without moving to take the phone. "Yes. Maybe later— Oof!"

Bertie has landed a vicious blow on Matt's chest, and finally Maud raises her voice.

"Bertie! Stop attacking Matt! Just . . . You *mustn't* . . ." She takes another gulp of cava, then heaves a massive sigh. "Oh *God*. It's my *birthday*."

I exchange looks with Nell and Sarika, because this is what always happens on Maud's birthday. She gets drunk and morose and starts saying she's ancient and usually ends up weeping in a taxi.

"I'm so old," she says, right on cue. "So *old*. Where's the other bottle?"

As she gets to her feet, she sways dangerously on her wedges, and I see that she's been quietly getting more drunk than I've realized.

"Maud, you're not old," I say reassuringly, as I always do. But she ignores me, as she always does.

"How did we get this old?" she says with a dramatic flourish, grabbing the last full bottle of cava and swigging from it. "How? You realize we're going to disappear?" She narrows her eyes. "We'll be invisible women, all of us. Ignored and belittled." She takes another glug of cava and sweeps a hand around to include all of us. "That's the wretched society we live in. But I *won't* be invisible, OK?" she gives a sudden impassioned cry, gesticulating with the cava bottle. "I refuse to disappear! *I will not be invisible!*"

I bite my lip to suppress a smile, because Maud could not be invisible if she tried, with her flowing vivid hair and maxi dress patterned with pink and violet flowers. Not to mention the cava bottle in her raised hand. In fact, the people at the next picnic rug have turned to stare at her.

"I exist," she proclaims, even more passionately. "I exist. OK? *I exist.*"

I glance at Matt and he's staring up at Maud, looking freaked out.

"Sorry," I murmur hastily. "Should have warned you. Maud always gets drunk on her birthday and makes a speech. It's her thing. Don't worry."

"I exist!" By now Maud's voice is *fortissimo*. "I EXIST!"

"Could you stop shouting, please?" comes a voice from the next picnic rug, and I swivel to see a woman in a stripy top regarding Maud with disapproval.

"My friend's allowed to shout if she wants to," objects Nell at once. "It's her birthday."

"You're frightening our children," persists the woman, gesturing at a pair of toddlers who look about two years old and are watching Maud avidly. "And is alcohol allowed in the park?"

"Frightening your children?" counters Nell in outrage. "How is it frightening to hear a strong, wonderful woman saying she exists? I'll tell you what's frightening—our unequal society. *That's* frightening. Our politicians. *They're* frightening. If your children want to be afraid of something, be afraid of *them*."

She glares at the two-year-old girl, who gazes at Nell's furious face for a moment, then bursts into tears.

Meanwhile, Maud has staggered over to the other rug and leaned down so her face is close to the woman's.

"It's my birthday," she says in slow, precise tones. "And that's fucking . . . *terrifying*."

"You're drunk!" exclaims the woman, recoiling and putting her hands over the nearest toddler's ears.

"Oh, puh-lease," says Maud, lurching back to our rug. "Did you never get drunk? Oh, that reminds me. Matt, I have a teeeeny little favor to ask you. . . ."

Matt instinctively backs away and gets to his feet. "Think I'll take Harold for a walk," he says, avoiding Maud's eye. "Get a bit of air."

"Kung fu!" Bertie lands a kickbox on him and Matt winces, then grabs Harold's lead.

"You know what else is frightening?" Nell is still on a

rant. "Global denial of the facts. *That's* frightening." She turns to Matt. "And you know something, Matt—"

"I'm taking Harold for a walk," he cuts across Nell hurriedly. "Back in a bit," he adds to me. "Just need . . . a break. Come on, Harold."

He strides away across the grass so fast that Harold has to scamper after him. When he's about a hundred meters away he swivels to look at us, then turns again and strides even more quickly.

"Matt OK?" says Sarika, who's watching him along with me.

"I *think* so," I say thoughtfully. "I mean, we can be a *bit* full-on, I suppose. When we're all together."

"I'm a *woman*, OK?" Maud is once more addressing the general populace of the park, her arms sweeping around dramatically. "With a soul. And a heart. And a libido. A libido to *die for*."

"What's a leebdo?" asks Bertie with interest, and I exchange looks with Sarika.

"Ooookay," she says. "Speeches are over. Who's got some coffee?"

It takes a bit of persuading to get Maud to drink two espressos followed by a flask of water. But we manage it with a mixture of cajoling and threats—we've done this before—and soon Maud is looking much more perky. She opens her presents and weeps effusively at each one of them and hugs us all. We collect up the paper for recycling, then Sarika produces the birthday cake, which is from this lovely, very expensive patisserie near her house.

"We should wait for Matt, though," Sarika says, looking around. "D'you think he's gone far?"

"He's been a while," I say, suddenly realizing how much time has elapsed. I scan the horizon and feel a clench of anxiety. Because Matt took Harold with him. And what if his delay is because something happened to Harold?

Something bad. Oh God. Please. No.

Already I'm standing up, scanning the busy park, trying to stop frightening images from piling into my head. I should have texted Matt. I should have gone with them. I should have—

"Matt!" Sarika's voice interrupts my frenzied thoughts, and I swivel round with a gasp—then gasp again at the sight in front of me. Matt is approaching, his face and shirt splattered in mud. Harold is at his side, still on the lead but also covered in mud.

"What *happened*?" I hurry toward them. "Is Harold OK?"

"Harold's fine," says Matt, in a slightly odd voice.

"Thank *God*." I sink down and cover my beloved Harold with kisses. Then, as a slight afterthought, I look up at Matt and say, "Wait. Are *you* OK?" I rise to my feet and take in his appearance properly. He's got a new graze on his cheek and a twig sticking out of his collar and looks generally disheveled. "What happened?" I demand again.

"There was an incident," says Matt shortly. "With a Great Dane."

"Oh my *God*!" I say, horrified. I'm already feeling a surge of fury toward this Great Dane. I can picture it, with its monstrous slavering jaws and killer instinct. "Did it attack Harold? You need to tell me exactly what happened—"

"The Great Dane was blameless," says Matt, cutting me off. "Harold was . . . Harold."

Oh, right.

For a moment I'm halted. Maybe I don't want to know exactly what happened, after all. I glance down at Harold, who gazes up with his usual bouncy, mischievous expression.

"Harold." I try to sound chiding. "Did you get Matt muddy? Were you naughty?"

"Naughty is an understatement," says Matt, and he's drawing breath as though to say more when his phone buzzes.

"Sorry," he says, glancing at it. "I'll just get this. I'll be quick."

"Just *look* at that dog," says Nell as Matt walks away. "Completely unrepentant." She adopts a sprightly Cockney accent. " 'Weren't me, guvnor. Weren't me. It were the other feller what started it.' "

"Shut up!" I say, a little indignant. "That's not Harold!"

"It's *so* Harold," says Sarika, giggling.

" 'Law-abiding citizen like me, guvnor?' " Nell continues, on a roll. " 'Start a *fracas* in a public vicinity? Me, what only wants a quiet life? I tell you, it were the other feller.' "

She raises her eyebrows comically high, and I have to admit, she does look a bit like Harold at his most bright-eyed and innocent. "Oh, hi, Matt," she adds, and I look up to see him returning. As he sits down, he lands with a bit of a thud, and for a few moments he's motionless, staring ahead.

"Sorry about your shirt," I say guiltily, and he comes to.

"Oh. It's fine." He reaches for the twig in his collar and looks at it absently for a moment before dropping it on the ground. "Listen, Ava. I know we booked a table for brunch on the tenth, but that was my parents on the phone again. They're convening a big meeting that day at the house. I've *tried* to get them to shift it, but . . ."

"At the weekend?" says Nell, in carefully neutral tones.

"We hold a lot of family meetings at the weekend," says Matt. "Away from the office. It's more private, I guess."

"Well, don't worry," I say supportively. "Brunch was just an idea. You go to your parents', that's fine—" I break off as I see both Sarika and Nell making weird faces at me behind Matt's back.

They're surely not trying to say—

I can't just *ask myself along to his house*. Can I? Should I?

Now Sarika is whirling her arms wildly and pointing vigorously at Matt. Any minute she'll clonk him on the head by mistake.

"And . . . er . . . maybe I could come along!" I add in a self-conscious rush. "Meet your parents properly!"

"Do *what*?"

Matt peers at me, apparently astounded. He doesn't exactly sound enthusiastic. But now I've suggested it I'm not backing down.

"I could come along!" I repeat, trying to sound confident. "Not for the meeting, obviously, but for coffee or whatever. Get to know your family better. You know, bond with them."

"*Bond* with them!" Matt echoes with a bark of laughter, which is a bit weird, but I'm not going to unpick it now.

My attention is suddenly drawn by Nell making jabbing gestures at Harold, followed by a finger across the throat. Oh, right.

"And I won't bring Harold," I add hastily. "He can stay at home."

"Really?" Matt seems newly astonished. "It's a long drive to my parents' place, Ava. You'll leave him at home all day?"

"He can stay with Nell. You don't mind having Harold, do you, Nell?"

"Of course not," says Nell. "Good idea, Ava."

Matt doesn't say anything. He sips his coffee while all three of us watch him curiously, his eyes distant with thoughts. Then, as though coming to, he exhales.

"Well, if you want to," he says at last.

He still seems a bit blindsided by my suggestion. Honestly, what's the big deal? It's only his parents and family home and business and whatnot. It'll be fun! I mean, it might be fun.

I mean, it could be.

Fifteen

~~~~~~

Positive, positive, positive!

As we drive down the M4 two weeks later, I'm determined to be upbeat. The sun's shining, I look good, and I've bought the most amazing cake from Sarika's patisserie, all covered with almonds. It's sitting in the boot in a beautiful cardboard box, and every time I even think about it my mouth waters. Matt's parents are sure to love it.

Charm and bond is my mantra for today. *Charm and bond*. It's all good.

And as for negatives . . . What negatives? There aren't any!

Well, OK, maybe just a couple of tiny things. Teeny glitches. Sleep is the thing, really. I need sleep. *I neeeed sleeeep*. I'm actually rethinking the whole children thing. How do people have babies and get no sleep and not actually *die*?

I'm becoming almost phobic about Matt's bed. I swear it

gets harder and more plank-like every time we sleep there. I lie, staring at the ceiling, listening as he falls asleep, and then I doze a bit, but then I wake up in 3 A.M. misery. Even Harold can't make me feel cozy in that bed.

Partly because he's started sleeping on Matt's feet whenever we stay there.

Which is . . . You know. It's lovely. Obviously.

I'll admit I was a bit surprised that first time I woke up and Harold was on the other side of the bed, snuggled up to Matt instead of me. But I *absolutely* don't feel rejected or anything. My darling Harold can sleep where he likes.

However, it doesn't help my sleep deprivation. At the moment we're alternating nights at each other's flats, and every so often we spend the night apart. Yesterday I tried to suggest to Matt that we sleep over at my place all the time. I didn't mean he should *move in,* not exactly, I just meant . . . Anyway. Didn't work. Matt looked a bit appalled and said he thought the arrangement worked well at the moment.

So the sleep is a problem. And I suppose there are a couple of other issues which have popped up. Tiny little annoyances which I never predicted. Like, Matt can't relax in my flat. He keeps going around finding fault with it. Looking at things I never notice. The wiring is dodgy. (He says.) One of the radiators needs sorting by a plumber. (He says.)

And his obsession with security is driving me nuts. He still keeps going on about my lovely picturesque back door onto the fire escape, just because the wooden frame has gone a bit soft. He says it's an invitation for thieves. Last time he came round, he actually started quoting crime statistics for the area. He wants me to either replace the door or buy six billion chains and padlocks, which would *totally* ruin the look.

I actually got a bit impatient with him. I said, "Look, Matt, you don't get it. The whole point of that door is, you can go out whenever. You can sit on the fire escape and watch the sun set and play the saxophone and not have to unlock twelve padlocks first."

Whereupon he asked if I play the saxophone, which is not the point. Obviously, I don't play the saxophone; it was just an *example*.

Anyway. Then we went shopping together, and that didn't go brilliantly. I thought it would be no big deal. Pop to the supermarket together! Stock up! Easy-peasy! I've seen other couples shopping in the supermarket. They calmly put things in the trolley. They chat unconcernedly. They say things like, "Shall I get the eggs?"

They don't peer at each other's items in disbelief as though they're watching a Channel 5 show called *Britain's Weirdest Trolley Choices*.

If there was a Venn diagram of my shopping tastes and Matt's shopping tastes, I think we would overlap at recycled loo paper and ice cream. That's it.

I mean, he buys crap. He just does. Terrible processed breakfast cereal. Nonorganic apples. Juice boxes. (*Juice boxes*.) I had to take everything out and replace it. And I was thinking, *It's so tragic that he just doesn't care what he puts in his body* . . . when suddenly he woke up in the wine section. I had put my usual bottle of white wine in the trolley. The one with the lady on the front (I can't remember what it's called). At which Matt blanched.

"No," he said, taking it out. "No. Just no."

"What's wrong with it?" I said, affronted.

"Don't skimp on wine. It's better to have no wine than shit."

"I'm not skimping!" I retorted. "That's a nice wine!"

"*Nice wine?*" He looked scandalized. "*Nice wine?*"

Anyway. We had a bit of a discussion-slash-heated argument. It turned out that we disagreed on what was a "nice wine." And on what count as "essentials." And on the principles of nutrition. At which point it turned out that Matt had never even *heard* of kefir. Who hasn't heard of kefir?

Then we passed the meat counter, and I'll draw a mental veil over what happened there. It was too distressing. And that butcher did *not* have to fall about laughing; it wasn't funny.

I mean, it was fine. We got the shopping home. We cooked supper. But it wasn't . . . I guess it wasn't what I imagined when I sat eyeing up Dutch in Italy. I was in a blissful rosy glow. I saw us kissing romantically in the sunset. I didn't see us standing in a supermarket, bickering about organic yogurt.

But, then, I guess all couples bicker about something, don't they, I tell myself firmly, trying to stop my torrent of thoughts. It's only teething troubles. We're still finding our way.

And there have been lots of precious, tender times too. Matt bringing home peach juice the other evening, so we could make Bellinis, like we had in Italy. That was magical. Or the way he did tai chi with Harold on his shoulders yesterday morning, just to make me laugh. Or the way that, when Nihal was gloomy about work the other day, Matt said, "Ava'll cheer you up, she's better than champagne," so affectionately it made me blink.

At the memory, I glance fondly at him, and Matt winks back, then turns his attention to the road again. I love how he's a responsible driver, not like Russell, who sometimes actually scared me, he was so erratic.

And *that's* why we're compatible, I tell myself firmly again. Because we have shared values. We care about each other's safety. He drives carefully, and I give him turmeric supplements every day. (He was skeptical, but I won him round.)

So it's all good. We're here in the beautiful Berkshire countryside. I love Matt and he loves me and that's all we need. Love.

At a mini roundabout I see a poster for a new Apple Mac and peer at it with interest.

"Should I upgrade my computer?" I muse thoughtfully. "God, these trees are *beautiful*," I add, as we approach a forested area. "What trees are these?" As Matt draws breath to answer, I notice one of my nails is broken. "Shit!" I exclaim. "My nail. Oh, that reminds me, what did you think of my idea earlier?"

"Idea?" Matt seems startled.

"You know!" I say, a little impatiently. "My business idea. Pitching for beauty work."

"Ava . . ." Matt pulls the car into a service station and looks at me. "I honestly can't follow. Are we talking about your computer or the trees or your nail or a new business idea?"

"All of them, of course," I say in surprise.

Honestly, what's the problem? It's not like I'm unclear or anything.

"Right," says Matt, looking beleaguered. "All of them. Got it." He rubs his face, then says, "I need to get fuel."

"Wait." I draw him in for a hug, closing my eyes, burying my face into his neck and feeling myself relax. There. *There.* Sometimes I just need the smell of him. The touch of him. His strong chest and his heartbeat and his hand stroking my back. Everything I fell in love with in Italy. We pull apart and Matt gazes at me silently for a few moments, while I wonder what he's thinking. I'm hoping it's something really romantic, but at last he draws breath and says, "You can still go to the pub, you know."

Matt's running riff these last few days has been that I'm going to change my mind and duck out of the visit. He's even identified a nearby pub that I can sit in all afternoon; it has Wi-Fi and a TV room. He pretends he's joking, but I think he's half serious. As if I'm going to come all this way and *not* meet his parents.

"No chance!" I say firmly. "I'm doing this. And I can't wait!"

OK. Wow. The house is big. Like, *big.*

And ugly. Not like Matt's flat is ugly, a different kind of ugly. As I peer through the humongous wrought-iron gates, I make out turrets and gables and strange brickwork surrounding rows of forbidding windows. It all adds up to a house of giant impressiveness which could equally well be a Victorian school of punishment for delinquents.

"Sorry," says Matt, as the gates slowly edge open. "They take ages."

"It's fine," I say, shrinking back in my seat. I suddenly, ridiculously, want to run away. Nothing about this house looks friendly. But instead I jut out my jaw and say determinedly, "Amazing house!"

"Well," says Matt, as though he's never given the house any thought. "It has offices too," he adds after a pause. "So."

"Right." I nod.

Matt parks the car tidily at the back of the house, next to a Mercedes, and we crunch over the gravel to a kitchen door. I'm half expecting some ancient retainer to appear and exclaim, "Master Matt!" But instead, Matt leads me through a vast, tidy kitchen, where I leave the cake box on a counter, and into a massive hall. It has a tiled floor and a stained-glass dome above us and is filled with shiny glass display cases.

"Wow!" I exclaim. "This looks like—" I stop, because I don't want to sound rude.

"A museum," Matt finishes for me. "Yup. Go ahead, have a look if you like." He gestures at the cases.

I wander up to the biggest glass case, which holds a vintage-looking Harriet's House and a load of Harriet doll characters and actual typed-out labels, saying things like *1970 Harriet the Air Hostess* and *1971 Harriet the Gymnast*.

Most of the cases contain Harriet's House displays, but one is filled with swirly pink-and-green china. I go to look at it and Matt follows me.

"That's my mum's family business," he tells me. "She's half Austrian."

"Oh yes," I say, remembering his golf-playing grand-mother. "But she doesn't have an accent."

"No, she grew up in the UK. But we have Austrian cous-ins. They run the china company. Mum's on the board," he adds. "She used to be in charge of the UK operation."

"I think I've seen that stuff." I crinkle up my brow as I stare at the gilded patterned plates. "In Harrods or some-where like that?"

"Yeah." Matt shrugs. "You would have. It's . . . you know. A big deal. That's how she met my dad, at an export confer-ence. She was selling china; he was selling dollhouses."

"It's . . . spectacular!" I say. Which is true. It's spectacu-larly ornate and frilly. And it has a *lot* of gold twirls.

Matt doesn't respond. He doesn't seem wild about the china. In fact, he doesn't seem wild about anything. Ever since we arrived, his shoulders have been slumped and his face seems frozen.

"You must be really proud!" I say, trying to enthuse him. "All these dolls . . . and the famous china . . . what a heri-tage! What's this . . ." I peer closer to read a typed label. " 'Salmon dish used by Princess Margaret in 1982'! Wow! That's . . ."

I have no idea what to say about a salmon dish used by Princess Margaret in 1982. I didn't even know there were such things as salmon dishes.

"Mmm," says Matt, eyeing the china cabinet without en-thusiasm.

"And what's this?" I say brightly, heading to the only cabinet which doesn't seem to exude pink. "Trophies?" I peer at the shelves of silver cups and boxed medals and framed photos.

"Yeah." Matt seems even more leaden. "Like I told you, my grandmother was Austrian ladies' champion, back in the day. And my brother turned pro. Guess we're a sporty lot."

Silently, I run my eye over the photos. There are several of a lady in a 1960s hairdo, swinging a golf club. There are group shots of what seems to be a skiing team, plus a black-and-white shot of a guy in a sailing boat. Then there are some modern photos featuring a guy in his teens and twenties, either swinging a golf club or receiving a trophy. He's good-looking and resembles Matt but is slighter in build and not as appealing. His smile is a bit too cheesy for me. He's Matt-lite, I decide.

"Is that your brother?" I gesture at one of the pictures.

"Yeah, that's Rob. He's in the States now. Runs a chain of golf clubs. Robert Warwick Golf and Leisure. They're successful," he adds after a pause. "So."

"Great," I say politely. I'm searching for a picture of Matt among all the silver frames, but I can't see one. Where's the photo of Matt? There must be one. Where is it?

"Matthias!" A brittle voice sounds behind us, and I turn to see Elsa. She's wearing a dress with leaves printed all over it and court shoes and frosted pink lipstick.

Her hair's good, I think as I watch her kiss Matt. I have to give her that. It's gorgeous. And her figure is svelte and she has a pretty face. In fact, everything about her is really lovely.

Except the way she's looking at me, with little splinters of unfriendliness.

"Hello again, Ava," she says in a neutral voice. "We're so glad you could join us. No dog today?"

Her eyebrows rise sardonically, and I force myself to smile.

"No, I left him behind."

"So our books are safe, I hope!" She gives a tinkle of laughter, and I try to join in, although my cheeks are flaming.

"I hope so. And again, I'm *so* sorry about the book. . . ."

"Don't worry." She lifts an elegant hand. "It was only an irreplaceable first edition."

"Mum," says Matt, and Elsa tinkles with laughter again.

"Just my little joke! Matthias is showing you around, I see?"

Charm and bond flashes through my mind. Quick. Say something flattering.

"Matt's been showing me your amazing displays," I say gushingly. "They're stunning. The dollhouses are out of this world!"

"I remember you said you *didn't* have a Harriet's House as a child?" Elsa looks at me with cool appraisal.

She's going to hold this against me forever, isn't she?

"I would have loved one," I say earnestly. "Only we couldn't afford it."

Her face freezes slightly, and at once I realize my error. Now I sound like I'm saying her company is evil and elite, with its exploitative pricing.

(Which, by the way, it is. Harriet's House prices are a shocker. I went and had a look the other day. Fifteen quid for a Harriet's Bag and Scarf Set. *Fifteen quid*.)

"Your china is *so* beautiful." I hastily move on to a different subject. "The detail! The brushwork!"

"Are you interested in china, Ava?" says Elsa. "Do you collect?" She tilts her head, regarding me with a piercing stare.

Collect? I'm guessing she doesn't mean *click and collect* from Ikea.

"I mean . . . you know. I have plates," I flounder. "And some saucers . . . Wow, these *photos*." I quickly step toward the sporting cabinet and gesture admiringly at the cups and medals. "All these champions in the family!"

"Yes, we're proud of our achievements," says Elsa, her gaze sweeping over the array.

"I can't see a photo of Matt here, though," I add lightly.

"Oh, I was never the sports champ," says Matt after an infinitesimal pause. "Not like Rob."

"Matthias never turned professional," adds Elsa crisply. "He never had that competitive edge. Whereas Robert was a scratch golfer at the age of thirteen. We all knew he would be special, didn't we, Matthias?"

"Sure," says Matt, his eyes fixed on a far point.

"Matt does play golf, though, doesn't he?" I say brightly. "Don't you have any photos of him doing that? Or martial arts. You could fit one in there." I point helpfully at a spare stretch of glass shelf, and Elsa's nostrils flare.

"I don't think you understand," she says, her smile rigid. "This is a display of professional sportsmanship. These are *tournament* mementos. Matt never competed at this level."

Tournament mementos? I'll give her a bloody memento. . . .

I suddenly realize that I'm seething. Which isn't ideal for charming, nor for bonding.

"I brought you a cake," I say, turning away from all the cabinets. "It's in the kitchen, in a box; it's from this really nice patisserie. . . ."

"So kind," Elsa says with a distant smile.

How does she make everything sound like the opposite of what it means?

"Matthias, I've just been speaking to Genevieve," she continues, "and she will be Skyping in for the meeting this afternoon. Very generous of her to give up her weekend. Don't you think?" Elsa's splintery eyes swivel to me as though expecting a response.

"Yes!" I say with a nervous jump. "Really generous."

Matt shoots me a slightly astonished look, and I try to smile back. But now I feel like an idiot. Why did I say that? Why am I bigging up Matt's ex-girlfriend, whom I've never even *met*? It's Elsa. She's put an evil spell on me.

Then I catch my own thoughts in horror. No. Stop it. Elsa's my future mother-in-law and we're going to love each other. We just have to find common ground. There must be *loads* of stuff we have in common. Like for example . . .

Look. She's wearing earrings and so am I. That's a start.

"Right," says Matt. "Well. Shall we have a drink?"

"*Yes,*" I blurt out too desperately. "I mean . . . why not?"

Sixteen

~~~~~~~

*C*ome on. I can find common ground with Elsa. And with all of Matt's family. I *can*.

It's an hour later and my cheekbones are aching from my fake smile. I've smiled at Elsa. I've smiled at John. I've smiled at Walter, who was introduced to me as the chief finance officer of Harriet's House and is sitting to my left. I've smiled at Matt's grandpa, Ronald. I've even smiled into thin air, so that no one can glance over at me and think I'm a moody cow.

We're sitting around a very shiny dining table, with more swirly china and crystal glasses and an atmosphere of silence. They really don't talk much, this lot.

I've done my best. I've complimented everything, from the spoons to the bread rolls. But all my conversational efforts have either dwindled into silence or else Elsa, who seems to be conversation czar, has cut off the topic. She does this in two ways. She has a weird tight-lipped shake of the head which instantly silences everyone. Or else she says, "I *hardly* think . . ." which I've realized basically translates as "Shut up."

I asked John how the business was going, but Elsa immediately cut in: "I *hardly* think . . ."

Whereupon John shook out his napkin and said, "No business talk at lunch!" with an awkward laugh.

Then Matt began to his father, "You know, Dad, those U.S. figures can't be right. . . ." whereupon Elsa glared at him and gave him a ferocious tight-lipped head shake.

Fine. *Don't* talk business in front of me. I get that. Although what does she think? That I'll be emailing everything I hear straight to the dollhouses editor at the *FT*?

The food's good, at least. Which is to say, the vegetables are. Everyone else is eating chicken, but Elsa forgot I was vegetarian, so I'm just munching my way through a mound of carrots and peas.

"Delicious!" I say for the ninety-fifth time, and Elsa gives me a frosty smile.

"Are you going to the meeting?" I say politely to Ronald, who has just turned away from talking to John about the governor of the Bank of England. Ronald shakes his head.

"I'm retired, my dear," he says.

"Oh, right," I say, racking my brains for something to say about retirement. "That must be . . . fun?"

"Not so much fun," he says. "Not so much recently."

He sounds so downcast, my heart twangs. He's the first member of Matt's family who's shown a human side.

"Why not?" I ask gently. "Don't you have any nice hobbies? Golf?"

"Oh . . ." He exhales a long, gusty breath, sounding like a deflating balloon. "Yes, golf . . ." His blue eyes go distant, as though golf is irrelevant to his life. "The truth is, my dear, I ran into some trouble recently."

"Trouble?" I stare at him.

"Very bad. Very embarrassing . . . To think that a man of my education . . . a former *finance* director . . ." He trails away, his eyes misty. "It's the feeling stupid, you see. The feeling like an old fool. A stupid old fool."

"I'm sure you're not an old fool!" I say in dismay. "What was the—" I break off awkwardly, because I don't want to pry. "Is the trouble over?"

"Yes, but it stays with me, you see?" he says, his voice shaking. "It stays with me. I wake up in the morning and I think, 'Ronald, you old fool.'" As he meets my gaze, his eyes are brimming over. I've never seen such a sad face. I can't bear it.

"I don't know what happened," I say, my own eyes hot with empathy. "But I can tell, you're *not* a fool."

"I'll tell you what happened," says Ronald. "I'll tell you." To my horror, a tear falls down from his eye onto the tablecloth. "It was a scam, you see—"

"Really, Ronald!" Elsa's voice interrupts, bright and brittle, making us both start. "I *hardly* think . . ."

"Oh." Ronald shoots her a guilty look. "I was just telling . . . Emma here . . . about . . ."

"I *hardly* think," repeats Elsa with an air of finality, "that Ava is interested. *Ava,*" she repeats distinctly.

"Ava." Ronald looks stricken. "*Ava,* not Emma. I'm sorry."

"Don't worry!" I say. "And I *am* interested. I don't know what happened, but . . ."

"It was an unfortunate incident." Elsa's mouth tightens even further, as though she's zipping it up.

"Dad, it happened, it's over, you need to move on," says John, sounding slightly robotic, as though he's said these words before, many times.

"But it shouldn't be allowed," says Ronald in distress. "They shouldn't be able to do it!"

Elsa exchanges looks with John.

"Now, Ronald," she says. "It doesn't do to dwell. As John says, it's best forgotten." She gets to her feet to clear the plates and I quickly rise to join her. As I carry a pair of vegetable dishes into the kitchen, I spy the patisserie box, still on the counter, and say helpfully, "Shall I unwrap that?"

"Oh, I don't think so," says Elsa, looking at the cake blankly. "Now, I'll make some coffee. Are you a sportswoman, Ava?" she adds as she fills the kettle, and I cough, playing for time. I am *so* not a sportswoman. But this place is sports central.

"I like yoga," I offer at last. "And I've started tai chi with Matt."

"I know little about yoga," says Elsa thoughtfully. "But I believe it's a challenging sport."

"Yes," I say uncertainly. "Although I wouldn't really say it's a *sport* so much as a—"

"Do you compete?" she cuts me off, and I gaze at her, perplexed. Compete at *yoga?*

"Yoga isn't really . . ." I begin. "Does that even exist?"

"Here we are." Elsa looks up from where she's been tapping busily at her phone. "There are yoga championships being held in London. You should train and compete. I'll send the link to Matthias." She eyes me with a steely gaze. "I'm sure you want to practice at the highest possible level."

"Um . . ." I swallow. "That's not really why I do yoga, but . . . maybe!" I add, as I see her frown. "Yes! Good idea!"

As I watch Elsa making the coffee, I add timidly, "Excuse me for asking, but what was the thing that happened to Ronald?"

There's a pause, then Elsa says, "An unfortunate incident." She shoots me an off-putting smile. "We don't talk about it. If you wouldn't mind taking the tray of cups?"

Obediently, I follow her, and as I'm sitting back down at the table, a beautiful sleek Doberman pinscher appears at the doorway. Oh my God. What a gorgeous dog.

"Mouser!" Matt greets him, smiling. "One of my dad's dogs," he explains to me, and I beam back in relief. Finally! Something I can relate to! I'm longing to meet Mouser and pet him—only he seems strangely pinned to the spot.

"Why isn't he coming in?" I ask, puzzled.

"He's not allowed in here," says Matt.

"He's not allowed in the dining room?" I say, baffled.

"He has his zones," explains Matt, and I try to hide my horror. *Zones?* That sounds sinister, if you ask me. It sounds like a spaceship from a dystopian movie. I smile sympathetically at Mouser, who is still standing at the threshold. Mouser gives a single bark, and John immediately frowns.

"Now, Mouser," he says. "Behave. Lie down."

Immediately, Mouser lies flat on the floor, as I stare, slightly flabbergasted. I've never seen a dog like that. He's like a robot dog.

"Why's he called Mouser?" I ask. "Because he catches mice?"

"No, *Mauser*. After the gun," says Matt, and I nearly drop my coffee cup in horror. A *gun*? They named their dog after a *weapon*?

"Mauser's on good form," says Walter, who has barely spoken all lunch.

"Ava has a dog," Matt tells Walter, who lifts his eyes toward me with the barest interest.

"Oh, really?"

"I have a beagle," I say eagerly. "A rescue beagle. He was found on the side of the A414." As ever, when I talk about Harold, my voice starts overflowing with love. "He's . . . would you like to see a photo?"

"No thanks," says Walter shortly, as John pushes back his chair.

"Matthias, Walter, I think we should get on."

"Sure," says Matt, draining his coffee cup. "Will you be OK, Ava?"

"I'll sort out something for Ava," puts in his mother, before I can reply. "You go along, Matthias. I'll join you."

"Nice to meet you," says Walter to me, and I muster a smile.

"You too!"

John strides out of the room along with Walter and Matt.

Mauser follows them, practically in step, and as I watch them go, I realize I'm mentally singing the Darth Vader theme tune. Oh God, I hope no one can hear.

"Ronald, your massage therapist will be here soon," adds Elsa, and Ronald gets to his feet.

"Very nice to meet you, Ava," he says, and squeezes me briefly on the arm before heading out of the room.

"Ava," says Elsa with her chilly smile. "I'm afraid we will be in our meeting for some time. But you are welcome to use the pool. It's indoor," she adds. "You'll find the pool complex in the garden."

I gape at her in surprise. The *pool*? I never expected a pool.

"Amazing!" I say. "Except . . . I didn't bring a swimsuit."

"We have spare swimsuits for guests at the complex," she says. "Help yourself."

"Thank you!"

I beam back at Elsa, all my antipathy melting away. Here we are. *This* is our common ground. Swimming! I may not be a sportswoman, but I can drift around a pool with the best of them. I'll loll around in the pool all afternoon and have a lovely relaxed time and then maybe we'll have the patisserie cake for tea, since we haven't had it for lunch.

"Oh, I should warn you," adds Elsa as she reaches the doorway. "My aunt Sigrid and cousin Greta are over from Austria with some friends, and are coming to stay. You may meet them. They're very charming."

"Awesome!" I say happily. "And maybe I'll have a little walk in the garden first."

"Be our guest," says Elsa, waving a hand at the French windows, and she almost sounds friendly. I can't believe it. This visit has completely turned around!

The garden is quite large and complicated, with walled sections and orchards and grassy bits that look like other grassy bits. As I'm trying to find my way back, I get drawn into a WhatsApp debate between Sarika and Maud about vitamin C serum and perch on a bench to join in. So it's quite a long time before I make my way to the pool complex, which is a glass-fronted wooden building.

The pool is stunning, all blue and glittering, just like something in a posh hotel. There are several sun beds and even a steam room and sauna. I can't help giving a little whoop of exhilaration as I look around. Why didn't Matt tell me about this in the first place? That is *so* typical of him.

Then I become aware that I can hear voices. I follow the sound, through a curtain, and find a group of women getting changed and chattering loudly in German. Three seem to be in their forties, and one is older. They look up in surprise as I enter, and I raise a shy hand.

"Hi," I say. "I'm a friend of Matt's. Ava."

"Hello!" replies a beaming, athletic-looking woman with short curly hair. "I am Greta, Elsa's cousin. This is Heike, Inge, and Sigrid." She gestures to the older-looking woman. "My mother. We are visiting with our husbands, who will be joining us here shortly. We are conducting a short tour of the UK. A road trip."

"After staying here for a few days, we go to Stratford," chimes in Heike. "I have never been to Stratford." She puts on a bathing cap with a snap. "Ready to swim," she adds cheerfully. "Bring it on."

"You all speak really good English," I say in admiration.

"No, no," says Heike modestly. "We do our best, but we are sadly lacking."

Is she kidding?

"There's no way I could say 'sadly lacking' in German," I say frankly. "Not a chance. So you win."

All the women laugh, exchanging pleased looks with one another, and I feel a glow rising through me. They're *nice*!

"The pool's amazing," I say, starting to take off my clothes.

"Yes!" says Greta cheerfully. "We're looking forward to our swim. See you there."

They all disappear out to the pool, and I take a swimsuit from a basket marked *Guests*. As I put it on, I'm actually smiling to myself, because this is so not what I expected of today. A lovely lazy afternoon in the pool with Matt's extended family! There are sun beds to lie on, I've already noticed. Or maybe we'll sit on the side, dangling our toes in the water, and chat about stuff. Maybe they can tell me what happened to Ronald.

But as I head out, no one's lying on the sun beds, nor dangling their toes. All the women are swimming hard. Like, seriously. Front crawl. Back crawl. The whole pool is like some sort of Olympic training session. Even Sigrid is performing a professional-looking breaststroke, and she must be seventy, at least. Who *are* these people? As I stand, flabbergasted, Greta reaches the near end of the pool and smiles up at me.

"It's refreshing!" she says. "Come in!"

"Right." I hesitate. "You're all . . . really good swimmers."

"We met through the swim team," says Greta cheerfully. "Although our technique is not what it was!"

As she speaks, Heike thunders toward the edge of the pool, turns a somersault underwater, and streaks back in the opposite direction.

"Do you swim?" adds Greta politely.

"Well." I swallow. "I mean, I can keep afloat. . . ."

"Enjoy!" she says, and then pushes off into a deft front crawl.

I make my way cautiously down the steps into the water, which is colder than I expected, and try a few cautious breaststrokes. Then I hastily move out of the way of Inge, whose arms are like pistons in the water. Oh God, I can't drift around with this lot thrashing up and down. It's like the M1 in here. Maybe I'll leave the swimming for now, I decide. Maybe I'll try the steam room and the sauna. The relaxing stuff.

"Just going to the steam room!" I say to Greta, as she pauses at the end of the pool, and she nods cheerily. I grab a towel and pad over the tiled floor to the steam room, and as I enter, I can feel all my muscles unwinding. This is more like it. *This* is the life.

I close my eyes and let the steam engulf me. My head is spinning with all the weird moments of today, from the salmon dish used by Princess Margaret in 1982 to poor tearful Ronald. After a while I can almost feel myself nodding off. But my chin jerks up as I hear voices again. It's Greta and the other women. They're obviously out of the pool, and I can hear some booming male voices, too, which must be the husbands. I should go and say hello.

It's a good strategic move to be friendly with Greta, I've concluded. And indeed her whole group of mates. They seem very nice (far nicer than Elsa), and it's a great way into the family. But as I emerge from the steam room, the pool area is empty. Where've they all gone? I look around—then notice two pairs of flip-flops outside the sauna door.

Of course! Well, even better. What could be more bonding than sharing a sauna together?

I wrap my towel around my body and cautiously open the sauna door, feeling a blast of heat hit me. I take a step inside—then stop in dumb horror.

They're all in here. All the women, at least. They're sitting on towels and looking up with friendly smiles—and they're all naked. Naked. Stark naked. All I can see is breasts and stomachs and . . . Oh *God*.

What do I do now? What? Am I supposed to be naked too?

"Shut the door!" says Greta, gesturing at me, and before I can get my thoughts straight, I'm closing it.

"Sit down!" adds Heike, shifting up on the bench, her veiny breasts swaying as she does so.

No. Do *not* look at her breasts. Or her . . .

Oh God, stop. *Don't* look. I hastily swing my eyes from Heike, to find myself peering at Inge's pale nipples, which are at eye level. In horror, I whip my head away, to find my-self regarding a mound of bushy pubic hair.

No. Noooo.

OK. Keep calm. Basically, no line of sight is safe. So I will stare at the door. Yes. Sweat is already pouring down my face, which is nothing to do with the heat of the sauna. It's sheer stress.

Should I leave? But what if that looks rude?

"Sit on your towel, Ava," says Greta encouragingly, and gingerly I place it on the wooden slats. As I sit down, I can see Sigrid peering at me with detached interest.

"Why do you sit in a costume?" she inquires politely. "Are you ashamed of your pubis?"

Am I . . . ?

What?

"No!" I say, my voice shrill. "I mean . . . I don't think . . . Gosh. I've never really . . . It's quite hot in here. . . ."

My floundering is cut short by the sauna door opening. Three men troop in, all wrapped up in towels and smiling broadly.

"Henrik!" exclaims Greta. "This is a friend of Matt, Ava."

"Hello, Ava!" says Henrik cheerfully. And I know it's my cue to reply, but I can't speak. I'm paralyzed in dread. The men are all busily unwrapping their towels, revealing hairy chests and thighs and . . . They're not going to . . . They're not . . . *Surely* they're not . . .

Oh my God. Yes, they are. All three of them.

Look at the *door,* Ava. Look at the *door.*

My head is rigidly fixed ahead. My gaze is locked on the

wooden slats. I'm trying to blank out that glimpse I just caught of Henrik's . . .

I mean, just as a sidebar, no wonder Greta's so cheery. . . .

No. *No.* Stop thinking, Ava. Stop looking. Just . . . stop.

I realize I'm clenching my towel so hard that tendons are standing out on my hands—and Greta seems to notice. "Ava, are you feeling quite well?" she says in concerned tones. "Is the heat too much? If you are not used to saunas, it's better not to overdo it."

"I'm fine!" I say. "I just . . . I suppose I'm not used to the . . ." I trail off and take a deep breath. I might as well come clean. "In England we don't tend to . . . We wear bathing suits."

Greta's eyes instantly pop with understanding.

"Of course!" she exclaims. "Of *course.*" She says something in rapid German to the others, and they all start exclaiming, too, including the men.

"We must apologize!" says Greta brightly. "Poor Ava. You must find this very strange! You see, to us it is normal. Imagine, Henrik! She walks into the sauna expecting to see bathing suits. Yet she finds naked bodies!"

Her arm sweeps around the sauna, and before I can stop myself, I follow it with my gaze, and . . .

Okaaaay. I've seen the whole lot. Can't unsee that.

"Quite a misunderstanding," Henrik is saying jovially. "Very hilarious."

"We will eat out on this!" Greta nods, then turns to me, her breasts flopping about. "Is that the correct idiom, 'eat out'?"

"I . . . guess," I say, desperately trying not to see her nipples. "Or 'dine out' would be more—oh!" I gasp, as Henrik gets up, swaying all over the place.

"Elsa and John are just coming down as well, by the way," he says conversationally to Greta. "The sauna will be packed!"

As his words impinge on my mind, I stop dead. Elsa and John are—

What?

It takes a moment for me to comprehend the full horror of this scenario. My possible future in-laws? In a sauna? *Naked?*

Already I'm on my feet, clutching my towel, my heart thumping, sweat pouring down my face in rivers.

"It was lovely to see you all," I gabble. "I mean, meet you all. I mean . . . But I think I'm sauna-ed out. So . . . er . . . have fun!"

As I push my way out, my legs are trembling. I need to get changed very, very fast. I need to *not* see Elsa or John naked. This is my priority.

I drench myself briefly in a shower and dump the wet suit in what seems to be a laundry hamper. Then I shove my clothes on any old how and hurry out of the pool complex, in a state of slight panic. As I'm hurrying up the path, I see Matt approaching from the house and accelerate till I meet him.

"Did you have a nice time?" he begins. "We finished sooner than I—"

"Oh my God," I cut him off. "Oh my *God,* Matt. You should have warned me!"

"What?" Matt looks puzzled.

"The sauna!" I half-whisper, half-squeak. "Your family and their friends were in there! Naked!"

"Oh, right." His face relaxes with understanding. "Yeah."

I wait for him to say more—but that seems to be it. Is that really all he's going to say?

OK, I am *not* a needy person, but in my opinion, "Oh, right. Yeah," is not a sufficient response at this time.

"Naked," I repeat for emphasis. "They were *naked*. All of them. You know how when you do a speech, they say, 'Imagine they're all naked, it'll give you confidence'? Well, that's a lie! It doesn't!"

"It's just the Austrian tradition." Matt shrugs.

"But it's not my tradition! I was freaked out! I was like, 'Oh my God, I can see . . .' You don't want to know *what* I saw," I finish meaningfully. "You don't want to know."

Matt laughs and I glare at him. He thinks this is funny?

"Did you set me up for this?" I say accusingly.

"No!" He seems astonished. "Ava, I didn't know anyone else would be there, it didn't occur to me that you'd take a sauna . . . basically I forgot. I'm so used to it, I forget. And really," he adds, lowering his voice as his parents approach us down the path, "is it such a big deal?"

"*What?*" I begin—then stop. Already Elsa and John are in earshot and Elsa is addressing me: "Hello, Ava. Did you have a good swim?"

"Wonderful, thanks," I respond with a polite smile. "Such a lovely pool!"

But as she starts telling me about the garden, my head is churning. Indignation is sparking around my body. *Is it such a big deal?* Is he for real?

Seventeen

~~~~~~~~~~

By the time we get into the car, an hour later, I'm bursting. I'm actually bursting. Arguments have been mounting up in my mind like planes waiting to land. First, Matt doesn't warn me about the naked sauna. Then he makes out like I'm overreacting. Then, over tea, he tells his parents that Harold needs training, even though he *knows* I don't like him saying that.

Then, as I'm still reeling from that, his parents launch into a half-hour lecture on the eighth wonder of the world that is Genevieve. I know that Genevieve has appeared on the cover of three magazines. And she's going to film a TV documentary. And she has to have two assistants to deal with all the fan mail she receives.

And OK, yes, Matt tried to steer the conversation away, but maybe he *didn't try hard enough*.

And, oh my God, *what* was that with the cake?

I'm breathing hard as I get into the car and wave at Matt's

parents. "Thank you *so* much!" I call through the window. "I had a *lovely* time. It was *wonderful!*"

"So," says Matt as he puts the car into reverse to turn. "How was that for you?"

Even his question flicks me on the raw. How does he *think* it was?

"Oh, I'm just super-thrilled I'll get an A-plus in my test on 'Genevieve the wonder woman,'" I say, still smiling sweetly at his parents through the window, and Matt sighs.

"I know. I'm sorry. My parents are . . . They can't let go."

He puts the car into first gear, and we shoot forward with a little spurt of gravel under the wheels. As we exit the gates, we both breathe out.

"But it was OK otherwise?" says Matt after a few moments. I know he wants me to say it was lovely. And I know I should. But I can't. I'm feeling tetchy and stroppy.

"Apart from Genevieve and the naked sauna and you insulting Harold, it was fab," I say, unable to keep the sarcasm out of my voice.

"Insulting Harold?" Matt sounds perplexed. "How did I insult Harold?"

"You said he needs training."

"He does need training," replies Matt, and I feel a spurt of rage.

"He does not! And why didn't they open my cake?"

"What?" Matt looks baffled. "What cake?"

What cake?

"I spent an absolute fortune on a cake from a patisserie, and they just left it in the kitchen!"

"Oh."

"And then they just served biscuits at tea, and I kept think-ing, 'But what about the *cake*? Why don't we have the *cake*?' "

Matt shoots me a wary look. "They're probably saving it up. I think you're overreacting."

"Maybe," I say morosely. "But it's no wonder." I suddenly feel weariness crashing over me and rub my face. "Matt, lis-ten. You *have* to move into my place. I can't sleep a wink at yours."

"Move into yours?" Matt sounds aghast. "What— No. Sorry, no."

"But my flat is more conducive. It's more comfortable. It's more welcoming."

"More *welcoming*?" Matt echoes incredulously. "Ava, your flat is a liability! Fucking . . . nails sticking out and stuff toppling down everywhere, and you *never* screw jars closed properly. . . ."

I stare at him, baffled. *Jars?* Where is this coming from? *Jars?* I open my mouth to defend myself, but Matt carries on as though the floodgates have opened.

"There are bloody 'rescue plants' everywhere . . . your 'rescue bed' is impossible to sleep in. . . ."

"At least my flat has character!" I snap. "At least it's not some monolithic concrete box."

"Character?" Matt gives a short, incredulous laugh. "It's crummy! *That's* its character! *Rescue books?* Rescue books are not a thing, Ava. You're not making a noble gesture by housing crap."

"Crap?" I stare at him, incensed.

"Yes, crap! If no one wants to buy *An Illustrated Guide to the Cauliflower* published in 1963, guess what? It's not because it's an unloved gem which needs to be rescued. It's because it's a *shit book*."

For a moment I can't speak for shock. I don't even know where to begin. And by the way, I do *not* own a book called *An Illustrated Guide to the Cauliflower*.

"So, what, you hate my flat?" I try to sound calm.

"I don't hate it." Matt signals left and changes lanes. "I think it's unsafe."

"Not this again. You're obsessed!"

"I would just like to go about my life without being injured!" says Matt with heat. "That's all I ask. Every time I set foot in your flat, I get some injury or a bloody rescue yucca falls on me or my shirt gets shredded by Harold. I've had to buy six new shirts since we started dating, you know that?"

"*Six?*" I'm momentarily halted. I didn't realize that. I would have said maybe . . . three.

"I love you," Matt sounds suddenly weary. "But sometimes I feel like your life hates me. I feel attacked. Your friends . . . Jeez . . . You know, every day Nell sends me some piece trashing Harriet's House: 'Why Harriet's House is misogynist.' 'Why all feminists must boycott Harriet's House.' It's a dollhouse company, for God's sake. We may not be perfect, but we're not *evil*."

I feel a slight qualm, because I hadn't realized that, either—but that's just what Nell's like.

"That shows she respects you," I say defensively. "Nell only fights with people she likes and respects. It's a compliment. And at least she engages! At least she doesn't ignore you. Your dad said nothing to me, all lunch! Nothing!" I know my voice is getting shrill, but I can't stop. "And my flat might not be perfect, but at least it's tasteful! At least I don't have robots everywhere!"

"What's wrong with robots?" shoots back Matt.

"It's ridiculous! It's adolescent! Who has their snacks brought to them by a *robot*? And as for your *art*—"

I break off, because I didn't mean to mention the art. Raindrops have started to spatter onto the car, and for a moment neither of us speaks.

"What about my art?" says Matt evenly, and for a few moments I'm silent. What do I say? Should I backtrack?

No. Nell and Sarika are right. I have to be honest. No more denial.

"I'm sorry, Matt," I say, looking out of the window. "But I find your art disturbing and . . . and weird."

" 'Weird,' " Matt echoes, his voice hurt and scathing. "One of the greatest, most acclaimed artists of our time, 'weird.' "

"He may be great. But his art is still weird."

"Genevieve didn't think so," Matt says in cutting tones, and I gasp inwardly. Oh my God. We're doing *that*, are we?

"Well, Russell loved my rescue bed," I say, equally curtly, "and he loved my rickety windows *and* he thought Harold was lovely as he is. So."

Matt pulls up at a red light, and there's such a long silence I feel like we're redrawing the lines.

"I thought you said Russell never stayed over at your flat," he says at last, without moving his head.

"No. He didn't."

"If he never slept in your rescue bed, how could he love it?"

"He dozed in it," I say with dignity. "And he found it very comfortable."

"Kind of strange he never stayed over," Matt presses on.

"He couldn't because of his work—"

"Bollocks. No one 'can't stay the night' in a five-month relationship. Never met the guy, but I'm guessing the reason he didn't have any opinions about anything in your life was, he didn't give a shit. He didn't care, so he said whatever you wanted to hear. He played you, Ava. The difference is, I'm not playing you. I *do* care. And I'm being honest."

I stare at him, stung. I should never have told Matt anything about Russell.

"Oh, really?" At last I find some words of retaliation. "You think that, do you?"

"Yes. I do."

"Well, let me ask *you* a question. How do you know Genevieve liked your art?"

"She said so—" Matt breaks off as he realizes the trap I've led him into. "She displayed interest in it," he adds stonily. "We went to exhibitions together. She had a genuine appreciation for it."

"She was playing *you*, Matt!" I give a derisive laugh. "I've seen Genevieve's Instagram page, I've seen her style, and take it from me, she did *not* genuinely like your art. No one likes it! My friends—"

"Oh, we're back to your friends," says Matt in a hurt, angry roar. "Of course we are. The Greek chorus. Do you ever leave off consulting them for five minutes of your bloody life?"

"Five minutes?" I shake my head. "You exaggerate about *everything*."

"You're addicted to WhatsApp," says Matt. "That's not an exaggeration."

"Well, I'd rather be addicted to WhatsApp than some stupid . . . website counter!" I say shrilly. "The number of Internet users in the world, for God's sake?"

"What's wrong with that?"

"It's weird!"

"So, everything in my life is 'weird,' " says Matt, his hands tightening on the steering wheel. "Again, Genevieve didn't think it was weird."

"Well, Russell loved my friends!" I lash back furiously. "And you know something else? He was vegetarian. Whereas you haven't even *tried* to be vegetarian—"

"I never said I was vegetarian," Matt interrupts.

"I'm not saying you did, but you could make an effort—"

"Why?" says Matt, and I nearly scream in frustration. How can he even ask that?

"Because you *should*! Because you said you would! Because the scientific evidence shows—"

"Ava, I'm telling you now," says Matt flatly, "I will never be a vegetarian. Limit meat, yes, buy responsibly, yes, give up completely, never. *Never*," he repeats, as I gasp. "I *like* meat."

I feel as though he's slapped me. For a few moments I can't even draw breath.

"OK," I say at last. "So . . . that's it, is it?"

"I don't know." Matt's face tautens. "Is it, Ava? Is that some sort of deal-breaker for you?"

"No!" I say, taken aback. "I don't believe in deal-breakers."

"Because you could have let me know in Italy," Matt continues relentlessly. "That's all I'll say. You could have let me know if being vegetarian was some kind of requirement."

"Well, I could ask the same of you!" I retort. "Is my being vegetarian a deal-breaker for you? Because, equally, you could have let *me* know."

"Don't be ridiculous," says Matt irritably. "You know it's not."

For a few minutes we're both silent as rain starts to thunder down on the car roof. Hurt is crackling around the car like a lightning storm. I can't bear it. How are we like this? *Why* are we like this?

We were so happy, standing on the Pugliese hillside. If I close my eyes I'm back there, under the olive trees, the garland round my head, suffused with love and optimism.

Then I open my eyes and I'm back here in the rain and misery.

"So, are you regretting what you said in Italy?" I say with an offhand shrug.

"What did I say in Italy?" Matt squints at an electronic sign about delays on the M4, and my face flames—because how can he not remember? Was it not *important* to him?

"Oh, sorry, you've forgotten." My voice ripples with hurt sarcasm. "Obviously it wasn't very important to you. I *thought* you said, 'I love this woman for keeps,' but maybe it was 'Could you pass the olive oil.'"

"Of course I'm not regretting that," says Matt irately. "And of course it was important to me. I didn't know what you were referring to. I said a lot of things in Italy. You always expect me to read your mind—"

"I do not!"

There's another silence, then Matt breathes out.

"Look, Ava, we need to talk. Properly. This is just . . . Shall we go for a drink or something?"

Before I can answer, my phone buzzes with a new Whats-App and automatically I check it, whereupon an incredulous, bitter smile grows on Matt's face.

"There we go. Chat to your friends. Greater priorities. Don't worry, Ava, I know my place."

My face flushes again, because that was an instant reflex. And if I'd been thinking harder, I wouldn't have opened it. But it's on my screen now, and—

Oh God.

My heart falls to the floor as I take in Sarika's words. For a moment I can't react. But at last I raise my head and say, "I have to go to Nell's. Could you take me there, please?"

"*What?*" Matt emits a disbelieving laugh. "That's your answer? I ask you out for a drink, I'm trying to build bridges, I'm trying to do something about this . . . and you say you want to go to *Nell's*? Ava, you accuse *me* of not caring, but . . ."

As he continues, I'm hardly listening to him. My mind is torn in two. I can't tell him, I never tell people about Nell without her permission, but this is different, he should know, he *has* to know . . .

"Nell's ill." I cut him off, mid-stride.

"*Ill?*" His combative tone falls away and he shoots me an uncertain look. "What do you— Has something happened?"

"I wasn't going to tell you till . . . I mean, she likes to tell people herself, but . . . Anyway." I take a deep breath. "Nell has lupus. So. That's . . . what this is. That's why I need to go there."

"Lupus?" Matt turns his head briefly toward me and away again. "That's . . . Shit. I had no idea. I mean, she doesn't look . . . I would never have guessed."

"I know. That's why it's so hard. It comes and goes. She was going through a really good patch, so . . ."

"Lupus." Matt still sounds a bit shell-shocked. "I've never—I mean, isn't that serious?"

"Yes. I mean, it can be. I mean, it depends." I blow out in frustration.

I know I sound short. Angry, even. But I'm not angry with Matt, I'm angry with sodding lupus. With illness. With all the *shit*.

"OK," says Matt after a long pause. "Got it."

He reaches out and puts a hand on mine and squeezes hard. I squeeze back, harder than I meant to, and realize I don't want to let go. So we stay like that, clinging tightly to each other's hands, till he has to change gear and releases me.

"What can I do?"

"Sarika says she's having one of her bad flare-ups. We try to stay over, and it's my turn. So just drop me there. Thanks."

For the next few minutes, we're both silent, then Matt says, "Tell me about it. Wait, no, don't waste your breath," he hastily amends. "I'll google. Whatever."

"It's OK," I say wryly. "It has a million symptoms, so if you google it you'll just get confused. It's an autoimmune disease. It can go a lot of ways. Nell has had a bunch of different problems. Her joints . . . heart issues. A couple of years ago she had to have surgery on her intestine. It's not fun."

"Shouldn't she be in hospital?" Matt sounds alarmed.

"It might get to that. She hates it, though. She likes to try to stay home. When she has these episodes, we try to be there for her. You know, distract her, just be company, get her stuff when she needs it, that kind of thing."

There's silence, and I can sense Matt taking it all in. At last he ventures, "It sounds grueling."

"Yes." I turn my head gratefully, because he found the right word. "It is grueling. And she seemed to be so much better." I can't help my frustration bursting through. "You know? She hadn't had a flare-up for months. We all thought— We hoped— It's so unfair—" As I recall Nell in the park, looking so uncharacteristically optimistic, my voice suddenly breaks. "*Shit.*"

"Ava, you're allowed to be upset," says Matt gently.

"No." I shake my head. "I'm not allowed to lose it. That's Nell's rule."

My voice has softened. As I glance over at him, all I can feel is affection. All our jumpy, irritable problems seem to have melted away. Everything felt so hugely important while we were yelling at each other two minutes ago—but now I can't even remember why I got so stressed out. In fact, I feel ashamed. Matt and I aren't in pain, we're not ill, we're not struggling. We're the lucky ones. We can work it out.

As I input Nell's postcode into Matt's satnav, he asks quietly, "How long has she been ill?"

"Diagnosed five years ago. She was ill before then, but no one knew what it was."

I'm silent for a moment, remembering those hateful, complicated years when Nell kept falling ill and no one could work out what it was. It was so unlike bolshy, energetic Nell to be tired. But she would lie in bed for days, unable to move and in pain, while her doctor talked about anxiety and viruses and chronic fatigue syndrome. She swung between rage and despair. We all did.

Then she was diagnosed, and it was almost a relief to know what was wrong but scary too. Because now it was a real thing. *Is* a real thing.

"And you all look after her?" I can sense that Matt is trying to work out the parameters.

"Not look after her. Just, you know, be there. And not just us," I add quickly. "Her mum stays over a lot, although they have quite a volatile relationship. And there's her brother and his wife, although they're down in Hastings, so . . ."

"Right. And is there a guy on the scene? Or girlfriend?" he adds quickly.

"There've been a couple of guys since she was diagnosed. But neither of them stuck around. They got bored when she had to cancel things, over and over." I shrug. "I mean, it's tough."

"I'm sure."

"I didn't tell you before because she's . . ." I hesitate. "She hates people knowing before they have to. But now you have to. I mean, you would have found out sometime." I pause, staring at the windscreen wipers, then add, "This is part of my life, as well as Nell's."

"I get that." He nods, and we sit quietly for the rest of the journey. Not in a bad, toxic silence but in a peaceful silence. I'm not sure we've fixed things exactly, but at least we've put down our weapons for a breather.

As we pull up outside Nell's block of flats, Matt says, "Shall I come in?" but I shake my head.

"Better not. Nell's quite private."

"But I'd like to do something." He looks troubled. "Ava, I want to help—"

"You did. You brought me here. Really." I nod reassuringly. "I can take it from here."

"OK." He turns off the engine, rubs his face for a few seconds, then turns to me. "Well, look. Before you go: Can I take you out for a drink? Or dinner? Let's go out for dinner. A *date,*" he adds, as though finally arriving at the correct word. "We haven't had a proper date. It's ridiculous."

"We haven't, have we?" I smile. "Unless you count jumping into the sea."

As I say the words, a vision of that long-ago day dances across my mind, and I feel a visceral pang of longing. Everything seemed so simple on that beach. Sun blazing down, sea salt in my hair, and a super-hot, perfect guy. Nothing to do but sunbathe and kiss. No rest of life. No wretched messy, stupid, bloody *life* to get in the way.

And I know it wasn't real, I know that.

But real is hard sometimes. Real is really *hard*.

"Speaking of jumping into the sea . . ." Matt breaks my thoughts—and I look up, wondering where he's going with this. Then, to my surprise, he opens the car door and gets out. "Wait there," he adds.

I hear him open the boot and rummage around. Then the boot closes again and he's back in the driver's seat, holding a bulky parcel.

"This is for you," he says, placing it on my lap. "It's a present. I wasn't sure when to give it to you, so . . . Anyway. Careful, it's heavy."

He's not joking: Whatever this is, it weighs a ton.

"What is it?" I say in astonishment.

"Open it. You'll see."

Shooting him bewildered looks, I peel off layers of brown paper, then bubble wrap, and finally tissue paper, to reveal—

"Oh my God," I breathe. My throat is suddenly tight. I can't believe it.

I'm holding the pebble tower. The one we made on the beach in Italy. It's somehow been stuck together in place and mounted on a plain wooden plinth, and it's the most beautiful thing I've ever seen. As my eyes run over the stones, I'm back there for an instant, under the dappled shade of the olive tree, intoxicated by sunshine and romance.

"I appreciate that we don't have quite the same taste in art," says Matt wryly. "So I'm not sure if you'll like it. *I* like it—"

"I love it." I swallow, my eyes hot. "I love it so much, Matt. It's perfect. And it's us, it's a souvenir of us. . . . How did you *do* it?" I swivel my head incredulously. "How is this here?"

"I sneaked back," says Matt, looking pleased with himself. "The next morning when we were writing those scenes. Hired a car, drove to the beach."

"You said you were writing in your room!"

"Yup." He grins. "That was a white lie. When I got there, the stack was still there. I numbered them in pencil, brought them back, found a sculptor online. . . . No big deal."

"It is a big deal," I say, stroking the smooth surface of the pebbles. "It's a huge deal. Thank you *so* much . . ." My voice wobbles. "Matt, I don't know what to say. I'm sorry I shouted. I don't know what got into me."

It's surreal. A moment ago we were yelling at each other—and now I'm almost in tears, because no one has ever done something as lovely for me as this.

"I'm sorry too,'" says Matt gruffly. "And I also wanted to thank you for something. The other night, when you were making me smell all those aromatherapy oils? I'll confess, I was skeptical. I thought it was bullshit. But that oil you made me for the office . . ."

"You like it?" I look up eagerly.

"I put it on my temples at work, like you said. I rub it in. And it's good. It makes a difference." He shrugs. "Makes me feel more chill."

"I'm *so* pleased!"

I stroke the pebble tower again, and Matt reaches out to touch it too. Our fingers graze and we smile a little warily at each other.

"I never thought I was the kind of guy who would use aromatherapy oil," says Matt suddenly, as though speaking with some effort. "Nor bring a load of pebbles home from Italy. It never would have even crossed my mind till you said you wished you could take them. But I'm pleased I did both.

So . . ." He hesitates, searching for words. "Thanks for expanding my horizons, I guess."

"Well, thanks for making my wish come true," I say, my fingers curled tightly around the pebbles. "That's a pretty impressive superpower."

"I don't have superpowers," says Matt, after a pause. "I won't pretend I do. But . . . I would like to take you on a date."

His face is square-on to mine, his eyes dark and earnest. This kind, complicated guy, who might not be vegetarian or perfect or get on with everything in my life but is thoughtful to a degree I could have never predicted. And still super-hot. And it's not his fault if he likes weird art.

"I'd love to go on a date with you," I say, and touch his hand gently. "I'd love to."

As I let myself quietly into Nell's room, she's lying in a hunched, curled-up position I recognize, and I bite my lip.

Nell once said to me, "Pain is the least romantic partner you can have in your bed. *Fucker.*" A few minutes later, she said in a strained voice, "It's like some total bastard's hammering my joints with a mallet," and ever since then, that's how I've envisioned it. I've seen pain leach the color from her face. I've watched it diminish her, drawing her into a private space, just her and her tormentor, till the drugs kick in. If they do.

"Hey," I say softly, and she turns her head briefly. "How's the fucker? Taken anything?"

"Yup. Getting there," says Nell, her voice shortened by the effort of talking.

I can tell she's bad, because she's not trying to read. Her hands are swollen, I notice. They often are. Her skin goes blotchy; her fingers go numb. Often she can't use an iPad, and even a remote control is a struggle.

But I don't refer to any of this. We have a shorthand, all of us, based on Nell's basic aversion to talking about her illness, even when she's unable to move. This doesn't go down too well with medical professionals, but the four of us are used to it. And I know that "Getting there" means she doesn't want to talk about it.

"Great." I sit down by her bed and open up my phone. "So, I've got a new one for you." I put on a super-dramatic voice. *"A Zombie Kiss."*

My way of distracting Nell is to read books aloud to her, and the latest genre we've found is horror romance novels. Some of them are pretty gruesome—*The Blood-Soaked Bride* was frankly traumatic—but Nell says that's what she likes.

"Excellent." Nell's voice is muffled by the duvet. "Wait, hang on. How were Matt's parents?"

"Oh." I cast my mind back to Matt's parents' house. "Fine. Bit weird. You know."

"But was it OK?"

"It was OK apart from the naked sauna. Right, Chapter One." I draw breath—but then out of the corner of my eye I suddenly notice the duvet shaking.

"Nell. Oh God . . ."

My stomach is hollow as I put down my phone and get to my feet. *Please* don't say she's crying. I can't bear to see wonderful, strong Nell felled. Plus if she cries, I'll cry . . . and then she'll yell at me. . . .

But as I peer fearfully over the folds of the duvet, I realize she's not crying, she's laughing.

"Pause on *A Zombie Kiss*," she manages between painful chortles and swivels her face to look at me. "Ava, you can't leave it there. What bloody naked sauna?"

Eighteen

~~~~~~~~~

Four nights later, Matt and I have our date. We've chosen a vegetarian restaurant in Covent Garden and have decided to come separately, just as though it really is a first date. I get there on the prompt side, but even so, Matt is already at the table, and I feel a massive pang of love as I see him. That's so him, to arrive early.

He gets up to greet me and kisses me lightly on the cheek. The waiter pulls out my chair for me, and Matt and I smile at each other with almost nervous anticipation.

"You look lovely," says Matt, gesturing at my dress.

"So do you." I nod at his crisp blue shirt.

"Oh, thanks. It's new." He seems about to add something, then stops himself.

"What?"

"Nothing." He shakes his head quickly. "What do you want to drink?"

Why's he changing the subject?

"Oh *God,*" I say in sudden realization. "You had to buy a new shirt because Harold wrecked your old one. Sorry." I bite my lip and Matt shakes his head quickly again.

"No! That's not what I was going to— I needed some new shirts, anyway. How's Nell?"

"Better." I smile at him. "I mean, not *better,* but, you know. Improved."

"Excellent. Menu looks good," he adds, with determined enthusiasm, and I feel another wave of love. He's not complaining about Harold ruining his shirt *and* he's being positive about vegetarian food. He's making a real effort here. I need to do the same.

"Why don't you teach me golf?" I say in an impulsive rush, and Matt looks slightly stunned.

"You want to learn golf?"

"Er . . ." I push back my hair, playing for time. Maybe "want" is overstating it. But I *do* want to bond with Matt, and also I should try to get over my prejudice. Plus, I might be naturally brilliant at it. Who knows?

"Yes!" I say firmly. "It could be a new joint hobby! I'll buy some tartan socks."

"Tartan socks aren't necessary." He grins. "But, yes, if you want, I can teach you." As he speaks, his phone buzzes with a call and he flinches slightly as he sees the number. "Sorry. My dad. I *told* him I was out for dinner, but . . ." He breathes out. "I'll just send him a quick text, remind him I'm busy."

As Matt sends the text, our waiter approaches the table and we order our drinks. Then, as we're left alone again, I draw breath, because I have some important stuff I want to say.

"Matt," I begin. "I think we need to talk. Can I be frank?"

"Frank?" Matt looks alarmed.

"Honest," I elaborate. "Truthful. Candid. Maybe blunt." I think for a moment, then backtrack. "No, not blunt. But the others."

Matt is looking more and more wary.

"I guess," he says at last.

"OK. So, here's the thing. It's been six weeks, give or take."

"What has?" Matt looks blank and I feel a tiny spurt of impatience, which I try to suppress. But honestly. What does he *think* I'm talking about?

"Us," I say patiently. "Us."

"Right." Matt thinks about this for a moment, then ventures, "I would have said longer."

"Well, it's six weeks. We've had six weeks so far for me to get used to Matt-land and you to get used to Ava-land. And I think you'd agree that our progress has been . . ." I pause, to pick the right word. "Patchy."

Matt breathes out, as though he was expecting something quite a lot worse than "patchy."

"That's fair." He nods.

"Sometimes everything is wonderful between us. Whereas other times . . ." I pause again, not wanting to dig up old, painful stuff. "But you know what? That's no surprise, because six weeks is nothing! I understand everything now! I've been reading this brilliant book."

From my bag I pull the paperback I've been studying for the last few days. I ordered it after doing a quick google, and honestly, it makes everything clear! It's littered with high-lighter and Post-its where I found useful tips, and I can't wait for Matt to read it.

" 'In a Strange Land,' " Matt reads off the front cover. " 'How to Acclimatize to a New Country.' "

"Look!" I say, flicking through it with enthusiasm and showing Matt chapter headings. " 'Chapter One: So You're in Love with a New Country! Chapter Two: The Shock of the First Few Days. Chapter Three: Getting Used to Strange New Customs.' See? It could be about us!"

"Right." Matt seems confused. "But it's not a book about relationships."

"It's about being expats in a foreign country," I explain. "Well, we *are* expats in foreign countries. Matt-land and Ava-land! It's the same!"

As I flick farther on, I come to "Chapter 7: When the Charm Wears Off." But hastily I turn the page, because that's not relevant to us.

"Anyway," I continue firmly, "everything in this book spoke to me. And what we're in right now is called 'culture shock.' We need to adjust. And maybe we're underestimat-ing how hard a job that is. Listen to this. . . ." I riffle through the pages till I find the right Post-it, then read aloud: " 'Even small differences between cultures can be disconcerting, from body language to food choices. You may often find yourself thinking, "Why?" ' "

"One beer . . ." A waiter interrupts us. "And one kombucha-fermented cocktail with extra wheatgrass shot?"

"Fab!" I smile up at him. "Thank you!"

As the waiter departs, Matt looks silently from his bottle of Budweiser to my green, foamy drink garnished with a bean sprout.

"Yes," he says at last. "I think I can relate to this."

"Well, what the book says is, don't expect instant results. It takes six months to acclimatize, minimum. Cheers." I lift my drink to his.

"Cheers. Six *months*?" he adds, after sipping.

"Minimum." I nod. "It also says you have to be open-minded, curious, embrace the quirks of your new adopted nation. . . . What else . . ." I open the book again and flip through. " 'Research your new country carefully before-hand . . .' No, that wasn't it. . . ."

"Bit late for that!" says Matt with a short laugh.

"Here we are." I read aloud again: " 'The more you explore and immerse in your new culture, the more quickly you will adapt.' You see?" I lean forward with animation. "Explore and immerse."

"Right." Again, Matt looks wary. "What exactly does that mean?"

"You know! Explore aspects of each other's lives. I'll explore your area of London; you explore mine. I'll explore golf; you explore . . . er . . . astrology, maybe."

Matt's face ripples with something unreadable.

"OK," he says, and swigs his Bud again.

"But the point is, we need to be nonjudgmental," I add earnestly. "Listen: 'You may find elements of your new culture unfamiliar. Perhaps even unpalatable. But try not to cling to your biases and prejudices. Widen your compassion and empathy.'" I look up, glowing. "Isn't that inspiring? Compassion and empathy."

"Mr. Warwick?" Our waiter approaches the table hesitantly. "I'm sorry to disturb you, but you have a phone call on our landline."

"A phone call?" Matt looks startled.

"A Mr. Warwick Sr."

"My dad?" Matt seems baffled. "He must have asked my assistant where I was eating and got the number."

"Maybe it's an emergency," I say in sudden fear. "Maybe something's happened to your grandpa."

"OK, I'd better find out. Sorry." Matt pushes back his chair and throws down his napkin. As he strides away, I take the opportunity to answer a WhatsApp thread on whether Maud should dye her hair, but I shove my phone away as Matt returns, looking a bit thunderous.

"What's up?"

"Nothing. My dad wanted my opinion on something." He sits down and slugs his beer.

"But he knew you were busy."

"Yup," says Matt shortly. And he opens his menu as though closing the discussion.

He sounds both pissed off and as though he doesn't want to talk about it, which is the *worst* possible combination. As I open my own menu, I can't help seething. I know it's a big family business, massive global brand, blah blah, whatever, but his parents treat Matt like they own him. Twice this week they've sent Geoff to pick him up from home when he wasn't expecting it, just like they did that time at the airport. Geoff isn't Matt's personal driver, as I assumed at first. He works for Matt's parents and does their bidding.

When Matt questioned Geoff's unexpected appearances, his mother got all defensive and said they were trying to "make his life easier." (I could hear her through his cellphone.) But it seems pretty controlling to me. Like all these phone calls and dropping in unexpectedly. Where are the boundaries?

"That's a bit weird," I try again. "Calling you at a restaurant just to get your opinion."

"Yup," Matt repeats, without looking up. "Well, that's how they are."

For a while we're silent, while my brain whirs. Here we are, then. This is culture shock. This is me, faced with an unpalatable aspect of Matt-land, thinking, *Why?* But Matt seems to accept it. Is this just how they behave in his world? Am I biased? Should I try to understand rather than criticize?

Yes! I decide. I should immerse and learn, with compassion and empathy.

"Matt," I announce firmly, "I want to visit your office."

"My office?" Matt seems staggered.

"Of course! I love you, but I hardly know what you do! I want to see your work, watch you in action, get to know that side of you. *Understand* you."

"You could come to the Harriet's World Expo," says Matt reluctantly. "That would be more interesting than coming to the office. It's in three weeks' time. We hire a conference venue, Harriet's House fans come from all over, there's entertainment. . . . It's fun."

He says "It's fun" in such flat tones, I almost want to laugh. But that wouldn't be compassion, nor empathy.

"Great!" I say. "I'll start by coming to the expo. And in return, you can ask me anything you like about my work." I sweep a generous hand around the table. "*Anything.* You must have a million questions!"

"Er . . . sure," says Matt. "My mind's a bit blank right now," he adds quickly, as he sees me waiting. "But I'll let you know."

"OK, well, I've had another idea," I press on with energy. "Let's bring our friends together. Let's have a party for them and they can all immerse with one another!"

"Maybe." Matt looks dubious. Honestly. He really should try to *engage* with this process.

"What about you?" I say encouragingly. "Do you have any ideas to help us acclimatize with each other?"

"Ava . . ." Matt takes a long sip of beer, looking beleaguered. (Which is his *dad's* fault, not mine.) "I dunno. This all seems like overthinking to me. Couldn't we just . . . you know. Go with the flow?"

"No! We have to be proactive!" I open the book and find a pull-out quote. " 'Don't shrink from culture shock, but launch yourself bravely toward it. Only then will you have a chance of success.' "

I jab at the words significantly with my finger, then clap the book shut and take a deep sip of my cocktail. Just saying those words has emboldened me. I'm going to launch myself bravely at Matt's work. And his parents. And golf. I just hope they're ready.

Neither of us wants dessert, so when we leave the restaurant it's still a light, balmy evening. The air is almost Italian-warm, and there are crowds of people outside every pub and clustered in the piazza, watching a busker. As we wander over, drawn by the shrieks and gasps of the crowd, I hear Matt's phone buzzing in his pocket and see the rocklike look start to come over his face.

"Don't think about your phone," I say as gently as I can. "We're in Covent Garden and it's a beautiful night. Let's have fun. *Fun*. Remember that?"

My words seem to prick Matt, because he says, "I'm fun!" defensively.

"Of course you are," I backtrack hastily. "I just meant . . . you know . . . let's chill out. Enjoy ourselves."

"Volunteer!" The busker's amplified voice rises above the crowd. "I need a brave, even *foolhardy* volunteer. . . . No takers?" he adds, as there's a nervous giggle in the crowd. "Are you all cowards?"

"Me!" Matt shouts suddenly, raising his hand. "I'll do it!"

"*What?*" I gasp.

"Live a little," he says, and winks at me before marching forward to join the busker. I watch, flabbergasted, as they cheerfully exchange a few words. Volunteering at one of these things is my idea of the *opposite* of fun.

"Ladies and gentlemen, our very brave volunteer . . .

Matt!" bellows the busker, and the crowd erupts. As Matt grins at me, I can't help laughing. Maybe I'd hate this—but he looks delighted to be there, standing beside a guy in neon-pink shorts and a headset, who's telling the audience to clap along and cracking jokes about health and safety.

I wasn't paying attention to the show earlier on, so I don't know what the act is. Some kind of acrobatics? Or comedy? I'm prepared for something quite cringeworthy, maybe involving hats. But then, as the busker starts issuing instructions to Matt and gets out his equipment, it becomes clear what the act is—and my smile freezes. Is this for real? Is this busker seriously intending to juggle flaming torches over Matt's prone body? And Matt's *agreeing* to it?

He's not just agreeing, he's laughing along. He's joining in with the busker's jokes about whether he's made a will or funeral arrangements. He's sitting on the ground and waving around. And the crowd is clapping and cheering.

I watch, petrified, as the busker lights the flames. He wasn't joking: That's real fire. My stomach is all twisted up; I can't even watch. But I can't not watch either. In the end I compromise by watching through my fingers, holding my breath. Oh God . . .

The buildup seems to go on forever. But at last, after an unbearable amount of banter, the actual stunt occurs—a blur of whirling, flaming torches to the sound of huge applause. And as soon as it's over, it seems obvious: Of *course* the busker was never going to drop a flaming torch on Matt and set him alight. But even so, I feel weak with relief.

"Ladies and gentlemen, give it up for Matt!" thunders the

busker, and, finally finding my voice, I cheer and whoop as loudly as I can.

As Matt rejoins me in the audience, he's flushed and his smile is wider than I've seen it for weeks.

"Awesome!" I say, hugging him, my heart still thudding with adrenaline. "That was amazing!"

"Couldn't resist." He flashes a grin at me. "Your turn next."

"No!" I recoil in genuine horror. "Never!"

"He's juggling a chainsaw next, if you're interested?" Matt deadpans, then laughs at my expression.

He seems somehow transformed, just by that one experience. There's a light in his eye and a lift in his voice. He sounds teasing, not rocklike. I've got my playful, carefree Dutch back, I suddenly realize. And I hadn't appreciated how much I'd missed him.

"Hey, look, gelato!" I exclaim, seeing a stall at the side of the piazza. "Proper Italian ice cream. Let's get you a nocciola as a reward."

"And let's get you a stracciatella," rejoins Matt cheerfully— and arm in arm we head in that direction.

As we walk, my mind can't help whirring. Does Matt realize how much his personality changes? Does he realize how much less carefree he is in London than he was in Italy? I want to raise the issue—but how do I put it? I can't say, "Sometimes you turn into a rock." I need to phrase it *positively*.

"It's really great when you relax and stop thinking about work," I venture as we join the ice-cream queue.

"Yup." Matt nods easily.

"Can I be honest, Matt?" I press on. "I think you should try to switch off more. Shed your worries."

"I guess work gets everyone down," says Matt, after a pause. "Sorry if I'm antisocial sometimes."

There's a tiny knot of frustration inside me. I want to retort, "It's not just that you're antisocial, it's more than that," but at the same time I don't want to ruin the mood. It's a gorgeous balmy evening and we had a lovely dinner and now we're getting ice cream. Matt's face is shining and animated; he looks supremely happy. I'm not going to rain on that parade.

As he hands me my stracciatella cone, I sigh contentedly. "Just so you know, ice cream is incredibly important in Ava-land."

"Ditto Matt-land," he counters with a grin. "In fact, we have National Ice Cream Day. Three times a year."

"Amazing!" I say admiringly. "We need to introduce that custom into Ava-land. Wait, I'll pay," I add more seriously, as he reaches for his wallet. "You got dinner."

I hand over the money—then we head to a nearby wall and perch there, licking our ice creams and watching people as they stroll by. Music is coming from a nearby bar, and there are gales of laughter from the busker's audience. The sky above us is a deepening blue, and there are twinkling lights all around the piazza. It's an enchanting sight.

"Speaking of money," says Matt presently. "Something I've been meaning to ask you, Ava—did you ever get the money for that piece of freelance work?"

It takes me a moment to work out what he's talking about,

but then I recall. A few months ago I wrote a leaflet for a nearby independent pharmacy—then weeks later I realized I hadn't invoiced them. Matt was with me when I sent the invoice out, and I guess he's remembered, all this time.

"No," I say vaguely. "But it's fine. It hasn't been that long."

"Well over a month," he contradicts me. "And it was long overdue, anyway. You should chase them."

"I will." I shrug. "I'm sure they're on it."

"Threaten them, if necessary," adds Matt.

"*Threaten* them?" I give a shocked laugh. "We're not all karate warriors!"

"You don't have to be a warrior, but you've done some good work for them and they should pay you; it's only right. I think you're sometimes too—" Matt cuts himself off, shaking his head. "No. Sorry. Wrong time, wrong place. Forget it."

"Forget what?" I say, my curiosity piqued. "What do you think? Say it."

"Doesn't matter. We should just enjoy the evening." He spreads his arms around. "It's beautiful here. I really enjoyed our dinner."

Does he think I can just sit here now and *not* hear the end of what he started?

"Matt, too late!" I retort. "I want to know! Whatever you were going to say, say it, or I'll keep bugging you."

There's silence, punctuated by another roar of noise from the piazza. I turn my head to see that the busker is now having some kind of confrontation with a policeman, while the crowd jeers. Oops. Wonder what happened there.

Then Matt exhales, drawing my attention back to him.

"You were honest with me a moment ago, Ava. Now can I be honest with you?" He takes my hand in his as though to soften his words. "Sometimes—just sometimes—you're overoptimistic about people. And situations."

I gape at him. Overoptimistic? How is that even a thing?

"Optimistic is *good*," I retort. "Everyone knows that!"

"Nothing too extreme is good," counters Matt. "I love that you see the best in everything, Ava. I do. It's one of your most lovable qualities. But everyone needs to deal with reality sometimes. Otherwise . . . they risk getting hurt."

I feel a prickle of resentment. I know about reality, thank you. And OK, yes, I sometimes choose not to look too hard in its direction. But sometimes that's because reality is inferior to what life *should* be like.

Out of the corner of my eye, I can see the busker packing up his things with stiff, angry gestures. There. *That's* reality, in all its shittiness. It's not the heady moment of cheering and glory; it's a policeman bringing you down to earth.

I crunch my ice-cream cone and eye Matt over the top of it.

"Real is *hard*," I say, almost as though it's his fault.

"Yup." Matt nods.

He doesn't crack a joke like Russell would. Or tell me I'm stupid. Or try to distract me. He's prepared to sit patiently with me and my thoughts. He's good at that, I've noticed.

"I'll chase the invoice," I say after a while.

Without speaking, Matt tightens his hand round mine, and I feel a swell of something warm inside. Not the white-hot rush of first infatuation, but maybe second love. Solid love. The love that comes of knowing what's inside as well as outside a person.

I love this man because of who he is and in spite of who he is. All at once. And I hope he loves me the same way.

Nineteen

~~~~~~~~

We decide to hold the party a week later, by which time my enthusiasm for exploring Matt's life has very slightly dimmed.

I tried to launch myself bravely at golf. But that did *not* go well. I was actually quite galvanized beforehand. I was prepared to deal with any obnoxious people. I was all set to follow the rules. I was ready to stand at the golf-club bar, talking casually about "par 4" and "birdies."

But none of that came into it, because we didn't go near a golf club. It turned out that my big challenge of the day wasn't the people or the rules or even the outfit, it was hitting the golf ball. Which turns out to be *impossible*.

Matt took me to a driving range, gave me a bucket of balls and a club and a quick lesson. He said that I would probably miss the first few times I tried to hit the ball, but after that, things would fall into place.

Things did not fall into place. I aimed carefully at every

single one of those wretched bloody balls, and I missed them all. All! Do I need to get my eyes tested? Or my *arms* tested?

It was *so* embarrassing. Especially because a couple of other golfers noticed my failure and started watching. Then one of them clocked Matt as being Rob Warwick's brother and they called over a friend. They all thought it was *hilarious*. When I got to the last ball in the bucket, I could actually hear them laying bets. By this time my face was beetroot and I was panting, and I was so determined to hit the last ball that I gave an extra-energetic swing. Which meant I didn't just miss but wedged the golf club right into the ground, practically dislocating my shoulder.

I will say I have more respect for golfers now. Because what they do—hit the ball all round the course, without once missing it—feels like a superhuman feat to me.

On the way home, Matt asked, did I want to try again? And I said, maybe we should stick to the tai chi for now. And that's how we left it.

So golf was a bit of a fail. And then that night we had a row because Matt decided to "tidy up" my flat and got rid of some essential notes for my book. Like, *essential.*

"They were ratty Post-its," he said, when I confronted him. "You hadn't looked at them for weeks."

"But I was going to!" I said furiously. "They were *vital* to my novel!"

I was quite cross, I must admit. The notes were all about Clara's upbringing in Lancashire, and I'd come up with a brilliant anecdote about a mangle and I'll *never* remember it.

"To be honest, I thought you'd given up on the novel," he said with a shrug, and I stared at him in shock.

"Given up? Matt, it's a *work in progress.*"

"Uh-huh." He surveyed me warily. "But you never do any writing."

"I have a job, if you remember, Matt," I reminded him, in prickly tones.

"Right." He nodded. "But all you've done this week is talk about the *other* book you want to do. I suppose I got confused. Sorry."

At first I didn't know what he was talking about. Other book? Then my brow cleared. It's not his fault he can't keep up with my portfolio career.

"That's not a book, that's a *podcast,*" I explained kindly. "Totally different."

I'm quite excited by my podcast idea, actually. I want to start a craft discussion, inspired by my Etsy batik. I'll interview other crafters and we'll talk about how our projects enhance our lives. I just need to get the equipment and decide on a name for it.

"Speaking of which," I added, looking around, "where *is* my batik?"

"D'you mean that chewed rag under the sofa?" Matt said, and I bristled again, because what is it with the pejorative language?

(It was under the sofa. And to be fair, Harold had chewed it a bit, but it'll be fine.)

(Also: I must find time for my batik, because the materials cost quite a lot and I was planning to sell five cushions, but I haven't made any yet.)

Anyway. Never mind. Golf is a minor detail. And everyone has little arguments. And there have been brilliant times too. Like this morning, when we tried a more advanced tai chi routine and we aced it! Then Topher sent us a video he'd secretly taken of us doing tai chi at different times, set to "Eye of the Tiger." It's really funny—in fact, I can't stop watching it.

But the most positive thing of all is that tonight we're holding our drinks party! We've decided to host it at Matt's flat, and as I bustle around, filling bowls with crisps, I feel quite excited.

"Nihal," I say, seeing him sit down at his workstation and put on his headphones. "You know we're throwing a party in, like, five minutes?"

"Sure." He nods, squinting at the screen. "I'll be there. Deffo."

As he starts typing, I quickly put up a picture which I've bought to brighten up Matt's flat. It's the same poster that I've got at my place, with the silk-petal frame and the message "You can cut all the flowers, but you can't stop spring from coming."

I've put it right next to the Bastard Chart, which is frankly hideous. Especially since someone's written *Fuck Off Topher* in green pen across the bottom. As I stand back to admire my new addition, I notice Nihal reading it.

"What do you think?" I say. "Isn't it a gorgeous poster? Those petals on the frame are real silk."

"I don't follow," he says, peering at it. "Are you defining 'spring' as the season in which vegetation starts to appear?"

I feel a tweak of frustration. Not another one.

"Well," I say with a relaxed smile. "I don't think it really—"

"Because in terms of flora, if you really were to remove from the entire earth's biosystem—"

"I know!" I cut him off before he can mention dead bees. "I know about pollination. It's not supposed to be *literal*, it's just a beautiful, inspiring thing to have on your wall. Better than the Bastard Chart, you have to admit," I can't resist adding.

"I like the Bastard Chart," Nihal replies.

"You can't like looking at it," I object. "You can't actually *enjoy* looking at the Bastard Chart."

"I do," says Nihal. "I find it peaceful."

He looks at me mildly and I gaze back at his sweet-natured, brainy face with a mixture of frustration and affection. I've got quite fond of Nihal, despite him being *even more* literal-minded than Matt.

"OK, well, the party starts soon," I say. "My friends are arriving any minute."

"Yes, I'll be there," says Nihal, peering at his work again. "Can't wait to meet them," he adds politely.

I head back toward the kitchen and look around. Where's Matt got to? Doesn't he realize we're hosting an event here? I know I'm a bit wired, but I can't help feeling nervous about this little gathering. This is our two worlds mingling—and what if they're oil and water? What if they all fight?

At last I track down Matt to his bathroom. He's perched on the edge of the sink unit, his phone clamped to his ear, looking stressed. I don't even need to ask who it is. Or what it's about. I catch his eye and point at my watch, and he winces.

"OK, Dad, look . . . Yup. I know. I have to go. Let's discuss this later. . . . Dad, I have to go. . . . Yes. Yes, I know. We'll talk about it later. Bye." At last he turns off his phone.

"Sorry," he says heavily. "I was just . . ." He exhales and closes his eyes. Oh God. I can see him turning into a rock before my eyes.

"What's up?" I ask, because I'm trying to get to know Matt's business as much as I can, in a supportive and empathetic way. "Is it the Japanese theme park again?"

Harriet's House is building a new theme park in Japan, and every day there seems to be some new nightmare. Just from overhearing Matt's conversations, I've learned more about Japanese employment law than I ever thought I would, not to mention the general pitfalls of construction. (My takeaway has been: Don't ever construct anything.) There was a brief saga about pumping water out of some stretch of land and I had a few helpful ideas about that, but that seems to be done with now.

"My parents want me to go over," says Matt flatly, and for a crazy moment I think, *Go over what?* until I realize what he means.

"Well, I guess that makes sense," I say after a pause. "You *should* go and visit."

But Matt shakes his head. "For the duration. For six months, till the build is finished. Although in practice it'll be a year, if not more."

"A *year*?" I stare at him. "A year in Japan?"

"They have a point." Matt rubs his head wearily. "We need someone on the ground. The guy they hired is way out of his depth."

"But why does it need to be you?" I say in dismay. "And what about the rest of your job?"

"They want me to supervise everything else from Japan. They're worried this project is spiraling. They want family out there."

"What did you say?" I gaze at him in dread.

"I said I'm not going to do it. We'll have to find someone else."

"*Is* there anyone else?"

Matt doesn't reply, and I feel a clenching in my stomach. I know I'm trying to empathize with Matt's world, but I'm running out of empathy.

"Matt, tell me something," I say impulsively. "Are you happy doing what you're doing?"

"Of course I am," says Matt without missing a beat. He looks at his watch. "We should get going."

"No, wait." I put a hand on his arm. "I'm being serious. I feel like you're two different people. Sometimes you're alive and fun and smiling. Like last week in Covent Garden, that was wonderful! But other times—in fact most of the time, to be honest . . ." I bite my lip. "You seem like someone else."

"Ava, what are you talking about?" replies Matt irritably. "I'm the same guy."

"You're not! The guy I met in Italy was easygoing. Relaxed. But now you're back, you're . . ."

"A miserable git," supplies Matt.

"No!" I say quickly. "Not a miserable git, but . . ."

"It's fine." He hunches his shoulders. "I know I'm a miserable git. Well, sorry to disappoint you, Ava. The holiday was a blip. Dutch was a fabrication. When the sun's shining, anyone can be a nice guy." He gestures at himself. "But this is who I really am."

He looks so resigned. I can't bear it.

"It's not who you are," I retort passionately. "I *know* it's not. If you're a miserable git, it's because you're unhappy. Maybe there are aspects of your life that you should change."

"I know you have problems with my life, Ava," Matt says, his face tightening. "You've made that abundantly clear."

"I *would* love your life, if it made you happy!" I erupt in frustration. "But when I see you so closed up, so rigid . . . I'm just looking at the evidence, Matt," I add, remembering what he said in Italy. "I'm just going on what I see in front of me."

Matt doesn't respond, so I put out a cautious hand to touch his shoulder.

"I want you to live your *best* life," I say in loving tones. But if I hoped that would touch him, I was wrong. He flinches.

" 'Live my best life,' " he echoes scathingly. "How incredibly exhausting. The thing is, Ava, I'm content with my mediocre-to-disappointing life. So, sorry about that."

I should stop the conversation here. But I can't resist one more attempt, hoping that somehow I'll find the magic button that gets through to him.

"Matt, *why* do you work at Harriet's House?" I ask gently. "Is it because you love it?"

Matt glances up with a frown, as though he doesn't quite

compute the question. "Someone has to do it," he says. "Since I've taken over, profits have increased year on year. We've expanded into ten more territories. Communications have improved. There were a bunch of inefficiencies and I've ironed them all out." He comes to a finish, as though he's covered everything.

"Right." I nod. "That's great. But none of that is about you, is it? None of that is about your happiness. Your *fulfillment*."

"Fuck's sake." Matt sounds at the end of his tether. "This is work. It's *business*."

"It's your life!"

"Yes, Ava. *My* life."

He snarls it like a warning, and I feel a jolt. If I push this any more now, we'll end up in a massive argument, just as the others arrive.

"OK." I smile, trying to hide my hurt. "Well, I'll go and be ready for the guests."

As I head out, my stomach is churning in distress, and I find myself looking for Topher. (This shows how desperate I must be.) I discover him in his bedroom, doing crunches on a yoga mat, dressed in his customary black athletic shorts and an inside-out T-shirt.

I'm not even going to mention the fact that he's supposed to be attending a drinks party in two minutes. I want to get straight to the point.

"Matt's parents want him to go to Japan for a year," I say, sitting on Topher's bed.

"Figures," says Topher, between crunches.

"He doesn't want to go, but it doesn't seem like they've got anyone else."

"That's because they're stingy fuckers," says Topher between pants and gasps. "Of course they don't have anyone else, not of Matt's caliber. He does way too much for that organization. You need someone to supervise a construction project in Japan? Well, you know what? Hire the staff. Hire the fucking *staff*."

I can hear genuine anger in Topher's voice, and I stare at him in surprise.

"Do you think Matt enjoys his job?" I venture.

"Of course not," Topher replies, so briskly that I blink.

"Not at *all*?"

"Oh, he has successes like anyone. He has family pride in the company. But overall, deep-down, contented happiness? No."

"He says profits have improved since he joined."

"Yeah, whatever." Topher comes up to a sitting position on his mat and regards me quizzically. "You have to understand, it's not a job for Matt. It's an answer."

"An answer to what?" I say, confused.

"To the nightmare of being Rob Warwick's brother." Topher swings over and starts doing press-ups. "Matt had to be the older brother of the champion golfer his whole life. He always felt inadequate."

My mind shoots back to that glass cabinet full of sporting prizes and photos. I've never felt able even to mention that to Matt. It feels too sensitive. Too raw.

"What's Rob like?" I say curiously. "Have you met him?"

"Few times," Topher says, his breath short. "He's pretty insubstantial. Weaselly. Superb at golf, give him that." He sits up on the mat again and reaches for a towel to mop his neck. "When Matt finally joined Harriet's House, he was the family savior. He got kudos. He still gets kudos, approval, one up over Rob. . . . And he can't let that go, even if he doesn't realize it. You know originally he said he would only join Harriet's House for two years?" Topher adds, glancing up. "He wanted to turn around its problems, then go and do something for himself."

"Really?" I stare at Topher.

"That was six years ago." Topher shrugs. "He's gone stale. The kudos are less every year, his parents take him for granted . . . but he still stays. I've offered him a job myself," Topher adds. "But I can't compete."

"*You've* offered him a job?" I stare at him.

"Partnership, in fact. Several times. I could use his business skills, he's very talented, interested in what we do, so . . ."

As he speaks, I have a vision of Matt sitting with Topher at his workstation, the pair of them engaged in animated, passionate conversation. Matt loves nothing better than to sit with Topher, late into the night, and talk about his latest figures. *Obviously* they should work together.

"He's turned me down every time, of course," Topher adds, and his voice is offhand but I can hear a thread of hurt.

God, Matt's parents have a lot to answer for. I have so many more questions for Topher, but at that moment the doorbell rings, and I feel a spurt of excitement-slash-panic. Someone's arrived!

"I'll get it!" Matt calls from outside the room, and I turn back to Topher.

"Are you coming to the party?"

Topher heaves an unenthusiastic sigh. *"Really?"*

"Yes! Really!"

"I'm inherently antisocial," says Topher discouragingly. "As I've mentioned before, people don't like me."

"I like you."

"You're dating Matt. You have no taste."

"Will you come anyway?" I say patiently, and Topher rolls his eyes.

"Fine. Kill me with your feminine wiles."

"I didn't use my feminine wiles!"

"Coming to my room and asking me in person is using feminine wiles," says Topher, as though it's obvious. "Matt and Nihal would text. Except they wouldn't ask in the first place, because they know I'm a recluse."

"I'll see you there," I say firmly, and hurry out. I find Matt outside the front door, and a moment later Nell, Maud, and Sarika come piling out of the lift, all in party outfits and heels and greeting me with exclamations.

"We're here!"

"You made it!"

"Matt! Look at your flat!"

As we all hug and kiss in the atrium, I can smell alcohol and Maud is particularly giggly. They must have gone for a stiffener first. (I slightly wish I could have gone too.)

"Guess what?" announces Maud in excitement. "Sarika's new man is on his way. They're going to have their very first date *at your party.*"

"Really?" I stare at Sarika.

The great WhatsApp excitement of yesterday was Sarika announcing that she'd finally whittled down her shortlist to one man, who fulfills all her criteria, and saying she was going to contact him for a date. But I never expected to meet him so soon!

"That's OK, isn't it, Ava?" adds Sarika. "The others made me text him from the pub, but I never thought he'd say yes. . . ."

"Of course it's OK!" I say. "It's great! What's his name again?"

"Sam," says Sarika lovingly, summoning up a picture on her phone of an Asian guy. "He grew up in Hong Kong, but then he went to Harvard Business School and now he's moved to London. He cycles and he plays percussion and *every single one* of his food preferences chimes with mine. Every single one!" She opens her eyes wide. "We're totally compatible!"

"Where does he live?" I ask mischievously, and Nell snorts with laughter.

"Five minutes from Golders Green tube," says Sarika, lifting her chin. "You can mock me, but I know this guy. I know what podcasts he listens to, and I know what he would put in a time capsule on the moon. And I agree with every single choice."

"Well, great." I hug her. "Can't wait to meet him."

I sling everyone's coats and bags onto the leather footstool, whereupon Matt silently opens the coat cupboard and hangs them up.

Oh, right. Yes. Somehow the coat cupboard never occurs to me; in fact, I forget it exists.

"*Wow,*" says Sarika, clocking the sculpture with the outstretched hands. "That's . . . In the flesh, it's even more . . . challenging." I can see her trying to overcome her revulsion, and I shoot her a grateful smile.

We had a little WhatsApp exchange yesterday in which I explained how sensitive Matt is about his art. The whole squad said they understood and promised fervently to be positive about it. But now they're here, I can see everyone struggling. Maud did a double take as soon as she entered, and I've seen Nell snort once or twice.

"It's definitely challenging," says Maud. "But, then, art *should* be challenging," she adds quickly.

"It really is," says Nell, walking up to the straining eyeless face, then abruptly turning away. "I mean, the raven is . . ." She seems lost for words. "And the *space* is fantastic."

At once, everyone seizes on the topic of the space.

"The space." Maud nods fervently. "Just look at the space!"

"Amazing space!" chimes in Sarika.

"Well, come through," I say, ushering them into the main living area, where I pour out champagne for everyone. We're just lifting our glasses in a toast when Nihal timidly approaches. He's brushed his hair flat and put on a tie and he looks about twelve years old.

"How do you do," he greets everyone, shaking hands formally. "I'm Nihal."

"Nihal!" Maud swoops down on him, her eyes glittering with interest. "You're the computer expert!"

"Yes," says Nihal. Then he seems to reconsider his answer. "'Expert' is a somewhat vague term. It would depend on your definition of—"

"*So* clever of you," says Maud breathily, blinking at him.

Nihal looks taken aback. "Knowledge of computers isn't inherently clever," he says politely. "It's merely an application of—"

"Well, I think it's tremendous," Maud cuts him off in a gush. "Just tremendous. I so admire your skills. So *useful*."

"Ava," murmurs Sarika in my ear. "Did you warn Nihal about Maud?"

"Oh God." I look at her in consternation. "No."

"Well, tell him, quick!" she says in an urgent undertone.

"How can I?" I whisper back. "It'll ruin the party atmosphere!"

"You have to! The poor thing's defenseless!" She prods me—but it's too late.

"Nihal," Maud is saying in her super-charming manner, "I *don't* suppose you could come round and look at my laptop? I have no idea what's wrong with it, and you're *so* clever, I'm sure you could sort it out."

She bestows her most dazzling smile on him, and Nihal blinks at her a few times.

"Maud," he says mildly, "you're a friend of Ava's and you seem like a very nice person, so obviously I would like to help you. But I think that was an inappropriate request, bearing in mind that we only met a few minutes ago. So I'm afraid I will be turning you down on this occasion. With apologies." He gives her a sweet, implacable smile.

Maud's mouth has slowly dropped open, and her cheeks have turned pink.

"Oh," she says at last. "Oh. Of course. I'm . . . so sorry!" She takes a deep sip of champagne, and I can feel Sarika descending into giggles beside me.

"I take it all back, he's a genius," she murmurs. "What did you say he does, runs Apple?"

"Apologies for my tardiness." A familiar dry, raspy voice cuts across the conversation, and we all turn our heads.

I've got used to Topher's hulking, powerful, ugly frame. But as I see him afresh through the viewpoint of my friends, I realize again how unconventional he looks, with his fleshy, cratered face and huge eyebrows. He's obviously taken his T-shirt off and put it on the right way around, as a concession to the party, but is still wearing black running shorts and sneakers. As he approaches, he glowers uncompromisingly at Maud, Nell, and Sarika.

"Hello, Ava's friends," he says.

"This is Nell, Maud, Sarika," I say, gesturing at each of them in turn. "Topher."

"Are you all vegetarian too?" asks Topher, and at once Nell's eyes flash dangerously.

"What would you think if we answered yes?" she shoots back in her most confrontational manner.

Topher raises one dark eyebrow. "You want the truth?"

"Of course I want the truth." Nell squares up to him, her chin set. She's looking as bolshy as I've ever seen her, and I feel slight dismay. Are they going to have an argument *already*?

"Does it really matter?" I chime in brightly. "So anyway . . . who saw that news story about the Shetland pony?"

Both Nell and Topher ignore me. In fact, everyone ignores me.

"Of course I want the truth," Nell repeats, and a glimmer of amusement passes over Topher's face.

"OK." He shrugs. "The truth is, whatever you answered, I'd think, 'That's another rung up this pointless ladder of conversation. What shall I ask next?' I'm not sociable," he adds, taking a glass of champagne from Matt. "No offense."

An expression of appreciation is slowly growing on Nell's face. I can tell that wasn't what she was expecting.

"I'm not sociable either," she replies with the tiniest of grins. "No offense."

"Hmm." Topher looks skeptical. "When I say 'not sociable,' I mean I'll happily go a week without seeing anyone except these guys." He gestures at Matt and Nihal.

"I sometimes go a month without setting foot outside the house," Nell responds, and Topher surveys her with renewed interest.

"You hate people?"

"I do hate a number of people, as it happens." Nell nods. "People are shit."

"*Yes.* Agreed." Topher lifts his glass to her.

"Also, I have lupus," she adds in an offhand manner.

"Oh." As Topher digests this, his face is impassive, but I can see his deep-set eyes scanning Nell's face intently. "Bummer."

"Yeah."

I'm agog, and I can tell the others are too. Nell *never* tells people she has lupus when she first meets them. What's going on?

"I don't know anything about lupus," Topher says at length. "But I should imagine it's fairly unpleasant."

"Has its moments," Nell replies with a nod.

"Nihal, why the *fuck* haven't you cured lupus yet?" Topher whips round to address Nihal in suddenly accusing tones.

"I'm not in medical research, among other reasons," Nihal says patiently.

"That's no excuse." Topher swings back to Nell. "I'm so sorry. It's all my flatmate's fault. He's a lazy bastard." He pauses, then adds, "So, here's a pertinent question. Are you allowed to drown your sorrows in tequila?"

Twenty

Everyone gets drunk really fast. It's not just the tequila; it's the slightly weird boys-and-girls vibe—my friends and Matt's friends, getting the measure of one another. It almost feels as though we're all back at the school disco.

Within forty minutes, Maud has got up on a chair and started her usual drunken speech about refusing to become an invisible woman. Topher and Nell are in the middle of some sort of heated discussion, and Nihal is showing off his robot to Sarika; meanwhile, Matt and I are trying to retrieve Matt's new scarf from Harold's jaws.

"You're so, *so* wrong," I can hear Nell saying vehemently to Topher. "That's the *worst* theory."

"Out of how many theories?" demands Topher.

"Out of all the theories!" she shoots back. "All. The. Theories."

"What on earth are they talking about now?" Matt mutters to me.

"No idea," I mutter back. "Global warming? Economics? Making Swiss rolls?"

"Harold, you total *bastard,*" Matt exclaims in exasperation as Harold dodges away triumphantly, the scarf still in his jaws. "OK, that's it. He's going on the Bastard Chart."

"What?" I stare at him, half wanting to laugh, half dismayed. "No!"

"He's going on," repeats Matt adamantly. He marches up to the chart and adds *Harold* to the list, then draws a fat strike next to it.

"That's so unfair!" I try to grab the pen out of his hand. "Harold's not a bastard."

"He's the *biggest* bastard!" Topher joins in. "Admit it, Ava. All he does is scheme and plot against us. He's the Bond villain of dogs."

"And he's never sorry," volunteers Nihal.

"Correct," says Topher, as though he's making a case in court. "He exhibits zero remorse, he's *far* too clever for his own good. . . ." As Harold reappears without the scarf, looking all bright and bouncy and innocent, Topher's eyes narrow at him. "What's your diabolical plan for world domination, doggo? And *don't* pretend you haven't got one."

"OK, everyone!" Sarika exclaims suddenly, looking up from her phone. "Sam's here."

"Sam!" exclaims Maud, waving her arms in excitement, as though Sam is a boy band and she's fourteen. "Sam's here! Yay!"

"Oh God," says Sarika, looking at her as though for the first time. "Maud, how much have you drunk?"

"Not much," says Maud at once. "Less than . . . him."
She points at Topher.

Sarika's the most sober person in the room, and as she
surveys us all, I can see qualms in her face. I mean, it *was* a
little ambitious to have a first date with all the rest of us too.

"Is Sam a feminist?" demands Maud, still addressing the
room from her chair. "Because if he's not, *if* he's not, then—"

"Yes, of course he's a bloody feminist," says Sarika impatiently. "Maud, get down off that chair. And don't ask Sam
for any favors. And *don't* be weird," she adds, taking in everyone with a sweeping glare. "That goes for everyone. Be
nice. Be . . . you know. Normal."

"Normal!" Nell barks with laughter.

"OK, then, *pretend* to be normal. I'm going down. I'll be
back up soon." She gives us all another ominous look. "I'll
knock on the door."

As Sarika disappears, we all exchange glances like guilty
children.

"We need fresh supplies," says Topher at last. "And then
you need to tell us who this character is." He heads to the
kitchen, then returns with a new bottle of tequila. "OK,
spill," he says, filling my glass. "Who's Sam?"

"All we know is that he's the perfect guy for Sarika," I
explain. "She met him online."

"After the most fearsome vetting procedure," puts in Nell.

"God, yes." I nod. "Terrible! Like . . ." I cast around.
"Like, worse than the Foreign Office exams."

"It would be easier to get a job at NASA than to date
Sarika," affirms Maud.

"But Sam got there," I say. "He beat all the others. He meets all her requirements. Every single one!"

I almost feel as though we should give this guy a round of applause and present him with a trophy as he enters the flat, just for surviving the process.

"What requirements did she have?" asks Topher.

"Oh, a million," I say. "She kept adding more. He couldn't be super-tall or be a dancer or an oil-rig worker . . . or vegetarian . . . What else?" I look at the others.

"He had to chime precisely with her views on the environment and social media and Ed Sheeran and Marmite," says Nell, wrinkling her brow. "Oh, and there was a question about hair washing. She's obsessed by clean hair."

"And live within ten minutes of a tube station," puts in Maud, with a gurgle of laughter.

"Yes!" I exclaim. "That's one of her big things. She's tired of guys who live in the middle of nowhere."

"Wow," says Nihal, digesting this. "Ten minutes from the tube. Ed Sheeran. Marmite. She's quite . . . picky."

"Not picky," I say, automatically coming to my friend's defense. "Just realistic. Her theory is, the more groundwork you put in beforehand, the more chance you have of success."

"D'you think she's right?" says Topher as a knock sounds at the front door.

"Dunno," I say, giving a sudden giggle. "I guess we're about to find out."

As Matt opens the front door, the rest of us are utterly agog, facing the door like a reception committee. Harold skitters to join us and barks twice, as though to assert that his opinion matters too.

"So, everyone . . . this is Sam!" says Sarika, ushering in a guy with the cleanest, shiniest hair I've ever seen. He has a sweet face—far handsomer than in the photo she showed us—and smiles around with a disarming grin.

"Hey," he says, lifting a hand to greet us all. "I'm Sam."

"Matt," says Matt, shaking hands with him.

"I'm Maud," says Maud, tossing back her hair and giving him a dazzling smile. "You're an accountant, right, Sam? That's *such* a coincidence. Because—"

"It's a coincidence because we don't need any accounting work doing," Nell cuts her off firmly. "At all. Do we, Maud? Hi, I'm Nell."

"Nihal," says Nihal shyly.

"Hi, Sam," says Topher. "Great to meet you. We were just talking about Marmite. Work of the devil, right?"

"No way!" says Sam, his eyes brightening in good humor. "I love Marmite."

"You're *Marmite lovers?*" Topher surveys him and Sarika with disfavor. "Well, no wonder the pair of you found each other. There are only two of you in existence. You revolt me."

"Have some tequila!" I add quickly to Sam, who looks a little nonplussed by Topher, as well he might. "I'm Ava."

"Sure," he says, then glances around the flat. "Amazing art, by the way. Oh, awesome robot," he adds, catching sight of Nihal's creation. "And I have to say . . . *what* a great dog."

———

Half an hour later, the truth has become apparent: Sam's perfect. He's absolutely perfect. Sarika is the queen of dating and the rest of us should all just give up.

He's witty, bright, obviously into Sarika, and has interesting yet palatable views. He's endearingly enthusiastic about his percussion playing, and he's fit, because he's climbed Everest. (Or maybe some portion of Everest. Whatever.)

We've reached the mellow, sitting-around stage of the party. Any minute now someone will suggest a curry or pizza. Maud's quizzing Matt about Harriet's House because—this is *so* Maud—she's only just clocked what Harriet's House actually is, by idly picking up Genevieve's book five minutes ago.

"Oh, *those* houses!" she exclaimed in astonishment. "*Those* dolls! I know those! They're really famous!"

"Maudie, what did you *think* we were talking about, this whole time?" said Nell in fond exasperation, and Maud replied vaguely, "Oh, I had no idea. I never know the names of things."

Now she's sitting next to Matt, saying things like, "So who chooses the curtains?" and "How do you choose the color of the dolls' hair?" while Matt answers patiently and I bite my lip.

"Hey, Ava." Nell's voice whispers in my ear. "Sam's a bit of a star, isn't he?"

She's come over to my side without my noticing and nods her head toward where Sam and Sarika are sitting together on the sofa, heads tilted toward each other, speaking in soft voices.

"He's *amazing*," I say in an undertone. "I bet he can cook."

"Of course he can cook!" says Nell, rolling her eyes. "Are you kidding? Sarika put in about ten cooking requirements. If the guy couldn't make risotto"—she draws a finger across her neck—"deal-breaker."

"Risotto!" I say, my eyes widening. "That's punchy."

"That's Sarika," counters Nell. "Knows what she wants. A guy who can make risotto."

We both turn to survey the happy couple again, and I notice that Sam has leaned even closer to Sarika. *I bet he knows who Ottolenghi is,* I find myself thinking—then hastily thrust the thought from my mind. It's irrelevant. Matt and I have a different kind of relationship. Not so matchy-matchy. More . . .

Well. More un-matchy-matchy.

"I mean, we were engaged, but only briefly. . . ." Matt's voice travels across the room, and I stiffen. What? Engaged? *What* is he saying?

"Engaged!" exclaims Maud with interest. "Ava never told us you'd been engaged."

"Well," says Matt, shifting uncomfortably on his seat. "It was only . . . I mean, 'engaged' is probably overstating it. . . ."

I'm blinking hard, my head trying to process this bombshell. Engaged? He was *engaged*? I suddenly remember asking Matt how serious it was with Genevieve and his answer: "Depends what you mean by serious."

How could that be his answer? Engaged is serious!

OK, I have to speak to him. Now.

"Oh, Matt!" I say, already on my feet. "I never told you

about . . . that thing you were asking about. That really important private thing that we need to discuss?"

As Matt turns his head, I shoot him my most fearsome daggers, and he blanches.

"Right." He swallows. "The thing."

"So shall we do it now?" I smile ominously at him. "Get it out of the way?" I'm already plucking at his arm, quite hard, and he gets up reluctantly. "Won't be a sec," I add over my shoulder to Maud. "It's just a private . . ."

"Thing," she supplies. "Yup. Got it."

I wait until we're both in the bedroom and the door is safely closed. Then I round on Matt.

"*Engaged?*"

"Just for twenty-four hours," he says hastily. "Less than twenty-four hours."

"To Genevieve?"

"Yes."

"And you didn't *tell* me?"

Matt stares at me, bewildered. "No! Why would I? We're not doing baggage, remember?"

"We're doing *some* baggage!" I almost explode. "We're doing context! You should have told me when we did those five extra questions. *That's* when."

"But you didn't ask, 'Have you been engaged?'" Matt says, looking flummoxed, and I suppress the urge to scream.

"OK." I try to speak calmly. "Let's start again. So, you were engaged to Genevieve."

"No!" Matt puts a fist to his head. "I mean, yes, strictly speaking; she proposed to me and it was very hard to say no. So for a matter of hours, yes, we were engaged. Until I broke up with her. But that was it. I mean, it really *was* it. Relationship over.”

“Right.” I’m still breathing hard, poised to fight, but I can’t think of my next move. Because this doesn’t actually sound *quite* as heinous as what I was imagining. (Genevieve at the altar and Matt backing away, still clutching his top hat.)

“I never bought her a ring, we never planned a wedding. . . .” He shakes his head. “It barely happened.”

“Did anyone know about it?”

“A few,” allows Matt. “My parents. Her parents. Her followers on social media.”

“A few?” I stare at him. “She has *thousands* of followers!”

“But they’ve all forgotten about it by now,” he adds unconvincingly. “It was like . . . a flash in the pan.”

He looks so troubled, I start to relent. Anyone can be engaged for twenty-four hours by mistake.

“OK, well, I’m sorry I overreacted. It’s just . . .” I hesitate, breathing out. “It’s quite hard, you know? Genevieve’s not like a normal ex, who disappears off the scene. She’s still around . . . your parents love her . . . you obviously had super-hot chemistry—”

“What makes you say that?” Matt stares at me, and I flush. That just kind of slipped out.

“I saw you in this video online,” I confess, feeling a familiar gnawing in my stomach as I recall it. “Doing a presentation with Genevieve about some new nautical line? And you were *awesome* together. You had such a spark. I guess it made me feel—” I break off, not knowing how to continue. Matt is peering at me, perplexed. Then his face clears.

"The presentation in Birmingham."

"Yes. The one where you kept finishing each other's sentences and you looked really happy," I add for good measure.

"I was happy," Matt says slowly. "You're right. But I was happy *professionally*. You don't know the backdrop. We'd had a lot of acrimony in-house. We'd lost a key member of staff. There was a lot of arguing about what direction we should go in. Then Genevieve came on the scene, she knew the fans, she got the brand—and we instantly agreed on a lot of issues. *Business* issues," he clarifies quickly. "She was a great new asset and it was a relief for me. I guess that's why I looked happy. Seems a long time ago now," he adds with a wry twist to his mouth.

I have a flashback to Topher talking about Matt being "stale" in his job. But I've said enough on that subject for one day.

"It can't just have been professional chemistry," I challenge him instead. "You fancied her too. And she fancied you."

"Well," says Matt, looking uncomfortable. "Maybe. But we weren't even a couple yet in that video. We were just two colleagues agreeing with each other."

"So how did it turn from business into romance?" I persist. "Did you ask her out? Or did she? Or what?"

"Ava." Matt surveys me seriously. "Do we need to do this?"

I open my mouth to say, "Yes!" then close it again, because I'm not sure it's the right answer.

"I'm with *you*," he continues. "I love *you*. We're hosting a party." He gestures with his arms. "We shouldn't be huddling in here, going over old ground; we should be out there enjoying ourselves. Everything's great and Genevieve is just a shadow from the past. Genevieve *who*?"

He draws me close for a slow, deep kiss, and I feel the Matt-magic working on me again. He has a point. Where are my priorities? I'd actually almost forgotten we were hosting a party, just for a minute.

"OK," I say at last, smiling up at him. "You're right. Genevieve *who*?"

"Exactly." Matt clasps me tightly, then releases me. "Shall we get back?"

As we head toward the others, I whisper to Matt, "Sam's pretty perfect for Sarika, isn't he?"

"Seems to be." Matt nods. "Good for her!"

We both sit down, and Maud shoots me a quick "Is everything OK?" look. I nod surreptitiously, then tune back into the conversation.

"I'm visiting her tomorrow," Sam's saying. "Just talking about my colleague," he adds to me in explanation. "She had a baby a couple of weeks ago. He's called Stanley."

"Stanley!" exclaims Nell.

"I know." Sam grins. "Great name, isn't it? I've just arranged to see them. Can't wait. I spent like an *hour* trying to choose a present." He rolls his eyes ruefully. "I was like, 'I'll be original. I won't just get some massive fluffy teddy bear.' But in the end what do I buy? A massive fluffy teddy bear."

"D'you want children, Sam?" says Nell provocatively. There's a tiny, tense pause—then Sam laughs, glances briefly at Sarika, and says, "One day. With the right person."

Oh my God. Just when I think he couldn't get any more perfect—he does!

"Shall we get some food? Like . . . pizza?" says Maud, looking around vaguely, as though hoping it might just spring up. Meanwhile, Sam turns to Sarika and touches her gently on the arm.

"D'you want to . . . We could go on somewhere?"

"Sure." She smiles happily at him. "Love to. I'll go and freshen up."

As she heads off to the bathroom, Nell addresses Sam again.

"That's very nice of you, visiting your colleague."

"Well, she's my neighbor too," explains Sam. "We both live right next to Queenwell Park—do you know it?"

"I thought you were five minutes from Golders Green?" says Nell, frowning.

"I was." Sam nods. "But I just moved. Last week."

"How close are you to the tube station now?" queries Nihal, who has been following this exchange with interest.

"Not sure," says Sam easily. "Maybe half an hour? But, you know, it's worth it for the extra space and greenery."

Beside me, Nell splutters on her drink, and Maud's head whips round. He lives *half an hour from the tube*?

"Does Sarika know that you've moved?" asks Nihal in a slightly strangled voice.

"Don't know," says Sam. "I'm not sure I've mentioned it to her yet."

As I look around the group, I can see identical expressions of somewhat hysterical consternation. Sam *can't* live half an hour from the tube. He *can't* be eliminated now.

"Sam, I really think you need to decrease your commute time," says Maud seriously. "For your own good. It should be your highest priority."

"I agree," chimes in Nell.

"I don't mind the walk," says Sam, shrugging. "It's not a problem."

"It *is* a problem!" Nell contradicts him forcefully, and he blinks in surprise. "It's more of a problem than you realize."

"Could you walk more quickly?" I suggest. "What road are you on?"

"Fenland Street," says Sam, looking a bit confused, and instantly Topher, Nihal, and Maud pull out their phones.

"I know that area," says Nell, summoning up a map. "What route are you using?"

"Down the hill," Sam replies. "Takes you straight there, pretty much."

"No," she says firmly. "Take Launceton Road. That'll shave off five minutes."

"Are you cutting through the shopping center?" chimes in Topher, squinting at his screen. "Because that'll cut down your time too. Are you jogging?"

"Jogging?" Sam looks startled.

"You should jog." Topher taps his chest. "Health."

"What about a skateboard?" suggests Nihal.

"Yes!" exclaims Topher. "Genius, Nihal. Use a skateboard," he instructs Sam. "Get you there in no time."

"A *skateboard*?" echoes Sam, looking around at our faces. "Listen, guys, I appreciate your suggestions, but—"

"If you use a skateboard and take Launceton Road, I reckon we've got it down to ten minutes," Nell says firmly.

"I'd say eight minutes with the skateboard," chimes in Matt. "You can power along on one of those things."

"Even better," says Nell. "Got that?" She swivels to Sam, who looks totally bewildered. "You're eight minutes from the tube. Remember that, Sam. *Eight minutes.*" She catches my eye and bites her lip, and I have a horrible feeling I'm going to burst into laughter, when Sarika appears and says brightly, "Ready to go, Sam—*aaargh!*" She suddenly screams in horror. "Harold! What the *hell?*"

"What's wrong?" I leap up in alarm. "Oh no!"

As I catch sight of Harold, my stomach swoops in horror. There's a dismembered furry paw sticking out of his mouth. It looks very much like the paw of a massive fluffy teddy bear. I glance beyond him and see a furry head lying on the floor, with two glassy eyes staring reproachfully at me. *Shit.*

"Oh God." I clasp my head. "Sam, I'm *so* sorry, he must have got hold of your teddy—"

"That *bloody* dog!" exclaims Sarika, making a swipe for Harold, who darts merrily away.

"Harold!" I say. "Drop! Drop it!"

"It's fine," says Sam, in a voice which suggests it's really not fine.

"Welcome to my world," says Sarika wryly.

"*Now* will you agree he's a bastard?" says Topher to me, but I ignore him.

"Come here, you bad dog!" Nell gets to her feet.

"Who's got a snack?" says Maud helpfully.

Soon all of us are pursuing Harold while he dances around the flat, occasionally dropping one piece of mutilated teddy bear, barking at us, then triumphantly grabbing another.

"We need to have a *strategy*," says Matt for the third time. "We need to form a circle around him . . . stay *still*, Harold!" As the landline phone rings, he turns his head briefly and says, "Get it, someone, will you?"

We approach Harold, who's clutching the teddy's head and eyeing us with bright defiance.

"We need to close in on him slowly . . ." says Matt in a low voice. "Then, when I say, 'Now,' we all make a grab. . . . Now!"

We all swipe for the teddy's head, Maud manages to grab it, and she starts a tussle with Harold.

"Drop!" she exclaims breathlessly. "Drop!"

"Drop!" I join in.

"Bastard dog!" says Topher, and Harold lets go of the teddy to bark at him.

"Got it!" exclaims Maud, lifting the dismembered, mangled head aloft while Harold's barking rises to a frenzy.

"Matt, it's for you." Sam tries to make himself heard over the racket. "Someone called Genevieve?"

Twenty-One

~~~~~~~~~

I mean, it's fine. Genevieve can phone Matt. In fact, Genevieve *has* to phone Matt, on occasion. They both work for the same organization and are obliged to be in contact. I do understand that. But I don't see why Genevieve has to call *quite so often.*

For a "shadow from the past," she's pretty bloody present. It's two weeks since the party, and since then she's been on the phone every night. Matt talks in short, sharp monosyllables, but still the calls seem to go on forever. Whenever I query them (in a lighthearted manner), Matt says, "We're doing a presentation together at the expo. We need to talk."

And then he looks beleaguered. And puts his golf ball for hours on end—which I've realized is not about enjoyment at all. It's stress relief.

Things are generally good, I keep reminding myself. The party was deemed a massive success—in fact, it went on till

2 A.M. and ended with everyone drunkenly swearing lifelong friendship. But I still feel tetchy. The more I watch Matt, the more I can see that Topher's right: He's stale. But I can also see how conflicted he is. Even I feel conflicted, and it's not my family company.

I mean, it's an amazing heritage. Whenever I see a Harriet's House ad on the TV, I feel a vicarious flicker of pride. But at the same time, I can't help resenting it. The day after our party, Matt had a closeted phone call with his parents, in which he told them he wasn't going to Japan, and ever since then he's been even less communicative than usual.

I haven't said a word on the subject, because Matt's been too preoccupied by the upcoming expo. But at last, thank God, Harriet's World day has arrived. Matt's event is at midday and we're in a taxi on our way to the venue, and then it will be over. Genevieve won't have an excuse to phone every night, and maybe Matt and I will sit down for a good talk. Meanwhile, I'm trying my hardest to keep an open mind. As our taxi drops us at the conference center, I notice a pair of girls walking toward us on the pavement, and I can't help gaping.

"Look!" I nudge Matt. "They've dressed up as Harriet."

"Oh. Yeah." He glances up without interest as they approach. "They do that."

Both girls have auburn wigs on, I notice as they get near. And turquoise shoes and dresses which they must have made themselves. How many hours did they devote to these outfits?

"Here's your VIP pass." Matt hands me a printed pass on

a lanyard, and I stare at it, slightly astonished. I've never had a VIP pass in my life.

"VIP, huh?" I say. "You do treat me well."

Matt laughs and gives me a kiss, which is interrupted by a voice saying, "Matt?" One of the girls has come to a halt nearby and is staring at Matt, bug-eyed. "Are you Matt Warwick?"

"Yes, I am." Matt smiles at her, looking uncomfortable. "Welcome to Harriet's World. Enjoy your day."

"Is that Genevieve?" asks the other girl, pointing at me in excitement.

"No," says the first girl. "They broke up. And Genevieve's blond. Don't you know *anything*?"

"So who's that?"

"Dunno." The first girl addresses me with an air of antagonism. "Who are you?"

"I'm Ava," I say, bewildered.

"We have to go now, guys," says Matt hurriedly. "Have a great day at Harriet's World. Catch you later."

"Wait, can I have a selfie?" says the first girl, and my jaw drops. A selfie? With *Matt*?

I watch as he poses awkwardly with each of the girls, then chivvies me into the conference hall through a side entrance. I'm already drawing breath to question Matt urgently, but as we step into the giant space, my queries melt away. Because . . . oh my *God*.

I'd pictured the expo, of course I had. But I hadn't imagined the *scale* of it. Everywhere I look, there are life-size dollhouse-room sets. Or stalls piled high with merchandise.

Or real-life Harriets walking around. It's all a little creepy, if you ask me.

"This way," says Matt, leading me briskly past the stands. But I can't stop swiveling my head to look at all the attractions: little stages with entertainers already in full swing, and cotton-candy stations, and life-size toy ponies standing in a life-size toy stable.

"You make *life-size toy ponies*?" I say incredulously, and Matt glances at them as though he'd never noticed them before.

"Oh. Yeah. I mean, we put on this expo in a few locations around the world, so it's cost-effective to produce them. I guess they're popular. . . ."

He's so dispassionate, I almost want to laugh. Everywhere I look I can see bright, exhilarated expressions—except on him.

As I'm glancing around, I notice that a few visitors are holding Genevieve's book. Oh God, she's probably here already, isn't she? We'll probably bump into her any minute.

"Matt." I tug at his arm so he stops walking. "I need some answers. What *was* that outside? Those girls."

"Oh," says Matt, after a pause. "That."

"Yes, that! Why were they talking about you and Genevieve breaking up? How did they even know about you?"

"OK," says Matt reluctantly. "Well, a few superfans are interested in the company. The history. The family. All that. They can't get enough of it. And they became . . . Well." He hesitates. "Invested in Genevieve and me. As a couple."

"*Invested?* Because, what, they saw you on social media?"

"I guess," he says, looking slightly tortured. "They followed us, they chatted on the forums. . . . For some people this is their major hobby. They dig in deep. I mean, it was Genevieve's thing more than mine," he adds, just as his phone rings. "Hey, Dad. Yes, just got here."

As Matt chats with his dad, I whip out my phone and do a quick, very specific google: **Matt Genevieve gossip breakup Harriet's House.**

I've googled Matt before (several times). But I obviously wasn't using the right search terms, because I *never* happened upon this stuff. There's a whole forum called "Harriet's House gossip." I stare at it in disbelief, then click on an old thread entitled **Genevieve and Matt . . . where are they at?**

At once I'm greeted by online howls of despair.

WHY DID THEY BREAK UP?????☹☹

I know. They were so cute!!!

The cutest EVER couple.

Who broke up, Matt or Genevieve?

Matt's gay, it's all a big cover-up, my bf works there and told me.

Who's going to the new Harriet Reveal Manchester event? Because I feel like boycotting right now? Just sad.

I guess it's their business?

It's our business too. I *follow* Genevieve.

I blink at the screeds of chat, then hastily click off. My head is whirling. I don't even know how to process this. Matt finishes his call and says to me, "OK, let's go to the Green Room." Then he looks at me again. "Ava? What's up?"

"Oh, nothing!" I say, trying to stay calm. "I'm only wondering, Matt, why you didn't tell me that a whole bunch of people were apparently devastated when you and Genevieve broke up?"

"Right." Matt looks evasive.

"Apparently you were the 'cutest ever couple'?"

"Ava, don't look at those gossip pages," says Matt, sighing. "It's just online rubbish in a tiny niche world. A few obsessive fans thought they owned us—oh, hey, Genevieve." His face tightens into a dreadful fake smile. "Good to see you."

Shit. She's *here*?

I wheel round to see a vision in pink, with clouds of blond blow-dried hair, accompanied by two guys in jeans with headsets. I recognize her from the book, but she's even prettier in real life. She looks phenomenal, I have to give her that, all petite in her perfectly fitting pink trouser suit and sky-high fuchsia heels.

"You must be Ava!" she exclaims, as though meeting me is the high point of her life. "So good you could come!"

"You too," I say feebly as we shake hands, and her face squashes up in mirth as though I've said something hilarious.

"They couldn't really stage the event without me, could they? Of *course* I will," she adds charmingly to a hovering little girl in a Harriet's House hoodie. "Just an autograph or would you like a selfie?" She poses immaculately with the awestruck child, then turns to Matt and says, "Let's hit the Green Room."

"Genevieve!" calls out a nearby girl. "Can I have a selfie?"

"Sorry, guys," says Genevieve regretfully. "Be back soon!"

As the two men in jeans silently accompany us through the crowds, I realize they're some sort of security. Genevieve is wearing a headset, too, I notice, and ducking her head as she walks along like some sort of A-lister. Meanwhile, every thirty seconds some nearby fan calls out, "Genevieve!" or tries to grab her. She's like the Beyoncé of Harriet's House. I don't know whether to laugh or be impressed.

The Green Room is a separate area from the conference hall, with sofas and a snack table, and it's stuffed full of people in suits. I recognize Matt's parents and Walter, talking intently on the far side of the room, but all the others are new to me. I guess they're all Harriet's House corporate types. Matt instantly gets swallowed up into a conversation and everyone greets Genevieve effusively, but she seems to want to stay with me.

"Let me get you some coffee, Ava," she says kindly, ushering me through the throng. "I expect you're overwhelmed! I remember my first Harriet's World Expo. I thought I'd died and gone to heaven. I was six," she adds with a laugh. "Hardcore fan here."

"How long have you been an ambassador?" I say, trying to make polite conversation.

"I started the YouTube channel five years ago." She smiles reminiscently. "But I've only been full-time ambassador for three years. It's gone stratospheric," she adds with satisfaction. "Matt must have told you."

"Not really," I say, and Genevieve's eyes flash in slight annoyance.

"Well, it has. I can say this to *you*. . . ." She leans forward as though imparting a delicious secret. "My commission is through the *roof*. There are some very big celebrity collectors. And I mean *huge*." She hands me a cup of coffee. "You'd be *amazed* if I could tell you. Obviously I can't, but let's just say, household names. Let's just say, private jets." She shakes her hair back and checks her reflection in the back of a teaspoon. "There's one celebrity I assist with her collecting—I mean, if you knew who it was, you'd *die*."

"Wow," I say, trying to sound suitably impressed. At once Genevieve's eyes narrow, as though she suspects I don't believe her.

"I can show you what she wrote to me," she says. "I can't show you her name, but I can show you the kind of relationship we have. I'm not just her Harriet's House consultant, we're *friends*."

She whips out her phone and finds a page, then shows it to me, one manicured thumb plastered firmly over the name at the top. There's one text, and it reads: Thanks, babe.

"See?" says Genevieve triumphantly. "I can't tell you her name, but that's an *A-lister*."

Plainly, she's waiting for a reaction. What am I supposed to do, fall to my knees and kiss the phone?

"Amazing," I say politely. "Well done you, for knowing celebrities."

"Well." Genevieve gives a self-deprecating laugh. "In a way, I *am* a celebrity. In an itty-bitty way." She laughs again and smooths down her hair. Clearly what she means is "in a gigantic, colossal way."

I've really had enough of this conversation, and I glance around to see if Matt is nearby. But to my dismay, Genevieve grabs my arm as though we're best chums.

"You're the one with the dog, aren't you?" she says cozily, as though Matt has ten girlfriends, all with different pets. "I heard how you ripped my face to bits." She tinkles with laughter. "*So* funny."

"It was an accident," I say, and Genevieve smiles kindly at me.

"Please. Ava. You don't need to feel threatened. You *mustn't* feel threatened! I said this to the last girl too. I said, 'Look, I'm close to the family, I *understand* the family, I dated Matt for longer than any other girlfriend . . . but at the end of the day, what does that mean? That I'm still in the frame? No! It's his life. He's out there, having fun before he . . .'" She gives an easy shrug. "You know."

Her words are shimmering through my head and I'm trying to unpick them, but she's such a pink, toxic presence, it's hard.

"No, I don't know," I say at last.

"Oh my God." Genevieve puts down her coffee, blinking innocently. "I'm not saying he's going to *end up* with me. That's not what I'm saying. Who am I? I'm out of the picture! Biscuit?"

"No thanks," I say, trying desperately to catch sight of Matt.

"His parents still keep in touch, though, isn't that sweet?"

continues Genevieve in musing tones. "They actually fill me in on his love life, which is *hilarious*. The girl he dated straight after me? The one he met doing martial arts? She was loopy." She gives me a conspiratorial smile. "Elsa was straight on the phone to me: 'Genevieve, what am I going to do?' And I said, 'Elsa my love, relax, it's just a fling—he's not going to *marry* her.' And then of course it ended so acrimoniously." She smiles sweetly. "I'm sure Matt's told you."

Her eyes are probing me as though to find a weakness. As though she already suspects I know less about Matt's past than she does. Well, she can sod off, because who had sex with him last night?

"Actually, we don't look backward," I reply in pleasant tones. "Because we have so much to look forward to in our beautiful future together. In fact, Matt's *so* uninterested in his ex-girlfriends that the subject never comes up. For example, I'm trying to think of the number of times he's mentioned you, Genevieve." I crinkle my brow thoughtfully. "Oh yes. None."

"Well." Genevieve's smile freezes. "If I can be any help, please let me know. Oh, Matt, there you are."

"Hi." As Matt joins us, his eyes swivel uneasily from Genevieve to me and back again. "So . . . you guys have been talking. Great."

"Yes, isn't it great?" I say. "*So* great. But I'll let you two get ready for the event now," I add, seizing the chance to escape. "Have fun!"

As I stride out of the Green Room, I'm breathing heavily.

What was that? She's the most narcissistic bighead I've ever *met*.

"Wait. Ava." Matt appears at my side, dodging a pair of handsome young men wearing heavy makeup, Harriet wigs, and sequined evening dresses. "Sorry. Sorry. I know she's—"

"Matt!" A young guy in a well-cut suit interrupts us and pumps Matt's hand cheerfully. "Great to see you."

"Hi, Mike," says Matt, brightening. "Didn't know you were coming over. This is Mike," he adds to me. "Runs U.S. marketing. Mike, Ava."

"Hi," I say, smiling politely.

"I had some meetings in London anyway," says Mike. "So I thought I'd take in the expo. . . ." He glances around at the milling crowds. "Attendance looks good. Any news on the Harriet movie release?"

Movie? Matt tells me *nothing*.

"Nothing recently," says Matt. "But you'll be the first to know."

"Sure." Mike nods easily, then adds in a lower voice, "I hear you're going out to Japan for a while, Matt? Reading between the lines, I think they need you out there. It's pretty chaotic. Everyone breathed a sigh of relief when they heard the news."

My eyes dart toward Matt, waiting for him to explain that he's not going to Japan, but his face has frozen.

"Right," he says at last, avoiding my gaze. "Well, it's a complex situation."

Complex? What's complex?

"Sure is." Mike glances at his watch. "Oh, I have to go. Great to bump into you! And to meet you, Ava."

He strides off with a cheery wave and I turn to Matt, determined not to overreact.

"He's got the wrong end of the stick somehow!" I say with a laugh.

"Huh," says Matt.

I wait for more, but it doesn't come, and I stiffen. What's going on?

"Matt, I thought you talked to your parents," I say as calmly as I can. "I thought you said you wouldn't go to Japan."

"I did," says Matt, avoiding my gaze. "I told them . . . I said it was suboptimal."

"*Suboptimal?*" I echo, dismayed. "But did you say you wouldn't go? Did you refuse?"

"I made my views crystal clear," says Matt after another pause. "But it's sensitive, it's tricky, we haven't found a solution yet. . . ." He screws up his face and rubs it briefly with a fist. "Look, Ava, let's not do this now."

"Do you *want* to go?" I say, feeling a clawing misery.

"No, of course not," Matt lashes back irately. "You know I don't."

"Well, then, you need to shut it down!" I say in agitation. "The longer you let them think you're going, the harder it'll be to pull out. Don't you see that?"

"I know." Matt looks wretched. "I'll do it. But it's not straightforward. In my family . . . talking is . . . It's not easy. It can go wrong."

He gazes at me as though expecting me to comprehend.

And I want to, but I don't. Yet again I feel as though I'll never understand where Matt comes from.

"How can *talking* go wrong?" I say helplessly. "How can *being truthful* go wrong?"

Matt sighs. "Come here." He reaches for me and pulls me into a tight hug. But I notice he doesn't answer either question.

Twenty-Two

～～～～～

It turns out Harriet's House gummies are pretty damn good. Half an hour later I've bought three packets and stress-munched them while walking around stalls, looking at all the dolls and houses and clothes and makeup.

Nell's right: This is a totally misogynistic, retrograde brand, unsuitable for feminists in this day and age. On the other hand, I can see why it's addictive. There are so many accessories. So many worlds. So many *outfits*.

When I reach the Animal Zone, I become transfixed by the display of toy dogs that Harriet and her various pals have had over the years. Because toy dogs are a whole different thing from dolls. They're noble. They're beautiful. Anyone might hanker after a toy dog. And I'm just asking the price of the beagle when jaunty music sounds through the loud-speakers, followed by an upbeat woman's voice:

"Our main event begins in three minutes! Warwick family members and Harriet's House ambassador Genevieve Hammond will be appearing on the main stage in three minutes! Come to the auditorium for today's big reveal, news announcement, and panel discussion with Genevieve!"

Around me I can see people scurrying toward the back of the conference hall. I'd almost forgotten about the big event.

"I'll come back later," I say hastily to the stall owner, and hasten toward the auditorium, along with everyone else.

As I arrive, I flash my VIP pass, and am directed to a special section at the front. It's pretty full, but there's a spare seat on the end of the third row and I perch on it, trying to look inconspicuous, just as the lights dim and thumping music starts.

"Ladies and gentlemen," says a hushed, disembodied voice, "welcome to this year's Harriet's World London Expo!"

At once, cheering and applause break out, and slightly reluctantly I clap along.

"And now I'm going to welcome our host to the stage . . . Genevieve Hammond!"

At once, screaming erupts. The music ascends to earsplitting volume, lights dance around the auditorium, and, looking like a rock star, Genevieve strides onto the stage.

"Hello, London!" she cries to the audience, her hair gleaming under the lights, and I can't help snorting. Hello, London? Seriously?

But the whole audience loves her. They're cheering and they've got their phones out and some are trying to take selfies with Genevieve in the background.

"I have so much to share with you today," she says, beaming around. "News, fun stuff, the big reveal you've all been waiting for . . ." She waggles her eyebrows teasingly, and a couple of girls whoop. "But first, I want to welcome onstage the people who began it all . . . the family we love . . . our very special guests . . . John, Elsa, and Matt Warwick!"

Music sounds again, and the next minute Matt and his parents walk onstage. Elsa is dressed in a purple suit and frilly shirt and looks absolutely thrilled to be there, if self-conscious. John looks resigned, and Matt is standing with hunched shoulders, as though he can't wait for the ordeal to be over.

"Mr. and Mrs. Warwick, Matthias . . ." begins Genevieve gushingly. "We are *so* honored to have you here. Writing my book, *Harriet's House and Me: A Personal Journey,* which I'll be signing later at a discounted expo price, no refunds, please leave five-star reviews online . . ." She draws breath and twinkles charmingly at the audience again. "Writing that, I was privileged to spend time with the Warwick family and learn about their legacy." She blinks earnestly at the crowd. "It all began back in 1927, when Gertrude Warwick constructed a wooden dollhouse for her daughter. And now the magic of Harriet's House has spread to every corner of the globe. You must be so proud of your heritage."

She hands a microphone to John and waits, smiling.

"We're very proud, yes," says John stiffly.

"Extremely proud," chimes in Elsa, grabbing the microphone from him. "And of course we're very proud of *you,* Genevieve, for writing your wonderful book."

She leads a round of applause, while Genevieve simpers.

"Well, you all helped me," says Genevieve, looking bashful. "Especially Matt, of course. Ladies and gentlemen, this man is a hero."

"I'm really not," says Matt, with a tight smile.

"It's true!" Genevieve opens her eyes wide. "He helped me so much with my research. And . . . this is no secret to any of you guys . . ." She lowers her voice to an emotional throb, looking around at the faces as though to make as much eye contact as possible. "He's helped me so much . . . *personally*. Harriet's House is about love and heart." She blinks earnestly at the crowd. "And this man is all about love and heart."

What? I stare at her furiously. She doesn't get to say Matt is about love and heart. *I* do.

Genevieve grasps Matt's hand and holds it up, and a cheer rises from the crowd.

"Get back together!" yells a voice from the rear, and Genevieve scrunches up her face as though she can't hear.

"Sorry? What are they saying?" she says to Matt, with a laugh.

"Get back together!" The voice increases in volume.

"We love you, Matt!" cries a girl about three feet from me.

"You're perfect together!" shouts another girl hysterically from across the room. "Genevieve and Matt forever!"

"Look, this really isn't what we're—" begins Matt, but Genevieve cuts straight across him. (I swear her microphone is turned up to a higher volume than everyone else's.)

"That would be lovely in so many ways." Her face droops a little sadly. "Because we *did* have a special magic together. But it's not meant to be. Is it, Matt? No matter what these guys think." She gestures at the audience with a rueful, wistful smile.

My entire face has flamed. *What* is she saying? *How* is this appropriate? In fact, why am I even sitting through this? Abruptly, I get to my feet, reach for my bag, and start edging along the side of the auditorium.

"Oh no!" Genevieve suddenly trills charmingly. "I'm *so* sorry. Ladies and gentlemen, I think we've upset Matt's new girlfriend. Ava, don't be shy, you're part of the Harriet's House family now!"

She gestures in my direction, and to my horror, a spotlight finds me. Immediately, the whole audience swivels round. And it's all very well Matt saying it's "online rubbish," but these people aren't online. They're right here, gaping at me and even taking photos.

"She's not that pretty, is she?" murmurs a girl in front of me to her friend, and I glare back indignantly.

"Hi," I say shortly. "I'm sorry, I have to go. Enjoy the show!"

I head to the door, murderous thoughts swirling round my head. All I can say is, there'd better be a Harriet's House bar and it'd better serve Harriet's House vodka and they'd better do double shots.

There is a Harriet's Bar, it turns out, and it's half empty, which I guess is because so many visitors have flocked to the main auditorium. It doesn't serve vodka, but it does sell "Bubblegum Bellinis," and I sit down on a barstool and order two in quick succession. I know I shouldn't let Genevieve get to me.

Or the superfans. Or this Japan business. But I can't help it: I'm bubbling over with stress.

Every time I discover a new layer to Matt's life, it's a more toxic, complicated layer. And he doesn't even seem to *see* it. He doesn't seem to *recognize* it. He walks around with blinkers on, like some sort of horse pulling a heavy wagon, and his job is the wagon. . . . No, his *family* is the wagon. . . .

Abruptly I realize I'm muttering to myself like a crazy person. I glance up, hoping that no one's watching me, to see a face I recognize. It's Matt's grandpa. What's his name again? Oh yes, Ronald. He's sitting at the other end of the bar, dressed in a pinstripe suit, drinking a glass of wine, and he's such an incongruous sight on his pink fluffy barstool, I can't help smiling. He catches my eye, clearly wondering if he knows me.

"I'm Ava," I say, sliding along to join him and extending a hand. "Matt's friend? We met at the Warwicks' house?"

"Ava!" His eyes brighten. "Yes, I remember. Are you enjoying the expo, my dear?"

"Kind of," I say. "Aren't you at the event? Everyone's onstage right now. Matt, his parents, Genevieve . . ."

"I know." A faint shudder passes across his face. "Very entertaining, I'm sure. It's the audience that I find difficult. They shriek."

"Yes," I agree. "They do. I guess you've been coming to the expo forever?" I add, as it occurs to me that Harriet's House has been his life too.

"Well." Ronald seems to consider this. "We didn't have an expo in my day. Everything was different. Less . . . *excitable*. I always come and see how things are getting along." He gestures vaguely toward the auditorium. "But I prefer to be out here." He lifts his glass to me in a toast and I follow suit. "And you?" he queries politely. "You didn't want to watch Matthias onstage?"

"I started watching. But . . ." I trail off and slump slightly. I don't particularly want to get into discussing Genevieve and her superfans.

"Another drink?" he asks, noticing my empty glass, and nods to the barman.

"Drowning our sorrows," I say, and it's meant to be a joke but comes out sounding more heartfelt than I meant.

"Indeed." Ronald smiles, but he sounds pretty heartfelt, too, and his hand trembles slightly as he lifts his glass.

Underneath his courteous demeanor, this elderly man seems just a bit fragile. I can remember Elsa shutting him up repeatedly at lunch, then Matt telling me that in his family, talking "isn't easy."

And suddenly I feel a surge of impatience. What *is* it with these Warwicks? Things *should* be talked about. Things should be out in the fresh air, not locked up to fester.

"May I ask you something?" I say, turning to Ronald. "You started telling me a story, the first time we met. Something bad had happened to you. But we got interrupted before you could finish. Well, we've got plenty of time now. And I wondered—only if you felt like it—could you tell me the story now?"

To say that Ronald looks startled is an understatement.

"You don't want to hear my troubles," he says at once, his eyes swiveling away.

"I do," I insist. "Really. We're not doing anything else, are we? And at the house I felt as though you wanted to share with someone. Well, here I am. Ready to listen."

It takes him a good half hour, what with repetitions and explanations, but at last he gets the sorry story out. And it really *is* a sorry story. It's a desperate story. It's the kind of story that makes you want to punch someone, hard.

Some people scammed him by pretending to be his doctor's surgery and requesting intimate photos of him, "for their records." After some puzzlement, he provided them— not consulting any other members of the family but instead feeling proud that he'd managed to use an iPhone.

As he tells me how the scammers then demanded fifty thousand pounds, I feel an incandescent rage. These people are evil. Who would even think of doing something like that? The police had to be involved, and he had to show the photos to his own children, and I can understand why he was mortified. Is still mortified.

"It's the *embarrassment,* you see." He smiles, but his pale-blue eyes are glimmering. "Everyone tells me to move on. But I look at myself in the mirror every morning and I think, 'You wretched old fool.' "

"How long ago was it?" I ask.

"A year ago or so," he replies, and I feel a pang. He's been miserable like this for a *year*?

"Have you spoken to a counselor about it?"

"A counselor?" He looks astonished. "Oh no."

"Have you talked to anyone about it? Like . . . John?"

"We don't . . ." He stops, then begins again, his eyes fixed on the bar. "My son is ashamed that I could have been so foolish. Quite rightly."

"I'm sure he isn't!" I say quickly, although I'm not sure at all. The embarrassment that was crackling around the lunch table at Matt's house makes more sense now. His family clearly didn't want Ronald downloading his story onto me. Maybe they thought it was inappropriate. I can hear Elsa's clipped voice now: *I hardly* think . . .

But where was their compassion? Where *is* their compassion?

"Ronald, if you ever want to talk, call me," I say impulsively. "I love talking. The more talking, the better. Shall I put my number into your phone?"

"That's very kind of you," says Ronald, watching as I input it. "You're a thoughtful girl."

"Not really," I say, wondering whether to tell him that "girl" isn't the correct word these days, then deciding against it. "I expect they've finished by now," I add, glancing at my watch. "I should go and find Matt. Are you coming to this lunch?"

"In a while," he says. "I might just sit here for a few more minutes." I hand him his phone back and he pats it. "Thank you. And you *are* a thoughtful girl. Matthias will miss you when he's in Japan."

Japan? *Again?*

I continue smiling, but my stomach has clenched. I was right. This thing is out of control. Matt needs to shut it down without delay.

"If he goes," I say casually.

"He's moving there, isn't he?" says Ronald, looking surprised. "They need him. I've heard all the plans."

"I think the plans are up in the air. I don't think it's definite."

"Ah." Ronald nods politely as though he doesn't want to contradict me. "I see. Well, enjoy your lunch."

The lunch is being held in an upstairs room. It's light and bright, filled with flower arrangements and tables covered with white cloths. Every table has a small model of a Harriet's House on it, and there are place cards with names on. A waitress is holding a tray of drinks, and as I enter I take a glass of wine, but I don't sip it. I'm too busy looking around for Matt.

"Ava!" A bright voice greets me from behind and I wheel round to see Genevieve bearing down on me, her cheeks flushed and her eyes sparkling. She looks wired, which is no surprise. "I'm *so* sorry to put you on the spot like that!" She tosses her hair back. "Had to improvise! The show must go on!"

"No problem." I smile tightly. "Well done. It was a really good event. Congratulations."

"Well, it's easy when I'm working with Matt," says Genevieve modestly. "We have a great rapport onstage. We're a natural duo. Everyone says so." She sighs with a happy air and looks around the space, which is filling up with people. "Aren't they wonderful?"

I don't know what on earth she's talking about. The flower arrangements? The chairs?

"Matt's family," she clarifies, gesturing at Elsa and John,

who are standing a few meters away, and I blink in shock. Matt's family? Wonderful?

"Sure," I say, and take a gulp of wine.

"Matt's a sweetheart, obviously, but his family are even lovelier. Elsa and John are like second parents to me," she adds in sincere tones. "They're so wise. And such fun!"

I know she's probably exaggerating to wind me up. But even so, I can't help feeling a twinge of sadness. Because that's exactly how I hoped I'd feel about Matt's parents. I *wanted* to love them. I *wanted* to bond and have little in-jokes. I was so optimistic. But, truthfully, I can't even imagine Elsa having an in-joke.

"I don't know them as well as you do," I parry. "Not yet."

"Well, they couldn't be sweeter. Elsa just gave me this—look!"

She shows me a brand-new watch on her wrist. It's baby-pink leather, covered in a flower print. Maud's four-year-old, Romy, would adore it. As I peer at it, a sudden thought crosses my mind and I look up.

"Matt told me you love his art collection, Genevieve?" I say lightly. "The Arlo Halsan pieces," I add, just to be totally clear. "The ones at his flat."

"Oh, I do." She nods vigorously. "I love his work!"

Ha. Ha! Caught her out. She does *not*. She cannot possibly like both a pink watch covered in daisies and a grotesque sculpture of a hairless wolf. It's not feasible.

"What exactly do you love about his work?" I press her, not bothering to hide my skepticism, but Genevieve doesn't seem to notice. She sips her drink, thinking.

"I love that it startles me but then makes me think," she

says at last. "I love that it's grotesque but beautiful. I love the concepts behind each piece. Although I think you have to read Arlo Halsan's autobiography to *really* understand what he's trying to do," she adds. "*Monster Dreams*. Have you read it?"

I'm having a horrible, terrible dawning as she talks. She genuinely does like the art. She likes it! As I gaze at her immaculate, pretty face, I feel a deep sinking inside. I don't want to compare myself to Genevieve. But, oh God. There she is, *oozing* compatibility with Matt-land. She adores Matt's art and his parents and his family business. She probably loves a well-trained dog, too, and a rare steak every night. And I don't like any of them.

"What about the naked saunas?" I say, sounding more confrontational than I meant to. "Did you ever get used to those?"

"Oh, I *love* being naked in the sauna!" says Genevieve earnestly. "So freeing. I think it's a wonderful tradition. I'm so grateful to Elsa and John for introducing me to it!"

What did I expect? Of course she loves the naked saunas. I expect she has gravity-defying boobs and is super-proud of her pubis. It probably has its own Instagram account.

"So, are you coming out to Japan with Matt?" Genevieve's chirpy voice interrupts my thoughts. "I've been looking at apartments to rent, but I don't know *where* to start."

"*You're* moving to Japan?" I stare at her stupidly.

"Didn't Matt say?" She blinks at me. "I'm writing a book about the Harriet's House phenomenon in Japan. I'll be in Tokyo to do my research. I'm going to use an office in the Harriet's House building. Oh!" She brightens as though with a new thought. "We can all hang out! If you come with Matt. Though maybe you can't get away from your work, Ava. Or your dog."

She tilts her head pityingly, a sly look in her eyes, and everything falls into place. I gaze back furiously, trying to transmit the words that are forming in my head. *I see you. You're planning the big Matt and Genevieve reunion in Japan, aren't you?*

"Yup," says Genevieve sweetly, as if she heard every word.

My hand is clenching my wineglass more tightly. How could Matt not have told me this?

"Matt!" Genevieve exclaims, and I whip round to see him approaching.

"Matt!" I say, a notch louder, and grab him by the arm. "Brilliant show . . . well done . . . Can I have a quick word?"

Without even looking at Genevieve, I hustle him away to a quiet place at the side of the room.

"Ava, I'm sorry," he says at once. "Genevieve shouldn't have mentioned you; they should never have beamed that spotlight on you—"

"It's fine." I brush his apology away. "But listen, Matt. Everyone thinks you're going to Japan. You need to put them straight."

"I know," he says after a tiny pause. "I will."

"But shouldn't you do it sooner rather than later?"

"It's fine," he says, and I feel a flare of frustration.

"Who says it's fine? Did you know Genevieve's planning to hang out with you in Tokyo? Even your grandpa thinks you're going!"

"Well, they're wrong," says Matt.

"Then tell them!"

"Canapé?" A waitress interrupts us, proffering a tray. "We have mini Yorkshire puddings with beef or spicy fish rolls."

"No thanks," I say, as Matt takes a fish roll. "I'm vegetarian."

"*Vegetarian?*" The waitress surveys me in alarm. "We weren't told there was a vegetarian guest. I'm not sure . . ."

Matt sighs. "Sorry, Ava. I'll talk to my mother."

"No, no," I say hurriedly. "It's fine. I'll just have some vegetables."

"Right." The waitress still looks anxious. "Only, the vegetables are poached in chicken stock and finished with a veal glaze."

Of course they are. I expect the profiteroles are garnished with pork pies.

"Please don't worry," I say. "I'll have . . . Is there a parsley garnish? I'll have that."

The waitress moves off, still looking troubled, and Matt says, "Sorry. This is my fault. I should have reminded my parents you were vegetarian."

"It's OK," I say automatically. But deep down, I feel as though nothing's OK. I feel . . . what exactly?

Hurt, I suddenly realize. I'm hurt by Genevieve's goading and Matt's parents' indifference to me and Matt's refusal to deal with this Japan situation. I'm even hurt on Ronald's behalf.

As I'm examining these feelings, one by one, Matt's parents come up, both flushed in the face.

"Wonderful show!" exclaims Elsa to Matt, ignoring me completely. "They loved you, Matthias! And Genevieve was a rock star! This new project of hers will be tremendous. The Japanese fan base is *so* passionate. . . ." She shakes her head wonderingly. "Well, you'll find out yourself, Matthias, when you're out there—"

"Matt's not going to Japan." My voice utters the words before I can stop it.

For a second no one moves. Elsa looks thunderstruck, and I feel a small flurry of nerves mixed with glee.

"Yes!" I continue, trying to sound like I'm just being chatty rather than landing a bombshell. "We were talking about it and Matt said he didn't want to go. Didn't you, Matt?"

Matt's silent, and my stomach plunges.

"At least, that's the impression I got. . . ." I glance desperately at Matt, but he doesn't even meet my eye.

"Yes, well," says Elsa, her face closing up tightly. "We'll discuss all these matters another time. Enjoy your lunch." She shoots me a flinty smile and stalks away, followed by John, and I turn to Matt in despair.

"Why didn't you back me up?"

"Why didn't you just keep your mouth shut?" he retorts in a furious undertone. "Jesus, Ava, we're about to have lunch! I have to be diplomatic! This is my family firm!"

"More like your family prison!" I spit back. And I know I was going to wait till later, but I can't stop my words tumbling out. "Matt, you're so careful of your parents' feelings, but they're not careful of *your* feelings! They take you for granted! I know you took on this job for all kinds of good reasons: your heritage, your brother—"

"My brother?" Matt's face jolts, and I see a wounded look in his eyes. Oh God. I was right. He is raw. "What's my *brother* got to do with anything?"

"Don't know." I backtrack quickly. "No. Nothing. I didn't . . ." I clear my throat, trying to regroup. "Look, Matt," I say more calmly. "I'm sorry I blabbed about Japan. But *someone* had to say it, didn't they?"

I gaze at him desperately, willing him to respond, to soften. For us to be us. But Matt's not even looking at me. He appears . . . agonized. And as I gaze at him, a terrible feeling comes over me. The most hollowing realization. Oh God, I've been a fool. . . .

"Matt . . ." I swallow, barely able to say the words. "*Are* you going to Japan?"

"No!" he says at once, but his face isn't saying what his voice is.

"Are you?"

"I'm . . . That's not the plan."

"*Are* you?" My voice is suddenly shaky. "Matt?"

My thoughts are skittering around in a kind of panic, because how can I be so out of the loop? How can he be making momentous decisions without any reference to me? Aren't we a team? Aren't we a couple?

I open my mouth to say something—but discover I'm out of words. I can't do this anymore. All I really want to do is go home and hug my dog.

"I'm not hungry," I say. "Please apologize to your mother. I think I might leave now."

"Ava—" He looks desperate. "Please don't leave—"

At that moment, a fork tinkles on a glass and Matt automatically looks around to see who it is, and I dart away, almost running out of the room. Within thirty seconds I'm on the staircase down to the main conference area, and I'm not expecting him to come after me. I'm not even hoping.

Twenty-Three

OK, I was hoping. Because I always hope. It's my inner optimistic Alice.

But at the same time the Red Queen has been muttering meanly, *He won't come after you, don't be so stupid.* And of course she's right. I get downstairs without any hand touching my shoulder. I get through the crowded conference center without any urgent voice calling me from behind. I make it down the road without hearing frantic footsteps and Matt's voice yelling, "Wait! Ava!"

It's only when I'm on a bus back to north London, slumped in my seat and staring out of the window in utter misery, that the text messages start arriving.

I'm sorry.
I'm leaving as soon as I can.
We need to talk.
Are you there? Where are you?

As I read his missives, one after another, I can feel his distress through the phone. I don't think he's ever sent me this many text messages at once. And I can't help it, I feel myself softening. After a moment's thought, I type a reply:

OK, I'll go to your place. Let's talk there.

I head to his building, let myself in with my key, and make a piece of toast to make up for the missing lunch. I can hear music coming from Topher's bedroom, but the door is shut, for which I'm thankful. So I just walk around, my hands clenched, my head swirling with dark, upsetting thoughts.

I've said, "Let's talk," but what do I even mean by that? Where do we start? If Matt won't share something so important as moving to Japan, what chance do we have? Doesn't he want a joint future? What does he think is going *on*?

I could get over him eating meat, I find myself thinking in a frenzied whirl. I could try to be tidier. I could find another joint hobby for us, bond with his parents, master golf. . . . We could overcome those obstacles. But *moving to Japan*? Without *discussing* it?

His texts are still coming in, but I can't deal with them, so I turn off my phone. The more my thoughts swirl around, the more stressed out I'm becoming. Right now it feels as if Matt-land and Ava-land are on totally different sides of the world. They're completely alien to each other. And Matt's just fired a missile over my airspace.

Yes. I feel a sudden whoosh of comprehension. That's what's happened. He's launched a socking great cruise missile at me. But now he's behaving like, "What's the problem?"

So my dilemma is, do I get out my nuclear missiles? Are we at war?

Wait. Do I have nuclear missiles?

I feel a little unclear on this, because I am naturally a pacifist, but on the other hand, I need to do something. I need to retaliate *somehow*—

The doorbell rings and my chin jerks up defensively. Why's he ringing the doorbell? Is he making a point? I stride to the door and swing it open, ready to make some barbed, pithy comment—but my words wither on my lips and I blink in astonishment.

There's a girl standing in front of me. (No, not girl. Woman. I shouldn't say "girl," even in my thoughts. A female, let's say.) There's a female standing silently in the hall, surveying me with raised quizzical eyebrows. And I know her. Don't I? She has tawny, feathery hair and very white teeth and she looks *so* familiar, but I can't quite place her. . . .

"A guy let me in downstairs," she says, and the sound of her voice triggers a rush of instant, comprehensive recall. It's Lyric. From the writing retreat.

Lyric? *Here?*

"Hi, Aria," she says, with the slightly aggressive manner I remember her using in Italy. "I heard you two got together. Didn't expect you to last, though."

My jaw has fallen open. My mind is scrabbling about. *What* is this conversation? Lyric seems to understand it perfectly, whereas I'm flailing in bafflement.

"What's your real name?" she adds. "Someone told me, but I forgot."

What's happening? Am I dying and everyone from my life is appearing before me, starting with complete randoms? Because I can't think of any other reason that Lyric should be here on the doorstep. She only stayed on the course for an afternoon. I'd forgotten all about her.

"I was in London," she says, as though realizing I need an explanation. "Thought I'd swing by."

"Do you . . ." I swallow. "Do you know Matt?"

"Do I know Matt?" She gazes at me incredulously. "*Do I know Matt?* Oh my God." A smile of relish curves across her face. "He didn't *tell* you? That's hilarious. We were to-ge-ther. We were a cou-ple."

She enunciates the words in slow, deliberate tones, as though I have a low IQ, and I flinch, even as my brain is groping for answers.

"Is your name Sarah?" I ask, in sudden realization.

"Is my name Sarah?" She gives a throaty laugh. "Yes, *genius*. I'm Sarah. Matt and I were together. Lo-vers," she adds, savoring the word.

I have an unwanted vision of her slithering round, naked, with Matt, and I close my eyes, trying to get rid of it. Because things were shitty enough without this.

"We were going to give it another chance on that retreat," Sarah continues, clearly enjoying her story. "But then we couldn't stop arguing, so I was like, 'Fuck off, then.'"

I'm feeling a bit faint. They were a couple? All that time, while we sat in the monastery in our pajama suits, thinking we were all strangers . . . they were a *couple*? And Matt said *nothing*?

"I mean, I knew *that*," I say, trying my hardest to regain some ascendance. "I knew *that*."

"No you didn't." Her eyes mock me pityingly. "Anyway, I'm in London and I just wanted to swing by. Tell Matt I'm engaged."

She waves a ring at me, her eyes flashing in triumph. I dimly register that it's a band of yellow stones and that I really don't like it. (Which isn't the point, but you can't help what your brain thinks.)

"Congratulations," I say numbly.

"Yeah, thanks. Met him in Antwerp. He's Dutch. *Actually* Dutch. Not like, 'Call me Dutch.'" She gives a little laugh with an edge to it. "Speaking of which . . . when will Matt be back?"

"Don't know. Not for a while. Not for hours, in fact." I take a step forward, trying to force Lyric backward into the hall. Because it's come to me that I really, *really* want her to leave. "I think you should go now," I add for good measure. "I have things to do. So. Goodbye."

She takes a step back but then pauses, her eyes running over me as though for enjoyment.

"Fine. I'm off." She shrugs. "You'll tell Matt I was here?"

"Oh yes," I say, with a slightly savage smile. "I'll tell him."

As the door closes, there's a kind of buzzing getting louder in my ears. I think I'm going a bit mad. I knew Lyric was attracted to Matt at the retreat. I could tell by how she looked at him in that fixated way. But how could I ever have imagined she was attracted to him *because she was his lover*?

Everywhere I turn, I feel wrong-footed. I think I've got a

handle on who Matt is, I think I understand him and his life . . . but then something else weird pops up. Secret discussions. Private decisions. Girlfriends he never thought to mention. Why didn't he tell me? I feel like screaming. Why the hell didn't he *tell me*?

Hardly knowing what I'm doing, I pick up his putter, which is resting against the wall. His stupid bloody putter, symbol of his misery. I lift it high in the air and thwack the leather footstool. And it's such an excellent feeling that I do it again and again, venting my frustration, my bewilderment, my anger, until my muscles are aching, until I'm panting hard, until—

CRASH!!!

I don't know what hits me first: the smashing sound or the realization that the putter has slipped out of my hands on the backswing. For a moment I'm so shocked that I can't even imagine what destruction has happened behind me. Broken vase? But there aren't any vases in the hall. There's only—

There's only—

Oh God.

No.

Hyperventilating, hardly daring to move, I slowly turn round to see what I've done—and it's so terrible I think my legs might give way.

I haven't.

Please, *please* say I haven't. . . .

But I have. It's a nightmare, right in front of my eyes. I've smashed the raven. Matt's precious, beloved work of art. Only one fragment remains on the wall; the rest is pulverized. There's a broken piece of wing and a human tooth right by my foot, and I shrink away with a shriek, part revulsion, part dismay at myself, part just anguish.

Could I mend it? But even as the thought passes through my brain, I know it's ridiculous. As I pick up the putter and survey the black smithereens scattered across the floor, I feel utterly sick. I didn't mean to, I didn't mean to . . .

Then my stomach heaves as there's the sound of a key in the lock. The front door is opening, but I can't move. I'm paralyzed, clutching the putter, like the murderer at the crime scene.

"Ava," Matt greets me—then stops dead. His eyes widen and darken as they take in the scene of carnage. I hear him emit a tiny sound of distress, almost a whimper.

"I'm sorry," I gulp. "Matt, I'm so sorry."

Slowly, his aghast eyes travel to the putter in my hand.

"Jesus." He wipes his face. "You . . . you did this?"

"Yes," I admit in a tiny voice.

"But how? What were you *doing*?"

"I was . . . angry," I begin in faltering tones. "Matt, I'm so sorry. . . ."

"You were angry?" Matt's voice rockets in horror. "So you destroy a piece of *art*?"

"God! No!" I say in equal horror, realizing how I'm misrepresenting myself. "I wasn't aiming at the *art*. I was hitting the *footstool*! I just . . . I don't know how it happened. . . ." I trail off in misery, but he doesn't respond. I don't think he's even listening.

"I know you didn't like it," he says, almost to himself. "But—"

"No!" I say in dismay. "Please listen! It was an accident! I was in a state! Because I get back here from the expo and the doorbell rings and who is it? Your former girlfriend, Sarah. Or should I say *Lyric*? I had no idea who she was, and I felt like a total, utter fool—"

"*Sarah?*" Matt looks shattered. "Sarah was *here?*"

"Didn't you bump into her? She only just left."

"No. I didn't." Looking shaken, he sinks onto the same leather footstool that I was whacking five minutes ago. "Sarah." He closes his eyes. "I thought she'd disappeared. Moved to Antwerp."

"She's engaged. She came here to gloat, basically."

My eyes feel hot and I blink a few times. I know he has the moral high ground right now. But don't I have it too? Just a bit?

"Engaged." He lifts his head a smidgen. "Well, that's something."

"So, you were with her in Italy." I look away, hunching my shoulders. "Did you sleep with her right before you slept with me?"

"No!" Matt raises his head, looking appalled. "God, no! Is that what she said? We weren't together by then. She stalked me! She just turned up on the martial-arts course. I hadn't even told her I was doing it. I *still* don't know how she found out. She wanted to get back together; I kept telling her it was over. . . ." His eyes suddenly flash with memory. "Remember when I did my monologue about trying to escape someone? How a person wouldn't leave me alone? That was *her*! That was for *her*!"

I remember Matt lashing out furiously, unable to articulate his frustration. I mean, it makes sense.

"But why didn't you *tell* me?" I say, feeling like a broken record. "Why didn't you *tell* me any of this?"

"Because we weren't talking about exes!" Matt lashes back hotly. "Remember? Then we got back here to the UK and I hadn't heard from her . . . and you reacted so badly to Genevieve. . . ." Matt rubs his face. "Sarah was gone. I thought she was gone."

"But she wasn't gone, was she?" I say slowly. "Because baggage never is gone. You can't just pretend it is. It catches up with you."

I'm feeling a kind of ripping sensation inside. Like all my thoughts are tearing apart, exposing how badly they were joined together in the first place. I've been wrong. Wrong about everything.

"God, I'm stupid," I say in despair.

"No you're not," says Matt, but he sounds automatic rather than convinced.

"I am. I thought we could have a relationship without baggage. I thought it would be all light and free and wonderful. But Topher's right, it's impossible. When I look at you, Matt, I can see suitcases all around you." I wait until he raises his head, then gesture with my arms. "Heavy, bulky, awkward suitcases everywhere, all in a mess, spilling out crap. Japan . . . Genevieve . . . your parents . . . Lyric . . . And you don't take *ownership* of them," I add, with rising agitation. "You don't even *look* at them. You just go and putt golf balls and hope they'll sort themselves out. But they won't! You need to sort your life out, Matt. You need to sort out your own life."

There's silence for a few seconds. Matt is staring fixedly at me, breathing hard, his face unreadable.

"Is that so?" he says at last, his voice ominous. "Is that so? You think I'm the only one who needs to sort their life out? You want to hear about *your* suitcases, Ava?"

"What do you mean?" I say, startled.

"You've got so much shit in suitcases, I don't know where to start." He counts off on his fingers. "Novel. Aromatherapy course. Rescue furniture. Fucking . . . *batik*. Dog who won't do what he's told. Unsafe windows. Unpaid bills mixed up with, I don't know, horoscopes. Your life's a mess. It's a bloody mess!"

My life's a *what*? Somehow, through my shock, my brain pieces together a reply.

"I have a portfolio career," I say in my most lacerating tones. "Which might be challenging for you to comprehend, Matt. But I wouldn't expect you to understand how I live, because you have a very closed mind."

"Well, if you ask me, Ava, your mind's *too* bloody open!" Matt explodes. "It's open to every flotsam-and-jetsam piece of crap out there! You make a new plan every week. But you really want to achieve any one of these aims you claim to have? Then *focus*. Focus on one of them. Finish the aromatherapy course, find some clients, and *be* that. You'd be great. Or do the podcast. Or write your novel. Pick one and make it happen. Stop explaining how impossible it is, stop making endless excuses, stop faffing around . . . and just do it!"

Blood is beating in my cheeks as I stare back at him. I don't make endless excuses. Do I?

Do I?

"You've never . . ." I pause, trying to keep my voice steady. "You've never said that before."

"No. Well. Sorry."

He doesn't sound remotely apologetic. He sounds matter-of-fact. Like he's saying real stuff. Like he's finally saying what he thinks instead of what he thinks I want to hear.

"That's what you've thought of me all this time?" I say, my head feeling hot. "That I'm a flake?"

"I haven't thought you're a flake," says Matt. "But I've thought it's a shame. You could get somewhere, you know?"

The remaining piece of sculpture falls off the wall with a little crash, and we both jump, then stare at it lying on the floor.

"It was an accident," I say yet again, but my voice is hopeless, and I'm not sure I even believe myself.

"There *are* no accidents," chimes in Topher, whizzing into the hall on a child's scooter, then stopping abruptly as he sees the damage. He glances swiftly from me to Matt, and I can see him taking in the situation. "I mean, there are," he amends. "There are accidents that are just accidents. They have no other significance."

"Huh," says Matt gruffly. I can't even bring myself to answer. Topher looks from me to Matt and back again, his expression suddenly stricken.

"Don't break up, guys," he says quietly, and he sounds more sincere than I've ever heard him. "It's not a breakup thing. Whatever it is."

I don't move a muscle in response, and neither does Matt. My eyes are locked on his. We could be in a martial-arts ring.

Without saying another word, Topher backs his scooter out of the hall, and a few moments later there's the sound of his bedroom door closing. And we're still staring each other down.

"Is this a breakup thing?" says Matt at last, his voice flat. "Because I don't know what the fuck the rules are."

"I don't *have* any rules," I say, feeling instantly prickly.

"You don't have any rules?" He stares at me with scathing incredulity. "Ava, you have nothing *but* rules. Jeez! 'We're not telling each other anything. Now just one fact. Now five questions.' I can't keep up. I don't know where I am."

"*You* don't know where you are?" I feel white-hot with rage. "*You* don't know?"

I'm fighting two strong impulses. An impulse to make up and an impulse to hurt him the way I've been hurt. I guess the hurt impulse is just more powerful.

"I thought I didn't have any deal-breakers." My words burst out of me in a wounded stream. "I didn't even believe in them. But you know something? If I was looking at an online profile and it said, 'By the way, I'll lie about my ex-girlfriend and plan to move to Japan without mentioning it,' that would be a deal-breaker. Sorry to be blunt," I add, with an edge to my voice. "But that's just how it is."

Matt's eyes move slowly around the hall, over his ravaged art, and back to me.

"Well," he answers tonelessly. "If I read, 'I'll smash up your art with a golf club,' that would be a deal-breaker for me. I'd click on to someone else like that."

He snaps his fingers, and the sound is so dismissive, my heart spasms. But I manage to keep my face steady.

"OK." Somehow I find a shrug. "Well, I guess we know the truth now. We didn't fit all along."

"I guess we do."

I want to cry. My throat is so tight, it's painful. But I would die rather than dissolve into sobs. Carefully, I place the putter on the leather footstool.

"Sorry about the art," I say, my voice barely a husk.

"No problem," says Matt, almost formally.

"I'll get my stuff." I stare at the floor. "And I'll clean up this mess, obviously."

"Don't worry about that."

"No. I insist."

There's a short silence and I survey the scuffed toes of my shoes in a weird, surreal daze. My life just shattered, but somehow I'm still standing upright. So. Silver lining.

"So, what, are we breaking up?" says Matt, a harsh heaviness to his voice. "Or 'having some space'? Or what?"

"You're planning to go to Japan, Matt," I say, feeling suddenly bone-weary. "You're planning to live on the other side of the world for a year. What difference does it make what we call it?"

Matt draws breath to make some response but seems to change his mind. At that moment his phone rings, and he glances at it in irritation—then his face jolts.

"Hi," he answers, looking confused. "Matt here." He listens for a minute or so, then winces. "Shit. *Shit.* That's . . . OK. She's here." He offers the phone to me, looking grave. "They couldn't get through to your phone. It's Maud. Nell's been taken to hospital with chest pains. They think you should go. Right now."

"Oh God. Oh *God* . . ." My heart thumping in panic, I make to grab the phone, but Matt puts a hand on my arm.

"Let me take you," he says. "Please. I'll go with you. Even if we're not together . . ." He stops. "I can still . . ."

His face is so grave, so honest, so exactly the face I wanted to love, that I can't bear it. I can't be near him. I can't even look at him. It's too painful. I have to leave. Now.

"Please don't bother yourself, Matt," I say, swiveling away, each word like a needle in my throat. "It's not your problem anymore." As I reach the door, I shoot him one last glance, feeling my heart implode with sadness. "It's not your life."

Twenty-Four

~~~~~~~~~~~~~~~~~

Seven months later

A shaft of afternoon sunlight is falling on my table as I type my final words. The days are getting longer, the air warmer, and spring flowers are everywhere in the olive groves. Spring in Puglia is enchanting. Scratch that—every season is enchanting.

Winter had a few bone-chillingly cold days, to be fair. And some wet spells. Rain clattered down outside while I wrapped myself in blankets and lived in my sheepskin boots and huddled by the fire every night. But it was still magical. And it was worth it. It's all been worth it for this moment.

The End, I type carefully, and feel a knot of tension unravel deep within me. I rub my eyes and lean back in my chair, feeling almost numb. Eighty-four thousand words. Six months. Many, many hours. But I've done it. I've finished a first draft. A rough, scrappy, patchy first draft . . . but still.

"Finished, Harold!" I say, and he gives a celebratory bark.

I look around the room—the monk's cell, to be literal—

that's been home ever since I arrived here, back in October. Farida was waiting at the monastery door to welcome me with a tight hug and encouraging words. Since then, she's kept me constantly nourished with food and warmth and inspiration, not to mention a few bracing pep talks whenever I've lost motivation.

I'm not the only participant to have come back for what Farida calls an "extended self-guided writing retreat." There was a guy here before Christmas, working on an updated edition of his anthropology textbook, in a room across the courtyard. But we didn't chat. Or eat together. Or even communicate, really. We both just got on with it.

I've never felt so immersed in anything in my life. I've spent seven days a week thinking, writing, walking, and just staring up at the sky. The sky can take a lot of staring at, I've discovered. I'm the first guest to have spent Christmas at the monastery, and I think my request to stay here took Farida by surprise.

"Don't you have . . . ?" she began delicately, but I shook my head.

"I've got no family, really. And, yes, my friends would love to see me, but I think they'd love it even more if I stayed here, kept going, and achieved what I want to achieve." At which she clasped my hand and said I'd be very welcome, and it would be a quiet Christmas but a rewarding one.

It was after Nell got out of hospital and was safely home that I finally tackled the question burning in my soul. She was still on the fragile side and quite stroppy about needing lots of rest, but none of us minded her irascible outbursts. We were just so relieved that her attack had been diagnosed *not* as a potentially fatal cardiac arrest (OK, maybe that was just my fear) but as some sort of heart inflammation with a lengthy name and treatment plan.

It had been a long seven days, during which time I'd been processing not just the Nell situation but the whole Matt situation. The whole life-feeling-like-it-was-over situation. The whole big-black-hole-of-despair situation. To be fair, a hospital is a good place to be if all you can do is keep dissolving into tears. People leave you alone or steer you gently to a chair.

(Except that hospital chaplain who kindly started chatting, got the wrong end of the stick, thought I was grieving for a dead husband called Matt, and started praying for his soul. It was all very awkward, and thank God for Maud coming along at the right time and asking if he knew anyone in the Vatican, because she had a *tiny* little favor she wanted to ask.)

So anyway. Nell was back home and one night it was my turn to stay over. We were watching TV on the sofa with Harold when I drew a deep breath and said, "Nell. D'you think I'm flaky?"

"Flaky? No," said Nell at once, in forthright tones. "You're the most reliable friend in the world."

"No, that's not what I mean. D'you think I'm flaky about my career? Or, like, all my plans?"

This time there was silence as Nell stroked Harold's ears and considered.

"I mean, you're scatty," she said at last. "You're capricious. Changeable. But that's why we love you. You always have a new idea, and you're *so* passionate about them all."

"But I never see them through," I said, and Nell propped herself up on her elbow to stare at me.

"What is this? Ava, don't beat yourself up! It's who you are, sweetie. It's lovely! It's you!"

"But that's not who I want to be," I said, with a sudden fierceness that surprised even me. "I want to finish something, Nell. Really finish it. I started a novel, I went to Italy, I had a plan. But I got distracted. Like I always do."

Then there was another silence, because we both knew what had distracted me in Italy, and we weren't going there.

"I want to finish something," I repeated, staring ahead, my jaw set. "I want to get something done. For once."

"Right," said Nell slowly. "Well, good for you. How are you going to do that?"

"Don't know yet."

But already the idea was taking shape in my mind.

The next night, after I'd eaten supper, I sat at my kitchen table. I did some sums. I looked up pet passports. And I thought. I thought for about three hours, till my legs ached and my shoulders had frozen and my chamomile tea had gone cold and Harold was whining to go out. But by then I knew. As I walked him along the chilly midnight street, I was smiling, even exhilarated, because I had a plan. Not a little plan: a huge, ambitious, drastic, exciting plan.

And once I told the others about it, they embraced it even more enthusiastically than I had. I mean, you'd have thought it was Maud's idea in the first place, from the way she reacted.

"Ava, my darling, of course you must go!" she exclaimed.

"Of course you must. And don't you worry about a thing. You've done *so* many favors for me over the years, it's payback time. I'll keep an eye on your flat, water your plants, upcycle those bits of furniture I've been meaning to do, keep it tidy, that kind of thing. I love playing house with other people's things," she added with a beatific smile.

"Maud!" I said, slightly stunned at her altruism. "You don't need to do that."

"*Darling.*" She gave me a fond hug. " 'From each according to his ability, to each according to his need.' I heard that the other day. Isn't it fab?"

"That's Karl Marx," said Sarika faintly.

"Maud, you are *not* a Communist," Nell said in outrage. "Do *not* start pretending you're a Communist."

"I'm not anything!" Maud blinked at her. "You know that, Nell, my love. Except founding member of the Ava-writing-her-book support group."

"The most important thing is, we won't disturb you, Ava," said Sarika, hauling the conversation back on track. "We're here when you need us, but if you need to ignore us, that's fine too."

"Take as long as you like." Maud nodded. "Focus on what you're doing. Don't worry about anything else. It'll be great! Only, *don't* meet anyone," she added sternly. "Or you'll never finish."

"I won't." I rolled my eyes. "No chance."

Buoyed by their support, I then negotiated an unpaid sabbatical with Brakesons. I'd actually planned to hand in my notice. It was the head of department who offered a sabbati-

cal and said it would look good as data in their new Staff
Flexibility and Welfare initiative and would I mind writing
five hundred words about it for the recruitment webpage?

So it was all set. I couldn't have had second thoughts even
if I wanted to. But the truth is, I never did. Sometimes life
just needs to swerve a new way.

I let my gaze drift over my screen, over the story I've been
telling these last few months. It's not about Clara or Chester.
I got sick of them, and what the hell do they know about life
anyway, with their corsets and hay wagons?

It's about Harold. And me. It's the story of our relationship from the first moment I saw him and experienced an
overwhelming, instant love. I didn't know how much I had to
say about Harold till I started writing, and then I couldn't
stop. I could write six books about him. It's funny in parts,
because Harold has done some outrageous things (I'm really
quite embarrassed), but it's also painful. Because that's what
life is like. And you can't talk about dogs without talking
about life. I've written about my parents. And my childhood.
And . . . stuff.

Matt's in it, too, though I've changed his name to Tom.
And what I've written about him is also painful, in places.
But, then, it's real.

Real is hard. And you can't dodge that. As I've come to
learn.

Sensing my attention has drifted away, Harold gives a little bark, and I tilt my head to gaze down at my precious boy.
Undimmed, undaunted, forever Harold, gazing up as though
to say, "What next?"

"Ava?" A soft voice sounds at my door, which is ajar.

"Hi!" I swivel in my seat. "Come in!"

A moment later, Farida is in the room, wearing an elegant ensemble of flared black trousers and an embroidered tunic.

"How's it going?" she asks, with a bubble of anticipation in her voice.

"Finished!" I say exuberantly.

"Oh, my dear Ava!" Her face creases into a joyful smile.

"Only a first draft," I amend. "But I've typed 'The End.' That's something."

"Typing 'The End' is everything," Farida corrects me. "Especially for the first time. It answers a question you've probably been asking your whole life, even if subconsciously."

"Yes." I nod, rubbing my face, feeling suddenly exhausted. "I can't believe it. I never thought . . ."

"I did." Farida gives me a wise smile. "You must come and have a drink. We must celebrate! Felicity will be thrilled! We're in the anteroom."

"I'll be there in a minute," I say, and watch as she walks out, her leather slippers noiseless on the stone floor. She's been such a mentor. Both Farida and Felicity, her partner.

As my thoughts rest on Felicity, I smile for the thousandth time. I still remember that extraordinary moment after I'd arrived in October and was drinking a welcome cup of fennel tea in the refectory, hoping I'd done the right thing. Farida said casually, "Let me introduce you to Felicity, my partner." Then a familiar woman with salt-and-pepper hair walked into the room and I nearly fell over backward.

Because it was Scribe! Farida's lover is Scribe! Or Felicity, as I call her now. It turned out that throughout the retreat, when everyone's attention was on Dutch and me, the *real* blooming romance was going on between Farida and Felicity. And theirs lasted. Felicity spends two weeks out of every month here, and they're clearly besotted, in a low-key, elegant way.

Of course, I had a million questions for them both—and that's when my jaw dropped even farther.

"I'm not really a stay-at-home housewife," Felicity confessed that same evening, as we drank wine and dipped crackers into fava bean puree. "I'm a literary agent. But I couldn't divulge that to the group. I would have been besieged by manuscripts. It would have ruined the dynamic." She shook her head. "So I told a white lie."

"A literary agent?" I stared at her. "So, what, you were looking for writers? It was all a lie?"

"No!" she said, turning pink. "I *am* trying to write, in my spare time. After a fashion. But I suppose the *real* reason I came to the retreat is that I'd met Farida at a literary festival in Milan. Couldn't get her out of my mind." She looked at Farida fondly. "So I booked a week's retreat. Just to see. Just to . . . give it a chance."

"Thank God," said Farida emphatically. And she clasped Felicity's hand and I felt a little misty. Because it just shows, it can all work out. It *can*.

I brush my hair and teeth, apply lip gloss and scent, and throw an embroidered shawl over my clothes. (Farida's style is kind of catching.) Then I head with Harold through the courtyard to the anteroom, which is a small sitting room lined with books and made welcoming with a huge fire, heavy throws, and fat candles that Farida lights every night.

Felicity is sitting on a low ottoman, watching the flames, but she leaps up as she hears me enter.

"Ava! I hear you've finished! Congratulations!" She envelops me in a hug, and Harold barks in appreciation.

"I don't know if it's any good," I say as she releases me. "But I finished. That's what I wanted, to finish something."

As I say the words, I have a sudden, almost painful urge to tell Matt. *See? I finished. I did finish something.*

But Matt was a long time ago now. And I try not to think about him.

"I can't wait to read more of Harold's story." Felicity's eyes dance as they meet mine. "Ava, you know how much I loved the first ten chapters. May I read the rest?"

"Touting for business, my love?" says Farida briskly, coming into the room holding a terra-cotta bowl of olives. "Felicity *is* the best agent," she adds fondly.

"I'm one of many," corrects Felicity. "I'm merely petitioning to be considered. Ava must manage her career as she sees fit."

"I don't *have* a career!" I retort, smiling at them both yet feeling a bit unhinged. I've only just typed *The End* and my eyes are still bloodshot from peering at the screen and an agent wants to read what I've written?

"I have a feeling," says Felicity, and she pats my arm. "But tonight just enjoy your accomplishment. Relax!"

Farida pours me some red wine and we raise our glasses, while Harold settles down in his favorite spot by the fire. These two feel like old friends after so many months together. They've been my world, while the rest of my life has been shadowy and distant. I've WhatsApped with Nell,

Maud, and Sarika, but not in the same intense way as before. Not day to day. Not minute by minute.

It's not that I've been single-minded these last six months. Of course other ideas have popped into my head. (*Import Italian pottery! Learn about frescoes!*) But I've told myself, *Not now*, which is something I never did before. And instead of chatting on WhatsApp all day, I made myself strict rules for social media. I guess you could call them my own personal deal-breakers.

I feel like a different person now. A stronger person. A person in charge of herself.

"Oh!" Felicity's exclamation breaks my thoughts, and she looks up from her phone. "Oh, this is marvelous! Ava, have you seen?"

"What?"

"I've just received an email from Aaron. Remember Aaron—Kirk? I think you must have got it, too; you're on the list."

I pull out my phone to check. The Wi-Fi is alive (this room is one of the few hotspots), and sure enough, I have a new email. It's from Aaron Chambers, and it's an invitation to the launch of his self-published graphic novel, *Emril Announces*. He's holding it in a pub off Leicester Square, and he's added a message:

Hope to see all you guys from the retreat, couldn't have done it without you!!!

"Good for Kirk!" says Farida. "You really were one of my more promising groups."

"Are you going to go?" Felicity asks me, and I blink at her

over my wineglass. Go? How can I go? I'm in Italy. I'm writing a book. I don't "go" to things anymore.

But then it hits me, as though for the first time. I've achieved what I came here to do. I've typed *The End*. That was my goal and I've done it. So what do I do now? I never thought that far ahead; I never made any plans; I was too focused on the task in hand. I feel a tiny flicker of panic, which I try to suppress by gulping my wine.

"Ava, darling, you're welcome to stay here as long as you like," says Farida, reading my thoughts. "It's wonderful to have you. You don't need to rush into any decisions."

"Thanks, Farida," I say gratefully, and for a moment I let myself imagine a sunlit existence where I never leave these walls but just eat olives and drink wine and play with Harold till I'm ninety and fluent in Italian.

But already I know it wouldn't be the right choice for me. It would be running away. I've been cocooned all these months. I've had a single purpose. I've blocked out all the mess and difficulties of real, actual life. Now I need to get back. Find my place in the world again. Engage with people and challenges and work and shopping and buses and the washing up.

Plus, let's be frank, I can't afford to stay here forever. Farida doesn't charge peak rates over the winter, but she doesn't charge nothing either. Even with my discount as a former retreat guest, these six months have eaten substantially into my savings. It's time to go home.

And if I go to Kirk's launch, Matt might be there.

As I let an unguarded Matt-thought into my brain, my stomach churns reflexively, and I draw breath, trying to stay steady. I'm waiting for the moment that thinking of Matt *doesn't* make my stomach churn. It hasn't happened yet. But, on the other hand, I do manage to go hours without thinking about him now. Now.

At first, of course, it was impossible, and I found myself thinking, *What have I* done? *Why have I come* here *of all places?*

I wandered desperately about the monastery, searching for a safe, Matt-free place, but memories of him were everywhere. In every courtyard, every corner, every doorway, I could see shadows of Dutch. Shadows of Aria. Shadows of us, laughing, arm in arm, a baggage-free couple in matching kurta pajamas, on our way to certain bliss.

On the second night I spilled the whole story of our breakup to Farida and Felicity, thinking that it might help. It was a very bonding evening and I'm glad I did, but it didn't solve my problem.

In the end, it was like an exorcism. I walked around the whole monastery, my hands in my pockets, my chin stuck forward, muttering, "Bring it *on*." Positively encouraging all the painful images to swoosh through my mind. And that did work, kind of. The more I forced myself to think about it, the less raw the hurt became. I started to laugh again and see just a courtyard, not a scene from our romance.

But Matt's shadow didn't leave me completely. I still went to bed every night, brooding. Thinking: What went wrong? Did it *have* to go wrong? *Could* we have made things work? I tried to retrace the steps to our split. I tried holding all our conversations again, with different outcomes. I drove myself a bit mad. Because let's face it: We did break up. And Matt hasn't turned up, hammering on the door of the monastery. Or even sent me a text.

In fact, the last time I saw any Warwick family member face-to-face was when I made a quick delivery to Matt's parents' house in Berkshire, before I left for Italy. I rang the doorbell, and as the door swung open, I couldn't believe my luck, because it was Elsa herself.

"Oh, hello," I said briskly, before she could speak. "I've got a present for you." I reached into my carrier bag and pulled out a framed photo of Matt swinging a golf club, which I'd harvested from Facebook. "That's for you. . . ." I reached for another framed photo of him, this one in a martial-arts tournament. "And that's for you. . . ."

I produced photo after photo, until eight framed pictures of Matt were teetering in a pile in her arms and Elsa was peering at me over the top of them, looking shell-shocked.

"I noticed you didn't have any," I said politely. "I should think your son noticed too." Then I turned on my heel and left.

I thought that would be a nice clean finish. And at first it was. For the first few weeks here, I managed not to look Matt up online at all. Then I crumbled. I couldn't help myself. So I had a quick peek, expecting to see photos of him in Japan with Genevieve. But to my astonishment, there was a news story from a trade magazine: *Matthias Warwick steps down from Harriet's House.* It said he was leaving for "fresh challenges" and there was lot of blah about his achievements and family history, which I skimmed, feeling stunned. He didn't just refuse to go to Japan, he quit! He quit Harriet's House!

Of course, I had a burning desire to know everything. I wanted to know how he'd decided, and how his parents had responded, and how he was feeling, and whether he'd gone to work with Topher or was doing something else. . . . But I'm not Sarah. I'm not a stalker. Plus, if I'd started down that rabbit hole, I would *never* have got my book written.

So somehow I managed to be strong. I didn't go on a trawl of the Internet, nor try to contact him, nor even text Topher on some casual pretext. I assumed I would never see him again, never know the answers. Case closed.

But now it's opening up again, just a chink. If I go to that pub in Leicester Square, Matt might be there. Just the thought of seeing him again makes me feel half sick with nerves, half heady with exhilaration.

What if he's with someone else by now? the Red Queen instantly demands inside my brain. *Because he's bound to be. You don't think he'll still be single, do you? A man like that gets snapped up at once. At* once.

By Genevieve?

No, not Genevieve, but some beautiful, amazing woman who loves Japanese punk and held his hand while he quit Harriet's House and is already pregnant with his baby.

(I have a sudden urge to hit her.)

(No. Retract. That would be a hate crime and I'm not a violent person and she doesn't exist.)

Well, what if he is *with someone else?* optimistic Alice answers in my head. Then I'll get closure. Exactly. So, in fact, however you look at it, it would be a mistake *not* to go. Yes. I should go.

I come to and realize that Farida and Felicity are both

quietly watching me process my thoughts, in that patient way they have.

"I think I'll go," I say, trying to sound casual. "I'll go along to Kirk's thing. I need to go back to the UK anyway, sort out my life. It would be supportive. And nice to see the group again. And . . ." I clear my throat. "Anyway. I think I'll go."

"I'm sure that's a good idea," says Farida, and Felicity nods, her face creased with empathy. And neither of them mentions it again, but I know they're thinking what I can't bring myself to say. Matt might be there. He just might be there.

Twenty-Five

He's not here.

As I lean against the bar, breathing in beer fumes, clutching a glass of terrible wine, and listening to Aaron's lengthy speech about his graphic novel, the last vestiges of my smile have fallen away. My cheeks have drooped. I've stopped swinging my head toward the door like a hopeful dog. If he was going to come, he would have come by now. It's over.

Of course, everyone expected us to arrive hand in hand, or even married. Everyone demanded to know what had happened. I batted away the questions with carefully curated, positive sound bites:

I'm all good! Really good! So good!

Yes, Dutch and I split up, but it wasn't meant to be, so. Yes, I know, a shame. These things happen.

I've just returned from the monastery, can you believe it? Got back yesterday. Yes, it is amazing in winter. Farida sends her love. . . .

No, I haven't seen Dutch for a while.

No, there wasn't anyone else involved, it just . . . Anyway! Enough about me.

But all the time, the disappointment was inside me, heavy and warm, weighing me down. I'd hoped. I'd really hoped. I'm not even sure what for, exactly. Just . . . something good. Yes, something good.

Because here's the thing. You can cut all the flowers, but you can't stop spring from coming. I don't care what they say, you *can't.* It pops up. It won't be subdued. It's there all the time, deep underground, dormant, waiting. The minute I saw that email from Kirk, I felt a daisy spring up, bobbing its head around as though to say, "You never know. . . ."

It wasn't overoptimism. It wasn't some deluded fantasy. It was just . . . *maybe.* Everyone's allowed a *maybe,* aren't they? And that *maybe* feeling propelled me all the way through packing up, saying my farewells to Farida and Felicity, flying home, choosing an outfit, applying my makeup, and coming out here tonight. Hope. Just a little daisy of hope.

But now a brisk wind is blowing and the daisy's feeling pretty buffeted. Actually, I might leave now. I've said hello to everyone from the group and we've promised we'll have another reunion, and it's been nice to see them in a way. Although it's not the same. How could it be? In Puglia we were a group of unburdened souls in kurta pajamas. In this London pub, Richard has turned into an anorak-wearing bore, and Eithne can only talk about her grandchildren. Anna has told me endlessly about her brilliant career and looked gleeful when I told her that Matt and I had broken up. Everyone's just a little paler and frownier than they were in Italy. Including me, I'm sure.

Mouthing a general vague apology at Eithne, I step outside the pub and into the drizzly London street, then breathe out, trying to shed all the feelings that have been building up over the last few days. And I'm just peering at a passing bus, wondering if I should catch one home, when my phone jangles with a FaceTime request. It's Ronald, wanting to chat, and I smile wryly. Of all the moments.

Ronald is the one member of the Warwick family I've stayed in touch with. I speak to him maybe twice a month, sometimes more. He called me soon after I arrived in Puglia, and we had a nice, aimless chat. He was interested to hear about Italy, and he had a few things to say about the news. Then he started telling me about his awful scam again, and even though he was repeating what I already knew, I listened sympathetically. I sensed he needed to say it, and he doesn't get a chance to at home. We didn't talk about Matt. When he strayed in that direction, I said, "Actually, could we *not* talk about Matt?" And we haven't mentioned him ever since. Or any of the family. But we've chatted. And it's been nice.

Not now, though. It's not the time. I decline his request and send a quick text suggesting we talk another day. Then I start walking briskly, trying to put distance between me and the pub. I need to move on from all this, both literally and mentally. Enough. Regroup. Onward.

As the word "onward" passes through my mind, I think of Sarika, and my heart contracts. Because *that's* where I should be. With my friends. With my squad. I haven't even told them I'm back yet. Not sure why. I suppose I hoped . . .

Stupid daisy.

With firmer resolve, I turn my steps toward the tube. I'll go round to Nell's and surprise her. Should have thought of that before.

It takes me about half an hour to reach Nell's street, picking up some flowers on the way. As I stride along the pavement toward her building, it really hits me, what I'm doing, and I start to feel excited. Exhilarated, even. Because it's been months! And I've finished my book! And I've missed my friends so much. *So* much. And they have no idea I'm back!

I have to thank Maud especially, because my flat looks amazing. So tidy! She's upcycled the shelving unit *and* the kitchen chairs *and* the dresser, which is now blue with wallpaper inside the cupboards. It's gorgeous. It's all gorgeous. It was definitely worth waiting for.

The trees on either side of Nell's street are covered with blossom, lit up by streetlamps, and the sight of it makes me smile wryly in spite of myself. There we are. The spring. Can't stop it.

It's only when I'm on the forecourt of her building that I suddenly feel nervous. No, not *nervous,* but . . . Should I text her at least, rather than just arriving on the doorstep?

I find myself a discreet place to perch, on a low bollard between two parked cars, dump my flowers on the ground, and get out my phone. But I can't think what to text that won't sound totally cheesy. Also: Should I tell the others I'm back too? In fact, should I have thought this through a bit more?

I'm just about to summon up WhatsApp when the sight of an approaching car draws my attention. It's a navy-blue Fiat that I recognize, because it belongs to Nell's neighbor, John Sweetman. And he's parking in the disabled spot. Again. As I see his calm, bespectacled face through the windscreen, reversing as though nothing's wrong, I feel a surge of rage at him. Still? I mean, really, *still*?

You go away for six transformative months and you return, all full of positive energy . . . and then this. Some things never change. Wearily, I thrust my phone back in my pocket, and I'm about to get up to challenge him, when a voice breaks the silence: "Hey!"

It's a deep, furious male voice. A voice I . . . recognize?

I must be dreaming. I must be hallucinating. But . . . I'm not. A moment later, he comes into view, striding toward John Sweetman like an angry bull, and I can't help gasping.

Matt?

"Move your fucking car," he says, and bangs on John Sweetman's car window. "Don't you *think* about parking there. Don't you even *think* about it. My friend needs that space. *Move*."

I don't hear what John Sweetman says in reply, if anything. I'm not sure I'm functioning. My hand has moved to my mouth and I can't breathe. I mean . . . *Matt?*

"Move!" Matt sounds like he's about to explode. He's quite a menacing sight, tall and stacked and eyebrow lowered. He looks as though he's about to demolish an opponent in the fight ring. If I were John Sweetman, I'd be terrified.

Sure enough, a moment later, John Sweetman's engine

starts up. Matt steps back, out of the way, waiting for him to move. Then he turns and beckons, and another car approaches. Nell's car. What . . . *what* is happening?

Nell's car maneuvers into the disabled space, and a moment later the door opens and Topher gets out, then leans back in.

"OK, careful . . . carefully . . ." I can hear him saying.

An arm goes around his shoulders and Matt comes to help him, so for a moment my view is blocked by the two men's backs, but then Topher stands up straight, and he's holding Nell in his arms.

Nell?

I feel a chill as I glimpse her face. She's so pale. What's happened? But she smiles at Topher and he adjusts his arm around her, as though he's done this a thousand times. Meanwhile, Matt has retrieved an overnight bag from the boot and banged it shut again. And I should say something, I should move, I should announce my presence to them . . . but I can't. I'm transfixed, and my eyes are somehow wet. In fact, they're so wet that my vision's blurry.

John Sweetman has meanwhile parked his car elsewhere and is walking toward the building with slow, reluctant steps. Matt swings round toward him.

"Apologize to my friend," he says shortly, and John Sweetman visibly gulps. He takes in the sight of Nell in Topher's arms, Matt holding her bag and cane, and his defensive demeanor starts to slip.

"I had no idea," he begins. "I had no idea the young lady . . . I didn't realize. I'm . . . sorry."

"You should be," says Topher, his dark eyes tiny with contempt. "Excuse us, please."

Matt has already opened the front door with a key—he has a key?—and he holds it open for Topher and Nell. A moment later, they've all disappeared.

I breathe out and wipe my eyes. This bollard I'm on is very hard and my legs have started to ache and I should stand up. But I can't while my thoughts are whirling.

Then I hear another sound, which makes me blink in fresh astonishment.

"We're here!" It's Maud's distinctive, top-volume voice. "Yup, got it all. Yes, Nihal found the elderflower cordial. *So* clever. See you in a sec!"

As I watch, bewildered, she sashays into sight, talking animatedly to Nihal, who's walking in step with her. Both are holding bulging shopping bags and they look like old friends.

"I know you all believe in it. And I *do* absolutely respect your beliefs, Nihal. But I just think it makes no sense," Maud is saying to him. "How can something change if you measure it? And what does quantum *mean,* anyway?"

"I'll try to explain," says Nihal in his mild way. "Do you know what an electron is, Maud?"

"No," says Maud emphatically. "Does that matter?"

As she's speaking, she lets them both into the building and they disappear. I exhale slowly, my thoughts even more mixed up than before. It's impossible. It's unreal. What's going *on*?

And suddenly I can't sit here anymore, a spectator on my own life. With trembling legs, I get up and venture toward

Nell's door. Her keys are in my bag, as they always are. I let myself into the main lobby, then approach Nell's flat. My stomach is screwed up with nerves. I've never felt so apprehensive about seeing my friends in my life.

My hand is actually shaking as I put the key to the lock, but I turn it, step inside, and hear a roar of laughter from the sitting room.

"No way!" I hear Sarika exclaim, and I feel another jolt. Is *everyone* here? "OK, Sam says he'll be half an hour. I'll just get some more wine. . . ."

She appears in the hall and sees me, and for a moment I think she might pass out.

"Ava?" she whispers. "Ava? Ava!" Her voice suddenly rips up to a scream. "Ava's *back*!"

It's pandemonium. Nell's hall isn't huge, but within ten seconds it's full of people. Sarika is first to hug me, and then Maud is squeezing me tight. I emerge from their huddle to see Nell standing there, using her cane, her face happier than I've ever seen it, and we sink into each other's arms while Nihal says shyly, "Welcome back," and Topher adds, "Excellent entrance, Ava. Excellent."

And then there's just Matt. Holding back from the melee, a few feet away. His eyes are dark and questioning. But I don't know what the question is. I don't know.

My throat has closed up and I can barely meet his gaze, but I say, "Hi."

"Hi."

He comes forward and reaches out a hand to touch mine briefly. "Hi."

"I don't . . ." I swivel around to take in everyone. "I don't get it. I don't *get* this."

"Poor Ava." Sarika laughs. "Come on, my love. Have a drink. We'll explain."

Of course, it's all very simple. Matt and I split up, but our friends didn't. Our *lives* didn't.

We all gather in Nell's sitting room with drinks and snacks. Then I sip my wine, trying to listen to everyone at once and to piece together the story.

"So, when you broke up," Sarika begins, "we were like, 'Oh no,' because we *liked* one another. But we didn't get together straightaway. Except Nell and Topher—they were in touch the whole time."

"We had arguments to finish," says Nell, glowering good-humoredly at Topher.

"Still do," Topher agrees, nodding.

"But the time when we *really* all got together was . . ." Maud hesitates, darting me a quick look. "When Nell went into hospital again."

"*Hospital?*" I interject, feeling a cold chunk of dread. "What's been going on? You didn't mention any of this."

"We weren't allowed to," Maud puts in quickly. "Ava, I wanted to. I really did. But Nell reckoned you would fly home. So we had to keep schtum."

"If you'd said a word, I would have had you assassinated," Nell growls.

"I know," says Maud regretfully. "You would. My children would have been motherless. So we didn't tell you."

"Tell me what?" I look from face to face. "What?"

"Just another surgery. Intestine. No big deal. *No big deal,*" Nell repeats firmly, as I draw breath to demand more details.

"Anyway, the guys were great. Topher stayed up all night—"

"Couldn't get rid of him," says Nell, with an eye roll. "Cluttering up the bloody hospital the whole time."

"I was playing online poker, so I was up anyway," says Topher with a shrug. "And who doesn't enjoy listening to Nell swear at nurses?" He touches her hand, with a look so fond that I blink in surprise. Is he . . . ? Are they . . . ?

"Then, when Nell got out of hospital, Nihal was absolutely *brilliant,*" says Maud, giving him a dazzling smile. "He should get the Nobel Prize. He said, 'Nell, sweetie, what you need in your life is robots!' "

"*Robots?*" I echo, baffled.

"I saw a possible function for robot usage," Nihal explains in his usual measured manner. "I suggested a number of ways in which we might facilitate Nell's everyday operations."

"Look!" Maud moves off her seat, pointing to something behind her—and for the first time I see the robot arm by Nell's side. It's mounted on a stand and is holding an iPad with a super-long stylus clipped to it.

"It's changed my life," says Nell, and Nihal instantly looks abashed.

"They're all over the house," says Maud, as proudly as though she'd invented the robots herself. "There's one in Nell's bedroom, and one in the kitchen. . . . Oh, look! There you go!"

A robot is approaching us over the wooden floor, just like the snack robot but holding Nell's medicine bottles instead. It's so simple and brilliant that I'm silenced. Because I'm remembering what I said to Matt about Nihal's geeky hobby—and now all I can feel is shame. He's a genius.

"What I'd *really* like to develop is an ocular motor control system," says Nihal thoughtfully, surveying Nell over his beer glass.

"What's that?" says Maud excitedly. "Is it a bionic arm?"

"You're not turning me into a bloody cyborg," Nell warns.

"Oh, go on, have a bionic arm," says Maud. "Go on, Nell."

"Yes, go on, Nell," says Sarika. "Don't be a spoilsport." She winks at me, and I feel a bubble of intense happiness. I've missed these guys *so much*.

"So, I take it you're still with Sam?" I ask her.

"Moving into his place next week," says Sarika, a smile spreading across her face.

"That's amazing! And where does he live again?" I can't resist asking innocently. "It's pretty near the tube, isn't it?"

"Fairly near," says Sarika, avoiding my gaze. "It's . . . I mean, I walk pretty quickly. And sometimes I cycle. So. It's ten minutes max."

"Ten minutes *if you're on a motorbike*," says Nell sardonically, and Maud explodes with laughter.

"OK, it's miles away," says Sarika, suddenly caving in. "It's bloody miles from the tube. But I don't care. I just want to be with him!"

She looks so happy, I feel a tiny wistful tweak in my heart.

There we are again. It can work out. You just have to have faith.

"And so now we need to know, Ava," says Nell. "It's nearly killed me not asking you, but . . . the book?"

I let a tiny pause elapse, then say triumphantly, "I finished it!" There's an explosion of whooping and Maud high-fives me, her face lit up with delight. "And an agent likes it," I add, still feeling a pinprick of disbelief as I say the words. "She . . . she wants to represent me."

Felicity read the rest of my memoir while I was packing to leave Italy. She said she can't make any promises, but she thinks Harold's story will make it into bookshops. My beloved Harold, in a real book!

Nell reaches forward to put her mottled hand on mine, her eyes shimmering.

"There," she says, her voice a little choked. "*There*. Knew you could do it." She grins, and I grin back, and I know we're both remembering the conversation we had in this house, months ago.

And as we're sitting there, hands clasped, I study Nell's face for clues. Because I have to know. That sparky, affectionate vibe between Nell and Topher is . . . It's *real*. Surely?

"Nell," I say, *sotto voce*. "Tell me something. Are you and Topher . . . a couple?"

"No," says Nell at once, withdrawing her hand as though in protest. "Jesus! No."

"Yes, we are," says Topher, listening in to our conversation.

"No, we're not."

"Well, I think we are. Sarika, are we a couple?"

"Don't ask me," says Sarika, lifting her hands at once.

"Of course you are!" says Maud passionately. "You're a lovely couple!"

"Maud, you're insane," says Nell, but she turns a little pink and shoots a quick look at Topher.

"Thank you for your support, Maud," says Topher gravely. "It will be remembered." Then he turns to me, his face crinkled in amusement. "To answer your question, we're in negotiations, I guess. More wine?"

I shake my head and take a sip, smiling at them both, just absorbing the atmosphere. The feeling of being home again, back with my friends. Everything's moved on but in a good way.

"How's Harold?" comes a deep voice behind me, making me start. I swivel to see Matt, sitting a few feet away, cradling a glass of wine. He hasn't joined in the uproarious conversation or said much at all since I arrived.

I mean, I get it. It's weird. And a bit painful. But here we are, and we can't ignore each other.

"He's really well, thanks," I say.

"Good." Matt nods. "Say hello from me. And well done on your book."

"I finished it," I say, because I want to hear the words out loud again, in front of him. "I finished something." I swallow. "So."

"Yes." His eyes are warm. "It's brilliant."

"And you've left Harriet's House?" I add, trying to make polite conversation. At once Matt's expression shifts to an unreadable place.

"Ah," he says after a pause. "You know about that."

"Yes. I saw it online. But I don't know what you're doing now."

"Working with Topher." His face expands into a smile. "Partner, in fact."

"Oh, *Matt*!"

"I know. It's pretty good."

He looks so thrilled, I can't help leaning forward to give him an impulsive hug—then instantly withdraw, mortified.

"God. Sorry. I didn't. *God*—" My cheeks are burning, and I lift my wineglass for a quick swig. "Anyway, so you've been well? You look well—"

"Ava." Matt cuts me off and waits till I raise my head. "Ava. Could we . . . I don't know, have dinner?"

His face is grave but hopeful, and I stare back at him, my head a cascade of thoughts. He had hope too? All this time, he had hope?

"I'd like that," I say at last. "Yes. I'd like that."

Twenty-Six

~~~~~~

We're both wary. We're so wary that at first I don't know how we're going to manage a proper conversation. I mean, we can barely make eye contact.

Matt has booked us a table at a vegetarian Italian restaurant, and we start off by talking stiltedly about the menu. Then Italian food more generally. Then we recall meals we ate at the monastery.

"That pasta with the herbs. That was good."

"The broad beans in the broth."

"And the bread every morning. So fresh."

"Yes! The *bread*."

But exchanging memories of food can only last for so long. At last the conversation peters out and we both sip our wine, exchanging the kind of polite smiles you do when no one has any idea what to say.

I draw breath, then stop dead, because I have a kind of brain freeze. I can only think of things *not* to talk about.

"I know who Ottolenghi is now," Matt volunteers into the silence, and I give him ten marks for conversational guts, because that's punchy. Right into the heart of things.

"Amazing." I smile at him. "You're a new man."

"I even bought some harissa," he adds, and I laugh.

"D'you like it?"

"Not really," he admits, and I laugh again, properly this time. "But you're right, I am a new man," he says, more seriously. "I eat tofu sometimes."

"You don't." I gape at him. *Tofu?*

"I do. I tried it and, you know, it's OK. It's protein. It's fine. I think I could be . . . semitarian, maybe? Half vegetarian? It's a thing," he adds, a little defensively.

"Wow." I rub my face, trying to absorb this new, unfamiliar Matt. *Tofu? Semitarian?* When did he even learn that word? "That's . . . different."

"Well, a lot's changed since we saw each other." He shrugs. "A lot."

"New job," I say, lifting my glass to him. "Congratulations again."

"Yes. New job. Really great new job," he adds with emphasis. "It's working out better than we could have hoped."

Matt's work was one of the conversational areas I was definitely going to avoid. But now we're in it, I can't resist asking what I've been burning to know all these months.

"It must have been a difficult decision, though," I venture. "How did your parents react when you told them?"

"My dad got it," says Matt after a moment's pause. "My mum, not so much. She says she's OK with it now, but at the time . . ." He winces. "I mean, she had no idea there was even a problem. She was expecting me to go to Japan. Not tender my resignation. She lost it a bit. She sent me a long letter all about my 'betrayal.' It was toxic."

"Wow." I can only imagine a long, toxic handwritten letter from Elsa. "But your dad didn't mind?"

"He *did* mind," says Matt. "But at the same time, he understood. He's lived in the Harriet's House world his whole life. Worked for the company, man and boy. He never tried to escape it, but I think he could see why I wanted to. Whereas my mum . . ." Matt sighs. "She's more passionate about Harriet's House than my dad, weirdly. I think it's because she came to it late. Like a religious convert. She's more zealous than any of them. But I think she's made peace with it now."

"And who took over your job?"

"Oh, a really great woman called Cathy," says Matt, his face lighting up. "She was promoted from within. Only been with us for three years. Before that she was at Mattel. She's sharp. She's hungry. She's *so* much better suited to the job than I was. She's out in Japan at the moment, in fact, with—" He stops dead, and I make an internal bet of a zillion pounds that he was about to say "Genevieve" but caught himself. "They're all out there," he amends, taking a sip of wine. "So. It's all fine."

"You still call Harriet's House 'us,' I notice," I say, raising my eyebrows, and Matt nods.

"Touché. Look, it's my family business. I'm still on the board, I still care about it . . . I just didn't want to make it my life. I realized I was trapped in . . . I don't know." He shakes his head. "A comfort zone. A miserable, toxic comfort zone. The worst kind."

"Well, I'm glad you stepped out of it," I say softly. "I'm glad."

"Me too." He blows out as though it's been a battle. But he looks stronger for the battle, I find myself thinking. He looks straighter, happier, prouder of himself. His face is glowing. He couldn't look less like a rock. "And I have you to thank," he adds.

"Oh." I shake my head awkwardly. "No. Really. No."

"*Yes,*" he contradicts me. "Before you, I always felt like I didn't have a choice. Somehow you made me see things differently. So here I am. A whole new guy. 'Living my best life,'" he adds, his mouth twitching, and at once I flush. I know he's trying to be nice. But just hearing that phrase is painful. It takes me back to our endless arguments and the way we were then. Matt, moody and obdurate. Me, shrill and hectoring (I realize now).

I really don't think we were at our finest.

"Matt, I said a lot of things," I blurt out guiltily. "I said a lot of things while we were together. And some of them were . . ." I raise my eyes to him. "I'm sorry. But I need to thank you, too, because you made *me* see life differently. I never would have written my book if you hadn't said I don't finish things."

"Oh God." Matt winces at the memory. "Ava, that was unforgivable. I should never have said that—"

"You should!" I cut him off. "It was true! But it's not true anymore. I achieved my goal and it was just . . . I don't know." I gesture vaguely with my hands. "It transformed me. I feel like I'm a new person too. We both are. You look different. Happier."

"I'm happier in a lot of ways," agrees Matt, then adds in a lower voice, "Although not in all ways. Not all ways." His dark gaze brushes over mine, and my stomach gives a little flip.

"Right." I swallow. "Well . . . me too."

"I didn't contact you in Italy," he says, his face averted, his fingers folding his napkin over and over. "We'd all agreed to let you write in peace. It would have disrupted you if I'd got in touch. But . . . I wanted to. I thought about you."

"I thought about you too," I say, my voice suddenly wobbly. "All the time."

His eyes meet mine again, with unmistakable intent, and my heart starts to thump. Is he . . . ? Are we . . . ? Might we . . . ?

Then Matt looks away, breaking the tension of the moment.

"I have something for you," he says, reaching for a plastic bag I noticed earlier.

"I have something for *you*," I reply eagerly, and reach into my tote. I place a solitary pebble on the table, large and smooth—then feel instantly foolish, because who brings a stone to dinner? But Matt's eyes soften.

"Is that from . . . ?"

I nod.

"Wow." He closes his hand around it. "All the way from Italy."

"I went back to that beach. That same olive tree. I sat

there and thought about . . . things. Then I saw this pebble, and I decided that if I ever saw you again—" I break off, flushing slightly. "Well. Here it is. A souvenir."

"Thank you. I love it. Mine isn't as special, but here goes. . . ." Matt hesitates, then draws a battered hardback out of the plastic bag.

"*Bookbinding for Amateurs, 1903,*" I read aloud.

"It called out to me as I walked past a charity shop," says Matt, looking sheepish. "I thought . . . I have to rescue that. For Ava."

He rescued a book. For me. I'm so touched, I can't quite speak. Wordlessly, I turn the old, tattered pages, my eyes hot.

"It's not the only one," he confesses, watching me turn the leaves. "I have a few. I see them and I think, 'Well, if I don't buy it . . .' "

"Then no one will," I join in, finding my voice.

"Exactly."

We meet eyes again, and I feel breathless. Every impulse in my body is drawing me toward him, almost sobbing with relief that we might have another chance. But at the same time I feel cautious. I don't want to hurt him. I don't want him to hurt me. Are we actually *able* to be together without hurting each other?

"Excuse me?" The tension between us is punctured as our waiter approaches the table, a strange little grin on his face, holding two large jiffy bags. "I was given something to deliver to you."

"To *us*?" says Matt in surprise.

"It was given to the manager earlier in the day."

"By whom?" I say in astonishment, and the waiter turns

the jiffy bags round so we can see the front of them. One reads, *To Ava, from your friends,* and the other reads, *To Matt, from your friends.*

"Wow," I say, taking mine from the waiter. "Well . . . thanks."

We wait until he's disappeared, then look at each other.

"Did you know anything about this?" asks Matt.

"No! Not a clue. Shall we see what they are?"

We both rip open our packages and I pull out a red binder. On the front, in neat block capitals, someone has written in Sharpie:

MATT-LAND
A GUIDEBOOK

I glance up at Matt's—and it's the same but blue and the title reads:

AVA-LAND
A GUIDEBOOK

"Oh my God," says Matt, shaking his head with a disbelieving smile. He opens his binder and peers at the first page. "No *way.*"

"What?"

"This is priceless." He reads out loud: " 'Ava-land can be contradictory, unpredictable, and erratic. Yet it is always joyful, hopeful, and colorful. See page seven for Ava's Sense of Color.' "

"Who wrote that?" I demand, half outraged and half wanting to laugh.

"Don't know. Maud? Nell?" He turns the binder so I can see the page, but it's typed out in some anonymous font.

"Well, you listen to this." I read out from the first page of mine, which is headed *Introduction to Matt-land.* " 'When first approaching Matt, you may believe he cannot hear a word you say. He appears motionless. But as you become attuned to his manner, you will realize he can hear and will react according to his own timescale. See page four: How Matt Communicates.' " I slap the page gleefully. "Whoever wrote that knows you."

"This is incredible." Matt is leafing through incredulously. "Look, a contents page. 'Food . . . Traditions . . . Wildlife . . . National Dress . . .' "

"You've got one too," I say, laughing. " 'Culture . . . Technology . . . Habitat . . . History . . .' "

"Ha!" Matt barks with laughter. " 'The national dress of Ava-land may appear disconcerting at first. Do not be alarmed. Your eye will adjust in time to the myriad of colors and styles.' "

"What?" I say, in mock outrage. "OK, I'm finding yours." I flick to the right page and read aloud. " 'National dress of Matt-land. This consists of trousers worn with a blue shirt. No other color is acceptable. Attempts to extend the range of national dress have, thus far, failed.' " I start laughing. "That is so true. That is so, so true!"

"It is not!" Matt looks down at his blue shirt. "Blue's a good color," he says defensively.

"'Matt-land hovers around subzero temperatures,'" I read out. "'Travelers are advised to dress accordingly.'"

"'Venturers to Ava-land must prepare for the strange musical customs of this nation,'" he rejoins. "'Consider earplugs.'"

"What a nerve!" I say indignantly. "Oh, here's languages. 'Commonly spoken languages in Matt-land include English, football, and logic.'"

"'The languages of Ava-land include English, aromatherapy, and Harold,'" Matt replies. "Hey, I speak Harold too."

"'You cannot visit Matt-land without sampling ice cream.'"

"Snap!" says Matt, nodding at his binder. "'You cannot visit Ava-land without sampling ice cream.'"

We smile at each other, then I flip randomly to another section.

"'Wisdom naturally permeates Matt-land, as well as a strong, valuable seam: the ability to listen.' Yes." I nod, feeling a fresh swell of affection for Matt. "Yes, that's true. You do listen."

"'Ava-land is transformative for the weary of soul,'" reads out Matt. "'The fresh, optimistic air is a known tonic, although it can cause dizziness for those unaccustomed to its potency.'" Matt shoots me a little grin. "You made me dizzy. Still do."

"'Rare volcanic eruptions of spontaneity and playfulness give Matt-land an exciting prospect that belies its calm appearance,'" I read. "*So* true!"

"'The altitudes and extremes of Ava-land can be challenging, but travelers will find vistas and delights well worth their efforts.' " Matt meets my eyes. "Vistas," he repeats slowly. "And delights. That's very well put."

I have a feeling I know what he means by vistas. And delights. In fact, his gaze is so intent, I feel a tad flustered and look down again.

"Oh, look, there's a conclusion," I say as I turn to the last page. " 'In Matt-land you find a solid landscape of truth, integrity, and honor. Matt-land is a rare find' "—I break off, my throat lumpy, because this is so true. " 'Matt-land is a rare find for the discerning traveler disappointed by other, shallower terrains and will reward perseverance beyond measure.' "

"Wow," says Matt, looking a bit shaken. "Well, this is what yours says . . ." He flips to the end of his binder and starts reading. " 'Ava-land is a Shangri-La. A realm of magic, hope, imagination, and, above all, love. It is a place . . .' " He hesitates, his voice scratchy. " 'It is a place few want to leave.' "

My eyes are suddenly hot, because who wrote that? Matt looks up at me, his face burning with love.

"I couldn't have put that better myself," he says quietly.

"Same," I say, feeling flustered. "I mean . . . what yours said about you. Same."

"No author name, I notice." Matt jerks his head at his binder.

"It's all of them."

"Bastards." He grins. "They're all going on the chart."

"Are they trying to send us a message, do you think?" I

say, and I'm trying to sound jokey, but my eyes are hot again. Because . . . is this real? Really real?

"Yes," says Matt, as though reading my mind, and he reaches his hand across the table to grasp mine.

I let him hold it for a few moments, feeling some of the tension in my body starting to sag away. But then I twist my fingers free. Because if this is going to have *any* chance, I have to be honest. We both have to be.

"Matt . . . I'm nervous," I say, staring at the table. "I don't want to be. But I am."

"Of course," says Matt gravely. "Me too. But we'll go slowly."

"Carefully." I nod. "No rushing."

"Nothing impulsive," Matt agrees.

"We'll realize we have differences. And we'll work around that." I look at him earnestly. "We'll *respect* each other. I can't love everything about your life, and you can't love everything about my life. And . . . you know. That's fine."

"Agreed." Matt nods. "That's fine."

On the way back to my flat, we keep our talk light and inconsequential. I don't know what Matt's feeling like, but my heart is hammering with nerves. It feels like a first date but the second time around. Which makes it *so* much harder.

The first time around, I didn't have any reservations. All I could see was glorious, inviting terrain that I couldn't wait to explore. Now I'm traversing the same terrain—but this time aware of its hidden rifts and potholes and dangerous cliff edges. I'm not skipping ahead confidently; I'm tiptoeing. Ready to retreat at any moment.

"I read Arlo Halsan's autobiography," I say, suddenly remembering.

"You did?" Matt sounds staggered.

"It was recommended to me by . . . someone," I say, not wanting to mention the G-word. "And it's extraordinary. Oh my God, his childhood. So *sad*."

I hate to admit Genevieve could be right about anything, but you do look at his pieces differently when you know what's behind them. Especially the hairless wolf. It never even *occurred* to me that it might represent a childhood fantasy dog that Arlo Halsan conjured up because he was so traumatized.

"But I thought you didn't—" Matt begins. Then he stops dead, and I can tell he's wary of the terrain ahead of us too.

We walk on silently for a while, then as we reach my flat Matt says, "I haven't mentioned my grandfather. He's told me how you've been chatting to him. You're a good person, Ava."

"It's been a pleasure." I smile at him. "I like your grandpa. Out of all your family—" I stop dead, too, because I think I'm getting near a pothole. "Anyway. He's cool."

"Well, he likes you too." Matt's gaze runs silently up to the porch light, which is *still* missing a bulb, and I know what he's thinking.

"I'll replace that," I say hastily. "I've been away."

"I wasn't going to say anything." Matt lifts his hands.

I feel a bit dismayed as I push the front door open, because we're still prickly. We're still not quite natural with each other. But maybe it'll come. We just need to keep talking.

"So, guess what? Maud finally refurbished all my rescue furniture!" I tell Matt as we mount the staircase to my front door. "Wait till you see the kitchen dresser. It's blue. It looks *amazing*. And no nails sticking out."

"Good to hear. Can't wait to see it. Can't *wait* to see Harold," he adds, and I feel a swell of fondness for him.

"Why isn't he yelping?" I say in puzzlement as we approach my flat. I open the door and wait for Harold to greet us with his usual paroxysm of joy—but there's no dog. No excited barking. It's eerie to come home without a greeting from Harold.

"Where is he?" I say in surprise. "Something's wrong. Harold?" I raise my voice. "Where are you?"

I hear a sudden distant growl and stare at Matt.

"What the— *Harold?*" he calls loudly.

A moment later there's the sound of breaking glass and Harold barking more frenziedly than I've ever heard him. Matt draws in breath sharply. "Fucking . . . fuck!"

"What?" I say in terror.

"Intruder," says Matt over his shoulder, and my whole body spasms in fright.

Matt's already thundering through the flat into the kitchen, and I skitter behind him. The back door is ajar, there's glass all over the floor, and Harold is at the top of the fire escape, barking his lungs out.

"Harold!" I make a grab for him, but he hurls himself out of my grasp, past Matt and down the fire escape, with the wildest barks I've ever heard. "Harold!" I yell in horror.

"Stop! Come back!" I make for the fire escape, but Matt grabs my arm, hard.

"Stay," he says. "I'll go."

He clatters down the fire escape and I stand there, my heart pumping, unable to hear either Matt or Harold, thinking, *What do I do? Do I call the police? Will they even come?* I get as far as pulling out my phone—but then Matt's back again, coming in through the back door, panting hard.

"Couldn't catch the intruder," he manages, between breaths. "Fuck knows where they went. Harold went haring after them. I called him back, but . . . you can guess how much notice he took of me. Ava, are *you* OK?"

He gazes at me, his eyes dark and anxious, and I feel as though some sort of unbearable swell is rising up inside me.

"Matt, I'm sorry!" My words burst out in a hot, desperate torrent. "I'm so, so sorry. You were right all along! I should have fixed the door. I should have bought padlocks. I should have listened to you about the crime stats. I should have listened about everything—"

"No!" Matt holds me by the shoulders, his own eyes glistening. "*You* were right all along. Harold's a star. He's a champion. There's nothing wrong with that dog, nothing. He protected you tonight. Protected you better than I did. I love your dog. I *love* your dog," he says again, almost fiercely.

"Really?" I falter.

"Are you kidding?" He stares at me, his face working with emotion. "Ava, I love your life. I love your flat. I love your rescue books. And your stupid hot baths. And your vegetarian food. And your . . . I don't know, your shit everywhere. And your friends. And—"

"Well, I love *your* friends," I cut in, my voice shaking. "And your ugly building. And your Internet countdown. And I love your art," I say with passion. "I love the hairless wolf and the freaky hands and all of it . . . because it's you. It's you, Matt. And I love you."

"Even when you smashed up my art, I still loved you," says Matt, his gaze resolute. "I loved you *even more*."

"You didn't."

"I did."

Tears have started streaming down my face, and I wrap my arms around Matt, suddenly feeling as though I could hold on to him forever.

"Let's never split up again," I say against his chest, my voice a little shuddery.

"Never."

"Ever."

"Do you . . . *really* love Harold?" I can't help adding as we finally draw apart a little, and Matt gives me a wry smile.

"I really love Harold. Don't ask me why, but I do. I love when he steals my food, I love when he shreds my shirts. . . ."

"No you don't," I say with a gurgle of laughter.

"I do," says Matt adamantly. "I love that dog more than I thought I could ever love a dog. Speaking of which, where *is* he?" Matt's head swivels around. "We need to go and find him. I assumed he would run back."

"What if the burglar's kidnapped him?" I say in fright, and Matt gives me one of his looks.

"Unlikely," he says. "Can you imagine kidnapping Harold? But we should track him down."

We head down to the garden and check that first, but there's no sign. Then we go out to the street and walk along, hand in hand, calling out at intervals through the dark night air.

"Harold? *Harold!*"

"Where *are* you, stupid dog? HAROLD!"

"What if he's lost?" I say anxiously as we reach the corner of a cross street.

"He won't be lost. He's probably showing off to the street dogs. He's probably got a gang by now. Harold!" Matt raises his voice. "Harold, you idiot! Come HOME!" Then he freezes. "Wait. Hear that?"

We stand motionless, and I suddenly hear it, too: the sound of distant, familiar barking.

"Harold!" I say in relief. "There he is! Except . . . where?" I turn around on the spot bewilderedly, trying to work out which direction the noise is coming from. We're in a warren of residential streets, with paths and gates and gardens. He could be anywhere.

"There." Matt points. "No, wait. There. Harold. HAR-OLD!"

The barking is getting louder, and now it's clearer where it's coming from. I start running along the road toward the sound, calling out at top volume till my lungs are burning.

"Harold? HAROLD!"

I reach another corner and skitter to a halt, breathing hard, still confused. The barking seems to be in a different place now. Where the hell *is* he? Is he in someone's garden?

"He's coming toward us," says Matt, arriving at my side. "Listen."

Sure enough, the barking is really loud now. He *must* be nearby, he must be . . .

"Is he behind us?" I say in confusion, and I turn around to look. And that's when I hear it. A screech of tires. An unearthly howl.

Harold.

No. *Harold.*

"Fuck," Matt mutters, breaking into a sprint. I match him, pace for pace, my brain hollow with dread, and as we round the next corner, we see him lying on the road. He's only just visible in the glow from a streetlamp, but I can already see the pool of blood.

I can't— I can't even—

I move faster than I ever have in my life, but still Matt gets there first and cradles Harold on his lap, his own face white.

Harold's breathing is hoarse. There's blood everywhere. There's mangled fur . . . I can see bone . . . Oh, Harold, Harold, my world . . . I crash down onto the road beside Matt, who tenderly transfers Harold's head onto my lap and gets out his phone.

"Fucking hit-and-run," he says, his voice taut as he dials. "Monsters."

Harold gives a little whine, and blood seeps from his mouth. I look at Matt and he looks at me. And it's all there. We don't have to say anything. It's all there.

Twenty-Seven

Six months later

Nihal wants to build Harold a new robotic leg. I keep telling him Harold doesn't *need* a new robotic leg. He already has a state-of-the-art prosthetic leg, which works really well. But every time Nihal sees Harold, he surveys the prosthetic leg and then his eyes go all pensive, and I *know* he wants to turn Harold into the bionic dog.

Me, I'm just grateful. I still wake up every morning and remember in a sickening rush and tremble with the dread of what could have been.

After we realized Harold was going to live (I nearly fainted with relief—*not* my finest hour), my biggest worry was that his spirit wouldn't survive. That the weeks of treatment and surgery and rehab he needed would somehow crush him. But I should have realized. This is Harold.

He practically swaggers along. He's all "Get me, with my cool metal leg." The veterinary physio said she'd never met a dog with such confidence. Then she got a puzzled look in her eye and added that he almost seemed to *lead* the sessions. At which Matt and I glanced at each other and Matt said, "Yup, that figures." Then he added, "Wait till he becomes famous. He's going to be *unbearable*."

It was a month after the accident that Felicity called to tell me that a publisher called Sasha wanted to turn my story of Harold into a book. A real book!

Sasha came to lunch and met Harold and I told her the story of the accident. (It was a bit of a therapy session in the end.) And then I said, surely I should put the whole incident into the book? Because this was part of who Harold was now?

Whereupon Sasha became thoughtful and said maybe leave that story for the sequel. And the next thing was, Felicity phoned me up and said the publishers had changed their mind: They now wanted two books! *Two* books about Harold! It's unbelievable. The whole thing's unbelievable. They offered me this incredible sum of money and I replied, "Wow, thank you!" before Felicity hastily stepped in and said my reply did not imply acceptance of the offer. And then she somehow got them to give me even more. I still don't know how. So I've been able to quit my job writing leaflets. I'm *totally* focused on writing another Harold book. (Except I do still want to get into aromatherapy; that's definitely going to be my sideline.)

Since then, Matt and I have worked out an arrangement where I sleep at his place—in fact, I live at his place, really—but work at my flat. That way, I still have my own office. We might buy a place together down the line. But in the meantime . . . drumroll . . . we've been bed shopping! It took a while, but we have the *best ever* bed now. Two different mattresses, zipped together. It's genius!

We've moved the hairless wolf, though. Since I know the unbearably poignant story behind it, I can't even *look* at it without my eyes filling up with tears. So we've decided the bedroom should be an Arlo-free zone.

Now I peer around Nell's sitting room to see where Harold's got to, and sure enough, Nell's nabbed him for a cuddle. She always had a soft spot for Harold—but even more so since his accident. Walking's been tricky for her this last month, and she told me that whenever she's struggling, she thinks of Harold.

"Ava!" she exclaims now, as she sees me looking at her. "You haven't told us! How was the naked sauna?"

"Oh my God." Maud perks up from her seat on the floor. "Yes! You haven't told us yet."

"We're not here to talk about me," I object. "We're here for the *launch*."

The exciting news is, Nell and Topher are launching a new political party! Its working name is the Real Life Party. It has ten members so far, because we all instantly joined, plus Topher's assistant and Nell's mum. But it'll grow soon, once they make a website and everything.

Nell and Topher both want to stand as MPs at the next election, but they've been quite cagey about any further details . . . until today! They've made a campaign poster and they want feedback, so this is why we've all gathered at Nell's place. The poster is standing on an easel by the window, draped in a sheet, and they're going to unveil it in a minute. Yesterday we started calling this the "unveiling," and then

Topher said, "Fuck it, let's call it the official launch," and bought champagne, which is why everyone's in such a tremendous mood.

(Also: They're totally a couple. Even if Nell still claims they aren't.)

"We'll have the launch in a minute." Nell bats my objection away. "First, naked-sauna story!"

"Naked-sauna story!" agrees Sarika firmly, and nudges Sam, who obligingly echoes, "Naked-sauna story!"

"*Fine.*" I glance at Matt, who chuckles into his drink. "Well, as you know, we went round to Matt's parents' place yesterday—"

"How is it with them?" interjects Nell.

"It's fine," I say, after a moment's thought. "It's a lot friendlier than it was. They remember to give me vegetarian food now. And they've forgiven Matt, pretty much. And they never mention Genevieve, obviously."

I glance at Matt again, who nods in assent, a wry smile on his face.

I don't add, "They never mention Genevieve, because she was caught dealing drugs in a sting." I don't need to. It was all over the *Daily Mail* two months ago: *Popular children's influencer offers cocaine to journalist posing as Hollywood agent.*

Elsa nearly collapsed. It was crisis central. Every single member of the board, including Matt, had to go and denounce drugs publicly in this grim press conference. But then Harriet's House sales surged on the back of all the publicity. So, you know. Swings and roundabouts.

"Well, that's good," says Maud encouragingly, and I nod.

"Yes. It is."

The other thing I don't say is, "I've felt warmer toward Elsa, ever since she put the framed photos of Matt in the glass cabinet." Because that's a secret between Elsa and me. The first time Matt saw them, he actually stopped dead. Then he said, "Wow. Mum. Those are new."

He looked so touched, it was kind of unbearable. Elsa glanced at me and I stared rigidly up at the ceiling, and at last she said, "Oh, yes. Yes. I thought . . ." She cleared her throat. "I thought, time for a change. We should all be represented. All the family."

That's the only time it's ever been referred to. But whenever we've been back to the house, Matt's lingered in the hall, and I've seen him looking at the cabinet and I've felt . . . content. That's the word. Content.

"Never mind all that!" says Sarika impatiently. *"Naked-sauna story!"*

"OK!" I take a swig of champagne. "Fine! Here goes. So, as you all know, I was pretty determined about this naked sauna. I was going to *own* it. I was going to be body confident."

"Had you waxed?" puts in Sarika.

"Of course I'd waxed! I had a whole plan. I was going to stride in there, stark naked and proud of it. You know? *Proud* of my body. *Proud* of being a woman. *Proud* of my weird veins."

"You don't have weird veins," protests Maud at once.

"Oh, I do." I turn to her. "Haven't you seen them? They're on my—"

"Stop it!" explodes Nell. "Tell us what happened!"

"Did you see Matt's dad's whatsit?" says Maud with a giggle.

"Were you there, Matt?" Sarika swivels to him.

"No," says Matt. "I got caught up on a call, so I missed it." His mouth twitches. "Unfortunately."

"OK." I resume my story. "So, I was waiting for Matt to finish his call, but at last he told me to go without him. I got down there, and everyone was already in the sauna."

"Who was, exactly?" demands Nell.

"Elsa, John, and two of their friends. So I got undressed in the changing room."

"Down to nothing?" says Sarika to clarify.

"Down to nothing." I nod. "I was pretty hyped up by this time."

"I bet you were!" says Maud, wide-eyed.

"I even gave myself a pep talk in the mirror. I was like, 'Ava, you *can* do this. You *can* be naked with your boyfriend's parents. Be *proud* of your body.' I had a towel, but I didn't wrap it round myself, I just trailed it behind me. Then I went to the sauna and I swung the door open with this big flourish, you know, trying to look sassy even though I was totally naked. . . ."

I shut my eyes, because the memory is just *too embarrassing.*

"And then what?" demands Maud.

"They were all wearing swimsuits."

"Nooo!" Sarika explodes, and I see Sam choking on his drink. Maud looks speechless, and Nell is laughing so hard, she's gone pink.

"It was hideous!" I say. "They just *looked* at me and Elsa said, 'You know, Ava, we have spare swimsuits for guests.'"

"But why were they in swimsuits?" Nell looks almost accusingly at Matt.

"That's what I said! *Why?* And Matt told me they'd worn them on purpose, to make me feel more comfortable."

"I think my mum *had* told me she was planning to wear a swimsuit," Matt says, with a guilty grin. "But I forgot to pass it on. Didn't think it was such a big deal."

"So what did you do, Ava?" asks Sarika, agog. "Did you sit down? Naked?"

"Yes, actually I did," I say, lifting my chin.

"Bravo!" Nell applauds.

"I styled it out," I say. "For eighteen seconds. And then I got up and ran." I drain my champagne glass. "And now that I've *totally* embarrassed myself, I think I need another one of these. Let me get another bottle."

My cheeks still flushed with embarrassment and laughter, I head to the kitchen and get a bottle of champagne out of the fridge, while simultaneously replying to Sarika's WhatsApp of a bikini emoji. Ha ha. She's so hilarious.

I'm still quite addicted to WhatsApp, if I'm honest. But Matt can talk! He's in the big WhatsApp group with all of us, and he chats as much as anyone else.

Although I suppose, to be fair, he's able to *compartmentalize* a bit better than I am. He can switch off his phone and attend to other things. The other night, Matt was trying to unbutton my shirt while I quickly argued a point with Nell (we disagreed about whether Maud should buy this dreadful car she was looking at). I was just trying to find a car-engine emoji when he flipped out. Before I could stop him, he had grabbed my phone and typed:

> This is Matt. I would like to have sex with Ava. Could she stand down from the WhatsApp group for a while please?

Then, of course, a moment later the replies started coming in.

> Sure!

> Have fun, you two!

> How long will you be? Just a ballpark?

> Nell, you can't ask them that!!!

> Just did.

Followed by a million eggplant emojis.

I mean, it was quite funny. It was even quite hot, in a weird way.

"Ava." Nihal interrupts my thoughts as he walks into the kitchen, a dreamy expression on his face. "I've been thinking about Harold. If not a robotic leg, what about a new means to communicate? He's *very* bright. If we could harness his brain patterns somehow . . ."

"Maybe," I say dubiously. "Although I think he can communicate quite well already, don't you?"

I'm about to add that Harold's not available for Nihal's pioneering sci-fi experimentation, when an alarm bleeps on my phone. I've had alarms set all day, just in case. I quickly load up my browser, search out the right Internet page . . . and, oh my God! It's time!

"Nihal!" I exclaim. "Come with me! It's urgent!"

"What?" Nihal looks alarmed but follows me back into the sitting room, where I clap my hands.

"Ladies and gentlemen! I have important news! The number of Internet users in the world is approaching . . . five billion!"

"*What?*" Matt puts down his drink. "How do you know?"

"Because I've been following it obsessively," I tell him proudly. "Every hundred words I write, I check the counter. It's like my reward. And now, look! You were going to miss it! We're on 4,999,999,992!"

I hold up my phone so everyone can see the giant number increasing. There's a breathless hush as the last digit inexorably rises. It's mesmerizing. It's addictive. I *totally* get this now.

4,999,999,997 . . . 4,999,999,998 . . . 4,999,999,999 . . .

"Oh my God!" squeaks Maud excitedly, and then the numbers turn over one more time:

5,000,000,000.

The room erupts into instant, ecstatic cheers. Matt and Nihal are high-fiving each other, and Topher is kissing Nell. And the whole thing is so silly, *so* pointless . . . but it's kind of special too.

"You're amazing!" Matt has come over to me, his eyes still bright. "I had no idea. You're a dark horse, Ava."

"Oh, I've just begun." I wink at him.

"Really?" He raises his eyebrows at me. "What does that mean?"

"Watch out, that's all I can say. But *now*." I turn to Topher and Nell. "Come on, you two. We've waited long enough. Show us your poster!"

"Right." Topher glances at Nell and puts down his champagne, then helps her out of her chair and escorts her over to the window.

When Topher helps Nell get along, it never looks like help. He manages to look like a guy who's just casually arm in arm with his girl. It's one of the reasons I'm so fond of him.

"So, ladies and gentlemen, welcome to our launch." Topher addresses the room. "The Real Life Party is at an early stage of development, as you know." He glances at Nell.

She takes over. "But we wanted to share with you this image and slogan. We've worked hard at making this poster say what we wanted to say."

"Exactly." Topher nods. "We feel it represents the *ethos* we are trying to present and the *future* we feel this country needs. So, without further ado . . ."

He reaches for the sheet and pulls it off the easel, revealing a huge mounted poster. And we all gape at it. Across the top, in a bold black typeface, are the words:

Life, huh?
It's a shitshow. But we're here for you.

Below this slogan is a photo of Nell with her cane, her pink hair on end, scowling straight ahead. And next to her is Topher, glaring at the camera, his eyebrows heavier than ever, and his skin looking particularly pitted.

I mean, I love Nell. I love Topher. But they look *terrifying*.

I swallow several times, wondering what to say and noticing that nobody else has spoken either.

"It's *powerful*," says Maud at last.

"It's a bit scary," ventures Nihal.

"Good font," says Matt. "Very solid. Very strong."

"Yes," I say, gratefully seizing on this idea. "The font's perfect! Couldn't be better."

"Can you say 'shitshow' on a political poster?" queries Sam.

"No," says Sarika firmly. "You wanted feedback, Nell? Well, Sam's right. You can't say 'shitshow.'"

"What are we going to say, life's a macaroon?" counters Nell combatively. "Life's a feather pillow? Life's a dumpling? No! Wrong! Life *is* a shitshow. It's chaos! It's a shambles! And if you don't agree, don't vote for us."

Glances are flying around the room, and I think we've probably reached the end of "feedback" time.

"OK!" says Maud brightly. "Well, it's a brilliant poster, and I'm sure you'll both be prime minister." She leads a round of applause, and we all join in with enthusiasm. "Shall we order pizza now?" she adds hopefully.

Sarika is already summoning up a pizza menu on her phone and working out the cheapest way to order, in that über-efficient way she has. Except now she has competition, because Sam is *also* working it out, but he's coming to a different result. (They really were made for each other.)

Topher helps Nell to the sofa, and they join in the pizza discussion with animation. While they're all arguing about percentages, I wander over to where Matt is standing in front of the giant poster. He's grown his hair out a little since he started working with Topher, and he's lost the uptight business attire. It suits him. In fact, the whole setup suits him so well, it's as if they've been working together forever.

"She's got a point," he says, looking up as I approach. "Life is a shitshow. But I wouldn't change it."

"Do you mean your life? Or mine?" I raise my chin teasingly. "Because my life is not a shitshow, thank you. My life is wonderfully under control."

"I meant both," he says, smiling.

"Both our lives are shitshows?"

"Not our lives. Our life." He hesitates, his eyes questioning. "Our . . . one joint life."

Our one joint life. As the words float in the air, I feel a little tingle, because that sounds almost like . . . Almost like . . .

"Our one joint shitshow life." I roll my eyes. "Sounds great. Where do I sign up?"

Matt's face crinkles in amusement.

"Sorry, should have been clearer. I meant . . ." He thinks for a moment. "I meant our one joint shitshow, hopeless, hopeful, messy, exhilarating life. With ice cream in the interval."

"OK," I say. "*Now* I get it. Sounds good. The ice cream does, anyway."

"That's what I thought."

He takes hold of my hand, low down, where no one can see, and his thumb rubs gently against my skin. Not wanting to be left out, Harold trots over to rub against our legs, and we both instinctively reach down to pet him.

"It's *twenty* percent off!" Sarika is exclaiming to Sam, so indignantly that I can't help laughing. Nell and Topher are now having a disagreement about the gig economy, and Nihal is sketching something, nodding politely as Maud makes suggestions. Harold is at my feet. And Matt is by my side. What more could I ever want?

I clasp his hand more firmly and breathe out sharply, listening to the voices, watching the faces. Wanting to save this precious-but-ordinary moment forever.

I don't know where we'll go from here, but right now I don't care. Because I'm here with everything that matters. Our friends. Our loves. Our life.

Acknowledgments

〜〜〜〜〜〜〜

Publishing a book is always a team effort. With this book I've felt the team spirit all the more, as we all communicated by various means through lockdown and beyond.

I would like to thank Frankie Gray and Kara Cesare for their wonderful, insightful editing, which helped me so much.

Thanks to Araminta Whitley and Kim Witherspoon, my fantastic agents, and the endlessly fabulous Marina de Pass.

Thanks to all my friends at PRH, especially Gina Centrello, Andy Ward, Avideh Bashirrad, Whitney Frick, Debbie Aroff, Jess Bonet, Sharon Propson, Madison Dettlinger, Belina Huey, Paolo Pepe, Loren Noveck, Dana Blanchette, Kristin Cochrane, Amy Black, Val Gow, Emma Ingram, and Dan French.

I would like to thank my dear friend Athena McAlpine for introducing me to Puglia while I was on holiday at her magical Convento di Santa Maria di Costantinopoli—a loose inspiration for the monastery.

Shout-out to the charming and charismatic Henry, who sparked my inspiration for Harold.

Special thanks to the residents of Windsor Close for the Bastard Chart.

I edited this book in lockdown and would like to thank my entire household for being brilliant throughout.

ABOUT THE AUTHOR

Sophie Kinsella is the author of the bestselling Shopaholic series, as well as the novels *Can You Keep a Secret?*, *The Undomestic Goddess*, *Remember Me?*, *Twenties Girl*, *I've Got Your Number*, *Wedding Night*, *My Not So Perfect Life*, *Surprise Me*, and *I Owe You One*. She lives in the UK.

sophiekinsella.com
Facebook.com/SophieKinsellaOfficial
Twitter: @KinsellaSophie
Instagram: @sophiekinsellawriter

ABOUT THE TYPE

This book was set in Sabon, a typeface designed by the well-known German typographer Jan Tschichold (1902–74). Sabon's design is based upon the original letterforms of sixteenth-century French type designer Claude Garamond and was created specifically to be used for three sources: foundry type for hand composition, Linotype, and Monotype. Tschichold named his typeface for the famous Frankfurt typefounder Jacques Sabon (c. 1520–80).